OPERATION LEBENSRAUM

OPERATION LEBENSRAUM

'NATIONALISM IS AN AVATAR AND CANNOT BE SLAIN' —SRI AUROBINDO

HIRANYA KUMAR BHATTACHARYYA

BLOOMSBURY

NEW DELHI • LONDON • OXFORD • NEW YORK • SYDNEY

First published in India 2018

ISBN 978 93 86643 63 6

10 9 8 7 6 5 4 3 2 1

Bloomsbury Publishing India Pvt. Ltd
Second Floor, LSC Building No.4
DDA Complex, Pocket C – 6 & 7, Vasant Kunj
New Delhi 110070
www.bloomsbury.com

Typeset by Manipal Digital Systems
Printed and bound in India by Replika Press Pvt Ltd

To

Dr. Tonmoy Das, MD, DM

CONTENTS

PREFACE

Without harbouring any intention of deluging the reader with statistical waves (which are available in abundance), an attempt has been made in what follows to present a holistic, if not amateurish, view of the proportion, assumed by the problem of illegal immigration all over the world with particular reference to West Bengal, Assam and other North-Eastern States of India. Also, efforts have been made to analyse the multifold problems engendered by unabated cross-border infiltration, all the more complicated by the appearance of Jihadis in the scenario. That the problem of immigration, both legal and illegal, has since become a global phenomenon; has been also highlighted and analysed, while also narrating the steps taken in this regard in Europe and the Western hemisphere.

In the course of equipping myself with proper data/ information for penning this discourse, I had to go through volumes of reports on the subject matter and relevant literatures, but sincere efforts have been made to present a dispassionate view and quoting correct data. The resurgence of political Islam within the framework of religious fundamentalism and its impacts, have been also highlighted to the possible extent. Let me make it very clear that I do not have the slightest intention of hurting anybody's religious feelings.

What have been presented in the book can by no means be the last words on this subject. There remains a vast scope for further research, study and amelioration of the none-too-happy state of affairs. I have dealt with and analysed this issue for almost six decades - first as a Police officer and then as a public activist. As such, my experiences of so many years, have been, to a great extent, instrumental in formulation of my observations and recommendations. Besides, interaction with knowledgeable quarters have also been of immense help. My heartfelt gratitude to Mr. P.C. Haldar for some of his invaluable suggestions. I am solely responsible for any error and/or omission in this book.

ACKNOWLEDGEMENTS

Possibly I would not have undertaken this venture but for the frequent goading by some of my dear and near ones. In this context, both my sons, Sanjeev and Rajeev, rendered invaluable assistance to me. On several occasions, they had made relevant data and literature available to me. My heartiest thanks and blessings to them. I am extremely thankful to Sriman Rabin Bhuyan, a senior journalist, for having put me in touch with Ms. Meghna Choudhury who helped me in completing the manuscript of this book. She not only helped me in picking up the complex operation of a 'laptop' which I was completely unaware of, but was also instrumental in speeding up the documentation process. How can I forget the long hours she spared for me despite her busy schedule as a research scholar and a government employee? **My heartiest thanks and blessings to her also**.

Also, I must thank my publisher for having undertaken the job of publishing this manuscript that shall henceforth, be known as a book!

Chapter 1
TIP OF THE ICEBERG

The horizon of the dark, still night was suddenly rendered aglow by the burning houses and the stillness disturbed by the fearful cries of the children and bellowing of the adults. Gun shots from AK-47s also reverberated intermittently, from far away hamlets situated in and around the fringes of the Manas Wildlife Sanctuary. The helpless inhabitants ran helter-skelter, out of their abodes for fear of losing their dear lives – many to the dense forest and many others, to the western bank of the river Beki. Quite a few were shot dead while trying to cross the river. The deep-rooted grievances of encroaching upon the land of the ethnic tribe suddenly burst open and the helpless migrants, irrespective of their status of domicile or otherwise, were thrown to the wolves, with nobody coming forward to rescue them. 'Humanity' was a meaningless word in this moment of absolute frenzy.

The atrocities resembling those committed at Nellie in 1983 were **ghastliness incarnate by themselves**. The kidnapping and subsequent molestation of a teen-aged tribal girl, was not forgotten and the recovery of her corpse with mutiliated genital, added fuel to the fire. (Source: A telephonic conversation with a Police officer who had worked under me). Ghastly and heart rending scenes were the natural consequences of the militant outburst, engendered by such violation of ethnic pride and the distinctive sense of self-preservation. The barometer of inhumanity was illustrated by the two-year old's struggle for survival - The two-year old was suckling her mother, when the other breast was chopped off; her throat slit open and still bleeding. The same officer informed me of having sighted an old woman, probably in her sixties or seventies. She was franctically looking for a pot that was belived to contain her silver ornaments, as she stood in the midst of ash heaps and rubbles, the only remnants of her otherwise charred house. Having lost her mental balance, she was insensitive to her surroundings and oblivious of the impending danger of being slain. Maybe, they were encroachers, illegal immigrants, criminals or even the *jehadis.* Certainly they could have been dealt with legally, under the laws of the land. However, the apprehensions of being extinct in all respect, obliterated such rational and humane approach which the administration completely failed to anticipate while the multiple Intelligence Agencies must have drawn a blank. Maybe, the victims were infiltrators or criminals or encroachers or even documented migrants, but the fact remained that they were human beings. If they were liable for prosecution under the law, why was no action taken against them, instead of allowing the marauders to take law into their own hands? These are some of the questions that the administration has never come forward to answer. There was a wakeful unwillingness to distinguish between human rights and political rights and in the process, human rights were totally ignored.

A mind-boggling ambience with smoldering residential huts, black smoke darkening the skyline, bellowing of children with their parents gunned down or missing, empty stomachs with uncertain future writ large in their faces and the ground littered with empty cartridges of AK series rifles, receives any visitor to these places of occurrences, be it police personnel or journalist, ever ready to blow up the situation beyond rational proportion or any NGO functionaries!

Needless to mention, that this was the repetition, if not magnification, of what had already happened in 2008. Of course, this time the only difference was that they had no opportunity to hoist the Pakistani flag, as was done in Darrang district during the disturbances of 2008.

Naturally, an inquisitive mind would raise the question as to how many marauders were arrested in 2008; prosecuted and jailed! All went scotfree and now, the result of such inaction on the part of the administration in general and law enforcing agencies in particular, is there for everyone to see. Now, the appearance of the *jihadis* in this scene has added a new proportion to the ever-expanding problem. Of course, of late, the administration seems to have woken up, after the exposure of the Burdhaman explosion coupled with the unearthing and extension of the jihadi network to Assam.

The origin of the recent disturbances in the BTAD areas is rooted in the distant past. These are neither sudden developments nor isolated incidents. In the past, there have been clashes between the Bodos and the immigrant Muslims as also between the Bodos and the other non-Bodos; but this time the most significant factor has been the emergence of fundamentalist forces in support of the migrant population, regardless of legal or illegal status of their domicile. The British policy of 'Divide and Rule' resulted in Assam being tagged with the new province of East Bengal, after the partition of Bengal in 1905 so that Assam could be turned into a Muslim majority province as a counterforce against the revolutionary outfits of Bengal. Though the annulment of the partition was announced in 1911, the overwhelmingly Muslim majority district of Sylhet was retained in Assam. Since then, there has been no respite of efforts for converting Assam into a Muslim majority province with the Muslim League playing a major role subsequently in this context. Sadulla's ministry followed the British policy of importing Muslim peasants from East Bengal in their thousands and settled them in Assam to the detriment of the interest of the indigenous people including indigenous Muslims also. Such official patronage attracted many more thousands land-hungry Muslims to occupy vast track of fallow land, VGRs, PGRs and riverine 'Char areas'. Abdul Hamid Bhasani emerged as their leader, as mentioned elsewhere and spearheaded the campaign for bringing as much land as possible under the occupation of these land-hungry Muslim peasants. His political clout became so deep-rooted that he was even returned as an MLA in 1937. He had certainly intensified the campaign for including Assam in Pakistan and the bad blood brewed thereby, was yet to be rectified

In the wake of such large scale encroachment upon Assam's land, clashes with the indigenous people became inevitable. In fact, way back in 1943, according to the old records of Gossaigaon Police Station, clashes had taken place beween the Bodos and the immigrant Muslims on the very issue of land ownership and allied matters. Chief Minister Sadulla's support was with the immigrant population in conformity with the Muslim League's and Bhasani's policy. One Deobar Bodo was shot dead by Sadulla's police. That is to say, the clash between the Bodos and the immigrant Muslims dates back to the earlier part of the twentieth century. It is worthwhile to mention that Lord Wavel in his 'Viceroy's Journal' had described Sadulla's policy of importing Muslim peasants from East Bengal as a 'Grow more Muslim' plan. In any case, Muslim invaders tried to conquer Assam almost for five centuries but could not. And now, Assam is being overwhelmed by unarmed hordes of Muslim infiltrators from Bangladesh with the help of a section of their co-religionists, unscrupulous Government officers/ employees and their political patrons. Even the Honorable Supreme Court of India while invalidating the controversial IMDT Act, had very significantly observed that '... there can beno manner of doubt that the state of Assam is facing external aggression and disturbance on account of large scale illegal migration of Bangladeshi nationals.' The Honorable Court had even directed the Union Government to invoke Article 355 of the Constitution, for protecting Assam from such external aggression and internal disturbance. The pro-infiltrator role is clearly discernible in the unwillingness of the political parties to introduce any fool-proof preventive measures against fresh infiltration. In fact, watertight preventive action is the only answer to retrieve Assam from the predicament she is facing. The lack of political will in this context emanates from the vote-bank politics, a phenomenon that the Bodo leaders have never approved of. Nor do they have to worry about the vote-bank politics for safeguarding their distinct identity, because the immigrant Muslims could not be organised into any vote bank in the BTAD area as yet. Hence, the emergence of some non-Bodo outfits in the BTAD area, thereby cultivating fresh ground for ethnic clashes. These immigrant Muslims have meanwhile been able to enroll themselves as voters, thereby causing apprehensions on another count.

Assam Public Works, a Guwahati-based NGO's petition was admitted by the Honorable Supreme Court. In the petition, it was alleged that there were names of forty lakh foreigners in the ERs of Assam. The petitioner prayed in the petition for the deletion of these alien names from the ER and for freezing the ERs until these names were removed from the voters' list. The Supreme Court, in this context, issued notices to the Central and State Governments and the Election Commission of India. Of course, the entire gamut of all the relevant issues raised in this context is presently subjudice in the Constitution Bench of the Apex Court of India.

Lord Curzon's policy of 'Divide & Rule' left behind its legacy: Indira Gandhi took the cue from this policy, while promoting the 'All Assam Minority Students Union' (AAMSU) during the peak period of the historic Assam Movement as a counterforce against 'All Assam Students Union' (AASU). On this occasion, Indira degraded herself to the level of a petty partisan politician. She failed to foresee that the formation of the AAMSU would pollute the socio-political atmosphere of Assam for a very long time. A statesman and a true patriot would never like to be instrumental in promoting permanent animus among different section of the citizens of one's own country. Obviously, she thought in terms of gains for her own political party and not for a harmonious future of the country at large. Her lack of farsightedness has been the source of many evils presently bedeviling the civic life of Assam. The adverse fallouts of such a divisive policy are now there for everybody to see. AAMSU has since played a crucial role in promoting the communal divide in Assam. Reaction to such divisive policy was simply natural. Now in BTAD area, 'All Bodoland Students Union' has emerged as a force to be reckoned with. A chain reaction has also surfaced and for quite some time now in BTAD area, 'All Bodoland Minority Students Union' (ABMSU) has raised its ugly head, asserting with full vehemence its presence in the latest round of conflicts in the BTAD area. Its role in impeding the preparation of the NRC also cannot be ignored. ABMSU's bitterly vocal and other objectionable activities are certainly not conducive to a perspicacious normalcy in the area. In other words, the possibility of a bitter confrontation between ABSU and ABMSU in the future cannot be rulrd out. In addition, more militant NDFB has also meanwhile thrown its hat into the ring. Thus, rehabilitation or no rehabilitation of the victims of so many riots, the entire area is still pregnant with dangerous possibility of bloody clashes in the future unless illegal migrants are evicted and future infiltration/encroachment upon tribal land prevented coupled with measures for restoring the land to the sons of the soil. That is to say, new battle line will be drawn up sooner or later.

Of late, anticipation of events likely to surface, has not been the strong point of the state administration of Assam — particularly of the Police functionaries. In this context, it may be in fitness of things to mention that the Bodo leadership may not be amenable to adhere to the terms of the infamous Assam Accord. The Bodo leadership was ignored while framing the Assam Accord, conveniently forgetting that the problem of Bangladeshi infiltration has been equally harming the Bodos. As such, the possibility of not accepting 1971 envisaged in the Accord as the cut-off date for detection of illegal alien migrants cannot be ruled out and how do the authorities and others associated with the issue, propose to deal with such an eventuality, is yet to transpire. In fact, non-implementation of the Assam Accord for over three decades, had already prognosticated such fate for the Accord. Some quarters are already thinking aloud about scrapping the Accord. The dilly-dallying tactics of the government is more likely than not, going to be counter-productive.

It will be quite pertinent of point out that the growth rate of population has recorded disproportionate increase as compared to birth rate. This unusual phenomenon is particularly evident in BTAD area, despite the fact that the birth rate among the Bodos is one of the lowest in the state according to the latest Census Report. This has been also reflected in the unusual increase of voters in the ERs. There is also enough data to substantiate this claim. As for instance, according to a media report, the number of Muslim voters in forty-nine LA constituencies has out- numbered the rest (DAINIK AXOM dt August 27, 2015) and eleven districts of Assam are reported to have become Muslim majority. At the time of Elections in 1983, the number of voters in Assam was 86,82,138 and in 1985, it went up to 98,83,304; the rate of increase being 13.83 per cent, whereas in five years, between 1978 and 1983, the increase was only by 7,07,662. Again between 1991 and 1996, the increase was by 2,26,955 whereas in the next five years, the increase was by 23,20,042, the percentage of increase being 16.07. The next five years recorded an increase of 17.17 per cent. So the picture defies all rational standards.

Such increase has not followed any particular pattern. It has been mainly been opportunities-oriented with a perceptible hurry to enter the names in the ERs on the eve of every election. In 2003-2004, the rate of such increase was 2.62 per cent only, whereas on the eve of Assembly Elections in 2006, the recorded increase was 14.52 per cent. Still more significant is the fact that most of the new entrants in the ERs are of immigrant origin. There is no reason to believe that BTAD area is an exception to such unusual development. Thus, the ground is ready for another round of fierce confrontation at the time of preparing the next ERs and resuming the process of updating the NRC. The pilot project of preparing the NRC of Barpeta and Chaygaon LA constituencies ran aground because of the lawlessness accompanying the bandh called by AAMSU. Such anti-national activities cannot but create apprehensions in the minds of the indigenous people. Besides, considering the present state of affairs, it may be well anticipated that there will be efforts galore by vested interest to include in the ERs and in the NRC as many names as possible from the post - 1971 stream of migrants from Bangladesh. In fact, many such instances have already surfaced. Such conspiracies will certainly precipitate another crisis, if not communal clashes. Symptoms of such clashes were already evidenced while conducting the aforesaid pilot projects for preparing the NRC.

To Sum Up:

The British legacy of promoting communal politics is very much alive even today, thereby converting Assam into a playground of communal fundamentalist forces — a phenomenon Muslim leaders like Badaruddin Azmal has not failed to take advantage of. Pakistan is not likely in near future to cease its efforts for avenging the loss of its Eastern wing. There are reasons to suspect that ISI will go on overdrive to promote inter-ethnic clashes with a view to frustrate all efforts, both official and non-official, for stabilizing the situation in the BTAD area with a section of the militant outfits going all out to take advantage of such destabilizing factors. The case in point is the unprovoked atrocities committed by NDFB (S) on the Adivasi community on the 23rd of December, 2014. This has, however, alerted the Central Government unlike before and the full scale anti-NDFB (S) operations are yielding perceptible changes. In fact, this outfit seems to be on its last leg with a section thinking in terms of coming to the negotiation table.

The fear of losing their respective identities, most of the ethnic groups will perforce intensify their struggle for survival with resultant consequences, thereby complicating the situation further, particularly after the BTAD riots. This time also, as in 1979, the point of ignition may be, in all likelihood, the preparation of the ERs for the ensuing General Elections, or the updating the NRC, if not earlier. Another agitation like the Assam Movement, is gradually surfacing, this time, of course, apparently in the entire North East. However, main focal points seem to be revolving round – (a) Foolproof preventive measures including reservation of seats for the indigenous people (b) Implementing the Assam Accord (c) Updating the NRC. AASU will certainly try to regain its lost credibility.

Needless to mention that AASU can avail of this opportunity to revive the composite character of the indigenous society of Assam, lost because of the lack of farsightedness and the policy of self-aggrandisement on the part of its predecessors – to be more precise, the two AGP Governments. However, in the latest election campaign for the general elections of 2016, the BJP-led alliance has largely succeeded in forming a united front of the Indian citizens of Assam, thereby reaping very rich harvest in terms of electoral gains. The immediate next need would be to sustain such a united platform.

Assam is burning! Despite all the betrayals perpetrated, it is still crying hoarse to the rest of the country, that neither is it suffering from a persecution mania, nor is the crisis exaggerated. This is not a class war. Nor is it a war cry sounded by the so-called Assamese middle class, as many of the theorists and westward looking progressivists would like to depict. Class war or no class war, every individual, as is natural, endeavours to preserve and promote his identity. And this trend or instinct for self-preservation gets magnified whenever a particular race or ethnic groups encounter the threat of being politically, economically and culturally extinct. The pressing need for socio-economic security can be ignored only at one's own peril. At least, the authorities of the District Councils of Assam created as per provisions of the sixth schedule of the Constitution, while preparing the ERs for the elections of the District Councils, may use their power under Rule number 128 of the Assam Autonomous Districts (Constitution of District Councils) Rules, 1951, for removing the names of illegal migrants from their respective ERs.

In any case, well-calculated anticipation of the shape of things to come, should be the keystone for prescribing necessary antidotes. In fact, pre-emptive measures taken on the basis of such anticipation might have mitigated the the extent of adverse fallouts of the mayhem committed on the 23rd of December 2014.

Chapter 2

NEW DIMENSIONS

The story of human migration is as old as the story of *homo sapiens.* People came out of the jungles, caves and so on, in search of better living conditions. The search for greener pastures proved to be an unending process. In the process, many civilizations sprouted, although mostly in riverine basins. In course of time, with the concept of private property emerging, the situation took a competitive, if not, a militant turn. The emergence of various ethnic entities on the basis of very many factors ultimately and gradually gave birth to nation states. The inborn tendency to survive, physically and otherwise, engendered the need for consolidating respective existence, which in turn gave rise to expansionist designs. Hence, the process of migration has since assumed a global proportion. This process of migration has completed a full circle and it has since assumed many new dimensions. Mainly, the rise of Islamic fundamentalism in the Middle East (ME) and in some other parts of Asia, coupled with the economic warfare surfacing in the wake of globalization, are two new phenomena afflicting the latest phase of human migration. One is to get the better of the other as yet. Such large-scale migration has brought in its train many unforeseen problems manifesting in multifold manners and adding new dimensions to political considerations and humane perspectives. Given the fact that illegal migration of alien citizens has never been welcomed anywhere, the exodus of Muslim migrants from the Middle East and other parts of Asia and Africa has of late, created new problems and serious tensions in quite a few countries. According to World Migration Report; WMR, 2011, 'The political transition in North Africa and the Middle East in 2011 have had a tremendous impact on migration pattern in the Middle East and North Africa region and beyond'. Besides, these regular migrants are also, of late, reported to have been involved in criminal activities. Incidentally, the incidence of criminal activities indulged in by criminals of Bangladesh origin are extremely high in Assam and now Europe seems to have fallen a victim to the same malady.

At the same time, vested political interests and human rights activists are gathering momentum in defense of these illegal migrants for promoting their causes, if not welfare. No less a dignitary than the Pope himself has appealed for sympathetic treatment of the entire issue and for humane treatment to the alien migrants. On the other hand, even in a country like the USA where illegal migration from Mexico had so far been receiving official and vocal opposition from the government and the public, a section of the politicians has been demanding to legalize the stay of these migrants and grant them voting rights. The latest from that country depicts a tell-tale picture: According to media reports, 'President Barack Obama today bypassed Congress to announce the most sweeping immigration reform in a generation that will protect 5 million illegal workers from deportation ...' This report further states that 'Obama rejected accusations by conservatives that he is offering a free pass to undocumented immigrants **and** warned in a prime-time address that he would bolster border security and make it harder for unauthorized outsiders to get into the country.' (Assam Tribune, 22nd of Novemeber, 2014). That is to say, while keeping an eye on political vested interests, he has not denied the presence of apprehensions against the ever present onslaught by Mexican immigrants. In fact, prior to his such sweeping reform, Obama had tried to amend the Immigration Reform Bill of 2007, by introducing the Border Security, Economic Opportunity and Immigration Modernisation Act of 2013. The Bill envisaged the creation of a new class of work-visas for low-skilled migrants and a Bureau of Immigration and Market Research. The bill was passed by the Senate but the House of Representative took no action on the bill. Many leading citizens of the US are now apprehensive, that the flow of Mexican migrants will now assume an upward trend.

In the wake of globalization, the concept of a global system of border management is also gradually emerging and the expansion of the labour market is bound to help in materialization of this concept.

Rapid globalization has certainly accelerated the pace of international migration, both legal and illegal, thereby creating fresh complications in the world situation which are bound to engender very many regional problems/imbalances. Thomas Nail of Stanford, California, has stated in his research paper captioned 'The Figure of Migrant' that 'The twenty-first century will be the century of migrants. At the turn of the century, there were more regional and international migrants than ever before in recorded history. Today, there are over 1 billion migrants.' He further stated that 'The twenty-first century will be the century of the migrant not only because of the record number of migrants today but also because this is the century in which all the previous forms of social expulsion and migratory resistance have reemerged and become more active than ever before.' Thus, the complex dynamics of human migration has lately ushered in, an unforeseen chapter of human civilization and this ever-growing problem aggravated by the rise of fundamentalist forces, has created an ambience of social, political, economic, cultural and above all, demographic tensions. Some instances may be in order:

According to a report published in a regional Assamese ***daily, Niyamia Barta*** on the 19th of June 2015, European countries had spent 11.3 Crore Euros for deporting illegal migrants. Preventive measures undertaken in their respective borders had accounted for another sum of 1.6 Crore Euros. According to the same report, a sum of 4,200 dollars had to be spent per head of deportees for executing their deportation.

Bertil Lintner, the famous Swedish journalist-writer, informed the present scribe on his query in an e-Mail in

November, 2015 that 'All that I can say is that Sweden has received more refugees per capita than any other European or Western country. And there has been a backlash against that among the public at large. An extreme right-wing anti-immigrant party (which was miniscule ten years ago) got 12.9 per cent of the vote in the most recent general election in Sweden (September this year), and thus became the third largest party in the parliament.' Sweden's population as on 31st of March, 2013, was 9,573,466 and in 2014, it was estimated to be 9.663 million, despite the strict birth-control policy. Meanwhile the Swedish government's decision to deport 80,000 immigrants who infiltrated in 2015, has created intense commotion all over Europe (Niyamia Barta; 29th of January, 2016). Most of these migrants are reported to have sneaked through the borders of Greece, owing to the weak border security arrangement. This is why there has been large-scale resentment in Europe against Greece. Within Greece itself, Greek citizens are strongly opposing the establishment of refugee camps in some of the small islands, as such steps may ultimately outnumber the indigenous people and overwhelm them; a situation being confronted presently in the North-Eastern States of India. In Europe, these immigrants are treated as refugees and unlike in Assam, not privileged to exercise any political rights. However, most of these refugees are availing in Europe all the benefits visualized in the relevant UNO resolutions.

Leaving aside the North Pole and the South Pole, there is possibly no corner of the earth where Bangladeshi and Chinese migrants have not set their feet, albeit with different motives and different reasons. Of course, Mexican migrants are yet to cross the Atlantic. They are struggling to find their feet within the Western hemisphere, particularly in the USA – mostly for economic reasons. But gradually, as already discussed, they are also developing their political muscles. As already hinted upon, globalization has certainly facilitated their international movement. What is still more significant, is that the mindset of the antagonists is also perceptibly undergoing changes in favour of the migrants. Economic benefits accruing from the presence of the migrants in various degrees and different ways have also proved to be advantageous to the migrants. As for instance, Bangladeshi labor operates at cheaper rates. But the availability of cheap labor has not been an unmixed blessing. This has been adversely reflected in the work culture of the young generation of indigenous stocks as, centuries back, slave labous were destroying the work culture of the American youths. In other words, international migration on large scale has added a new dimension to the labor market. In the ultimate analysis, it will transpire that the availability of cheap labor has, to a great extent, been instrumental in developing the system of 'outsourcing' which, in turn, has proved to be beneficial to quite a few developing countries. And the system of outsourcing, in turn, has been instrumental in engendering interaction among many countries in the field of economic activities. International co-operation has been the very much natural outcome of such global enterprises while at the same time, cut-throat competition has surfaced for economic domination the world over, thereby creating a new vista in world politics. That is to say, the concept of political domination and expansion has yielded place to the concept of economic domination, which has since given birth to neo-colonialism. As such, the conventional warfare for political domination and territorial expansion, seems to be on its way out, although the game of one upmanship continues in the field of nuclear capabilities. Of course, boundary disputes are still keeping the possibility of armed clashes alive in some regions. However, the days of China marching into Tibet with India betraying an utterly helpless stance and subjecting India into shameful performance in 1962 over the NEFA (now Arunachal) clashes, have been left behind long back. Of course, India's helplessness does not seem to end. India's manufacturing and marketing ventures are yet to match China's. Any territorial expansion into the Indian sub-continent, not being high now in its list of priorities, China is presently working overtime for expanding its trading and marketing dominance over the sub-continent and its neighborhood. China seems to be, in fact, trying hard to revive the long-forgotten slogan of 'Hindi

Chini Bhai Bhai' in the marketing sector. According to media reports, of late, Indo-Chinese armed forces had embarked upon joint military exercises in the Ladakh sector. However, Chinese traders are not known for any religious fanaticism and fundamentalism-oriented expansionist design like a sizeable section of Bangladeshi infiltrators who, with active help from various jihadi groups and ISI of Pakistan, are moving ahead in a planned manner for founding a 'Brihat Islamistan' in the North-Eastern part of India. The Chinese has, on the other hand, set up the 'String Of Pearls' in the Indian and the South-Pacific oceans for promoting their commercial and strategic supremacy over India as also building up a counterforce against the American role. Besides, China's aggressive and diplomatic efforts for establishing her supremacy over the small island-states in the South-Pacific region, tell the same story, although in this region, she may have been entertaining more than commercial interests. However, the fact remains that China has the largest population in the world and it has to cater to the need for the survival of such a huge population. The compulsion of the situation has, thus, been instrumental in large-scale Chinese migration to different parts of the world. Bertil Lintner points out in his book captioned '*World. Wide. Web*' (Page number viii) that 'Now, people from China are fanning out across the world, not to establish official colonies – that kind of migration is history – but in search of greener pastures, or freedom, or both. While exact figures are not available, Western intelligence officials believe that perhaps as many as two million people from the People's Republic of China, or PRC, have migrated legally or illegally since 1978. They estimate that 30,000 – 40,000 a year go to the United States – the preferred destination – and the same number to the rest of the world.' As pointed out by Lintner, earlier the Chinese migrants used to move out from the Southern coastal provinces, but now, the migrants come from all over China. Japan has very strict immigration laws which are strictly enforced. Even then, Japan has witnessed a large influx of Chinese migrants. Even, according to media reports, thousands of Bangladeshi migrants moving in ocean-going ships as *'khalasis'*, have managed to stay back in violation of the laws of the land, although they are yet to change the demographic structure, whereas Chinese migrants are fast changing the demographic pattern in the Russian Far East and the Pacific region. No doubt, remittances to 'Motherland', has also increased manifold. These Chinese migrants have been also instrumental in promoting friendly ties with quite a few countries, thereby being instrumental in enlarging the trading network of their motherland. Bertil Lintner also agrees in his above-mentioned book that '—remittances from overseas Chinese —old as well as new migrants —are a significant contribution to the Chinese economy'.

However, it cannot be gainsaid that there have been adverse fallouts as well. Firstly, some regions are experiencing gradual emergence of racism which bears the possibility of snowballing into major clashes, depending on the attitude of the leaders in power. Secondly, some Pacific nations have witnessed violent anti-Chinese clashes. Details of such clashes will be too much time-consuming and may not be relevant as well for this treatise. Thirdly, Chinese dominance over the economies of countries like Myanmar, Cambodia, Laos, is causing widespread resentment among the indigenous people. As such, China's future relation with these countries continues to remain uncertain. But China is trying her best to keep these recalcitrant elements at bay by promoting the insurgent groups of North-Eastern India and helping them with arms & ammunitions and explosives. This has also provided her gun-runners and arms dealers with a market to dispose of stocks no more in use in the Chinese army. Thus, the Chinese continues to remain a suspect in the eyes of the Indian intelligence agencies and the security forces. No doubt, China has been the major suppliers of illegal arms to the underworld of India, thereby cultivating not only worries but also suspicion about China's ulterior motives. Such illegal export of arms has been a constant irritation to Indo-China relations. On the other hand, Chinese traders have covered every nook and corner of the world for marketing, legally or illegally, consumers goods manufactured in China.

In the process, there have been violations galore of international laws and regulations, particularly in marketing pirated brands. According to media reports, 63.2 per cent of pirated commodities were of Chinese origin between 2011 and 2012 and in this context, American companies are suffering huge losses. Indian markets have been also flooded with such pirated consumers goods at cheap rates. It may not be impossible for China to build up its espionage network with the help of the micro-traders of the receiving countries.

Pew Research Centre, WASHINGTON DC, conducted a study in 2008 on the extent of Mexican infiltration into the US. According to this study, 11.9 million illegal migrants had infiltrated into the US. The main reasons for such influx were listed as an open border, lack of border security measures, and availability of cheap Mexican labor. Millions of these migrants came with valid travel documents but did not go back on expiry of the validity of their visas— a strategy adopted by many Bangladeshi migrants visiting India. For reasons of easy accessibility, Mexico has been also used as a transit point by illegal migrants from South and Central America. Also the business of smuggling alien migrants across the US border, has been very much rampant as has been the case at many vulnerable points of Indo-Bangla border.

John Dougherty, an investigative journalist has cited in his book 'ILLEGALS', many instances of US border violations by illegal migrants as also the modus operandi of infiltration. Dougherty has pointed out that unchecked immigration is destroying the very fabric of American culture and also endangering American lives. He has furnished specific evidence also. Dougherty contends that reckless policies and lackluster restrictions are allowing criminals, drug lords and even tourists to take advantage of American freedom. He asserts that 'If 9/11 can't get us to secure our borders, nothing will.'

Despite America being a nation of migrants, she has her own national ethos and heritage. As such, Dougherty is very emphatic in asserting that 'Despite ethnic diversity, most American can trace their roots to America, and America alone, for several generations. —As such, most of us have deep cultural, spiritual and social ties to this nation — despite a desire by certain quarters to hyphenate us along ethnic lines.

Immigrants, however, have no such ties.........' (Illegals, Page number v). This is precisely the case with the migrants from Bangladesh, both legal and illegal and fresh or old, as they are yet to develop a sense of belonging to Assam and have been intent only on exploiting the resources of the state.

Incidentally, this has been also the malady of Assam's community life, subjected to all the adverse effects of infiltration by Bangladeshi nationals. However, Mexican infiltration differs in much respect from Bangladeshi infiltration. The issue of Mexican immigration has been analyzed in details in Chapter 9 of this book.

Other Western countries also have been confronted with this problem of infiltration by alien nationals. Some available reports are as follows: More than one million illegal migrants were in Spain in 2003. In 2006, 500,000 illegal migrants were estimated to be living in Italy. Next to Spain and Italy, Portugal and Greece have been receiving alien infiltrators. Portugal had roughly 500,000 such infiltrators in 2004 and Greece about 550,000 in 2006 (source: M.K. Karaboytcheva's 'And the Evaluation of the last Reorganisation Process of Foreign Workers in Spain, February, 2005. ERISS, Madrid, 2006.'). Press release by the Greater London Authority has depicted similar picture in respect of UK. France has been also reported to be suffering from similar problem. Hungary's barbed wire-fencing on the international border is being cut from time to time, by migrants from Serbia. In February, 2016, Hungary is reported to have arrested 1200 Serbian migrants while violating its border.

Chapter 3

TRANSBORDER INFILTRATION

The case of Bangladeshi migrants presents a rather different story.

Geophysical factors and Islamic elements coupled with political machination have rendered the issue of migration from Bangladesh, both legal and illegal, albeit mostly illegal; a volcanic issue in those areas of India where the demographic avalanche from Bangladeshis, is changing the demographic pattern - particularly in Assam and its neighborhood.

Bangladesh has an area of 1,44,000 square kilometers (to be precise 1,43,998 square kilometers according to BBC). In 2015, its population was 160.4 million with a density of 1,033 per square kilometer. With early childhood marriage coupled with polygamous practice and unsatisfactory birth-control measures; the growth rate of population is yet to assume a declining tendency. Bangladesh is a country of millions of landless peasants who had been, through the ages, cultivating the land of the *zamindars*, an institution created under 'Permanent Settlement' system when Lord Cornwallis was the British Governor General in the eighteenth century. Under the extremely oppressive system resorted to by the landlords, millions of peasants were reduced to abject poverty, making it impossible for them to make both the ends meet. They were constantly on look out for better conditions of living which they could not hope to find in their land of birth. Thus, inhuman atrocities resulted in the exodus of large number of landless peasants into Assam as early as in the nineteenth century itself.

True, Assam was not subjected to Lord Cornwallis's system of 'Permanent Settlement' but the institutes of 'Mauzadar' and 'Mandal' were adequate enough for opening the gate to the landless migrants from East Bengal and thus, started the unending and unholy journey with no sign of a halt as yet. But for the sake of fairness, it must be mentioned that the large scale migration of the nineteenth century, did not create any adverse and tense situation in the political and cultural world of Assam. But apprehension of losing his identity did arise in the mind of the Assamese, though on a different count, The British introduced Bengali language in Assam as the official language in 1837. This step created apprehensions in the mind of the Assamese that he might lose his independent identity and all that was Assamese might become extinct one day. Thus, the struggle for survival as a distinct entity had commenced. Though the British authorities had, on the 19th of April 1873, restored the Assamese language to its rightful place, the fear psychosis of losing distinct identity did not vanish and this fear psychosis has reemerged with full vehemence in the face of unabated flow of Bangladeshi infiltrators into Assam. That they may be outnumbered by Bangladeshi infiltrators, both Hindu and Muslim, in their own homeland has been creating turmoils in the socio-political life of Assam for last few decades. Unscrupulous politicians and their respective political parties have spared no effort to build up their respective vote-banks by getting these Bangladeshi infiltrators registered in Assam's Electoral Rolls (ER) as voters.

Anyway, let us get back to where we had digressed from - analyzing the case of the Bangladeshi migrants.

The inadequacy of living space with no usually available alternative means of livelihood, the unemployed people of East Bengal/East Pakistan/and then Bangladesh were forced by circumstances to look elsewhere and the easily accessible regions were Assam, West Bengal, Tripura, say, the north-eastern part of India. To start with, there were no motives other than economic ones. But the fact remains that the Muslim element has been a major factor in determining the course of the life of the people of East-Bengal and it received a shot in the arm when the demand for Pakistan gathered high momentum. Still, Bangladesh declared herself as a secular country on being liberated with Indian assistance from the yoke of West Pakistan. But after the assassination of Skh. Muzibar Rahman, Pakistan worked its way up to cultivate its influence over the rulers of Bangladesh; ISI could dig deep into the affairs of Bangladesh.

During the regime of Maj. General Ziaur Rahman in 1977, the image of Bangladesh was given the look of an Islamic country by dropping secularism as one of the four basic principles of Bangladesh's constitution, the other three being democracy, nationalism and socialism. Lt. General H.M. Ershad, on assuming power, went one step further and in 1988, made Islam the State religion of Bangladesh. Ershad converted Islam into a political factor to be reckoned with. It was during this period that the Jamat leaders, who had fled the country in the wake of the Liberation War, came back from Pakistan and they imported with them the most fanatic variety of Islamic expansion. Consequently, the pace of illegal infiltration into Assam also increased manifold.

Here, a brief account of the political history of Bangladesh may be of interest to the reader:

The brutal exploitation of East Pakistan coupled with the denial of democratic rights by the western wing of Pakistan, culminated in one of the bloodiest civil war of history. The civil war ended in total defeat of the Pakistani army and on the 16th of December 1971, an independent, sovereign State of Bangladesh was born. Sheikh Mujibor Rahman took over as the Prime Minister of Bangladesh. But it was no bed of roses for Mujib. The country, devastated by the civil war, was facing famine-like conditions and Mujib had to approach several countries with a begging bowl. Only India and the Soviet Union had responded to his request. His relations with the USA was far from being friendly. President Nixon was unhappy with Mujib for having broken up Pakistan. So he did not get the benefits available under PL480. Also, his foreign policy not being a run-away success, his image suffered severe beating both at home and abroad. Fundamentalist elements and pro-Pakistan lobby started undermining him. When he attended the Islamic Summit at Lahore in 1974 against the advice of his trusted friends, reactionary forces got a chance to raise their heads with active connivance from Pakistan. His participation in the Summit imparted a severe blow to his secular image also. On the other hand, his participation in the Summit failed to bring in any perceptible material benefits. Even the Arab countries excepting Iraq, turned a deaf ear to his entreaties. Meanwhile, Pakistan's fifth column in Bangladesh was working overtime to cultivate a strong foothold. The Islamic countries had practically isolated him as he was held responsible for breaking up a Muslim country. Adverse economic conditions were further compounded by all-round corruption in the Administration. Even the crime map also started recording a rising graph. Mujib's downhill journey had commenced. Betraying desperate and despotic attitude, he changed the Parliamentary form of government into Presidential form of government and declared himself the President without any sanction from the Parliament. His hope of the Presidential form being the panacea for all the adversities also did not fructify. The change was only cosmetic and would have never succeeded without the necessary political and administrative infra-structure. Mujib went on committing one mistake after another. He went all out to throttle the voice of any opposition by banning all opposition parties and newspapers. He formed a new political party and clamped down emergency in the country with the purpose of arresting the downhill journey of his government. But he committed the monumental mistakes of dropping his two most trusted lieutenants, namely, Tajuddin and General Osmani, who had become a national hero because of his significant contribution to the Liberation War against Pakistan. Thus, he isolated himself without ever realizing that his lack of farsightedness was fast yielding ground to the fundamentalists who were constantly on the look-out for opportunities to destroy him. To be precise, counter revolution had already begun and the reactionary forces ultimately eliminated him in the early hours of the

15th of August 1975 and those members of his family who were present in his private residence, on that fateful morning, were also gunned down. Two of his daughters escaped because they were abroad. Many others were also slaughtered at different places of Dacca. Radio Bangladesh announced that the Mujib government had fallen and the Army seized power under the leadership of Khandakar Mushtaque Ahmed who had taken over as the President. However, this was not the end of political turmoil in Bangladesh as subsequent events proved. Khandakar Mustaque was a tool in the hands of the army officers who were instrumental in staging the *coup d'etat*. General Ziaur Rahman had been appointed the new C-in-C of Bangladesh Army who was conspiring to capture power himself. President Khandakar Mushtaque was reduced practically to a rubber stamp by the army officers. Now, General Ziaur was running the administration from behind the scene.

The Bangladesh Army was divided into two factions, pro and anti-Mujib factions. Brigadier Khaled Musharaf was leading the pro-Mujib faction and he had even staged the semblance of a *coup* on the 3rd of November1975 but he was outwitted by Khandakar Mushtaque and assassinated by a sepoy on the 7th of November1975, with tacit support from General Zia. Brig. Khaled had to sacrifice his life because of his serious differences with General Zia. Thus, General Zia advanced one step forward towards the seat of supreme power. The next step was to impose Martial Law and Zia himself became the Chief Martial Law Administrator. A reign of terror followed and ultimately, General Ziaur Rahman declared himself as the President of Bangladesh on the 28th of April 1977. Then Gen. Zia arrested many army officers and men, sending them to the gallows. Amongst the victims, were some of his ardent supporters who had helped him in the struggle for capturing power. Gen. Zia did not trust the senior army officers who had helped him in the assassination of Mujib as he was apprehensive of himself becoming a victim of the army clique. Not remaining content with court martialing hundreds of officers and men of the Armed Forces, he had sent almost a lakh of people to jail in order to curb dissidence. Such action made his own security more vulnerable. He had become very unpopular and he tried to woo over the people by converting Bangladesh into a theocratic state with the hope that the promotion of religious fanaticism would endear him to the common man. Secularism was given a goodbye, a tradition still being patronized by his wife, Khaleda Zia who was leading the fundamentalist and anti-India faction of politicians. But Zia failed to earn popularity in the real sense of the term. Rather, on the contrary, he was distrusted and despised by his countrymen. Even an abortive attempt was made to kill him on the 2nd of October 1977 by a clique of army officers and this was followed by more repressive action taken by Zia. But his luck ran out. Under the leadership of Maj. General Manzoor, a group of army officers assassinated him on the 30th of May1981, at Chittagong where he was camping. This fourth *coup* during last six years commencing with assassination of SK. Mujib, clearly indicates the state of instability that Bangladesh was suffering from. However, General Manzoor was also shot dead four days after the assassination of Zia. Presently, while Khaleda Zia, wife of Gen. Zia, is carrying on the trend set up by her husband. Sk. Hasina, the present Prime Minister of Bangladesh and daughter of SK. Mujib, is trying her best to restore normalcy in the country and revive the secular tradition. The fundamentalists have so far refused to reconcile to SK. Hasina's friendly attitude towards India and have been working overtime to cause her ouster.

In the wake of the anarchical situation following the murder of Zia, the army under the leadership of Lt. General H.M. Ershad, Justice Abdus Sattar was installed as the President but Justice Sattar failed to restore normalcy and usher in any qualitative change in the ever deteriorating situation. Ultimately, Justice Sattar stepped down and handed over the charge of the Administration to Lt. General H.M. Ershad, the Chief of Army Staff. Ershad remained in power for seven years. During his tenure he converted Bangladesh into an Islamic state by amending the country's constitution. In June, 1988, Islam was declared the State religion of Bangladesh. Ershad was a pro-Pakistan fanatic Muslim. It was during his tenure that Pakistan was able to bring Bangladesh under its sphere of influence and ISI was having a field day in cultivating anti-India conspiracies of various hues. General Ershad had no role to play in the 'Liberation War', as he was then in Pakistan.

During the military rules of Gen. Zia and Lt. Gen. Ershad, most of the tribal people from the CHT, the habitat of twelve ethnic tribal groups, were driven out and more than four lakhs of Bengali Muslims were settled in the land left behind by the evicted tribal people. Khaleda Zia after becoming the Prime Minister continued the policy of Zia and Ershad so far the CHT was concerned. She proved to be an equally fanatic Muslim. The CHT, the habitat of more than six lakh tribal people, had to face untold sufferings under the fundamentalist regimes of Zia, Ershad and Khaleda Zia. The CHT Commission based in Denmark, exposed the violation of human rights in the CHT. Then the Commission headed by Prof. Douglas Sanders of the University of British Columbia, Canada observed, that peace would not return to the CHT unless a political solution was found out. In fact, all democratic rights were denied to the indigenous people of the CHT. However, under growing international pressure, the District Council Act was passed in 1989 and three District Councils were set up as a face-saving measure. Face-saving measure, because the Councils were not given enough power to be autonomous in nature. The Councils were given little power to settle the vital issues pertaining to their honorable existence. Rather, on the other hand, the militarization of the CHT was perpetuated by setting up three permanent military garrisons.

Begum Khaleda Zia who had fought against the dictatorship of Gen. Ershad, failed to introduce any democratic measure for the benefit of the average citizen as her vision was blurred by her fundamentalist attitude like her two immediate predecessors. Her anti-India policy was also pronounced whenever she used to come to power. In fact, it was during her tenures as the PM that many insurgent outfits of North-East India were able to set up their strong bases within Bangladesh. Besides, she categorically denied the presence of any Bangladeshi infiltrators in India.

But when Sk. Hasina came to power, she not only adopted a very stringent attitude towards the fundamentalist forces and those who had opposed the 'Liberation War' but also started taking punitive action against them through proper judicial procedure according to the laws of the land. She was also responsible for uprooting the bases of the Indian insurgent outfits from within Bangladesh. The top-ranking leaders of ULFA were arrested and handed over to Indian authorities. (However, that is a different story altogether). Thus, she has, in a way, contributed to the commencement of 'Peace Talks' between the ultras and the Indian government. She has also given official recognition to those foreign citizens who had offered active assistance in bringing the 'Liberation War' to a victorious end. In fact, this humble self was also awarded 'The Friends of Liberation War Honour' for having trained up few companies of Guerrilla fighters of the 'Mukti Bahini' of Bangladesh. The economy is also getting stronger by the day under her stewardship. But, at the same time, it must be admitted that efforts for destabilizing her government have been unending while she has proved herself to be the *'Iron Lady' of Bangladesh.*

Still one piously hopes that Bangladesh will turn a new page of history and come to occupy a pride of place in the comity of nations.

Apart from natural calamities regularly causing devastation in Bangladesh, another serious threat is looming large in the horizon of Bangladesh in the shape of global warming. SK. Hasina, the Prime Minister of Bangladesh, had recently stated in an international conference held in Indonesia that global warming will raise the sea level in next few years. Consequently, extensive coastal areas of Bangladesh will go under water, thereby rendering these areas inhabitable. This phenomenon, she further said, will displace more than thirty million Bangladeshis, without adequate rehabilitation space. So what is on the cards? The natural consequence will be that these people, in search of safer havens, will spill over mostly to neighbouring India, its Eastern and North-Eastern parts being the most accessible areas. According to UNO's report on 'World

Population Prospects, "the climate of Bangladesh is already undergoing rapid changes causing displacement of a huge number of people"'. (Niyamia Barta, 22nd of April, 2016).

James S Pender of NORWEGIAN CHURCH AID states that '— However for the first time in the earth's history it has been firmly established that its human inhabitants are altering the climate through global warming as a result of greenhouse gas emissions'. He further writes that '— Greenhouse gases have mainly emitted by developed Western countries and it is these countries that must act to prevent climate change becoming more serious....' He further says that the severity of such changes will surface in Bangladesh, in the following manners: 'Average weather temperatures rising; more extreme hot and cold spells; rainfall being less when it is most needed for agriculture, yet more in the monsoon when it already causes floods; melting of glaciers in the source areas of Bangladesh's rivers altering the hydrological cycle; more powerful tornados and cyclones; and sea level rise displacing communities (emphasis mine), turning freshwater saline and facilitating more powerful storm surges. The impact will be intensified by the fact that Bangladesh is both one of the most populated and one of the poorest nations on earth." Pender has also quoted Bishop Michael S. Baroi, former Moderator of the Church of Bangladesh (2007), who stated that, 'It would be a serious catastrophe for my country and for the whole region if much of the land in Bangladesh disappears under the sea. I become friightened to think that my grandchildren will have no place to live on this planet earth. I really want to be sure that they, and their children after them, will be able to enjoy the beauty of my country that I have enjoyed, and will be able to have enough land to live and enough land for food.'

Laurie Goering writes that "Rising Tide of Climate Migrants Spurs Dhaka to Seek Solutions." She has further pointed out that 'Bangladesh's capital city of twenty million, is growing by close to 5 per cent a year, in part as rural families migrate to the city seeking work or having lost their homes to worsening river erosion and storm surges.

The stream of migrants, expected to surge as climate change problems like sea-level rise intensify, could double the already crowded city's population in fifteen years, said Omar Rahman, Vice Chancellor of Independent University, Bangladesh (IUB). '(http://thewire.in /2016/04/27/rising–tide-of-climate-migrants-spurs-dhaka-to-seek-solutions-31912/0—accessed on 11/5/16.

According to a news item published in the Assamese daily, Niyamia Barta of the 12th of May, 2016, five islands of the Pacific near Solomon, have already disappeared under the rising water level and six more are likely to meet the same fate in not too distant a future.

Such studies simply confirm that global warming has already started taking its toll. In December, 2015, the historic climate summit was held in Paris and a climate deal was agreed upon by 195 nations; but only 170 nations including India have so far signed the climate pact under the aegis of the UNO. But it has been apprehended that the process of implementing the pact is going to be rather tardy for various reasons. The concerns of individual countries in this regard will be a major factor. It may, therefore, be concluded that joint venture at international level in this front may not materialize as early as it should.

Such environmental changes are nothing but an alarm signal, particularly for the Indian states bordering Bangladesh. Besides, such changes are sure to cast very adverse impacts on the bio-diversity of these Indian States, particularly causing serious degradation of habitats of birds and animals endemic to these regions and creating unprecedented pressure on land.

Migration from East Bengal/East Pakistan/and then from Bangladesh, may be traced to the following phases:

(1) Immigration, mostly in the nineteenth century between 1826 (when Assam came under the British rule) and 1905, for avoiding the inhuman atrocities perpetrated by the *zamindars* as well as for finding out alternative means of livelihood free from atrocious exploitation.

(2) With the advent of the British, efforts were made between 1905 and 1947, to utilize the abundantly available fallow lands

of Assam for enhancing revenue collection and with this end in view, the door was thrown open to landless peasants of East Bengal and the process received tremendous boost with the introduction of the 'Grow more food' scheme during the World War 11.

(3) Muslim League's Sadulla ministry of Assam took full advantage of the situation and in the name of promoting the 'Grow more food' scheme; thousands of landless Muslim peasants were imported from East Bengal. They were given settlement in lakhs of acres of land. Between 1930 and 1950, these Muslim migrants had occupied 1,50,8000 acres of land. Compared to this, the area of land in possession of indigenous Muslims was rather insignificant. The real intention, as it transpired, was to turn Assam into a Muslim majority state with ulterior motive. Lord Wavell, the then Viceroy of India, ridiculed Sadulla's scheme as 'Grow more Muslim' scheme. The availability of large areas of fallow land, then the existence of large number of grazing reserves and the prevalent system of ownership of land, made the onrush of these land-hungry Bengali Muslims much easier. This apart, the government connivance added fuel to fire. According to the Census Report of 1961, only one-third of Assam's Muslim population was of indigenous stock. By now (2015), the situation must have worsened further. Sadulla's such conspiracy complicated the situation of the state with many adverse fallouts to follow—particularly socio-political tension on the eve of the partition of the country.

It will be of interest to mention here about the appearance of an evil star in Assam's horizon in the shape of one Abdul Hamid Bhasani during the pre-Independence era. Nobody had come forward to assume the leadership of the huge migrant Muslim population and taking advantage of this vacuum, came Bhasani in 1928, from the district of Pabna of East Bengal. He settled down in a riverine island of Goalpara district. In no time, he succeeded in occupying the vacant seat of the leadership of immigrant Muslims. It was mainly due to the tremendous organizing ability of Bhasani that the entire riverine areas under the occupation of the immigrant Muslims and the villages set up by them, were reverberating in the forties of the last century with the slogan 'Ladke lenge Pakistan'. And until the birth of Pakistan, Maulana Bhasani continued to be in Assam politics a force to be reckoned with. Having spread the virus of communalism, he tried his best till the last moment to include Assam in general and Goalpara district in particular, in Pakistan. All such efforts having failed, he went back to East Pakistan. But his ghost still roams about in most of the immigrant pockets. Even the other day, a road was named after him in the district headquarters town of Dhubri with the State Government looking the other way! No doubt, such adoration of Bhasani's memory has given a fresh lease of life to the virus of rabid communalism.

(4) The next wave of migrants surfaced with the partition of the country. The transfer of power coupled with the partition of the country on the 15th of August 1947, was followed by communal riots and atrocities of an unprecedented scale against the Hindus and Sikhs in West Pakistan. East Pakistan did not take much time to follow the same example. As a result, millions of Hindu refugees crossed over to Assam and West Bengal. All these refugees being Bengali speaking, West Bengal did not experience the degree of tension experienced by the Assamese in the wake of this large-scale influx of Bengali refugees. In the long run, the Assamese, already under tremendous pressure from the immigrant Muslims, had to face serious upheavals on the economic, political, social, religious and cultural fronts. However, Goalpara, since reorganized into four districts, continued to be an integral part of Assam.

(5) Migration from across the border had never ceased. The next big influx took place during the 'Liberation War of Bangladesh.' According to various estimates, both official and non-official, about ten million people crossed over to Assam during this war and most of them did not go back after the war ended.

(6) Bertil Lintner refers to another wave of migrants in his *Great Game EAST* in the following words: 'A third campaign against the Hindu minority began in 2001, as Islamic

fundamentalists went on a rampage through non-Muslim communities. Thousands of people fled to India' (Page 153).

(7) According to Ramchandra Guha, after Bangladesh came into existence, the number of voters in the electoral rolls of Assam jumped from 6.6 million to 9 million in the decade of 1970's, which is accounted for chiefly by immigrants from Bangladesh. (India After Gandhi, Page number 555).

[8] Apart from these main phases, unabated infiltration is still going on daily in absence of any foolproof preventive measures.

The process of illegal migration, thus, continues unabated, creating serious apprehensions in the mind of the Assamese. Late Gaurishankar Bhattacharyya, a most celebrated intellectual and poltical and literary luminary of Assam who was the leader of the Opposition in the Assam Legislative Assembly for a very long time as also the President of the Assam unit of the Janata Party during the post-Emergency period, has recently written that 'Foreign infiltration is the biggest problem of Assam today. It has impaired the political, economic and demographic balance of the State and has made a planned development of the State almost impossible. With the passage of time it is becoming a growing menace endangering the very existence of the State of Assam and the integrity and safety of India.' (Assam: An Epitome of India, Page number 78).

Baljit Rai, another intellectual from the Punjab, while writing on Muslim fundamentalism and Assam's problems emanating there from, says: 'Assam is on fire and will continue to burn till it is reduced to cinders and Bangladeshi Muslims hijack the State. Thanks to the policy of British rulers for setting unwholesome precedents and Indian leadership, both state and central, which adamantly refuses t o see ground realities' (Demographic Aggression Against India, page 122).

Way back in 1944, Dr. Rajendra Prasad, who went to become the first President of the Republic of India, had expressed grave concerns over the unabated influx of Muslims to Assam from East Bengal.

Dr. Birendra Kumar Bhattacharyya, a Jyanapeeth awardee and subsequently the President of the Sahitya Academi, observed that 'the politics of land-grabbing in Assam is ostensibly expressed in minority politics, which means an issue of land and jobs for Bengali Muslims and Hindus irrespective of their nationality. In reality, as the historical experience shows, it gives rise to a different kind of politics, the politics of demographic expansion and of gradually converting it into a politics of language, culture and finally of executive power.' (The Voice of Assam, published by Axom Sahitya Sabha, Page number 14 and15). 'He further quoted a veteran freedom fighter and journalist Harendra Barua as follows: "In the present census of 1971, out of nearly 15 million people of the State, over four millions, both Hindus and Muslims, were Bangladeshis. Hindus and Muslims are poised almost equally. In 1980 in an estimated population of 18 million, their number is estimated to be eight million. Assam today is faced with the twin problems of being either greater West Bengal or prospective Bangladesh. If this trend continues, sooner or later Assam may meet the fate of Tripura or Sikkim."'

> In 'Impereiled Frontiers: India's North-Eastern Borderlands', Nari Rustomji observed that 'The hopes and aspirations of the Assamese that they could absorb the hill districts of Assam within their own cultural stream were doomed from the very outset. The Assamese did not realise that people, however primitive, resent the imposition of alien culture. And so, one by one, the hill districts broke away from the parent state. The Assamese have since found themselves in their turn faced with the threat from cultural annihilation. Year after year, immigrants from Bangladesh have been infiltrating into Assam and getting themselves in the host state. But in getting themselves so absorbed, they have clung tenaciously to their own culture and made no attempt to assimilate with Assamese. The Assamese have a legitimate fear that if the influx continues the time will not be far when they will be reduced to a minority in their own state and lose

their cultural identity.'— This author would further add that the hill people also had a legitimate fear that if they remained within Assam, they would be, sooner or later, overwhelmed by the foreign infiltrators. No doubt, the people in Meghalaya, Mizoram, etc feel safer today than being in Assam, despite the pressure of illegal migrants in their states also because their societies and governments are more alive to the situation.

Lt. Gen SK Sinha, as the then Governor of Assam, had submitted a report to the President of India in 1998, with copies to the Prime Minister and the Chief Minister of Assam, on the problem of illegal influx to Assam. Relevant potions of his report is available ai Appendix 11 for favor of reference. He has once more written in The Assam Tribune of the 3rd of June 2016 on 'Tackling illegal migrants issue in Assam'. Some quotations from the article are as follows: '— In 1997, Prime Minister IK Gujral sent me as the Governor of Assam when insurgency and violence were at its peak in the state. I found that the root cause of the alienation of the people of Assam was the illegal migration from Bangladesh changing the demography of Assam with all its adverse political and economic impact. In 1998, illegal migrant voters were in a majority or near majority in 40 of the 126 Assembly constituencies in Assam. Their presence has increased in the last 18 years.' He further writes that 'The Illegal Migration Detection by Tribunal (IMDT) Act ostensibly to check illegal migration was actually designed to facilitate infiltration into Assam'. He also alleges that 'All the 14 Congress MPs from Assam wrote to the President calling for my recall as I was interfering in political matters.' He goes on to point out that 'To this day, hardly anything has been done to implement the recommendations in my report to the President submitted in 1998. -------------------Tarun Gogoi as the Chief Minister maintained that illegal migration was a non-issue.'

Still, given the present state of affairs, all other states of the North-East are likely to be confronted with the same menace as the network of the infiltrants, lately backed up by jihadis, are being spread out far and wide.

New Delhi's indifferent attitude towards Assam has been felt for over a century now. Late Ghanashyam Barua was the first representative of Assam in the Imperial Legislative Council. Way back in 1913, he had spoken about the pitiable plight of Assam in his maiden speech in the following words: 'Assam is indeed still very backward and poor; but I venture to think that the backwardness is greatly due to the indifferent treatment she received from the Government all along' and the tradition has lasted for over a century.

The indifferent attitude betrayed by New Delhi has unfortunately generated a feeling of alienation among the indigenous people of the North-Eastern part of India, which in some cases degenerated into secessionism. The thinking section of the indigenous population, particularly the younger generation, is quite disturbed over the issue of Bangladeshi infiltration with the result that the atmosphere has remained agitational for decades. In 1937, Ambikagiri Raichoudhury, Nilmoni Phukan and Satyanath Bora had submitted a memorandum, on behalf of the '*Assam Sangrakshini Sabha*', to Pandit Nehru during his visit to Assam, highlighting the ominous development generated by the incessant flow of Bengali Muslims from East Bengal. It was clearly explained to Pandit. Nehru that with each constitutional amendment and administrative change commencing from the days of the Partition of Bengal in 1905, the possibility of safeguarding the separate identity of the Assamese people and their characteristics, was receding. They had even informed Nehru that a section of Assamese intellectuals, being alarmed by these ominous development, was even thinking in terms of seceding from India. Not that the state of affairs has since improved. This state of affairs has not gone unnoticed: Myron Weiner wrote in his *SONS OF THE SOIL* that '—The Assamese often think of themselves as a "forgotten" and "neglected" State, within the Indian Union and as neglected people in danger of being overwhelmed by migrant peoples and absorbed by neighbouring states.'

Rajmohan Gandhi, a journalist of very high repute and grandson of Mahatma Gandhi has observed in the same context as follows : 'The rest of India does not see us. If seen, we are not recognized. If recognized, we are not remembered. And we are not heard. This has been the charge of the citizens of the North-east against the Indian majority.' (The Wounds of Indifference by Rajmohan Gandhi.)

Kamal Sadiq, an American Muslim scholar of Indian origin, cites a specific example of the indifferent attitude in his book, 'Paper Citizens' in the following words: 'It is significant that almost 288,109 persons reported themselves as having been born in Bangladesh during 1991 census. They remained so without being enquired into through the process of the Foreigner's Act and enjoyed all the facilities and privileges of Indian citizens'. (Page numbers 45 and 46).

Factors responsible for Bangladeshi infiltration:

Thus, the unending flow of Bangladeshi infiltrators into Assam and other neighboring states, may be attributed to the following inter-related factors: the inadequacy of living space, economic factors, religious factor like expansionist design of fundamentalist elements, very high rate of population growth, resulting from child marriage, polygamous practice and birth-control measures not being in wide vogue, environmental factor like global warming, ever increasing problem of unemployment in Bangladesh, needs of labor markets (being cheaper compared to developed regions, Bangladeshi unskilled and low-skilled labors are in high demand), and international and internal political factors. The porous Indo-Bangla border and the non-availability of a correct ER and non completion of the compilation of the NRC have been additional factors.

The indifferent attitude coupled with total failure of the Government of India and the Assam Government to maintain strict vigilance and seal the Indo-Bangla border, has practically amounted to an invitation to Bangladeshis to infiltrate. Whatever little measures were envisaged in the PIP scheme are also gradually becoming inoperative. The Assam Tribune dated. 25th of February 2016, reports that 'Nearly 30 per cent watch posts meant for keeping a tab on illegal infiltrators are lying nonfunctional in the state even as the law enforcing agencies continue to remain clueless about 37,789 untraced illegal Bangladeshi immigrants who came to Assam post 1971.' In the same report, a senior Assam Police official has been quoted to have complained that on most occasions, watch post personnel are unofficially attached with the local police stations where they perform duties other than they are required to do. This should suffice to inform the reader about the attitude of the Assam government. Ground realities also reveal that most of the watch posts set up under the PIP scheme are defunct.

It cannot but be admitted that the poor work-culture and the easy going habits of the young generation of Assam, also facilitates the employment of illegal migrants from Bangladesh, thereby creating avenues for fresh infiltration. In this context, one cannot help asking that if there are 23 lakhs of unemployed persons in Assam, how is it possible for millions of infiltrators to find employment in Assam? Of course, one must not ignore the fact that lakhs of infiltrators are adept in taking up illegal practices. Many Assamese youths have gone out of the State to take up jobs for a paltry salary of rupees seven thousand or so, instead of concentrating in the rural sector for self employment. The lure of salaried jobs is an important factor contributing to growth of poor work culture.

Assam, nay, India has certainly missed the bus, given the fact that, as already pointed out, the problem of illegal migration has since assumed a global proportion with manifold dimensions which are beyond the control of any particular country. The Prime Ministers of the country and those who became Chief Ministers of Assam since 1985, never considered the issue of alien infiltration seriously, let alone the question of detecting and deporting the illegal migrants. As a result, Assam is under siege today, confronting a fundamentalist network with, lately, the jihadis calling the shots. In fact, the latest dimension added to the problem of illegal migration, is the unearthing of jihadi activities, although the initial detection was not due to any enterprise on the part of the the law-enforcement agencies but carelessness on the part of the IED devices-making jihadi activists. It seems that we are walking into a tinder-box situation, with uncertainty writ large all over about the ignition point. Now, the illegal migrants have spread out to places like Delhi, Rajasthan, Maharashtra and so on. An excerpt from the report prepared in 2001, by the 'Group of Ministers on National Security' of the Government of India, as reproduced below, will speak for itself:

'IIllegal migration from across our border has continued unabated for over five decades. (it may be noted that by now it is for over almost seven decades.) We have yet to fully wake up to the implications of the uncheched immigration for the national security. Today, we have about 15 million Bangladeshis (which must have increased by now after 15 years of the submission of this report.), 2.2 million Nepalese, 70,000 Sri Lankan Tamils and about one lakh Tibetan migrants living in India. Demographic changes have been brought about in the border belts of West Bengal, several districts in Bihar, Assam, Tripura and Meghalaya as a result of large-scale illegal migration. Even states like Delhi, Maharastra and Rajasthan have been affected. Such large-scale migration has obvious social, economic, political and security implications. There is an all-round failure in India to come to grips with the problem of illegal immigration. Unfortunately, action on the subject invariably assumes communal overtones, with political parties taking positions to suit the interests of of their vote banks. The massive illegal immigration poses a grave danger to our security, social harmony and economic well-being.'

(The words within bracket are not parts of the report but 0bservation made by the writer.) It may be noted that the above-quoted report amounts to admission by the Central government itself but no follow-up action was noticed to write home about!

As already mentioned elsewhere, according to knowledgeable circles, the situation will further aggravate with upward trend of global warming, thereby displacing many Bangladeshi in their millions. Of course, same misfortune will overtake many other small island-countries; but that is no ground for consolation to Assam and West Bengal as all these displaced millions will swarm into these two Indian states bordering Bangladesh.

The Bangladeshi lobby has made significant inroads into Assam's politics and two MLA's belonging to this lobby lost no time in denying the existence of jihadi elements in their respective areas, although six jihadi activists had already been arrested from one of the two LA constituencies of these two MLA's. During the investigation of two cases of explosion at Burdhaman district, the international links of the jihadis have also been unearthed. As these lines were being penned, information poured in that eleven more jihadis were apprehended in Chirang districts of the BTAD within a span of five to six days in the third week of April2016, the total number of jihadis arrested rising to twnety-nine. It transpired that some mosques and Madrasas were being used for imparting training to the young recruits. The arrest of Imam Joynal Abedin of Rajapara Jame Mashjid in this connection, intensifies such suspicion. Two AK-47 rifles are also reported to have been recovered from their possession. This was confirmed by a Police officer of DGP's rank while speaking to the electronic media on the 21st of April 2016. As usual, protests have been made and mostly repeated slogan of harassing the minoroties has been also raised. But action against these demonstrators for interfering with Police investigation is yet to be taken. Certainly religious intolerance has been the main sustaining factor in activating the illiterate mass. Some organisations operating in BTAD area, are also reported to be organizing terrorist network under the banner of one 'Popular Front of India' in association with some International terrorist organisations (Editorial column of Dainik Axom dated 14th of October 2014) and they are certainly not operating to promote the cause of the indigenous population. Even it has been reported that these elements had been very active in fomenting the communal disturbances in BTAD area. They have been also reported to have been involved in attacks against the tribal people. The NIA is reported to have enough evidence on this count. That al-Queda had hatched a conspiracy, was sounded long back in 2002 by Alex Perry. Perry wrote in **TIME** on the 21st of October 2002 that 'Bangladesh has its fundamentalists. Its Southern coastal hills and Northern borders with India are lawless and bristling with Islamic militants armed by gunrunners. 'Having ascertained the emergence of Laden's al-Queda in Bangladesh, he has further reported that —'The emergence of al-Queda in Dhaka is merely the latest sign that Bangladesh's more radical Islamic groups are coming out from the forests. —On the 9th and 10th of May, sixty-three representatives of nine Islamic groups, Rohingya forces, the Islamic Oikya Jote and the ULFA met in Ukhia to form the Bangladesh Islamic Manch, a United Council under HUJI's leadership. So far the *Manch* has restricted itself to circulating speeches by bin-Laden and Mullah Masud Azahar, a Pakistani militant leader. But it has big plans, says the HUJI sources: 'The dream to create a larger Islamic land than the territorial limits of Bangladesh to include Muslim areas of Assam, North-Bengal and Burma's Arakan province. That dream, if Islamic terrorists are allowed to continue their operations in Bangladesh, could be nightmare for the rest of the region.' As such, efforts for expanding the Muslim-occupied areas must be viewed in the context of what Alex Perry had reported a decade and half back. The Government of India cannot be accused of reacting sharply to this piece of information involving the security of the entire north-eastern region of the country.

A critical and dispassionate review of various happenings, writings and studies, makes it crystal clear that Bangladesh's operation to flood the North-East with her nationals, is not only a well-planned strategic move but it is also backed up by well-defined philosophical/academic exercises, which do not seem to cause the least of worry to the Central and State governments. On the other hand, the tripartiteness of the unholy alliance of China, Pakistan and Bangladesh, has not failed to attract the attention of security analysts. A PTI report published in The

Assam Tribune on the 23rd of July 2007, should be an eye-opener for the doubting Thomases:

New Delhi, July 22: Warning that the threat to India's security in the North-east is 'most difficult' to handle, a security analyst has said vulnerability of the Siliguri corridor could be exploited by 'inimical regional powers' to cut off the region from rest of the country. Maintaining that the 10-12 kilometres wide and 200 kilometres long corridor had been facing turmoil for many years, the expert said: 'The area may well be further subverted by inimical regional powers. Chinese intention to bargain for Tawang to secure Tibet is deceptive.

In an Editorial in the latest issue of 'Indian Defense Review', its Editor Bharat Verma said: '................ If this critical corridor is choked or subverted or severed by force, Union of India will have to maintain the North-east by air.'

Noting that vote bank politics had led to illegal migration from Bangladesh in the past two decades, he said many border districts now had a majority population having illegal migrants from the neighboring nation. 'In the near future, this leverage will be used to create an internal upheaval against the Centre as in the case of the (Kashmir) Valley.' Verma further said that this would be a classic case of 'Asymmetric warfare' launched by Islamic fundamentalists. 'What cannot be achieved by conventional wars, can be done through infiltration and subsequently internal subversion. They call it *jihad*.'

Verma said with the internal turmoil in the Siliguri corridor, the low population surrounded by an over populated Bangladesh exporting Islamic terrorism under the tutelage of Islamabad, growing Chinese influence in Nepal and Bangladesh and Beijing upping its ante on Tawang – 'The danger to the region is great.' He said New Delhi continued to 'fiddle while the North-east burns' posing a grave problem to the territorial integrity of India. – PTI

Not that the experts of the MHA, External Affairs and Defense, are not aware of these possibilities; but the political leadership prefers to look the other way with the sole intention of perpetuating its vote banks. Thus, briefly speaking, the question of national security and integrity, is not receiving the topmost priority it deserves, thereby making the whole issue more complicated and bereft of any possibility of early solution. Latest developments emanating from the ouster of Bangladeshi migrants from Arunachal and Nagaland and their influx into Assam, have certainly notified in advance that a confrontationist is on the cards.

And the Burdhaman exposure confirms far beyond any doubt that international links are already operating in Assam. In the same context, it should not have been difficult to understand the reason behind the emergence of so many underground militant outfits of immigrant stock. Such development, however, is a pointer to the fact that things may quickly fall apart when the deficiencies of law-enforcing and intelligence agencies cause no concern to the power that be. These official agencies would have certainly done better if Alex Perry's report was anything to go by. An Assamese daily Amar Axom's correspondent from Gossaigaon of Kokrajhar district, reported on the 12th of October 2014 that some local fundamentalist organisations were receiving help from fundamentalist outfits of Bangladesh and indulging in anti-national activities in the guise of religious and voluntary organisations. These NGO's have set up in the name of Islam some educational institutions where uneducated youths are being motivated to join terrorist outfits. Such operations are taking place in the districts of Dhubri and Kokrajhar bordering Bangladesh. One cannot help wondering why the respective district Administration has so far drawn a blank. Religious sentiments are exploited and the uneducated poor youths are thus attracted to the fundamentalist networks with the Administration appearing to be a helpless onlooker. These recruits are subsequently trained up in handling of arms and explosives as also in subversive activities. Those arrested in connection with the Burdhaman incident, are also reported to have made confessional statement in this context. Also it has come to light that they are receiving funds and arms from countries like Afghanistan, Pakistan, Bangladesh, Iraq amidst others As a result, in many places innocent Indian Muslims are being eyed with suspicion, thereby fomenting communal tensions. Then, The Assam Tribune of the 13th of October 2014, further reports that 'The ethnic clashes in the Bodoland Territorial Autonomous Districts (BTAD) area in 2012, brought Assam within the radar of the international jihadi groups, while the Indian security agencies started getting inputs about the possibility of Al Qaeda expanding bases to the Indian sub-continent from early this year. 'According to the same report, the Ministry of Home Affairs (MHA) is of the opinion that these clashes of 2012, have since attracted the attention of the International jihadi groups.' The threat from the Al Qaeda increased after the emergence of the ISIS in the Middle East countries, says the same report.

The situation in the BTAD has already been highlighted at the beginning.

CHAPTER 4

RELIGIOUS FUNDAMENTALISM, TERRORISM AND THE IDENTITY CRISIS OF ASSAM AND ITS INDIGENOUS PEOPLE

These are matters of full-scale research. As such, efforts have been made in what follows below, to dwell mainly upon the salient factors involved in the issue briefly.

The instinct of self-preservation apart, religious fundamentalism and terrorism are not inherent in human nature. These are subsequent acquisition during the journey of human civilization.

While exercises for preserving ethnic and religious identity may ensure survival of the fittest, successful aggressive exercises of such nature may also engender the tendency to dominate, if not exterminate, others not falling in line. The lack of wider vision of human existence and co-existence with nature, accentuates a process, which more often than not, degenerates into fundamentalism and sheer selfishness. In recent times, the fight for monopolizing political powers has added extra wings to growing fundamentalism, both ethnic and religious. The basic democratic right to disagree is destroyed by any kind of fundamentalism.

Left alone, self-destructing fundamentalism would not have possibly surfaced in India. But cocooned existence was not possible in the march of human civilization. Which is why, the infiltration of different ideologies and ways of life was a natural development, and in the process, assimilation did result and where the process did not succeed, seeds of confrontation took various shapes. But the process of assimilation still continues and that has been the hallmark of the emergence and existence of the composite existence of India as also of Assam. In this context, it will be relevant to point out that in India, Hinduism with its multifaceted schools, has been, as already recognized by no less a body than the Supreme Court of India, is more a way of life than a religion of the bigots. Hinduism does not owe its origin to a single scripture or a single prophet with the result that over the millennia it has absorbed diverse schools of thoughts and practices, thereby developing rich tradition of tolerance. Even an atheist like CHARBAC has been acclaimed as a 'Hrishi' (saint). But with the advent of single Prophet/single scripture-oriented religions, the tradition of tolerance was put on heavy premium despite the respective Prophets' teachings to the contrary. As such, not the prophets but the extra jealous disciples have not hesitated to violet the teachings of their respective Prophets. Thus, the seeds of fundamentalism were sown, though not fertilized immediately. As unlike Christianity and Islam, swords were never used by Hinduism for extending its domain, thanks to the natural process of growth coupled with the tradition of tolerance. Ideas have fought against ideas, but not men/regions against men/religions. Hindu fundamentalism, if any, has been only a reaction to alien expansionist fundamentalism. In fact, in no ancient university, India ever cultivated any fundamentalist attitude to religion, as opposed to the thousands of Quami Madrasas controlled by Darul UloomMadrasas of Bangladesh, enriched by compulsive circumstances, despite its rich cosmopolitan heritage, Hindu fundamentalism in recent times did raise its ugly head, mostly as a reaction resulting in the demolition of the Babri Masjid and immediately after, politics took over. Since then, there has been no lull. With the help of hindsight, it may be deduced now that instead of promoting the Hindu cause, the Babri Masjid incident has been like a shot in the arm of the Muslim fundamentalists. Assam has been no exception. Even, Congress(i) members, while trying to polarize the Muslim voters during the electioneering campaigns, do not hesitate to take recourse to a communal approach. During the electioneering campaign of the infamous elections held in Assam in 1983, Abdul Ghani Khan Choudhury, a Congress (I) leader from West Bengal, had gone to the extent of instigating Muslim voters in an immigrant Muslim area in the following words: 'If Hindu kills one Muslim then Muslims should retaliate by killing three Hindus and the government would support you.' (An excerpt from the speech delivered on the 10th of February 1983 at Mairabari.) The camouflaged rise of the AIUDF immediately after the repeal of the IMDT Act, is an unmistakable pointer to that direction. And under its aegis, as many as three developments/phenomenon, may be said to have emanated from its hidden agenda of perpetuating fundamentalism:

- Open demand for an autonomous area for Muslims in lower Assam.
- Threat to drive out the Assamese from the districts of lower Assam.
- Demand for making 'Lungi' and 'Topi' the National attire of Assam.

Subsequently, in a *'dharna'* staged at Dhubri, besides shouting anti-India slogans, threats were held out to drive out the Indians from Dhubri district. In this connection, two cases were registered at the Police Stations of Gauripur and Hatigaon against one Mahibul Haque. The High Court had reportedly refused to grant anticipatory bail to him but he is yet to be arrested. No investigation has been done and Mahibul continues to thrive under political patronage of Dispur. He was the Chairman of a government Corporation and he was sighted by me in the company of the then Chief Minister Tarun Gogoi on a Television channel after those two cases were registered and bail refused to him.

If these are not well pronounced form of fundamentalism and anti-national activities, what else could be?

A word of caution: Hindu fundamentalism as a backlash, may be as nauseating and reactionary as any fundamentalism or bigotry. Still India continues to be a strictly secular State because of its predominant Hindu majority whereas the Muslims of the sub-continent lag far behind in accepting it as a political creed, thereby keeping the ground fertile for growth of fundamentalism. However, one must admit that there has never been any communal clash between the Assamese Hindu and the Assamese Muslim and both the communities have been maintaining harmonious relation for centuries on end. Which is why, communal riots did not break out in Assam in the wake of the partition of the country as elsewhere. No doubt, Chaglas are exceptions and not the rule. Besides, Madrassa education with heavy bias for Arabic tradition is not allowing any concession to Indian secularism. Needless to mention that in a Muslim theocracy (where Islam is the State religion), no minority group can expect to survive with dignity. The exampies of Afganisthan, Pakistan and Bangladesh are there to remind us of this grim reality. Religion receiving priority over the nation and national heritage, the Muslims of India excepting those with national outlook and particularly the power-hungry Muslim leaders, could not reconcile to the idea of a free India wth a Hindu majority, subscribing to the democratic principle of 'one man, one vote' (universal suffrage) and also ignored the promised creed of secularism. For them, India is a Hindu country only. Hence, the 'Two nation theory'. Their war cry was that 'Islam is in danger', the legacy of which is the fountain head of their ever-expanding fundamentalism with, however, no relevance to ground realities. Right on the heels of the partition of the country, emerged the Kashmir tangle, now hanging fire for almost seven decades and keeping the socio-political tension alive between the two major communities of the subcontinent on the one hand and on the other, contributing volubly to the expansion and consolidation of religious fundamentalism. Significantly, many of the fundamentalist outfits originated in Kashmir and its neighborhood. As already pointed out, the rise of Taliban and al-Quaeda has been instrumental in expanding the fundamentalist networks to Bangladesh, South-west Myanmar and to many areas of Assam, Mizoram, Manipur etc. in a planned manner. Alex Perry's words as quoted above, have proved to be prophetic. Now, Rohingiya Muslims of Myanmar have also appeared in the scene. Nandita Haksar, a writer and human rights activist, has pointed out in her book, 'Rogue Agent' that the Burmese government declared that the Rohingiyas were foreigners, thereby divesting them of their citizenship status, that they had to flee to Bangladesh after the military crackdown in 1990. She categorically states that 'Arakan resistance organisations have been traditionally hostile to the Rohingiyas and this attitude alienates the Rohingiyas even further and they are compelled to look for solutions in radical Islamic politics.' This is a glaring instance of ethnic forces joining hands with religious force. Consequently, areas inhabited by Rohingiyas have become breeding ground of Muslim fundamentalists as also safe havens for racketeers. Be that as it may, the situation in Myanmar is likely to undergo some change in favor of the Rohingiyas after a democratically elected government has captured power in Myanmar. Aung Sun Su Kyi, the Nobel Peace Prize awardee, who has been mainly instrumental in installing a democratically elected government, has since turned her attention to the problem of the Rohingiyas and treating the entire problem from the humane point of view, thereby raising hopes of a peaceful solution of the problem.

Little more details about the proliferation of the Madrassa network may be in order:

Jihadi activities in Bangladesh could not have proliferated without the active assistance and training imparted by pro-Pakistani elements in the government, political parties like the Jamat-e-Islami (JEL) which was a key constituent in the BNP government and the chain of 'Qaumi Madrassas', the breeding ground for Islamic militancy coupled with India-bashing. The revolt in Bangladesh Rifles some time back, is an indication of the damage that may be caused by the fundamentalist elements against a government perceived to be pro-Indian. According to available reports, 700 Qaumi madrassas are dedicated to support and train up Islami militants. These militants-manufacturing plants function mainly under three parent organizations: Darul Ulum madrassas in Chitagong Lakhan Bazar/Darul Ulum MounulMadrassas in Hathazari/and Jamiatul Islamia Jamia Madrassas in Patiya. These three parental Madrassas co-ordinate and produce thousands of Islamic militants. The Islamic Madrassa curriculum is controlled by Anjumane Itteihadul Madaris with planning and executing Islamic militancy Movement as its chief agenda. Jamiat-i-Islamia and its student wing Islami Chhatra Sibir are also directly involved in these activities. The Islamic student organisations of Myanmar and Rohingia-inhabited areas are closely working with Jamiat-i-Islami and Islamic Chhatra Sibir of Bangladesh with abundant fund flowing from the Middle East. Islamic militants are reported to have formed active relations with the Taliban and Harkatul Jihad groups through 'Bangladeshi Afghan Fighters' formation. The proliferation of these Islamic activities in Assam and occasional clashes with the Islamic ultras in Assam have been also evident.

The Jihadis based in Bangladesh and operating in Assam and other parts of the North-East are drawn from a vast cross section like government officials and political parties with 'India bashing and India baiting' as their primary motto coupled with aggressive design for creating the 'lebensraum' for over-flowing population of Bangladesh and their economic emancipation. These outfits/parties/officials have been very active in supporting insurgent outfits from the North-East like ULFA/MULTA/NDFB amidst others and help these organizations to reap rich harvest and create disturbances in the region in furtherance of fundamentalist expansionism. The blasts which took place on the 30th of October 2008, point to such unholy collaboration. Of late, the Jihadis are trying to acquire permanent moorings in Assam as they have done in West Bengal. The 'Jamatul Muzahidin, Bangladesh' (JMB) had, to start with, set up its camps in the areas inhabited by its co-religionists, namely, the immigrant Muslims. Gradually, it spread its tentacles to other areas, particularly in Barpeta district. It took full advantage of religious fanaticism of the illiterate section of the immigrant Muslims and succeeded in not only enrolling persons like Idris Ali and Shahanur Alam, but also started trading activities with the help of these recruits. NIA's investigation has revealed that one Zahidulla, a prominent leader of JMB, not only purchased land in village Bhaktardaba of Barpeta district, but also married a local girl, thereby cultivating close relationship with villagers of immigrant stock. Zahidulla indoctrinated a number of local youths for getting actively involved in jihadi activities. It is surprising that even without being either an Indian citizen or a permanent resident of the village, Zahidulla could acquire immovable property in violation of laws and rules of the country. But no action has been taken against those officers and employees of the concerned departments who had facilitated the acquisition of immovable property by Zahidullah. Even there are scopes for prosecuting those who had harboured this Bangladeshi jihadi leader. The case of Shahanur Alam is too well known by now for any elaboration. It was with Zahidulla's blessings that Shahanur succeded in spreading the jihadi network in areas like Howli, Kayakuchi, Bhabanipur amidst others. Of course, Zahidulla disappeared as soon as Shahanur attracted Police notice.

However, the situation in this regard is assuming a much more dangerous proportion. Of late, the jihadis are reported to have established contacts with the gun-runners of Nagaland and Myanmar for acquiring modern weapons. [The Assam Tribune, May 2, 2016].

Lakhs of immigrant Muslims including illegal migrants are mostly illiterate and prone to fall victims to religious bigotry. As a result, they are easily drawn to a larger game plan in Assam for capturing political power. To foment communal tensions and riots, may also prove to be a factor in furthering the aforesaid game plan, because such communal riots invariably lead to polarization of the population on communal line as in Gujrat. The reaction to such sinister design may also bring in its train untold sufferings to thousands of innocent immigrant Muslims. Certain indigenous ethnic groups, potentially more militant by nature, are even reported to be thinking in terms of ethnic cleansing! The fear factor invariably results in secular elements taking the back seat with parties nursing an entirely communal agenda emerging as the winner. In Assam, the Bangladesh lobby would reap the richest harvest in such a situation. Quite possible that tough policies adopted by the Hasina government in Bangladesh, may result in slowing down the progress of jehadi activities; but Assam will still stand to suffer, in the face of unabated infiltration because fundamentalist seeds have already been sown in the minds of millions. Unfortunately, the graph is still rising in the absence of any foolproof anti-infiltration measures.

The latest developments in North Cachar Hills, leading to the exposure of the role played by one John Mizo, has laid bare the fact that Manipur/Mizoram/Meghalaya/Assam are being used as corridor for importing arms and explosives illegally from China. China's role in this respect has always been a matter of serious concern for last few decades. On the other hand, drugs-trafficking has been a source of income for quite a few terrorist outfits. Bertil Lintner, a Bangkok based Swedish Journalist, has in his book, 'Land of Jade', given enough indications as to how drugs-trafficking has been developed as a thriving industry, mainly in North West Myanmar with North East India as the main corridor for export and the terrorist outfits of the region have not failed in taking full advantage of this situation.

The rise of terrorism in Assam is not only due to ethnic clashes but also due to short-sighted, partisan attitude on the part of the Central government. The tendency to treat any legitimate, democratic movement/agitation as a law and order problem has, more often than not, boomeranged as counter-productive. Indira Gandhi's attitude towards the historic Assam Movement is a case in point. The emergence of ULFA is the direct result of such hard-line, if not hard-headed, attitude. Insurgency of long standing in Nagaland, did not help matters either. Nor did the hostile foreign powers failed to take advantage of such fertile ground for promoting secessionism and so many ethnic groups did not lag behind taking the cue from ULFA/Nagas/Mizos amidst others. Lately, symptoms of religious radicalism joining hands with separatism have been also evidenced. In fact, in Assam (If not in Nagaland where 98 per cent of her population is Christians), they are complimenting each other. Samir Kumar Das, a writer and research scholar, in one of his discourses writes: 'In a region like the North East, radical religious discourses are situated within a very complex demographic and ethnic matrix. The process of community formation inspired by the emergence of radical religious discourses in the North East, has taken on an ethnic character as much as the prevailing ethnic lines of difference slowly get translated into religious divisions.' While concluding, it may be safely stated that religious fundamentalism has emerged as a big threat not only to Assam's distinct identity but also to national security as its concept does not admit of a secular nation-state. The concept of Islamic Brotherhood as understood by the fundamentalist cuts across diverse ethnic and national existence.

The situation in West Bengal is no less alarming and such alarming situation has even attracted the attention of foreign scholars and researchers. While writing an article captioned **'Greater Islamic Bangladesh is a serious threat to Indian Integrity, Sovereignty and Hindu Majority'**, Pamela Geller has quoted Dr. Richard L. Benkin, author of *'A Quiet Case of Ethnic Cleansing The Murder of Bangladesh's Hindus' in Benkin's words as follows:* 'I can confirm this. I have spoken with Bangladeshi schoolchildren and older students who are being taught that there is "no reason for Dhaka (capital city of Bangladesh) and Kolkata (Calcutta) to be separate" and that they should both be part of Bangladesh. When I ask them why both should not be part of India if they should be one (and given the fact that Bangladesh is a failed state), they are left without a response. But this is how they are being prepared. When we see how ruling WB (West Bengal) ruling parties are willing to lay down for this in order to hang on to vote banks, we see the importance of elections.'

Taking advantage of such anti-national politics, the Jihadis and Bangladeshi infiltrators are graduallbuilding up their own network of operation. Geller has further pointed out that 'The NIA (National Investigation Agency) has smelled a deeper conspiracy of the establishment of a Greater Islamic Bangladesh hatched by the ISI (Inter Service Intelligence) of Pakistan and DGFI (Director General of Foreign Intelligence) of Bangladesh with other terror modules engaged in the Burdwan Blast. Revelation through recovered documents by the NIA suggest that a bigger conspiracy was being materialized in different parts like Burdwan, Murshidabad, Birbhum, Nadia, Jalpaiguri and in different Madrasas stretched out in the border areas of West Bengal. The documents reflect that the terror modules working on brain-washing of the Bengal Jihadis to establish a 'Greater Islamic Bangladesh' considering the territory of the last nawab of Bengal Siraj ud-daulah (1733-1757) as on 1750 AD, who was infamous for his anti-Hindu cruelty and debauchery. The proposed Greater Islamic Bangladesh includes whole of present Bangladesh, West Bengal, Assam, Tripura, Meghalaya and parts of Bihar, Jharkhand and Orissa. 'The entire article written by Pamela Geller is reproduced in Appendix 9. Once, Shree Aurobinda had observed that 'Nationalism is an Avatar and cannot be slain.' That is to say, the struggle for survival as a distinct identity on the part of any nationality, becomes a continuous process, although under different circumstances such struggle may assume different proportion and complexion. True, as Jaswant Singh has opined in his book, 'A Call of Honour' that 'In our age, issues of international concern are being redefined, national sovereignties and boundaries down-graded, human rights, environment, globalization gaining primacy. We have to recognize this new agenda and work together to meet the challenge.' (Page Number 186). Unfortunately, the fanatic fundamentalist refuses to see the writings on the wall as very succinctly pointed out by Shree Singh in the above-quoted words. The ISIS activists have also refused to see the writings on the wall and dragging the entire human race to a self destructing confrontation.

Politics in general and democracy in particular being a game of numbers, the indigenous people of Assam are losing the game very fast. Any action taken in this regard, either by the State (the possibility of which is remote) or by the people is now likely to amount to only rearguard action. But the history is replete with instances of rear guard action also retrieving quite a few beleaguered situations. As such, it is felt that the situation is still retrievable, provided the authorities concerned take a leaf out of what the European Union (EU) authorities have been doing in similar situations. In the given circumstances, AASU and AJYCP may be seen as involved in such rearguard action only. The total betrayal perpetrated by two Mahanta-led AGP governments, has resulted in loss of credibility on the part of the middle-class leadership of the Assamese mainstream. No new leadership was allowed to emerge to stave off the identity crisis of Assam and her indigenous people. On the other hand, the lack of farsightedness on the part of the two AGP governments accentuated the ethnic divisions. The fear of being dominated by Assamese speaking majority, added extra wing to this process. The failure or unwillingness on the part of the successive central and State governments to take effective measures against trans-border illegal migration did also intensify the fear of being extinct. More infiltration means occupation of more land and jobs. Hence the growing demands for autonomous areas/councils for various ethnic groups. But this may not be the solution of the problem if the State government is dominated by the infiltration-lobby backed up by religious radicalism. In fact, in no Muslim dominated countries minorities could survive, and thus, the crisis of identity has assumed a serious proportion. A mere cursory look at the pattern of growth of electorates in Assam may be enough to indicate the dark cloud looming large in the horizon of Assam:

Years	Increase in Number of Voters
Between 1957 and 1970 (13 years)	12,08,446
Between 1970 and 1978 (8 years)	22,72,671
Between 1991 and 2004 (13 years)	14,37,608
Between 2004 and 2009 (5 years)	24,28,743

Thus, the phenomenal growth of Assam's population has been fully reflected in the bewilderingly bizarre increase in the number of voters registered by the Election Commission of India. What further proof is required in respect of the identity crisis faced by Assam and its indigenous people? The latest Census report has shown that the Muslim population of India has grown faster than other religious communities. The Muslim population increased by 24 per cent, whereas the national decadal growth of population is about 18 per cent. The case of Assam presents a more alarming picture in as much as the decadal growth of Muslim population has shot up to 34.2 per cent as against the rise by 30.9 per cent in the previous decade. Thus, the demographic profile of the state is totally changing and fertilizing the ground all the more for rapid spread of fundamentalism and communal politics. If anything, the last census report has laid bare the dangerous situation resulting from the demographic aggression by Bangladesh.

Because of weak-kneed policy of the Assam government, these immigrant Muslims are now spreading out to the neighbouing States of Assam. In 2003, Neiphiu Rio, the chief Minister of Nagaland had bluntly accused the Assam government of exporting illegal migrants into Nagaland, and Nagaland cannot take any action against them, for they were in possession of valid documents procured in Assam. These immigrant Muslims of Bangladesh origin have now made tremendous impact in the trading sector of Nagaland. In the editorial column of Nagaland Post dated the 31st of August 2002, it was observed that 'There is no denying the fact that in any Muslim religious day, at least half of the shops in Kohima and some 75 per cent in Dimapur remain closed. The point is that this is a clear indication of how much the migrants have been able to make an impact on trading.' The same phenomenon is being witnessed in all the main trading centres of Assam. In a ridiculous vein, Petricia Mukhim had written in the Telegraph (Kolkata) on the 4th of December, 2003 that 'It may not be too long before somebody with the power of numbers (population) demands a Union Territorial status in Dimapur. Its market areas already look like a mini-Bangladesh, albeit more lucrative.' Does not it remind us of the demand for an 'Autonomous Muslim Council' in lower Assam under the leadership of the Chairman of an Assam government's Corporation? The same leader had threatened to drive out the Indians from Dhubri. Conspiracies have been also hatched to enter many names in the NRC, presently under preparation. In this context, it is significant to note that in 2011, the Census Report had registered 63,85,577 families and now, 68.23 lakhs of families have applied for their inclusion in the NRC. This amounts to a tell-tale story of the extent of migration and the well planned design to overwhelm the natives of Assam.

It may be safely concluded that the ISI's game-plan has been that ' More the number of Bangladeshi infiltrators, more are the chances of committing subversive and anti-India conspiracies', thereby speeding up the operation for destabilizing the entire North East. And that such a base is rapidly materializing is evident from the rapid increase in the number of villages in Assam as shown below:

Years	Number of Villages
1901	10,133
1961	22,044
1971	23,001
1991	25,313
2011	26,395

Thus, within fifty years, between 1961 and 2011, 4351 new villages had surfaced in Assam, despite the fact that native people of Assam do not change their habitats unless compelled by environmental circumstances and other natural disasters. These apart, there are number of human habitations in non-cadastral riverine areas which might not have been covered during the census.

While analyzing the entire chain of development from the beginning of the twentieth century, it transpires that the absence of a firm purposeful and native people-oriented land policy had made it that much easier for the immigrants, both legal and illegal to gain a strong foothold all over Assam. In ancient India as well as in mediaeval India and under the Muslim rulers, India had an elaborate system of land & revenue which was developed on the basis of theories developed centuries back by Kautilya, Yagyabalka and in Mughal times by Todarmal. Of course, the British had introduced many changes in land & revenue administration for consolidating their colonial policies as well as to modernize the entire system. After Independence, the tenth chapter was added to the Assam Land & Revenue Act of 1886, in order to safeguard the land rights of the Scheduled Tribes and the Scheduled Castes. Further, in 1980, The Assam Alienation of Land (Regulation) Act. According to section 4 of this Act, if anybody not being an Indian citizen, is found to have purchased land, then his ownership of land will be forfeited and the right over such land will get vested with the government. With such provisions of law, it should have been impossible for any foreign citizens to acquire land rights, provided at the time of granting permission for purchasing such land and getting the same legally mutated, the authorities concerned had exercised their powers in terms of the laws and rules instead of ignoring these rules and regulations. Even there are instructions for not diverting agricultural lands for use in non-agricultural purposes but these provisions also have not been strictly observed. The farsighted, native people-oriented and liberal land policy but at the same time specific enough, adopted by Bordoloi, had been systematically undone by the skimming Sadulla and unfortunately, after the pre-mature death of Bordoloi, his successors till date failed even to visualize the significant role a sound land policy could have played in containing the infiltration problem. Of course, Bishnuram Medhi who succeeded Bordoloi, tried his best to pursue the land policy introduced by his predecessor but under the pressure of vested interests, Medhi was eased out of Assam politics and sent away as the Governor of Tamilnadu in 1957.

The communal outburst at Barpeta, Bohori and lately at Rangiya might have been dismissed by many as pre-election flexing of muscles, thereby ignoring a dangerous pattern in the matrix of fundamentalist exercises. How can one ignore that a particular section of a community is involved in creating all these disturbances? In the awake of the Rangiya disturbances, the demand for a separate territorial council for a particular community has been once more raised. The developing pattern does not certainly augur well for the future of the indigenous people of Assam. Obviously, communal passions are being built up so that polarization on communal lines becomes a reality. In fact, the symptoms of such exercises on the eve of Assembly Elections of 2016 have already surfaced. However, this time the indigenous people of the State seem to be realizing their past mistakes and trying to take the bull by its horns.

The intrusion of the immigrants into the field of economic activities at micro level, has accentuated the identity crisis for the young generation of indigenous stock. The worst effect of such large scale influx has been reflected in the work culture of the younger generation of Assam. As it happened in the Southern States of the USA, in the wake of the extensive prevalence of the slave trade during the mid-nineteenth century, so also the easy availability of services of Bangladeshi infiltrators in abundance and that too at comparatively cheaper rates, is making the youths of Assam allergic to hard labor with the result that the areas of economic activities involving manual labor are slipping into the hands of the Bangladeshis; both Muslims and Hindus. Needless to mention that *nature abhors vacuum* and the vacuum created by the poor work culture of the Assamese youths that has been emerging over the years, is being filled up by the Bangladeshis most enthusiastically. Besides, the engagement of Bangladeshi labor, both in the unskilled and semi-skilled sectors on massive scale, has added a new and serious dimension to the ever growing unemployment problem in Assam. As such, not only in political field, but the crisis of identity has expanded into economic, linguistic and cultural fields too. Linguistic because, millions of immigrant Muslims are being instigated to change gear and declare Bengali as their mother tongue.

So, the day may not be far off for raising the demand for declaring the Bengali language as one of the State languages!

The talks and discourses centering around the issue of assimilating the pre-1971 stream of immigrants into the main stream of Assam's community life, may become irrelevant in the context of numerical superiority being gained by the migrants from East Bengal; East Pakistan -and now Bangladesh. Fundamentalist Muslims were mainly responsible for partitioning the country in 1947, then breaking up Pakistan in 1971 and now their sinister game of going for the kill in the shape of usurping another chunk of Indian land, is gaining momentum beyond all shades of doubt. It is then noteworthy that Parsees could not survive in Persia(Iran), Christians in Lebanon and Hindus in Afghanisthan, Pakistanand Bangladesh. As such, our call to the young generation of the Eastern and the North-Eastern States of India, irrespective of ethnicity and religion, would be in the words of Walter Scott:

'Breathes there the man
With soul so dead
Who never to himself hath said
This is my own, my native land'

CHAPTER 5

THE AVALANCHE

Illegal immigration into India is not from Bangladesh alone. It has been happening from Afghanistan, Pakistan, Myanmar, Nepal, Tibet, Sri Lanka, Somalia amidst others places. But the illegal migration of Bangladeshi Muslims in their millions, is of much more serious concern for India in general, and its North-Eastern States in particular. The situation is worsening daily, particularly in view of the fact that immigration from Bangladesh is taking place in a planned manner whereas Assam, nay, India does not have any fool-proof plan to arrest the dangerous trend. Way back in 1931, the Census Commissioner, C.S. Mullan had observed in the context of migration from East Bengal that '"The whole structure of Assamese culture and civilization has been threatened by the invasion of a vast horde of land-hungry Bengali immigrants—mostly Muslims, from the districts of Eastern Bengal, and in particular, from Mymensingh. —it is sad but non-violence in Kokrajhar appears improbable, and that, in another thirty years, Sibsagar district will be the only part of Assam in which an Assamese will find himself at home.' Of course, lately (in 2016), the Union Home Minister interacted with some senior citizens of Assam in Guwahati and apparently, the MHA is gradually waking up. The Assam Tribune dated. the 29th of February 2016, reported that 'The Government of India is trying to chalk out a comprehensive plan to deal with the problem of infiltration of foreigners, while instructions have been given to the agencies concerned to expedite the construction of border roads and fencing to check infiltration.

—the Government has decided to chalk out a comprehensive strategy and the MHA is also taking the help of non-government organizations and experts in the field while trying to formulate the plan' According to the same report, 'The Government is also examining the feasibility of preventing foreigners from acquiring land and that is why, the issue of granting ST status to six communities of Assam is now viewed from the security point of view as such a move would protect land holdings of the persons belonging to the communities.'

Bangladeshis and their leaders have never ceased to think in terms of extending their domain to Assam. Leaving aside Jinnah's and his close followers' dream to include Assam in Pakistan, our attention deserves a close look at the attitude of the leaders of East Bengal in respect of their design for extending their domain east-ward. Way back in the fifties of the last century, no less a person than Sk. Muzibor Rahman, Indira's favourite, if not a blue-eyed boy, had without any reservation voiced his design in respect of the North East of India in his 'Eastern Pakistan: Its Population Determination and Economics', which, briefly speaking, may be surmised as follows: 'The huge population of Bangladesh is an asset. Assam is full of forest resources. Also Assam has abundant resources in the coal and petroleum sector. Which is why Assam must be a part of East Pakistan, (Bangladesh was then yet to be born) then only the economy of East Pakistan would prosper.....' That dream is not yet over.

The Assam Tribune of the 28th of October 1992, published a significant letter to the Editor captioned **'Some Alarming Aspects'**.

Sir,

Recently I have come from London and will return soon. I would like to put forward some of the alarming aspects, which are taking shape in London.

The *Islamic Cultural Center*, based in London, has been taking active role against the interest of India and Assam in particular. The Director of the Center, has taken some specific programmes for inclusion of a major portion of Assam, specially covering oil fields to Bangladesh with aids and help from a specific country and from the organizations of London. I may quote here few lines from newspapers, which may give little idea about the programme.

Arab Times (January 1990) says: 'Bedawi suggested a plan to attract Bangladeshi Muslims, which then could take the number of Indian Muslims to 200 million so as to give them more protection. He expressed his fear that such an opportunity might not come again and proposed that the plan be urgently carried out through European Islamic Council and to delegate one or two persons to carry out a field survey secretly and discreetly so that not to create doubts among the Hindu circles which worked to maintain its creed among its members. Bedawi also suggested that such preachers should be Urdu knowing Arabs and coordination of their work should be through the Center in London.'

'Bedawi also said that there is an opportunity to attract more than 800 million Harijan Hindus who are facing attempts to force them to leave this creed and choose their religion.'

It may be mentioned here that the number of Muslim tourists including tourists from Bangladesh has increased in India, vis-à-vis Assam and several confidential conferences were also held.

There are other significant aspects, which are difficult to be included in this column. It is more important that while transporting people from Bangladesh, large number of physically handicapped people and a number of people who were marked for several crimes were also deported to Assam.

I would also like to ask all people of Assam to look into this aspect very seriously, as it is already late to take any measures to prevent it.

Yours etc.

One observer from London"

Incidentally, there was no perceptible reaction whatsoever either from the government or from the Assamese to this international conspiracy of a tell-tale character. It is a matter of great doubt if ever the above-quoted letter attracted the attention of the State Intelligence Agencies and so many other Central Intelligence Agencies. On the contrary the Union Government had been until recently appeasing the Arabian countries no end; but the possibilities of any of these countries extending support to India over the Kashmir issue, ignoring the claims of Pakistan, did not even seem to be remote. Besides, the Bangladeshi intellectuals are also building up their case for acquiring more living space for their countrymen. *'The Question of Lebensraum'* authored by Sadique Khan as published in The Holiday Weekend of Bangladesh dated the 18th of January 1991, says: 'There is no reason why under-populated regions in the developed world cannot make room for planned colonies to relieve build -up of demographic disasters in countries like Bangladesh....'

'................ A natural outflow of population pressure is therefore, very much on the cards and will not be restrainable by barbed wire or border patrol measures. The natural trend of population overflow from Bangladesh is towards the sparsely populated lands of the South East in the Arakan side and of the North East in the Seven Sisters side of the Indian Sub-continent.'

Abdul Momin, former-Secretary, External Affairs Ministry of Bangladesh and ex-Ambassador of Bangladesh to China observed in Dhaka Courier dated the 22nd of November 1991 that '.......... Not only that Bangladesh has by far the highest density but also that others have several times more space to expand comfortably.....'

The situation has deteriorated so far that Bangladeshi nationals are now making it bold even to think in terms of contesting elections in Assam. One particular Kamaluddin, a Bangladeshi national, was detected in Nagaon district by the police on the 3rd of February 1998. Upon interrogation, Kamaluddin divulged that he hailed from Bangladesh. Son of late Modorisin Ali, Kamaluddin procured a passport through illegal means on the 25th of October, 1994 and entered Assam, arriving at Murajhar of Nagaon district. Kamaluddin was deported to Bangladesh on the 3rd of February 1998 itself. But he re-entered India and filed a case (CR No. 2501 of 1998) in the Guwahati High Court challenging his deportation from India, stating that he is a permanent resident of village Kapahbari, P.O. Murajhar with landed property in that village. Moreover, Kamaluddin claimed that he is an Indian voter and had even contested the 1996 election from No. 90 Jamunamukh LA Constituency. The State Government contested Kamaluddin's claims and produced before the court a passport and a boarding pass of Pakistan International Flight seized from Kamaluddin.

The Court of Justice J.N. Sharma, while disposing off Kamaluddin's petition answered the legal query as to whether a person can be deported from India without resorting to the procedure laid down in the IMDT Act (Since repealed by the Supreme Court) with the following words: 'Yes............. it is not the law if there is a clinching evidence or material, the authority cannot deport a person in view of this Act.' In its judgment, Justice Sharma also vacated the stay order passed earlier on the deportation of Kamaluddin and said that he may be deported from India by the authorities immediately, while holding that his petition also suffered from suppressing of material facts. Justice Sharma further observed that 'before parting with the record I only express my displeasure and annoyance with regard to the casual and cavalier manner in which voters list is prepared/made in Assam. On the basis of such an incorrect voters list a person was allowed even to contest the election...........' (The Assam Tribune, dated the 11th of July 2000).

It may be also considered that Kamaluddin could not have enrolled himself as a voter and contested the election without the active cooperation of his co-religionists of village Kapahbari. However, the reaction of the Election Commission of India after the above quoted judgment was delivered, was nothing to write home about. Also it would have been quite revealing if an enquiry was made to ascertain who had financed Kamaluddin's election campaign along with the names of those who had proposed him as a candidate for the election. One, however, need not go too far to determine where their loyalty lies! In fact, all of them should have been prosecuted for harboring a foreign national. So much for the administrative attitude towards such a dangerous situation! This one single instance should suffice to appraise the readers of the dangerous future Assam has been left to unwillingly move towards. Assam, as an integral part of India got its freedom from the British rule on the 15th of August 1947; but it is yet to get freedom from the fear of being extinct in the hands of Bangladeshi nationals!

An account of the extent of infiltration into Assam and the role played by the Election Commission of India will be very much in order:

Total lack of a firm land policy and the absence of any policy for international border management on a firm and internationally acceptable level, are considered to be the source of what is depicted below. However, the issue of border management is gradually receiving more active attention.

In nine decades, between 1901 and 1991, the population of India recorded a rise of 254 per cent and during the same period, Assam's population rose by 577.77 per cent. In 1901, Assam's population was 32,89,680. On the basis of average national growth, Assam's population in 1971 should have been 69,86,697 whereas it shot up to 1,46,25152. If the national growth is taken as the index for this period of seventy years, Assam had to accommodate an extra load of 76.38 lakhs of people Shri A.K. Roy, the Director General of BSF, had reported in October, 2008, that twelve lakhs of Bangladeshis had legally entered India between 1972 and 2005 but did not return. This abnormal growth has been reflected in the rapid increase of the number of villages of Assam as already shown above. Hence, the need for strictly maintaining a *National Register of Villages*. It may not be out of context to mention here that Indian migrants from other States have been mostly settling down in urban areas, industrial areas and other centres of commercial activities.

Growth rate of Muslim population in Assam:

1911	9.4 per cent
1921	9.4 per cent
1931	20.0 per cent
1941	25 per cent
1951	19 per cent
1961	34.4 per cent
1971	34.5 per cent
1981	No Census could be held in Assam because of the Assam Movement
2001	30.9 per cent
2011	34.2 per cent

The growth of Muslim population in Assam is much higher than the national growth of Muslim population. According to Census Report of 2011, out of total population of India, 14.23 per cent are Muslim. Compared to the national growth, Assam has 20 per cent more Muslim population and this is not due to the increase in the number of indigenous Muslims. The following table illustrates the growth of Muslim population in eleven districts of Assam decade-wise:

Districts	1971	1981	1991	2001	2011
Dhubri	64.5 per cent	no census	70.5- per cent	74.3 per cent	79.6 per cent
Bongaigaon	27.8 per cent	do	50.2 per cent	53.7 per cent	57.52 per cent
Goalpara	41.5 per cent	do	50.2 per cent	53.7 per cent	57.52 per cent
Barpeta	48.6 per cent	do	56.1 per cent	59.4 per cent	70.74 per cent
Kamrup	20.5 per cent	do	23.4 per cent	24.8 per cent	39.66 per cent
Darrang	23.9 per cent	do	32.2 per cent	35.5 per cent	64.34 per cent
Hailakandi	51.4 per cent	do	54.8 per cent	57.6 per cent	60.31 per cent

>>

>>

Districts	1971	1981	1991	2001	2011
Karimganj	44.2 per cent	do	49.2 per cent	52.3 per cent	56.36 per cent
Nalbari	15.4 per cent	do	19.9 per cent	22.1 per cent	35.31 per cent
Morigaon	40.4 per cent	do	45.3 per cent	47.6 per cent	52.56 per cent
Nagaon	39.2 per cent	do	47.2 per cent	51 per cent	55.36 per cent

Thus, leaving aside Kamrup and Nalbari, nine out of twenty-seven districts of Assam have become Muslim majority districts. Being situated on the border of East Bengal and having to face in the past all the Muslim invasions first of all the areas of greater Assam coupled with the consequences of the partition of Bengal, when Assam was tagged with East Bengal, Dhubri district had the distinction of having a larger Muslim population (which is why it had become the hot bed of Muslim League's politics) than other districts of Assam. But the case of Darang district causes the most consternation. According to the Census reports of 1971, this district had 23.9 per cent Muslim population and within next twenty years, it shot up to 64.34 per cent. In fact, the ignition point for imparting tremendous momentum to the historic Assam Movement was triggered off in this district. The untimely death of Hiralal Patowari, the Member of Parliament of the Mangaldoi Lok Sabha constituency, necessitated the holding of a bye-election in this LS constituency and during the preparation of fresh ERs, as many as 47658 objections were filed against alien voters included in the ERs of the constituency. Meanwhile, the Lok Sabha was dissolved on the 23rd of August 1979, thereby necessitating fresh preparation of the ERs of the entire State. Having witnessed the success of the operation of identifying foreign voters in Mangaldoi LS constituency, CM Golap Barbara passed an order for extending the operation for identifying foreign voters to 81 more Assembly constituencies prone to infiltration by immigrants from Bangladesh. During this second phase of operation, more than 5,83,000 objections were filed against suspected Bangladeshi voters in addition to 47658 objections already filed during the first phase of the operation. The Chief Election Commissioner succumbed to political pressure and kept these objections pending, although there is no provision in the Representation of People Act to keep such objections pending! The CEC knelt down when he was asked to bend! These objections were never disposed of, although it was legally mandatory to dispose them of in the prescribed manner.

Apprehensions have already been voiced that such rapid increase in Muslim population resulting from large scale trans-border illegal migration, may ultimately result in a demand for secession and merger with Bangladesh. In other words, what Jinnah could not achieve, would be accomplished by these illegal migrants, actively backed up by the fundamentalists! Commenting on such rapid growth of population in Assam, Ms. Audrey Cantley of London observed that 'In 1961 the Agro Economic Research Centre for North-East India carried out a resurvey of a village called *Chotahaibar,* in the vicinity of Nowgong town. The original settlers of the village were Assamese Hindus. In the 5 years 4 months between the first point of survey and the resurvey the population of the village rose from 600 to 1779 as a result of migration. The composition of the village at the time of resurvey was: Assamese Hindus 10 per cent, immigrant Bengali Hindus 33 per cent.' (The Assamese, Page number 24 by Audrey Cantley.) Thus, within a short period, the population of the village had undergone total change with the Assamese Hindus being ousted rather silently and predicting the shape of things to come in years ahead. Ms. Cantley recorded another example: '1961-62 the Centre carried out a resurvey of Dispur. —The village had been previously surveyed in 1955. One third of the total population had taken up residence there during the intervening 6 and half years.' (*ibid,* Page number 24). One Sri Sudhakar Rao, hailing from Andhra, had carried out a similar study in Morigaon district of Assam which was known to be an infiltration-prone areas. According to his study, in the post -1980 period when the Assam agitation against the foreign infiltrators were gaining momentum, as many as twenty-five villages of Morigaon district were totally 'deHiduised' and in many other villages also, the non-Muslim population was on the retreat. What is significant, is that those who were responsible for this phenomenon, were not Assamese Muslims. Sri Rao has specially mentioned the instances of the following villages:

Dhuti-Dimal/Bhutanimara/Bhogduba/Basundhari-Barajol amidst others of Uttarkhola mouza. Unfortunately, the State government had remained a silent spectator without realizing the significance and implications of such ominous developments. It also may not be out of context to mention here that in the wake of the Indo-Pak War of 1965, many infiltrators/immigrant Muslims of East Bengal stock, had run away to East Pakistan; but off late, they had re-infiltrated and laid claims on the immovable properties they had left behind, thereby creating a constant source of friction and tension. Likewise, many Rabha and Koch-Rajbongshi families of undivided Goalpara district have over the years been displaced in similar manner. An all Assam survey may expose a much more serious situation. As for instance, Diphu, the district headquarters town of Karbi Anglong district falling under the sixth schedule area did not have any immigrant Muslim pockets; but of late, two such large pockets have surfaced in the heart of the town, namely, Panbari and Harilal Basti. Harilal Basti is now known as Islampatty. In fact, within Bangladesh itself, the indigenous people of Chittagong Hill Tracks (CHT) were also ousted and their lands taken over by the Muslims. As a result, the CHT witnessed serious tribal militancy of serious proportion and in course of time CHT Peace Accord had to be devised for pacifying the native people. As such, it has been apprehended that such situation may surface in the tribal areas of Assam also as has already been evidenced in Kokrajhar/Bongaigaon/and Barpeta districts. To be more precise, the concept of ethnic cleansing is gradually gaining ground in the tribal areas of Assam.

The infiltrators' style of operation for land grabbing, by and large, takes the following shape:

Lands legally purchased.

Lands purchased outside the official procedure.

Lands illegally encroached upon.

Indigenous people engaging immigrant labors and then subletting to the immigrants their land, thereby giving a foothold to the immigrants to settle down permanently.

Indigenous people also mortgage their lands, at times, to the immigrants.

Mostly occupation of *khas* land/VGRs/PGRs/non-cadestral riverine areas and 'char' areas has been in vogue for many decades.

Immigrants also, at times, compel the indigenous people to move out to remote places beyond the reach of the immigrants by causing discomfiture to them in various ways.

Finance is made available through the fundamentalist channel. Even, petro-dollars are also suspected to have been playing a significant role. Unfortunately, corrupt Revenue/Forest/Police officers and unscrupulous politicians, ever ready to enrich their vote banks, facilitate such illegal, anti-national deals of land transfer. For sheer greed of money, some tribals were noticed to have sold their land at very high price to the immigrants.

Such rapid growth of the population of immigrant Muslims has been reflected in the composition of the Assam Legislative Assembly. In the elections held in 1946, when Sylhet, a Muslim majority district, was a part of Assam, 34 Muslim MLAs were returned to the assembly; of them thirteen were from the Brahmaputra Valley. But the trend of larger number of Muslim MLA's returning to the Assembly became more prominent even after Sylhet was included in East Pakistan. Following table will illustrate this trend:

Year	No. of Muslim MLA's	Muslim MLA's from Brahmaputra Valley
1952	15	9
1957	15	10
1962	14	10
1967	19	12
1972	20	15
1978	28	21
1983	33	25
1985	23	16
1991	24	21
1996	27	20
2001	26	20
2006	27	22
2011	28	23
2016	28	22

Between 1972 and 1978, a huge number of Muslim infiltrators had entered Assam and registered their names in the ERs. Hence, the increased number of Muslim MLAs in the Brahmaputra valley. The trend has since continued. In 1983, major political parties excepting Congress (I) had boycotted the election and Congress (I) therefore could return thirty-three Muslim MLA's, of whom twenty-five were from the Brahmaputra valley as shown above. In 1985 elections, because of Axom Gana Parishad's ascendency only sixteen Muslim MLAs were returned from the Brahmaputra valley. But the above mentioned trend has since reappeared with full vehemence. Also it may be of interest to note that most of the Muslim MLAs returned from the Assam valley, are not of the indigenous stock. Presently, there is only one Muslim MLA of indigenous stock out of twenty-three returned in the Assam valley. Here an account has been given only of the winning candidates. But if an account of all the Muslim candidates of non-indigenous stock contesting in the so many elections, is given, then a much more alarming situation will emerge. Even in the constituencies reserved for the SC/ST, voters of Bangladesh origin will sooner be dominant factor. Thus the voters of alien origin have laid a seizure of the ERs of Assam! Some simple tribal people, lacking in farsightedness have even sold off their land in some pockets to the immigrant Muslims at exhorbitant prices and moved out to remote areas. The appearance of immigrant villages in the basin of the Ai river, is one such instance. There are many others.

Sri Baljit Rai, in his 'Demographic Aggression Against India', has observed that 'But before we begin to narrate the long and dismal story of universal betrayal of Assam it will be instructive to go into the factors that have contributed to this national shame. The four main factors are:

1) The poor numerical strength of the Assamese,
2) Lack of interest articulation, on the part of the people of Assam and the absence of pressure groups among them in the pre-1947 period,
3) Gentle and tolerant nature of the Assamese and lastly
4) Almost total absence of assertiveness at the national level.'

Thus, Sri Rai has candidly focused on the absolute failure of the indigenous society of Assam. Such a dismal state of affairs could emerge because Assam had been practically mortgaged to the political leadership. Today in Assam, 'leaders' connote only political leaders who, under the present circumstances, are interested only in promoting their partisan and personal interests. Non-political leadership, which should have been the mainstay of the society in promoting its all round development, has surrendered itself to the political leadership and receded to the back bench. On the other hand, political leaders have failed for many decades to make their presence felt in the corridor of powers in New Delhi. Besides, the Members of Parliament from Assam and other North-Eastern States could never form a united platform for raising the problems common to all of them.

Data revealed by the Census of 2011 on the basis of religion, presents a consternating picture. As already depicted above, minorities have become majorities in nine districts and two other districts are proceeding in the same direction. In fifty Assembly constituencies out of 126, voters of immigrant stock are going to determining factor in deciding the result of any elections to be held in future. In twenty-seven of these fifty constituencies, indigenous people including indigenous Muslims will never win any election. These twenty-seven seats will be represented by people who do not belong to the mainstream. And in the remaining twenty-three constituencies the fate of the contesting candidates will be decided by immigrant voters. To be more precise, the winning candidates of these fifty constituencies will have deciding influence in formation of the state government. As such, the political future of Assam is proceeding in a very uncertain and dangerous direction. The day may not be far off when a leader of the immigrant Muslims will become the Chief Minister of Assam. The emergence of the AIUDF seems to be hastening that process.

The extent of infiltration by Bangladeshi nationals into India will be understood better if the Census Reports of Bangladesh are also analyzed along with those of India. Most of the states of India have much less density of population than Bangladesh. Bangladesh is one of the poorest countries in the world. Besides being regularly visited by devastating natural calamities, its political instability and corrupt administration, does not leave much room for social welfare activities and planned development. The Constitution of Bangladesh does not have any provision for the protection of ethnic minorities. The result is there for everyone to see. After partition, there was practically no exchange of population in the eastern sector as in the western sector. In 1947, the religious minorities of East Pakistan accounted for 29.7 per cent of its population including 28 per cent Hindus. Coupled with the lack of political and economic security for the minorities, are certain discriminatory laws like the *Vested Properties Act* and the *Enemy Property Act* which have been, over the years taken full advantage of, by Bangladesh to deprive minorities of the properties – not to speak of the regularly happening communal riots. Lakhs of people belonging to minority communities have been driven out of

Bangladesh, thereby giving rise to the problems of Chakma and Bengali Hindu refugees. The declining trend of Hindu population in Bangladesh is shown below:

Year	Percentage of Hindu population
1941	28 per cent
1951	22 per cent
1961	18.5 per cent
1971	13.5 per cent
1981	12.1 per cent
1991	Little less than 10 per cent

It will be quite in order to note the growth rate of Hindus and Muslims in India, for four-five decades, which will facilitate the appreciation of the fast emerging pattern:

Year	Growth rate of Hindus	Growth rate of Muslims
1911	6.87 per cent	24.83 per cent
1921	19.42 per cent	37.61 per cent
1931	24.68 per cent	43.91 per cent
1941	Not available	Not available
1951	47.99 per cent	56.51 per cent
1961	33.71 per cent	38.37 per cent
1971	37.18 per cent	31 per cent
1971 to 1991	41.89 per cent	77.42 per cent

(The increase in the growth rate of Hindus in 1951 may be entirely attributed to the partition of the country in 1947)

The Hindu population of Assam declined to 67.13 per cent in 1991 from 72.5 per cent in 1971. However, such decline in the percentage of Hindu population is not due to any emigration of Hindus from Assam, nor does it imply its decline in numerical strength; but this is mainly due to the addition of huge number of immigrant Muslims to Assam's population. On the other hand, the growth of Assamese Muslim population has invariably kept pace with that of the Assamese Hindu population. While analyzing the changes in the population pattern, it cannot be ignored that the district of Sylhet with its numerically predominant Muslim population had ceased to be a district of Assam since partition.

But the pace of infiltration has not slowed down even after the six year long Assam Movement and signing of the Assam Accord, way back in 1985. Some latest press reports published after analyzing the Census reports of 2011, are quite relevant: Niyamia Barta, an Assamese daily published from Guwahati, reported on the 9th of March 2016 that in nine districts of Assam, Muslim voters will determine the results of elections to be held in 2016. According to the same report, Muslim voters will determine the results of elections in 170 constituencies of West Bengal and in fifty-seven constituencies of Kerala. The same report is corroborated by another Assamese daily, Dainik Axom of the 27th of August 2015. Dainik Axom's report most relevantly pointed out that in 2001, Muslim majority districts in Assam were six and it had, now in 2011, shot up to nine. Significantly, this has been caused by the increase in the population of immigrant Muslims and not indigenous Muslims. This has been possible only because there is no effective preventive measures in operation. The Assam Tribune and the Times Of India, corroborated the same data after The Register General and Census Commissioner of India released the religion-wise data of population on the 25th of August 2015. As has been apprehended for almost a century, the indigenous people of Assam are on the threshold of being reduced to minority in their own homeland.

But how do they infiltrate and reinfiltrate? Unless this question is seriously addressed by the authorities, both State and Central, neither fool-proof preventive measures may be conceived, nor the demand for an electoral roll divested of the names of foreign nationals, is going to fructify. A comprehensive perception about the 'modus operandi' followed by these Bangladeshi Muslim infiltrates for expanding their base in Assam and its neighboring States is, as such, imperative for the serious students of the problem.

These Bangladeshis use all the three available routes: the surface route, the Railways and the riverine routes. After crossing over at various border points, they mostly entrain at Karimganj of Assam and a number of railway stations of West Bengal. With the improvement of the road system coupled with the extension of the railway network, one may well anticipate that the volume of such illegal Bangladeshi trafficking is bound to increase, given the present poor state of preventive measures Presently, there is no arrangement for any check during their train journey, although mobile checking patrols of the Border Police Organization had achieved remarkable success in the late seventies of the last century. Even Rohingya Muslim infiltrators from Myanmar were also apprehended by such checking parties; apparently the system was abandoned for mysterious reasons after the fall of the Barbara Government. The absence of such measures facilitates the inward journey of the illegal migrants. On the other hand, the intermittent connivance of the BSF personnel at the international border has also turned out to be a major factor. Quite a few arrested infiltrators had in the past made confessional statements about such unholy alliance. The riverine routes are almost exclusively used by the Muslim infiltrators. Unfortunately, the River Police Organization which was mainly conceived as a major anti-infiltration measure, today exists only on paper with no efforts in evidence for improving this very vital organ of the Border Police Organization. Besides, despite repeated demands, no action has yet been taken to register all kinds of rivercrafts, operating both in the Brahmaputra and the Barak, as also in all their tributaries. Movement by country-boats, is a favorite mode of travel by the Bangladeshi Muslims. Lately, they have been using motorized boats as well.

It is an open secret that after crossing over, the infiltrators do not find it least difficult to receive ready shelter with the help of some of their co-religionists. The lobby promoting planned infiltration, were also reported to have taken some cautionary measures so that the infiltrators after crossing over might come overcome probable obstacles. For instance, reports were available that some tutorial classes were held to train up the intending infiltrators in speaking the local language in vogue across the Golokganj sector of the border. Such measures might not have been necessary in the Karimganj sector, obviously because of the similarity of the colloquial language on both sides of the border. The imparting of working knowledge of Assamese language was intended to ensure that the illegal migrants do not find any difficulty in communicating with people inside the Indian border and merging with them without raising any suspicion. This strategy was resorted to, because the PIP scheme was then in operation in full swing. Immediately after, they merged with the local people who mostly used to be their co-religionists. Then they started working as day laborers, cycle-rickshaw pullers, push-carts operators and so on. Previously they used to work mostly as agricultural labors. But subsequently, steps were taken to disperse them eastwards, instead of keeping them confined only to immigrant areas. Now their presence in large numbers in almost all the urban areas including those of the upper Assam, is easily discernible. On being questioned, they invariably take the plea that they hail from certain villages of the districts of Goalpara/Darrang/Nagaon/Marigaon/Barpeta, etc which had since been swallowed by the Brahmaputra. Unfortunately, there have been no efforts for verifying such claims nor does the State government maintain a list of villages obliterated by large-scale erosion caused by the Brahmaputra and its tributaries. Which is why, the maintenance of a 'National Register of Villages' is imperative. It is, however, true that thousands of immigrant Muslims who are legitimately entitled to Indian citizenship, have been victims of the aforesaid erosion; but the authorities simply did not bother to keep any count of these erosion-affected people with the result that they were being eyed with suspicion in respect of their citizenship We have already pointed out that presently, infiltration is taking place in a planned manner. In pursuance of this plan, many organizations and individuals are reported to be maintaining large fleets of cycle-rickshaws/push-carts for providing ready employment to the infiltrators until, after being dispersed to various interior areas, they find their permanent moorings. In fact, according to a reliable report, within Guwahati city itself, more than 20,000 cycle-rikshaws are being operated by these illegal migrants without any valid license from the Municipality authorities. On the other hand, municipal authorities are not known to have been anxious to co-operate with the Police for detecting such violation of laws and rules. On the contrary, the said authorities do not bother to verify the citizenship at the time of issuing valid permits. Thus, organized and unorganized rackets have been facilitating to perpetuate the stay of these alien nationals. Besides, many of them are on constant lookout to avail of any opportunity befalling them for land-grabbing and for procuring ownership of land. The shape of the operation for land grabbing has already been narrated elsewhere. For last few decades, illegal occupation of *khas land/forest land/VGRs/ PGRs/Char (riverine islands) areas and so on*, has become the order of the day. Many tribal people are also reported to have sold their land at very high prices and then moved out to remote areas presently beyond the reach of the Muslim infiltrators. But where did they get the money from to purchase land, is indeed puzzling, which should have attracted the attention of the Intelligence agencies. Villages have been sighted to have surfaced in vacant plots of land overnight and this has been possible because of the culpable connivance of corrupt Revenue/Forest/Police officials and unscrupulous politicians. Thus, they reach the final round of a bigger game-plan and their mentors spare no efforts for getting their names enrolled in the ERs. It may also be mentioned that many forged documents are used to prove their eligibility for getting their names enrolled in the ERs. This apart, some politicians of their own religion have been also issuing certificates to some of them so that they may claim to be Indian citizens. A copy of such certificate is reproduced in Appendix 4. In this case, the politician who issued the certificate was an MLA and a cabinet minister at the same time! When exposed, this certificate had created a bitter furor in the media but the Chief Minister ignored the matter, despite strong public demand for taking punitive action. The Sentinel, an English daily published from Guwahati, had in this context, reported in its issue dated the 11th of November 1992, under the caption 'Criminal issuance of citizenship papers', that Mr. Afzalur Rahman had been issuing citizenship and permanent residence certificates on especially printed stationery in violation of prescribed rules and regulations. Another significant press report is available at Appendix 4. It may be mentioned here that citizenship and permanent residence certificates can be issued only by the District Magistrates, who are required to cross-check the antecedents of the applicants before issuing these certificates. An MLA is not authorized under the rules to issue such certificates. Such violation of the rules also amounts to criminal activity. The form, especially printed by Rahman, goes on to prove that he has been issuing such certificates in the past also, thereby being a party to the conspiracy against the indigenous people of the State. The issuance of such certificates entails other adverse impacts also. Such certificates issued by no less a person than a cabinet minister, besides facilitating the receipt of various licenses by persons of doubtful citizenship, are likely to influence the enumerators while preparing the revised ERs. This particular MLA represented the Jaleswar LA constituency. Quite likely that the pace of issuing such certificates gathered extra pace after the Central Government had announced its intention of issuing identity cards with photographs to the citizens of the districts bordering Bangladesh. Of course, the proposal for issuing identity cards was yet to materialize. In any case, such measures may not yield the desired result if the process is confined to border districts only, because the illegal migrants do not stay put at the border districts concerned and instead, have been spreading out to the nook and corner of the entire North-East. One possibly cannot ignore the fact that a few years back, Bangladeshi infiltrators were caught in most interior areas of Arunachal Pradesh; not known for easy accessibility. In any case, the issuance of identity cards must be preceded by steps to determine the real citizenship of the recipients. It must, however, be pointed out for enabling the reader to draw his/her own conclusion that many of the immigrant Muslim militant outfits were maintaining their training camps within the jurisdiction of this particular constituency. Records will prove that quite a few immigrant Muslim terrorists hailed from this region. It also may not be out of context to mention here that in the wake of the Indo-Pak war of 1965, many infiltrators/immigrant Muslims of East Bengal stock, had run away to East Pakistan but afterwards they had reinfiltrated and claimed ownership of immovable properties they had left behind, thereby cultivating a source for constant friction and communal tensions.

Even in the economic sector, the activities of these migrants are contributing to the impoverishment of the country's economy. Besides circulating forged currency notes, these illegal migrants have been responsible for causing huge outflow of money from India to Bangladesh. The Assam Tribune, dated the 6th of February 2015, referred to a World Bank report, 'Bangladeshi migrants are sending home huge amounts of money every year and according to persons who are well versed with economic affairs, such remittances can adversely affect the economy of the country, from where the money is sent out.' According to this report of the World Bank, Bangladeshi migrants sent home fourteen billion dollars in 2013, from foreign countries and India topped the list of these countries with 6.6 billion dollars sent from India. This sum of money amounted to 6 per cent GDP of Bangladesh, while it was 47 per cent of the money sent home in that year from foreign countries. According to this report, Bangladeshis prefer India the most because of the low cost of migration. Needless to mention that such huge outflow of money, is sure to cause low availability of fund for India's own use.

Thus, unknown to the rest of the country, a deep-rooted conspiracy is operating in full swing to obliterate Assam from the map of the epical 'Bharatbarsa'!

According to study conducted by a few scholars of Toronto University and the American Academy of Arts & Science, fifteen million Bangladeshi nationals have infiltrated into India. According to another study done by another American organization, namely, The Advancement of Science, twenty million Bangladeshi nationals are presently staying illegally in India. On the other hand, the number of Bihari Muslims staying in Bangladesh in 1991, according to Census Report of Bangladesh, was five lakhs and all of them were since missing from Bangladesh. Besides, according to a UN survey, the population of Bangladesh should have been 118 million in 1991; but the Census Report of Bangladesh had determined the population to be 108 million; in other words, ten million less than what the UN survey had calculated.

Such heavy influx of Bangladeshi nationals is rapidly changing the demographic patterns of Assam, West Bengal and Bihar. Now the presence of huge number of Bangladeshi nationals in metros like Mumbai and Delhi has also been confirmed officially. But so far Assam has been the worst sufferer. Which is why, our main focus has been on Assam. American Committee on Refugees also reports that ten million Bangladeshi nationals have already infiltrated into Assam and the rest of the North-Eastern States of India. This Committee further reported in 1993 alone, more than 3.5 lakh Bangladeshis crossed over to India.

According to such records, the Commission had removed twelve lakh names from the ERs of Bangladesh in 1996, on the eve of the country's parliamentary elections because they were no more staying in Bangladesh. The ERs of Bangladesh had 6,21,81745 voters in 1991. But during the revision of the ERs in 1995, the Commission removed the names of 61,65,567 voters from the ER because of their non-existence in Bangladesh. Where these missing people have gone, is anybody's guess!

The study carried out by the scholars of Toronto University had pointed out that in 1996, the population of Bangladesh was 120 millions. According to their opinion, in 2025, the population of Bangladesh will be exactly double of what it was in 1996; but the land and other relevant resources that will be available then, will not suffice to sustain this overflowing population of Bangladesh. Obviously, Sadiq Khan must have visualized this situation while pleading for the theory of *'Lebensraum',* albeit at the cost of Assam and its neighbors.

Kamal Sadiq is an American Muslim scholar of Indian origin. In 'Paper Citizens', a book authored by Sadiq, it has been observed that 'As a result of high rates of illegal immigration from Bangladesh, there are significantly high population growth rates among Muslim population. Consequently, these districts resulted in a Hindu- majority district becoming a Muslim majority district. (Page Number 44) (Earlier he had named these districts as Nagaon/Dhubri/Barpeta/Marigaon/ Goalpara/Karimganj/Hailakandi).

Rita Afsar, a research scholar in the Bangladesh Institute of Development Studies has a more significant and tell-tale picture to present. She spoke of a 'migration industry' in a paper submitted for panel discussion at the 20th European Conference on the Modern South Asian Studies held from the 17th of July 2008. She stated in her paper that 'Migration industry composed of well organized network of *dalals* in Bangladesh and India together with recruitment agencies, recruiters, touts, brokers, informers, travel agents and their employees and controls in many Bangladesh border side villages help escalating new forms of trans-nation flows.' Quoting from a report submitted by R.A. Ahmed to the UNDP in 1998, she further stated that 'Migration industry facilitates migration to India and minimizes the risk of settlement by offering necessary document e.g., passport, ration card etc. for substantial sum of money.'

Willem Van Schendel observed in his book, 'The Bengal Borderland, Beyond State and Nation in South Asia', that 'Identification of Bangladeshi immigrants was (further) hampered by the fact that Indian border-landers very often protected them. — Immigrants also found it easy to make use of the imperfect registration of Indian citizens: only 30 to 40 per cent of births in India are registered (as against an even smaller 12 per cent in Bangladesh). This provides ample opportunities for forgery. Many immigrants secured an 'Indian' identity fraudulently acquiring ration card, birth or school certificate, enrolloing as voters and — ultimate proof of Indian citizenship— availing themselves of the Election Commission's identity card. And for those with money and connections it was not difficult to manage a passport.' (Page Number 220)

Most of the Bangladeshi infiltrators migrate from the districts of Mymensingh, Sylhet, Bogra, Khulna, Noakhali, Faridpur, Commilla and Bakarganj. Consequently, the growth rate of population in these districts, is much lower than other districts of Bangladesh, as shown in the two tables, given below:

Districts	Percentage of growth during 1951–1961
Mymensingh	21 per cent
Sylhet	13.9 per cent
Bogra	22.8 per cent
Khulna	17.8 per cent
Noakhali	4.7 per cent
Faridpur	16.9 per cent
Commilla	15.4 per cent
Bakarganj	16.8 per cent

It will be seen that the following districts recorded a much higher growth during the same period:

Districts	Percentage of growth
Kustia	31.5 per cent
Jessore	28.7 per cent
CHT	34 per cent
Rangpur	29.6 per cent
Chittagong	28.6 per cent
Dinajpur	24 per cent
Dacca	24.8 per cent
Rajshahi	24.8 per cent
Pabna	23.3 per cent

Also, there was an exodus of thirty-nine lakh members of the minority communities of Bangladesh between 1971 and 1981; and another thirty-six lakhs went missing between

1981 and 1989. Both the phenomenon's have been reflected in the respective Census records of Bangladesh. Obviously, these seventy-five lakh members of minority communities of Bangladesh had crossed over to India, particularly to Assam, West Bengal, Tripura and Arunachal. Such influx of huge number of foreign nationals, besides changing the demographic pattern in Assam, many other problems have cropped up, particularly in respect of the political future of the North-Eastern region of India. According to the Report prepared by the Economic And Social Department of the UNO, published as the 'World Population Prospects', till April, 2016, the population of Bangladesh has shot up to 16,10,94,504 and daily, 4423 Bangladeshi nationals are immigrating to other countries. The social ambience in Bangladesh has reached such a stage that no alternative is left for the people other than to leave the country and immigrate to other countries, as was observed by the 'International Union For Conservation' in October, 2015. According to the Report of the Union, fifteen million Bangladeshi nationals will have to immigrate within 2050, because of rapid climatic changes caused by Global Warming. Vast area of agricultural land will go under saline water, thereby causing 10 per cent less production of paddy and 30 per cent less production of wheat. The resultant scarcity of food grains will create serious crisis in the country and the situation will compel a huge number of Bangladeshi nationals to seek shelter outside their country. Which is why, clashes with the neighboring countries will become inevitable as predicted by the Union. According to the Report of the Gulf Commission, the main target of these immigrants is India in general and Assam in particular because of easy accessibility. According to the Report of the 'World Population Prospects', the statistical account of Bangladeshi immigrants is as follows:

Between 1970-75	6,05,700
Between 1975-80	2,20,300
Between 1980-85	1,67,500
Between 1985-90	43,900

>>

> >

Between 1990-95	1,70,700
Between 1995-2000	1,51,200
Between 2000-2005	3,40,000
Between 2005-2010	7,14,200
Between 2010-2015	4,45,300

And in the first four months of 2016, 3,22,895 Bangladeshi nationals immigrated to other countries (Source: Niyamia Barta, the 22nd of April 2016). As such, it may be well anticipated the kind of serious challenge in store for Assam.

CHAPTER 6

ADVERSE IMPACT

Most adversely affected has been the socio-economic sector of Assam. Little illustration in this context may be of interest to the readers: According to the latest Census Report, the number of agricultural labors has shot up to 15.4 per cent whereas the number of real agriculturists has recorded a decline of about 13 per cent. Objective analysis of these data would expose a very dismal state of affairs in the agricultural sector, which implies that a large number of peasants has given up tilling the land themselves and instead, has hired labors for tilling their land. Why this has happened, calls for an explanaton: Some significant factors have certainly contributed to this development. Despite sounding unpleasant to some irrational ears, the fact remains that the Assamese people are, by and large, comfort loving and loathsome by nature. May be the environment has a role to play. Besides, the fertility of the land also makes the Assamese complacent. They remain satisfied with raising only one crop during the year. In fact, till now they had never thought of raising three crops during the year; a practice ardently followed by the immigrant Muslims. The Assamese peasants do not have to work as hard as their counterparts in Bihar or Uttar Pradesh or the South. In fact, this applies to Meghalaya as well. This mindset has played a big role in shunning hard work and entrusting the same to easily available cheap labor, which are now abundantly available from the immigrant stock. As such, the agricultural sector has been inundated by cheaply available immigrant labor. In the process, the Assamese has been divested of a healthy work culture as it happened with the American youths for abundant availability of slave labor. Thus, many Assamese peasants find it more convenient to engage immigrant labors for ensuring a more comfortable existence without realizing that they are indirectly helping the illegal migrants to perpetuate their stay in Assam. If they do not get employment, they would have no reason to linger their stay in Assam and would have moved out to other convenient location. Unfortunately, the rural/agricultural sector of Assam is thus slipping away from the hands of the indigenous people. I, for one, would blame most the unthinking Assamese peasant for this sordid state of affairs. They must consider how did their forefathers manage to do without the services of the immigrant labors. Of course, mechanization of the agricultural sector may lead to avoidance of immigrant labors. But such an eventuality will have to be created by a well planned scheme for modernizing the agricultural sector. Incidentally, it may be mentioned that agricultural holdings are getting divided into small plot of lands where the application of modern techniques on the part of the owner of a small plot of land may not be possible. Since economic opportunities are being shared by millions of illegal migrants with the indigenous people, the per capita income of the indigenous people has betrayed declining trend and planned development has been facing rough weather.

These illegal migrants have also crowded the coal and limestone mines of Meghalaya and occasional reports of violent clashes between them and the local people are also pouring in. They are now reported to be trying to establish themselves in Nagaland by marrying Naga girls. In Assam today. it will be simply impossible to find a single site of building or road construction where Bangladeshi labors have not been engaged. Even the government agencies have been noticed to have engaged them, the only reason seeming to be their easy availability at cheaper rates. When this author was the president of the Employee's Union of the Guwahati Oil Refinery in the last decade of the last century, he had seen immigrant labors being employed inside the Refinery by the contractors and on his query, it transpired that they were engaged without verifying their citizenship and still more surprising was the fact that there was no security check at the time of their entry inside the Refinery gate. This simply betrays the callous attitude of the authority concerned. The contractors have been the real culprits in respect of engaging immigrants as labors in various enterprises. In earlier days, labors from Bihar/Madhya Pradesh/Orissa etc. used to be imported. Even, most of the rikshaw-pullers and push-cart drivers used to be Biharis. But all these sectors have since been taken over by illegal migrants. Candidly speaking, these illegal migrants from Bangladesh have opened a full-scale labor market, thereby ousting the labors coming from other states of India. On the other hand, Hindu infiltrators/migrants from Bangladesh have been monopolizing the micro trading enterprises. Thus, these illegal migrants, in addition to creating pressure on land, have created tremendous pressure on job opportunities also, thereby causing the rise of the graph of unemployment amongst the the local population mainly attributable to availability of cheap Bangladeshi labors. Also the rate of employment of child labor for identical reason has recorded unprecedented rise, a phenomenon not witnessed in the indigenous society. Previously, prostitution had not assumed any alarming proportion; but now, the urban areas are in the grip of large scale prostitution by women of immigrant stock with consequent spread of venereal diseases including AIDS.

The more the number of infiltrators, the more is the need for living space. After they have fully occupied the riverine island ('Char areas') areas, now these migrants are moving out to jungle and hill areas and such movement has resulted in denuding the forest and hill areas on large scale, thereby hastening the process of environmental degradation. According to the Forest Survey Of India, Assam tops the list in the country, in respect of denuding the forests state-wise. The *Dainik Axom, an Assamese daily dated Apri 2016,* has quoted extensively from the reports of the Forest Survey Of India which presents a rather alarming picture. According to this report, 20,000 square kilometer of forests have been destroyed since 1991. Assam had 24.58 per cent forest areas within its total area of land mass. This accounted for 27,826 square kilometer. The Forest Survey of India reported that between 1991 and 2003, 12,833 square kilometers of deep forests had disappeared. According to the same report, by 2003 Assam was left with only 1,684 square kilometers of deep forests. The following table will give a vivid account:

Name of districts	Forest area in 1991	Forest area in 2003
Barpeta	199 square kilometers	35 square kilometers
Cachar	338 square kilometers	91 square kilometers
Darrang	85 square kilometers	17 square kilometers
Dibrugarh	1317 square kilometers	26 square kilometers
Dhubri	264 square kilometers	20 square kilometers
Goalpara	147 square kilometers	Nil
Jorhat	76 square kilometers	Nil
Golaghat	141 square kilometers	15 square kilometers
Kamrup	697 square kilometers	69 square kilometers
Karbi Anglong	6044 sqkm	684 square kilometers
Karimganj	376 square kilometers	2 square kilometers
Kokrajhar	1401 square kilometers	207 sqkm
Lakhimpur	330 square kilometers	4 square kilometers
Nagaon	685 square kilometers	72 square kilometers
North Cachar (now Dima Hasao)	1995 square kilometers	187 square kilometers
Sibsagar	245 square kilometers	15 square kilometers
Sonitpur	245 square kilometers	71 square kilometers

This table suffices to confirm the extent of environmental damage caused mainly because of the search for living space by the illegal immigrants. True, local people also must have contributed in lesser degree to this catastrophic happenings. In only two years between 2009 and 2011, 549 square kilometers deep forests have disappeared in the North-East. According to the another report from the same source, in the last ten years,

3,30,560,42 hectares of forest land have been encroached upon. The insensitive attitude of the State Government towards encroachment into even wild life sanctuaries and Reserve Forests, mostly by immigrant Muslims (most of whom are again likely to be Bangladeshi infiltrators), is illustrated by the following table:

Name of the Sanctuary/ Reserve Forest	Original area (in hectares)	Encroached area (in hectares)
Burhachapori-	4406	2850
Laokhoa	7013	400
Sonai-Rupai	22,000	1900
Nameri National Park	20,000	2100
Kazironga National Park	42,900	7790
Manah National Park	50,000	1700
Barnadi Sanctuary	2622	600
Dibru-Saikhoa National Park	34,000	300
Orang	7,881	800
Pabitora	3800	200

Both the above-tabulated charts should suffice to illustrate how the Forest Department has connived in perpetrating such anti-national and environment-degrading mal-practices. In this ontext, it is worth-mentioning that Assam, particularly the North bank of the Brahmaputra, is dotted with large water bodies, constituting 43 per cent of India's total number of water bodies. These lakes of Assam, have mostly emerged from the changes of the courses of many rivers. There are about 4,000 of such water bodies in the State, although according to official records there are 3931 such lakes in Assam. These water bodies are extremely rich natural resources of Assam and with little imagination and planning these could have been converted into profit-earning fisheries, instead of importing thousands of tons of fishes from other States of the country. Presently, only 25 per cent of these lakes has been utilized for pisciculture. Which is why, Assam has to import such a large quantity of fishes from outside Assam. Even a well sketched map of these natural water bodies, may not have been prepared either by the Revenue department or by the Fishery department. Still more significant is the fact that these water bodies possess the possibilities of being developed into eco-tourism centres like the 'Lake Districts 'of England. The Tourism department of the State does not seem to be capable of planning in such terms.

In the absence of well demarcated boundaries and a reliable map, it has been possible to encroach upon these lakes and in this respect also, the immigrant Muslims have been very enterprising. As such, the degradation of these natural lakes are also taking place rapidly. In many places, the system of wet cultivation has been extended by the immigrants into the bed of these lakes, thereby not only causing environmental degradation but also hastening the end of these water bodies. It may be mentioned here, that such wet-cultivation has been instrumental in reducing the original size and depth of the lakes. Ultimately, the lakes will dry up and put to use as paddy fields. Neither the government nor the indigenous people, seem to have realized that these immigrants are destroying the rich heritage and potentials of these lakes to the detriment of the interests of the State. By extending human habitation to the fringe of the lakes and extending cultivation into the bed of the lakes, these immigrants have contributed volubly to raise the level of pollution also, besides destroying the bio-diversities of the areas concerned. Necessary preventive measures are yet to be in evidence and the people at large have preferred to remain silent while the government is looking the other way as if such degradation of the environment is of no consequences.. The people must be educated to understand the long-term adverse impact of such depredation being caused by the immigrants. There is more to such anti-biodiversity activities:

Certain breeds of fish are endemic to Assam and its neighborhood. While conservationists are laying maximum emphasis and extending help for conservation of these breeds, the immigrants are undoing all efforts. These Bangladeshi immigrants are born and brought up in the riverine areas. Because of their proximity to the flowing water bodies, they become expert swimmers and take to fishing from their childhood years. Because of their poverty and struggle for existence, they adopt any means to eke out a livelihood. Under compulsive circumstances, they could never cultivate any enthusiasm for conservation of Nature; rather, exploitation of the Nature as much as possible, has been the main motivating force of their life and livelihood. In fact, this scribe had opportunities for travelling in immigrant areas extensively during the course of his service life and had noticed their aforesaid apathetic attitude to the conservation of Nature. As such, they have never been known for their anxiety for responding to conservationist programmes. Which is why, from the moment they enter Assam, they resort to indiscriminate fishing, even in the prohibited areas. Still worse, they bring with them unfailing means of catching the smallest of the small fish. They use fishing nets of very narrow mesh so that even the fingerlings cannot escape. This is how breeds of fishes endemic to Assam and its neighbourhood, are on the way to total extinction. They have been even poaching in bio-diversity areas like the river Manas/river Jiya Bharali/and so many lakes inside the Kaziranga Wild Life Sanctuary. I had myself once arrested eight such immigrant poachers in the Manas Sanctuary, with the help of Late Sanjoy Devroy, who was then the Director of the Manas Tiger Project. Many immigrants have encroached upon the land of the Kaziranga Sanctuary and its vicinity. Having taken up their abodes in these prohibited areas, they have been reported to have extended helps to the poachers of the world famous one-horn rhinoceros. Some of them have been arrested also for such criminal activities. Writ Petitions have been also filed in the Guwahati High Court with prayer for their eviction from Kaziranga and its vicinity.

Smuggling of cattle heads from India to Bangladesh, has been a regular phenomenon. It has been reported that beef and leather industries on the Indo-Bangla border inside Bangladesh, are surviving on cattle heads smuggled from India and media reports confirm that Golokganj sector of Assam bordering Bangladesh and riverine routes are being used regularly for carrying on such smuggling activities. Abundant presence of Bangladeshi immigrants in Assam has been facilitating such smuggling activities. There is no denial of the fact that corrupt police officers have been of great assistance to these smugglers. What a great shame indeed!

There are instances galore of clashes between hardened criminals of erstwhile East Pakistan and now of Bangladesh, on the one hand and Assam Police personnels on the other. Quite a number of dacoits have since been shot down by the Assam Police personnel in these clashes. Inside the geographical boundaries of Assam, criminals of Bangladesh origin, have been regularly involved in committing heinous crimes like murder, dacoity, rape, kidnapping, etc. A careful look at the list of criminals arrested in these cases, confirms this charge. Some criminals are also reported to have been deported from Bangladesh to Assam. In fact, the very incidence of illegally entering Assam is a cognizable crime.

Because of the presence of lakhs of infiltrators, the public utility services have to bear extra load and thus, fail to deliver the goods in adequate quantity to the indigenous people, whose welfare these services were aimed at. The basic infra-structure of these services were not adequate to cater to such extra requirements.

These immigrants, wherever they go, are invariably accompanied by their polygamous habits, the practice of child marriage and uncontrolled birth rate. Many immigrant girls and women are also reported to have resorted to prostitution, thereby spreading many deadly diseases. Some of these women have been also detected to have indulged in human trafficking. In fact, quite a number of immigrant women have been rescued from the red-light areas of many cities; again some of them have managed to escape. These immigrants are not concerned about promoting hygienic living conditions. The habit of defecating in the open is still in vogue, amongst a considerable percentage of their society. Whenever they move to urban areas, the area of their habitation is turned into a slum in no time! The dream of integrating them into the main stream of the civil society of Assam, continues to be a far cry. Their services are also being utilized in some other nefarious activities as narrated below:

Pakistan is determined to avenge the partition of the country and the humiliation it suffered in the 'Liberation of Bangladesh'. Having politically and militarily failed in its confrontation against India, Pakistan is trying to sabotage India's economy to whatever extent it may be possible. After gaining a foot-hold in Bangladesh, Pakistan has organized its spying network in Bangladesh, so that subversive activities may be directed against the Indian economy, and taking advantage of the presence of lakhs of Bangladeshi infiltrants in the North-Eastern part of India, the ISI has worked out a network with the help of these infiltrators, to build up a conduit for circulating fake Indian currency notes of various denominations, in this part of the country, as also the business of smuggling of various items harmful to India. Besides, the riverine habitats of the immigrants have been a safe haven for Muslim militant outfits.

Before concluding this chapter, it must be pointed out that the infiltrators have been receiving ideological support from the Islamic fundamentalist organizations and on close analysis, it will transpire that there is a close co-relation between the rise of Islamic fundamentalism and the unabated flow of infiltrators from Bangladesh. Though much has been uttered about integrating them into the Assamese main stream, such utterances are bound to remain confined to words only, for their loyalty lies elsewhere!

CHAPTER 7
DISTORTED ELECTORAL ROLLS

Distortion of electoral rolls: The abnormal growth of the population of Assam has resulted in unprecedented increase in the number of voters in Assam. This has been possible for naked violation of the provisions of the Representation of People Act. Needless to mention that vested interests have spared no efforts to enroll the names of lakhs of Bangladeshi infiltrators in the ERs of Assam and this is where the Election Commission (EC) has failed rather miserably in discharging its constitutional obligation of preparing a correct voters' list. This failure of the EC had resulted ultimately in launching the historic 'Assam Movement'. Since 1950, till date as many as twenty Chief Election Commissioners have been in charge of this autonomous body. All the names of the CECs who held office between this period, are available at Appendix – 1

The illegal migrants, after crossing over to India, had never applied for being granted Indian citizenship. They have been making an absurd claim that they are Indian citizens because they have been voting in successive elections held in India, at various levels. In all sovereign countries, only their citizens can exercise the voting rights. The relevant Indian law also stipulates the same condition. But because of total inefficiency and indifferent attitude of the Election Commission (EC) of India, well aided by the vested political interests, a total mockery has been made of the law. Even constitutional provisions have been also ignored with impunity. An analysis given below should be quite illustrative:

The abnormally high increase in the number of voters in all the infiltration-prone LA constituencies during last few decades, defies any rational explanation. Obviously, abnormal growth of Muslim population in some of the districts of Assam, has been followed by abnormal increase in the number of electorates. The following table is illustrative:

Year	Number of voters	Percentage of increase
1957	44,93,359	
1962	49,42,816	10 per cent
1966	55,85,056	13 per cent in 4 years
1970	57,01,805	Only 2 per cent increase in 4 years. (This decline might have been due to the tumultuous situation in Bangladesh.)
1971	62,96,198	10.42 per cent in only one year!
1977	72,29,543	14.82 per cent in 6 years
1978	79,74,476	10.30 per cent in one year
1985	98,32,826	23.30 per cent increase in 7 years
1991	1,18,92,078	20.94 per cent increase in 6 years
1996	1,25,83,895	5.81 per cent increase in 5 years
1998	1,42,81,511	13.49 per cent increase in 2 years
2011	1,81,45,914	26 per cent increase in 13 years
2016	1,98,66,496	9 per cent increase in 5 years

It may be quite revealing to observe that during seven years, between 1971 and 1978, the National Growth Rate of electorates was 12.63 per cent, whereas Assam's was 18.15 per cent, and thus, during this period, the pro-Bangladesh lobby entrenched themselves deeply, by dint of getting many Bangladeshi nationals enrolled as Indian voters. Unfortunately, the government of Assam and the EC remained silent spectators. In thirteen years, between 1957 and 1970, the number of electorates increased by 12,08,446 and during eight years, between 1970 and 1978, the increase was by 22,72,671 voters. This phenomenon defies all rational standards and it leads one to firmly believe, that those who had crossed over to Assam during the 'Liberation War of

Bangladesh', did not go back to Bangladesh after liberation. Instead, they preferred to stay back in Assam and managed to get their names enrolled in the ERs of Assam. A study of the above noted table is baffling even to a keen analyst. In other words, the increase in the number of voters in Assam has not followed any standard pattern, in variance with the national pattern. The national growth of electorates till 1966 was 80 per cent, whereas till 1966, such increase in Assam was 155.70 per cent - almost double the national average. Even there is the baffling instance of increase in number of voters within one year by 23 per cent This happened when the revision of the ERs of 1983 was done in 1984. Take the instance of Barpeta district: In 1983, its number of voters was 5,20,000 and in December 1984, it shot up to 6,36,900. Most of the infiltration- prone LA constituencies recorded such abnormal increase, as is evident from the following table:

Name of Constituencies	No. of voters in 1983	No. of voters in 1984	Percentage of increase
Sarbhog	68,986	94,700	37.27 per cent
Jania	56,892	76,900	35.16 per cent
Baghbor	53,450	69,800	30.56 per cent
Chenga	50,924	65,190	28.01 per cent
Sarukshetri	75,887	91,850	21.03 per cent

Patacharkuchi is a Hindu majority constituency in the same district, with insignificant presence of immigrants and this constituency recorded a rise of only 7.36 per cent. During this period, the 'Assam Movement' had peaked and apprehensions were writ large in the faces of all the Bangladeshi immigrants, that they would have to quit Assam. Therefore, there was unprecedented hurry to get their respective names enrolled in the ERs, so as to subsequently claim Indian citizenship on the absurd plea that *'they were Indian citizens because they had voted in elections held in India!'* This ridiculous claim has already been highlighted elsewhere. The friendly attitude of the State government elected in the forcibly held elections of

1983, also helped the immigrants in their efforts for Indianizing themselves without formally acquiring Indian citizenship. The EC remained a silent spectator. Needless to mention that the Congress (I) had actively connived in this unholy, anti-national exercise. Such manipulation of the ERs could be possible only because of the connivance of the State government with the EC failing to discharge its constitutional obligations. Even subsequently, the Congress (I) had resisted any move for cleansing the ERs of the names of foreign voters. It is significant to note that such abnormally high increase in the number of voters had been recorded only in the immigrant Muslim pockets. The constituencies which were not subjected to heavy infiltration till 1991, recorded a much lower percentage of increase in number of voters by only 50 per cent between 1966 and 1991, as compared to the following constituencies which recorded such increase by more than 100 per cent:

	Voters in 1966	**Voters in 1991**	**Percentage of increase**
Haflong	27,644	82,889	199.82 per cent
Bokajan	38,383	80,195	158.93 per cent
Howraghat	35,644	73,481	106 per cent
Baithalangshu	37,753	1,10,250	192 per cent
Dhubri	38,723	91,711	136.83 per cent
Kokrajhar West	42,641	99,352	133 per cent
Kokrajhar East	45,949	98,450	114.25 per cent
Sidli	43,445	1,18,195	172.54 per cent
Boko	42,503	50,656	148.57 per cent
Dalgaon	39,830	89,605	125 per cent
Dhing	36,393	99,991	174.74 per cent
Rupahihat	41,517	94,323	127 per cent
Sarupathar	49,735	1,26,884	155 per cent
Chhoygaon	47,225	85,988	82 per cent

The abnormal trend of increase in the number of voters has continued till now (2016), even after the signing of the Assam Accord and this has been prominently evident during the fifteen years of continuous rule of Congress (I), under the leadership of Tarun Gogoi. Only one single instance of Sonitpur district would substantiate this charge. According to a press report of Dainik Axom dated The 10th of March 2016, the percentage of increase of voters in five LA constituencies, is 42.57. In Dhekiajuli LA constituency alone, such increase is by 61.23 per cent. In these five constituencies of this district, the number of voters was 5,44,382 in 2001. But in 2016, the total number of voters has been 7,76,142. In other words, these five constituencies has recorded an increase of 2,31,760 voters, the percentage of increase being 42.57. Borsola constituency recorded an increase by 38.82 per cent, Rangapara constituency by 32.46 per cent, Tezpur constituency by 46.67 per cent and Sootea constituency by 33.74 per cent. In this context, one has to consider that the increase of the indigenous population in these constituencies, is much lower than the percentage of increase of voters. One instance should suffice: In Tezpur constituency, the percentage of increase of indigenous population in fifteen years has been 18.7 per cent, whereas the percentage of increase in the number of voters is 46.67 per cent.

Such indifferent attitude, particularly on the part of the EC, has amounted to distorting the ERs of Assam and betrayals perpetrated on the people of Assam. For last few decades, the role of the EC has not been adequate for preventing such manipulation of the ERs of Assam. Not that everybody had remained silent. The issue was agitating the minds of many! Some like me, had waited upon Mr. Seshan in 1996, during his vist to Guwahati for discussing about the revision of the ERs. To start with, he accused the people of Assam of remaining silent about the problem, whereupon we had to remind him of the Assam Movement and also attracted his attention to the *Writ Petition filed* by Indrajit Barua, a top-ranking civil engineer, in the Guwahati High Court in the same context as well as to the open letter written by me to the CEC and the

Chief Election Officer of Assam on the 27th of October 1992. In this letter, I had dwelt upon the large-scale distortion of the ERs and indirect connivance of the EC. The letter was released to the *Press* also and published in a number of *dailies* published in Assam without, however, attracting any reaction from the Commission. Mr. Seshan cut a sorry figure and failed to assure us about any positive action he would initiate in this context. The letter has been reproduced in Appendix 2, which will speak for itself.

The *Print media* also highlighted the points raised in my above-mentioned letter. Only one press report, *inter alia,* as published in *The Sentinel* should suffice to convince the readers that Assam was crying hoarse over this 'life and death issue' for its existence and distinct identity. This press report has been reproduced at Appendix 3.

The Commission was hoodwinking the people, by shifting the responsibility of identifying the infiltration-prone constituencies to the State government, whereas it should have no difficulty in identifying such constituencies on its own. On the other hand, the State government pleaded total ignorance about any foreigners-infested constituencies and it expected the Commission to furnish necessary data on such constituencies. Thus, ensued a tug of war between the Commission and the State government. The main issue of identifying alien voters was lost sight of. It may not be out of context to mention here that the State CEO was himself present in the All Parties Conference held on the 22nd of September 1992 and as such, he cannot be unaware of the State government's consent to implement the aforesaid guidelines. The CEO seemed to be more committed to please the State government, than to implement the guidelines issued by the Commission, so that he might not be subsequently harassed by a vindictive State government! On the other hand, the Commission never bothered to ensure that its instructions were carried out.

On an earlier occasion also, the Commission had totally ignored Assam's demand for an ER divested of the names of foreign voters. On this occasion, it was apparent that Indira

Gandhi had to be kept in good humor. The fall of the Janata Government necessitated holding of fresh elections in 1980. All the commitments made to the leaders of the Assam Movement were thrown to the wind and the Commission issued fresh instructions to the State government. The State government published these instruction in its Press-note number 88, dated the 18th of September 1979 in the following words:

'The Commission has instructed that no person whose name was included in the electoral roll should be eliminated on the ground of citizenship, as the process of establishing whether a person is a citizen or not is time consuming'.

What a plea! Because the process is time consuming, foreigners must be allowed to vote freely! Such irrational argument was nothing short of being self-defeating, if not downright anti-national. Thus the EC was once more responsible for perpetuating the distortions of the ERs. The entire situation was thus rendered favorable for lakhs of foreign voters. And the foreigners were placed in a position where from they started pleading that 'only citizens have the voting rights. Since we have been voting so long, we are certainly citizens!'

The Commission preferred to remain silent about the fate of more than six lakh objections filed against the inclusion of names of foreigners in the ERs. In fact, these objections are still (2016) pending. But the Commission tried to assuage the enraged feelings of the public in the following words:

'The Commission has further advised to take up scrutiny of Electoral Rolls after the ensuing General Election is over, with reference to the question of want of citizenship of any elector included therein in a systematic manner having regard to the provisions of section 22 of the Representation of People Act 1950 and general instructions issued thereunder. Action as per the instructions of the Election Commission is being taken.'

As usual, this promise was also never honored! The promise was made, as it transpired, only to stave off any outburst of public resentment. Such hopes of the EC were belied, as no election could be held in the Brahmaputra valley in the face of very stiff public resistance, although in the process many had to sacrifice their lives. Only in the Barak valley where the impact of the Assam Movement was not in evidence, elections could be held in two of the LS constituencies there.

Sri S.L. Sakhder, the CEC had visited Meghalaya in May, 1982. So some of us wanted to meet him and press our demand for a correct voters' list. Initially, he refused to spare any time for us. A personal factor helped us: I had worked as S.P. of Garo Hills district from 1962 to 1964. Meghalaya was yet to be born. It was during my stay at Tura, the district headquarters town of Garo Hills district that I had cultivated a close relationship with Capt. Wiliamson Sangma, who was the Chief Minister of Meghalaya at the time of Sakhder's aforesaid visit to Meghalaya. Capt. Sangma also wanted a peaceful end to the Assam Movement. I was aware of his sympathetic attitude. He persuaded Sakhder to meet the following persons at the Inspection Bungalow of Meghalaya State Electricity Board at Burnihat, about fifteen kilometers away from Guwahati: Indrajit Barua, Prafulla Kumar Mahanta and Bhrigu Kumar Phukan, the then President and the General Secretary of AASU and I met him on the 29th of May1982 accordingly. Ms. Sabita Goswami, a leading journalist of the State also accompanied us.

Sakhder was all praise for the ASSAM Movement. We had pinned great hopes in Sakhder because of a statement he had made in a conference of Electoral Officers, held at Otacamund in September, 1978. He had stated '— The influx has become a regular feature. I think that it may not be a wrong assessment to make on the basis of this increase of 34.95 per cent between the two censuses, the increase that is likely to be recorded in the 1991 census would be more than 100 per cent over the 1961 census. In other words a stage would be reached when the State may have to reckon with the foreign nationals who may in all probability constitute a sizable percentage if not majority population in the State.'

So, we were talking to the man who had visualized the shape of things to come and had made the above-quoted prophetic statement. Every word that was uttered by him, seemed to have been topped with oodles of honey. Indrajit with his witty anticipation, simply winked at me without being noticed by the rest. Sakhder's words were too pleasant to our ears as if the controversy about alien voters, was nearing an end! We discussed the entire range of issues involved in cleansing the ERs of the names of illegal migrants. Sakhder agreed with all our suggestions as if he was more royal than the king! Certainly, both I and Indrajit smelt a rat and suggested that the proceedings of our discussions and the decisions arrived at, should be reduced into writing so that the people of Assam and the functionaries of the Commission get a clear picture of what were on the cards. Sakhder pleaded shortage of time as he did not want to miss the flight to Delhi and instead, suggested, on our repeated insistence, that the matters discussed and the decisions arrived at, should be sent to him in the form of a letter which we sent immediately after. In order to maintain the continuity of the entire exercise and enable the readers to follow the course of events, the letter is reproduced below instead of treating it as an appendix

H.K. Bhattacharyya
The Wilderness,
Beltola, Basistha road,
Guwahati-781005(now 781028).
Date: 4th June, 1982. us

To Shri S.L. Sakhder, Chief Election Commissioner of India, Nirvachan Sadan, Ashok Road, New Delhi- 110001.

Sir

Kindly allow us to thank you for sparing your most valuable time on the 29th May last at Burnihat (Meghalaya) when you accorded us and our friends the privilege and the honour of being able to meet you and talk to you freely and frankly.

In that meeting, we had a threadbare discussion about the revision and correction of electoral rolls of Assam as well as the present circumstances. You may kindly recollect that the points discussed in the meeting were as follows:

1. You were kind enough to appreciate that the Assam problem is not one of *'Law & Order'* as it has been made out to appear.
2. The electoral rolls of Assam prepared for the last general elections including the draft rolls of 1979 did contain the names of a large number of foreign nationals, numbering lakhs, if not a few millions.
3. It is not possible to prepare correct electoral rolls without inviting and disposing of objections in this regard in Form No 7as prescribed in the rule 13(2) of Registration of Electors Rules-1960. Further the scope of eliminating the names of all foreign nationals from the electoral rolls by means of objection filed in Form No 7 being extremely limited and inadequate to meet the existing situation, recourse has perforce to be taken to the mandatory provisions of section 22 of Representation of People Act-1950(Act 43 of 1950). The Election Commission would therefore issue guidelines for taking action under section 22 of the R.O.P. Act-1950 well in advance so that the plea of non-availability of time cannot be taken as was done by the State Government vide its press Note No 88 of 18/9/79(copy enclosed). (This has already been quoted above.)
4. The final electoral rolls required under section 21 of the R.O.P. Act-1950 cannot be prepared without disposing of all the pending objections, numbering about 6 lakhs filed after publication of 1979 draft rolls, which is precisely the reason why the final electoral roll for 1979 could not be published till now
5. The stand of the Election Commission as explained by you is very clear on the matter. On more than one occasion, the Election Commission has instructed the State Government to proceed forward with the revision and correction of rolls. But the State Government has willfully ignored the Commission's instructions in this regard so far. That it has done so is evident from the fact that (1) it has transferred two successive Chief Electoral Officers without the knowledge & consent of the Commission, and (2) despite

the Commission's repeated instructions it has kept the post vacant for over a year. These omissions and commissions of the State Government have clearly proved its callous and indifferent attitude towards this vital matter. The Stae Government has shown that it could not care less to flout the Election Commission's lawful directions and orders.

6. Elections in Assam cannot be held without publication of the final electoral rolls as required by section 21 of the ROP Act-1950 and Rule 22 of the RER -1960. The publication of the electoral rolls must logically result in the inclusion of the names of Indian citizens to the exclusion of the names of foreign nationals, required by our Constitution and our law. It is also imperative that all necessary steps as laid down by the law are taken so that foreign nationals are not enumerated as voters in Assam in future.
7. For the purpose of deletion of names of persons who are not qualified to be electors, not only all the objections filed in Form No 7 shall have to be disposed of, but also the mandatory provisions of section 22 of the ROP Act-1950 shall have to be invoked to cover the large number of pockets of foreign nationals spread all over Assam—particularly the riverine islands and the border areas from where the likelihood of objection being preferred by a person whose name is already included in that roll and countersigned by another person whose name is also already included in that particular part of the roll in which the name objected appears, is practically nil for obvious reasons. To enable the Electoral Registration Officers to take action under section 22 of the ROP Act-1950 under their own motion or otherwise, the Election Commission would be pleased to take into account any enumeration or inclusion of foreign nationals as electors.
8. The Commission will not hold elections anywhere in Assam until and unless the process of exclusion of names of foreign nationals from the electoral rolls is completed as required by law. The plea of non-availability of sufficient time to delete the names of foreign nationals from the electoral rolls, or a

so-called need to fulfill constitutional obligation, will not be resorted to, as was done by the State Government in 1979. You were also kind enough to say that the Commission would satisfy itself through its own independent machinery whether it is really possible to hold free & fair election as required under the law, which process, you said, is a voluntary process that cannot be imposed on the people agaist their will.

9. The Election Commission certainly did not authorize or allow the imposition of curfew to enable any particular candidate for certain Lok Sabha constituency to file nomination in 1979. Curfew orders were resorted to, in the face of AASU's stiff resistance in quite a few constituencies to enable the Congress candidates to file nominations! There cannot be any such permission in future either. In fact, you very much appreciated that such a step is not conducive to hold free & fair election, and also mentioned that such a step may lead to annulment or countermanding of such elections.
10. It was very kindly clarified that the Commission does not intend to hold elections in certain specific constituencies in the state to the exclusion of certain other constituencies as such a procedure is not permissible under the law.
11. Various statement recently made by certain spokesmen and high dignitaries of the Government including a Union Minister of State have nothing to do with the independent and impartial functioning of the Election Commission, and as such, these statements do not reflect the views of the Commission in any way whatsoever.
12. Assam Govt.'s press Note No 88 of 18/9/79 mentioned that the inclusion of name in an electoral roll does not necessarily entitle the person to claim the right of citizenship. You have also kindly clarified that this does not *ipso facto* entitle such a person who does not have the primary qualification of being an Indian citizen to the right of franchise perpetually just because he might have voted in the past. In fact, to allow non-citizens the right of franchise is a sacrilege of our Constitution and election laws.

Sir,

We have attempted to put before you the sum and substance of our discussion with you on the 29th May, 1982. We feel greatly relieved that your considered opinion on the matter have coincided with our humble views. We shall deem it a great honour and privilege to receive your valuable reply and comments thereon. The disposals of objections filed in Form 7 and the application of section 22 of the ROP Act-1950 by the ERO may not cover all the cases of foreign nationals, the situation being what it is. We have every apprehension that political pressures will be exerted and manipulation attempted by vested interests. We have raised this vital point because we have bitter experience of such happenings. In this connection, it may perhaps not be out of place to point out that Mrs. Anwara Taimur in 1979 rushed inside the chamber of a particular Asst. ERO with a batch of her rowdies while hearing of objections was in progress not only to disrupt the proceedings but also to threaten the Assat. ERO to drop the proceedings. This is precisely the reason why we had suggested the use of an electronic computer to ensure the correct preparation of electoral rolls in a foolproof manner. The use of a computer would rule out the possibility of any manipulation in respect of pinpointing the names of foreign nationals. It would also overcome all the difficulties that may be presented by the time factor. We sincerely and earnestly pray that you will kindly consider our humble suggestion and do the needful in this matter also.

With kind regards,

Yours sincerely,

Sd./H.K. BHATTACHARYYA

Sd./Indrajit Barua'

Indrajit also followed up the matter by going to Delhi and personally meeting Sakhder in pursuance of our prayers and Sakhder's promises.

The oft-quoted adage that 'Delhi Door Aust' (Delhi is far away) was once more proved by Sakhder, our honored VIP of 29th May, 1982! Delhi was far off to reach the homilies performed at

Burnihat. Sakhder proved to be no exception to his predecessors and also successors. Obviously, it must have been under his instructions that the Secretary of the Commission sent us the following perfunctory reply, reeking of downright evasiveness and total blacking-out of the promises made at Burnihat. The letter is reproduced below:

From Secretariat of Election Commission of India
Letter No. 23/1/82 dated 10th June, 1982.

To

1. Shri P.K. Mahanta.
   President, All Assam Students Union.
2. Mr. H.K. Bhattacharyya
   "The Wilderness"
   Beltola, Basistha Road.
   Guwahati—781005
3. Mr. Indrajit Barua.
   C/O H.K. Bhattacharyya
   "The Wilderness" Beltola, Basistha Road.
   Guwahati – 781005.

Subject: General Election-Assam

Sir,

I am directed to refer to your letter dated 1/6/82, 4/6/82 and today that the Legislative Assembly has been dissolved and the state is now under President's Rule, the question of holding general election to the Legislative Assembly would arise only if and when it is indicated to the Commission by the Central Govt. that the Commission might proceed with the holding of the elections and that the Centre would revoke the President's Rule. In that event, the Commission will first have to revise the electoral rolls in the state with reference to the 1st January of the year in which the revision would be taken up and then hold the election. The electoral rolls of 1979 would be taken up as the base and they will be published as a draft roll. Adequate time will be given to raise objections to any entry in the in the electoral rolls. As and when objections are filed on any of the grounds mentioned in the law including the ground of want of citizenship they would be disposed of jn accordance with the provisions of law.

As regards the question of disposal of objections and application under section 22 of the Representation of people Act, 1950 by the Electoral Registration Officer is concerned, I am to say that those objections seeking deletion in the electoral rolls as finally published would also be disposed accordance with the provisions of the law.

As regards the holding of elections to the 12 vacancies in the House of the people from Assam, the above observations hold good.

Yours faithfully

Sd./(K. GANESAN)
Secretary.

What is most significant is that in the above-quoted reply, there was no mention about the lakhs of pending objections, as was mentioned in our letter. It is clear that the Commission visualized the submission of fresh objections was not a practical possibility. What confidence the people would have to come forward once again to undertake the exercise of filing objections in respect of lakhs of foreign nationals? When our meeting of Burnihat took place and the reply sent to our letter, the State was under the President's Rule and there should have been nothing to prevent the Commission from disposing the objections already filed in 1979. The impression created by the Commission was that it either did not want to displease the Congress (I), the lobby banking on alien votes or was simply scared by the enormity of the task that it would have to undertake! In fact, these objections were never disposed of in sheer violation of the law. Indrajit Barua and late Girin Barua, the then President of the Axom Jatiyatabadi Dal, had again written to the Commission inviting attention of the Commission on the same matter but there was no positive response with the result that the infamous elections of 1983 was pushed down the throat of Assam. R.K. Trivedi, who was the CEC at the time of holding the elections of 1983, refused to appreciate the ground realities and see the writings on the wall. Thousands were massacred in the wake of the election. That was, of course, another black chapter of Indira Gandhi's second tenure in office.

The Commission perpetrated another round of betrayal by forcibly holding the elections in 1983, which left behind a long trail of bitter legacies. The memory of the massacres committed at Nellie and Gahpur in addition to hundreds killed by Police bullets, still haunts the people of Assam. But what did this election achieve? The answer is not pleasant at all:

1) It brought a Congress (I) government to power which was never recognized by the people of Assam. In fact, more than 90 per cent indigenous people including the indigenous Muslims, had refrained from participating in the election whereas, the immigrant Muslims including the Muslim infiltrators, had come out in their thousands for voting.
2) It fostered sharp communal and ethnic divide in Assam, the adverse fallouts of which are still bedeviling the civil society of the State.
3) It enabled the immigrant Muslims including lakhs of infiltrators, to assume a more aggressive, if not belligerent, posture in an organized manner.
4) The autonomous character of the Commission was totally sacrificed. One frequently wonders why the Commission has so far failed to lift itself to a non-controversial level. With sagacious far sight, it could have certainly upgraded itself to the level of a judicial body, beyond the reach of the vested interests.

The people of Assam had already conveyed their unmistakable message to the Central Government, by not allowing the elections to be held in twelve out of fourteen LS constituencies in 1980. The government had declared large areas of Assam as disturbed areas under section 3 of the Assam Disturbed Areas Act. As such, the situation prevailing in the months of January and February. 1983, was by no means conducive to holding free and fair elections in Assam. The following remark was very significant: 'We also cannot avoid the conclusion that the party in power at the Centre ordered election with the sole object of capturing power and was determined to go through the process by availing the services of a tame bureaucracy and savage police.' (Mshta Commission's report, page 74:4, 1. The Freedom Fighters' Association of Assam had appointed an unofficial Commission of Enquiry headed by Justice Sri T.U. Mehta, the retired Chief Justice of Himachal Pradesh High Court, to enquire into the barbaric holocaust caused by the elections of 1983.) Unknown to the rest of the country, the findings of the above-mentioned unofficial Commission, are lying somewhere unattended. But the findings of this Commission will continue to be a huge storehouse of information/data for the historians of contemporary Assam

The ambience prevailing when the elections of 1983 were held, deserves special mention for exposing the role devoid of farsightedness, played by the Election Commission: Elections were to be held in three phases on the 14th, 17th and the 20th of February, 1983. Elections held on the 14th proved beyond all shades of doubt, that the situation was not conducive to holding free and fair elections. Elections were held in sixty-one constituencies on the 14th of February1983 and large-scale violence was witnessed in eighteen constituencies and in another fifteen, as many as hundred polling stations could not be established. Then, on the eve of the second phase of elections, a serious armed clash took place on the 16th of February1983 at Goalpara between some sepoys of Assam Police Battalion and sepoys of CRPF/Rajasthan Police, resulting in the death of two CRPF jawans, three Rajasthan Police jawans and one havildar of

Assam Police. Forty Assam Police personnel were subsequently dismissed from the force. Simmering discontentment against the inhuman repressive measures unleashed against the indigenous people of Assam, was already surfacing amongst the officers and employees of the State government and such widespread resentment had found expression in the ghastly clash amongst the Police forces of the same country. But, the Election Commission did not seem to bother about such unhealthy development and went ahead with the schedule of elections. In the second phase elections were to be held in thirty-seven constituencies. But the elections could not be completed in sixteen of these thirty-seven constituencies. Even then, the Commission went ahead with the third phase of the elections, held on the 20th of February 1983, despite the fact that large-scale rioting, arson and murders took place just before the 20th February. Atrocities were committed at Nellie, Gahpur, Samaria Satra and many other places. The latest version of King Nero in the shape of the CEC continued to play on his violin! Even on the 20th of February 1983, elections could not be held in eleven constituencies. Many of the voters were reported to have been transported in Police vehicles. Some mobile polling stations were also reported to have been created. Even in Guwahati city, non-Assamese voters did not venture to go out for voting. The Mehta Commission has most aptly pointed out that '— Even if the third round of poll was wholly adjourned in time, much of the bloodshed could have been avoided.' *(Ibid, Page 108)* Abdul Ghani Khan Choudhury was Indira Gandhi's main agent, perpetrating such unprecedented communal holocaust. During his electioneering campaign, he had openly asked the Muslim people in a meeting held at Mairabari of Nagaon district, that '— if Hindu kills one Muslim, the Muslims should retaliate by killing three Hindus and the Government would support you.'— Needless to mention that Ghani Khan went scot-free! Where was the EC's code of conduct? The Mehta Commission has further pointed out that despite the widespread nature of the Assam Movement, no clash had taken place between the Movement activists and the immigrant Muslims prior to the elections of

1983 but this election opened the floodgate of such large-scale violence. While appearing before the Mehta Commission, some prominent Assamese Muslim personalities had stated that Indira Gandhi herself had threatened the immigrant Muslims that unless they voted for the Congress (I), the Assamese leaders would drive them out of Assam! Even those immigrant Muslims who had appeared before the Mehta Commission, had admitted that 990 immigrant Muslims had lost their lives at Nellie and another 584 of them at Barbari, only because of the election. In the wake of the tremendous momentum gathered by the Assam Movement, the pace of fresh infiltration from Bangladesh, had certainly been slowed down. But with Indira Gandhi returning to power in 1980, the "infiltration lobby' became bolder and more active. The immigrant Muslims including the infiltrators, assumed an aggressive posture and engaged themselves in open clashes with the native people of Assam. In 1980, they attacked a number of Assamese villages and rendered 5000 people homeless, who had to take shelter in relief camps. In April, 1980, Mrs. Gandhi visited Assam and hopes were entertained that she would take steps to redress the grievances of the Assamese, highlighted by the Assam Movement. Instead, she planned in terms of weakening the Assam Movement by organizing the minority communities on the basis of religion and language. The result followed immediately after: The All Assam Minority Students Union (AAMSU) observed a 'Demand Day' on the 26th of April 1980 at Barpeta. They had the audacity to hoist the flag of Bangladesh while shouting the slogan 'Jai Bangla'! The Administration preferred to remain a silent spectator! Almost simultaneously, a large number of suspected Bangladeshi nationals attacked some villages of Assamese people in Nagaon district and rendered 1500 native people homeless in addition to torching houses of 300 families. These were all well planned, organized violence, which took place well before the forcibly held elections of 1983. There was no end to undemocratic and unconstitutional activities after Indira's return to power.

At this time, the Assam Assembly was under animated suspension with only eight MLA's of Congress (I). In the meantime, horse-trading was resorted to, on a massive scale and forty-three MLA's were won over to join the Congress (I). Still, Congress (I) could not command a majority in the Assembly. Even then, Anwara Taimur was sworn in as the Chief Minister of Assam, thus bringing in another reign of terror and atrocities. During her short stay in power (for about five to six months only), she had unleashed such a reign of terror that many knowledgeable persons compared the atrocities committed by her, with those of the Burmese invasion in the first quarter of the 19th century! Bitter memories of Mrs. Taimur's reign of short duration, will continue to haunt the Assamese mind for a very long time to come. During her short reign, Dispur had assumed the look of any fundamentalist Islamic country's capital, thereby possibly predicting the shape of things to come in the eventuality of the Assamese failing in his struggle for survival. Taimur's atrocious reign had even stirred the conscience of the neighboring States. Jubehu Lule, the President of the Naga Students Federation, came forward to extend their support to the Assam Movement. Stanley Nichols Roy, a prominent leader of Meghalaya cautioned all concerned by observing that if the Assam Movement failed, then the entire North-East would face a serious crisis of identity and his words had proved to be prophetic over the years. Again, Dr. Hiren Gohain, a leading intellectual of the State, subscribing to leftist ideologies, had prophetically observed as follows: The overall approach of the Centre to the problem ridden states of the North-East is to destroy the local popular base of the leadership opposed to it. Puppet regimes or something very like them, are being propped up everywhere with plenty of Police *bandobast*, CRPF deployment and army operations. There is an intensive drive to divide tribes and races against one another. Civil liberties have suffered. In Assam alone, more than eighty police station areas are under the *Disturbed Areas Act*. This kind of basis for government invariably breeds an irresponsible and cynical kind of corruption which turns the local people even more against these governments.

Terrorism is the desperate resort of rebels brought up against the wall. (Assam: A Burning Question. Page XX1X by Dr. Hiren Gohain.)

It deserves to be put on record that the majority of the Assamese Muslims of the Brahmaputra valley, had boycotted the election of 1983. In fact, sixty-two prominent Muslims of Guwahati had, in a joint statement, called upon the Muslims of Assam not to participate in the forcibly held illegal election as well as not get instigated by communal consideration as was being promoted by scheming brokers of power. Besides, Ataur Rahman of Titabar, Kader Ali of Sipajhar and Mehnur Ali of Barama had to sacrifice their lives in their efforts for resisting the forcibly held election, thereby once more proving that the Assam Movement was not organized by Assamese Hindus only. This apart, the tribals, the tea-labor community and the Bengali-speaking Hindus of the Brahmaputra valley had also overwhelmingly responded to the boycott call. What would have happened if the elections were not held forcibly in 1983? Three possibilities transpire immediately without going into detailed analysis: Firstly, there would not have been a Congress (I) government in Assam. Secondly, Indira Gandhi might not have had an open field for wrecking vengeance on 'Agitational Assam.' And lastly, the barbaric holocaust could have been avoided.

It will be in fitness of things to review how some of the Congress (I) leaders of the North-Eastern region, had in the past looked upon the problem of unabated infiltration from East Pakistan/Bangladesh.

As the Assam Movement had taken off the ground, Hiteswar Saikia, a prominent Congress (I) leader of the North-Eastern region and twice Chief Minister of Assam, wrote an article on the 'The Foreign Nationals Problem in Assam' published on the 20th of December1979 in Nagarik, an Assamese weekly, since defunct, and then edited by Homen Borgohain, a leading intellectual and litterateur of the State. Late Saikia, in this article, had dwelt upon most of the implications of unabated infiltration and the apprehensions caused in the minds of the native people of Assam. He had even mentioned about some international conspiracies to destabilize the entire North-Eastern region. Quoting Census Reports, he had also highlighted the abnormal growth of Muslim population. He had even claimed in this article that he, as the Minister of State for Home, had resisted the Centre's proposal to wind up the PIP Scheme. He had sounded words of caution against this growing menace. Of course, he had advocated for accepting 1971 as the cut-off year for detecting the infiltrators.

Five General Secretaries of the North-Eastern Congress (I) Coordination Committee, namely, R.C. Chiten Jamir, B.B. Dutta, H.K. Bora, D.D. Pugh and Liansuana, in a memorandum submitted to Prime Minister Narasimha Rao in July, 1992, had highlighted the serious problem of infiltration from Bangladesh. They had, *inter alia,* drawn the attention of the Prime Minister to the following important points involved in the issue:

1. 'The atmosphere of general repression of all minority communities makes them look forward to India as a haven of refuge—.'
2. 'Apart from the chronic influx of people in search of work and food, fundamentalist forces find it a fertile ground to utilize the leverage of aid and allied for anti-secular and anti-India campaigns'.
3. In the memorandum, it was admitted that 'The assumption that partition would solve the Hindu-Muslim question and that on both sides, Hindus and Muslims would be able to live in peace and unity, proved to be unreal.'
4. 'To remind ourselves, the religious minorities, which accounted for 29.7 per cent of population in the area comprising East Pakistan (now Bangladesh) in 1947, were reduced to 14.6 per cent of the total population in 1974, – the influx period being 1947-71. – Riots and killings have yielded place to other means of oppression. Minorities find that they are seldom able to protect their faith, property and women. Reports of forced marriages and conversions have been pouring in'.

5. 'Between 1971 and 1981, Bangladesh census records show a reduction of thirty-nine lakhs in the minority population, —. Between 1981-89, 36 lakh religious minorities were missing from that country.' It was also pointed out that 'In 1972, there were 7.5 lakh Bihari Muslims in the camps in Dacca. As a result of mediation by Saudi Arabia, only 33,000 of them were accepted by Pakistan. At present, there are less than two lakhs in the camps, where have the rest gone?
6. 'Shri M.M. Jacob, Union Minister of State for Home Affairs said in the Parliament in December 1991, in reply to a question that there were one lakh Bangladeshi nationals in Delhi and 5.87 lakhs in West Bengal.
7. 'From the above, we may infer: There are infiltrators-though it is a difficult task to examine the precise number. The infiltrations are not only by minorities of Bangladesh but also from the majority Muslims. In absolute terms, the number of Muslims crossing into India is likely to be much larger than that of non-Muslims.

   An ideological support is given to the phenomenon by the Islamic fundamentalists creating the vision of a larger Islamic country comprising Bangladesh and the entire North-East where the economic problems will be solved and security ensured. There is a direct co-relation between the rise of fundamentalism and increase in influx.'
8. Before concluding, it is pointed out that 'unfortunately the Government of India appears to be suffering from a half-hearted approach or no approach to this challenging problem. The Ministry of External Affairs; MEA, has not done the job it should have done. The concerned desk has virtually been a non-functioning one. For years, a practice has been if anything appears to be wrong there, ask Mr. So and So of West Bengal, who is im the limelight at that time. The desk is not asked to come forward with its findings. It is not realized that the problem is too deep for an active politician, however talented he is, to understand without the help of expert watchers. It is

> also not realized that the problem is not merely of West Bengal but of others as well.'

Now, what has been highlighted in this discourse in the foregoing chapters, may be considered in the light of what these prominent Congress leaders of the region had to say. Unfortunately all of them including the present set of Congress (I) leaders are fighting shy of confronting the problem, obviously because they do not want themselves to demolish their own vote banks. They had never in the past imagined that their vote banks would one day be infiltrated by a communal party like the AIUDF. To quote John Earls' Jacobian character '..........................the affectate traveler who hath seen all and perceived nothing'. No specific steps were taken over the years to determine the correct figure of Bangladeshi infiltrators staying in Assam. Now, of course, the exercise will be made much easier with the completion of the National Register of Citizens (NRC), the preparation of which is in progress.

CHAPTER 8

GONE WITH THE WIND

A frontline freedom fighter; Tyagabir Hem Chandra Barua was one of the first to ring the alarm bell for drawing attention to the uncontrolled immigration into Assam. In 1940, Barua had said, 'Assam has already reached a point where its role of or capacity for absorption has far exceeded its assimilation capacity. The Congress which stands for its ideal of wider nationalism embodied in the secure foundation of the cultural autonomy of the constituent units cannot view with equanimity the prospect of its distinct individuality being lost. The real problem is how to control immigration.'

Another veteran freedom fighter, Omeo Kumar Das was a member of the Constituent Assembly where in 1947, he had pleaded that 'In this list of subjects enumerated in the Federal List, I find migration and naturalization. To my mind, these two subjects should be on the concurrent list or the language so altered as to permit the province to have scope of action in these two subjects. I do not know what the other provinces feel, but it is a sore point to us. We know how mass migration into Assam has altered the very complex of population. With the system of Communal Award and communal representation it was not fair to allow mass migration on a large scale. In spite of the evictions that have been carried out in the province, I still find a large number of people who are not people of the province but only trespassers into government lands still hanging on to the province living with their relatives. I want the members, specially the mover of the motion, to think more clearly on the point and permit the provinces to have more scope in the matter. If Assam which is the homeland of the Assamese people cannot be protected, I have no justification to come to the House. — We must protect the Assamese people.'

While Mahatma Gandhi was against such mass migration, no concern was discernible in respect of other leaders. It is on record that Gandhiji had even gone to the extent of suggesting to Gopinath Bordoloi to resort to *Satyagraha* against such mass migration, so that popular sanction could be generated aginst such uncontrolled immigration. As such, the apprehensions and resentment against such unbridled immigration have been agitating the minds of the Assamese people for many decades. The attitude of New Delhi could not have been more indifferent! Now after the partition of the country and the emergence of Pakistan/Bangladesh, such immigration is illegal. In fact, the issue has since assumed ever-increasing serious proportion because of fundamentalist and political design, a phenomenon which may not be applicable to the problem of migration faced by Europe and America, at least for the time being.

In Gandhian terms, the Assam Movement was in reality, a *Satyagraha*, although vested interests did not hesitate to brand it as communal and in order to mislead the rest of the country, even blamed it as secessionist in nature, which certainly it was not. However, there was no dearth of efforts to derail the six year long non-violent Movement and degrade it into violent one. True, some exasperated young adults, both men and women, took to the path of violence; but the Movement was not responsible for this. In addition to geographical isolation, wrong policies pursued by the Central government since Independence, gave rise to a sense of deprivation which, particularly during the reign of Indira Gandhi, engendered a sense of alienation. As the sense of alienation became deep-rooted, it degenerated into secessionism. In brief, this was, inter alia, the root cause of the rise of militant outfits like ULFA.

As already narrated elsewhere, the ignition point for the commencement of the Assam Movement was the revision of the ERs of the Mangaldoi LS constituency. Steps taken by Barbara government to cleanse the ERs of foreign voters, amounted to blowing up the hornest's nest which ultimately became a major factor contributing to the fall of the Barbara government. However, little reflection on the past may be quite relevant for understanding the character of the historic Assam Movement.

The sense of deprivation and consequent alienation was gradually generating a very defiant attitude amidst the young generation for a very long time. They felt as if India was treating Assam as her colony, not the least bothered about the preservation of Assam's distinct identity and her development. Abundantly available Assam's natural raw materials were being exploited without any corresponding benefits accruing to Assam. An oft-repeated lamentation, if not a charge, has been that Assam never gets her dues without resorting to agitation irrespective of the fact whether it is a university or an oil refinery or a bridge over the Brahmaputra or the extension of the broad gauge railway line (Of course, this trend has, of late, undergone perceptible change, may be because of change of guards at New Delhi.), had already started doing the rounds. With the gradual spread of education and the increase in the number of educated youth, a sense of self-consciousness for ensuring one's due position under the sun had emerged. The desire for equal treatment, matching with other developed States of India, became a major motivating force for getting the benefits of development without sharing the same with foreign nationals. Meanwhile certain political developments also contributed to opening the eyes of the educated young generation.

Such political phenomena revolved around cases like the handicap experienced by the then Chief Minister, B.P. Chaliha, in implementing the PIP scheme and the roles played by two cabinet colleagues of Golap Barbara, namely, Golam Osmani and Zahirul Islam, in respect of pulling down the first ever non-Congress government of Assam. Certainly, such political manipulations did not go down well with the young generation, already smarting under apprehensions caused by the incessant flow of foreign infiltrators to the land of their birth. The overall ambience resulting from such political manipulations was certainly not conducive to building up mutual trust and understanding the burning problems of Assam dispassionately. Osmani's subsequent role in propping up the most communal government of Anwara Taimur, did not help matters either. Such happenings, involving the future of Assam were the key contributors to the arrival of AASU and consequently, the surfacing of the Assam Movement, with full vehemence under the leadership of AASU. The then AASU leadership succeeded in attracting the attention of the indigenous people to the dark cloud looming large in the horizon, which was brought about by the incessant flow of foreign infiltrators, causing demographic change in the State. The indigenous people responded spontaneously, cutting across the lines of caste, creed, language and religion and the six year long Assam Movement was born. The people came out to the streets, all over Assam with their three specific demands of detecting the infiltrators. their deportation and deletion of their names from the ERs and this came to be known as the 'Three Ds.' Tribals, non-tribals, Assamese Hindus, Assamese Muslims, non-Assamese Indian citizens and the tea-labour community, all participated in the Movement without any hesitation, thereby imparting a totally non-communal character to the unprecedented Movement.

In 1974, AASU had formulated a twenty-four points' Charter of Demands, wherein it had focused on the dangerous consequences of unbridled influx of people from outside Assam. Then it did not seem to be seriously concerned with the more serious problem of unabated infiltration from Bangladesh. But the success in detection of Bangladeshi voters in the ERs of Mangaldoi LS constituency in 1979, caused serious concern to the AASU and it analysed the problem more objectively. Some officers also had helped them in this venture. Some officers of the Border Police Organisation persuaded the AASU leaders to mobilize the AASU units spread all over the valley for filing objections against the Bangladeshi voters, in the wake of the revision of ERs being done by the Election Commission. The response was not only positive but tremendous. The Purbanchaliya Loka Parishad and the Axom Jatiyatabadi

Dal had already raised the demand for deletion of lakhs of foreigners' names from the ERs. AASU earnestly took up the issue and formed the All Assam Gana Sangram Parishad on the 27th of August 1979, which emerged as a common platform for the indigenous people of Assam for launching the historic Assam Movement. Meanwhile, CM Borbora also not only called upon the youth of Assam to be on guard against the dangerous consequences of foreign infiltration, but also appealed to the people of Assam to cooperate with the enumerators of ERs, so that only the names of Indian citizens could be enrolled as voters. Borbora's appeal while touching the heart of the people, set in motion the conspiracy of the vested political interest for pulling down his government, so that Borbora could not complete his mission of cleansing the ERs of alien voters. In the following political turmoil, Borbora had to ultimately resign on the 4th of September 1979. In fact, Golap Borbora happens to be the last Chief Minister of Assam, who took keen interest in solving the problems of Bangladeshi infiltration. Since then, the matter has been allowed to drift away from the control of the authorities, despite the fact that the AGP had formed the ministry twice. I had the opportunity of witnessing most of the crucial developments during this period, in my capacity as the DIGP of the Border Police Organisation of Assam, which should not be confused with the BSF, a Central Government's organization.

However, the catalyst for generating a mass upsurge had surfaced in the shape of the notification for elections to the Lok Sabha by the end of 1979, which had already been highlighted. As already told, the elections could not be held in the Assam valley for stiff resistance offered by the indigenous people of Assam. This single phenomenon suffices to indicate how much the Assam Movement was deeply rooted. Of course, there was no impact in the Barak valley. Apprehending electoral reverses, tremendous pressure was applied on the CEC to suspend the operation for identifying alien voters by the Congress (I), the Congress (U), the CPM and all other Leftist parties. The CEC, succumbing to the pressure, made a complete *Volte-face* and not only called a halt to detecting the names of alien voters from the ERs but also announced that Section 22 of the ROP Act, which empowers the EROs to delete the names of foreigners from the ERs on their own, would remain inoperative until the elections were over. Such irrational, if not unconstitutional, subversion of the ERs by the CEC himself, went a long way in consolidating the base of the Assam Movement and lengthening its duration. As a result, the movement assumed the proportion of an unprecedented large mass movement, even surpassing the Quit India Movement of 1942 in its intensity and expanse. Students came out of their schools and colleges, women from their homes, government, semi-government and non-government employees from their offices. They were all determined to prevent this unconstitutional election. Mass rallies were organized all over the valley. The huge All Assam mass rally held at Guwahati on the 6th of October 1979, was attended by people coming from all the districts of the valley including Karbi Anglong and the NC Hills districts. This mass rally further solidified the determination of the Assamese people irrespective of ethnicities to prevent the elections and the elections were prevented. This rally was followed by many other agitational programmes, all of which were unusually successful. Still, the central government, the CEC and the Congress/Leftist leaders refused to read the writings on the wall. The government went ahead with making full preparations for holding the elections, thereby turning a blind eye to the gathering clouds. In the face of the defiant attitude of the government, the decision to boycott the election and prevent the candidates from filing the nomination papers was spontaneous. As the zero hour approached for filing nomination papers, curfew was imposed in some of the district headquarters for enabling the intending candidates to file their nomination papers. But this too, didn't succeed in the face of the unprecedented popular uprisings excepting that Begum Abida Ahmed, the wife of late Fakaruddin Ali Ahmed succeeded in filing her nomination papers in Barpeta, under heavy police escorts led by a senior DIGP. However, fate ordained otherwise: her nomination papers were rejected by the Returning Officer on some technical ground! No election could be held in Assam valley, while elections were held in the two Lok Sabha constituencies of Barak Valley. But the elections held in Barak Valley didn't have any significant impact on the subsequent course of the Movement. The Assamese people in their thousands violated the curfew orders throughout the Assam Valley and thus, prevented filing of nomination papers in the Brahmaputra Valley. **The first phase of the Assam Movement had come to a successful end.** This phase of the Movement remained, by and large, non-violent. A few sporadic instances of violence, mostly resulting from provocations were, of course, reported and for this, the leadership of the Movement could not be held responsible.

The second phase of the Movement commenced on the 18th of December 1979, with the adoption of the 'public pledge' in public meetings held all over the valley. The said pledge read as follows:

'We pledge today, to sacrifice our lives for the national cause of Assam and promise, that we will continue to be active participants in the national movement started under the aegis of the AASU and we will save our motherland, from the grips of the foreigners and from any other threats that may befall.'

It must be noted by the rest of the country, that neither in this pledge nor in the speeches delivered by the leaders of the Movement, the message sent out by the Movement had ever reeked of secessionist tenor, although some quarters never tired of blaming the Movement as secessionist. Such motivated wrong publicity might have pleased the ruling class but could never endear the Assamese. The success in preventing the holding of the election in 1979, was not focused in the manner it deserved. The failure to attract the attention of the national media and the rest of the country, had set the Movement leadership thinking. The outcome of such deliberations was the decision to resort to a programme of 'Oil Blockade' which was expected to create an all-India impact, particularly in view of the fact that Assam was then producing more than 50 per cent of India's total oil production. The blockade commenced with effect from the 27th of December 1979. Thousands of men and women participated in the 'oil blockade' programme. Being starved of crude oil, the refineries at Bongaigaon and Barauni came to a grinding halt, although the refineries at Digboi and Guwahati were allowed to operate on the basis of a revised decision. Assam was resenting that 70 per cent of crude oil produced in Assam, was being refined outside Assam and in the process, it was deprived of a huge sum of sales-tax and opportunities of employment. Such corollaries had also imperceptibly contributed to the build-up of the Assam. Movement. Which is why, the idea of an 'oil blockade' had immediately caught the imagination of the people. (It may be noted that in order to address this grievance, the establishment of the Numaligarh Oil Refinery was envisaged in the Assam Accord). The oil blockade continued for almost three months. Serious confrontation with the security forces had become inevitable.

Meanwhile, anti-socials and agents of the 'infiltration lobby' started communal riots in North Kamrup as referred to elsewhere. The security forces swung into action, their targets being mostly the Movement activists. Immigrant Muslims also had become very active to wreck vengeance against the indigenous people. The climax of this chain of events came on the 18th of January 1980, in the shape of the infamous 'Duliajan Massacre'. The oil installation at Duliajan was put under virtual seize by the activists of the Movement since the 27th of December 1979. Thousands of picketers were picketing at Duliajan on the 18th of January 1979; they were all unarmed. Suddenly, on the 23rd day of picketing, brute forces were let loose on the picketers and the peaceful picketers were fired upon by the CRP forces, without any provocation and warning, only because the picketers refused to lift the blockade. Four picketers were killed on the spot and many others, seriously injured. As a retaliatory move, some rowdy elements from the gathering, killed Ravi Mitra, who was on that day, the in-charge of the Duliajan oil installation. This ghastly act did not fit into the Movement's plan of action and therefore, the Movement leadership condemned the murder. The whole intention seems to have been to create a serious 'law & order' situation for terrorizing those agitating, while forgetting the latter's unwavering determination to carry on with their mission. Confrontation with the security forces became frequent. As a result, the situation was deteriorating day by day, while the Central government still did not consider to start negotiation with those agitating. The State was under President's rule and the bureaucrats in charge of the Administration were not known for their anxiety to start the negotiation. Rather, the State Administration was eager to restore its sagging image in the Court of the 'North Block'. The turn of events had put the non-violent elements of the Movement under heavy pressure and the threat of being replaced by militant leadership. Even a section of AASU leadership had betrayed the tendency of taking recourse to armed militancy during this period and the idea of receiving training in use of arms and explosives, was no more treated as a mere facet of adventurous romanticism. It is quite significant to note, that it was during this period that **the United Liberation Front of Assam (ULFA)** was born, more out of frustration and disappointment emanating from New Delhi's apathetic attitude to all the legitimate dues and demands of Assam in preference to partisan causes, like patronizing the immigrant vote-bank, piping out Assam's crude oil to Bihar and the likes. Whether its emergence had any co-relation with the existing state of affairs in Assam, is a matter of full-scale and deeper research. In fact, Delhi had prepared the ground for the emergence of militant insurgency, as Lenin had once most aptly observed that **'Society prepares the crime and the criminals commit it.'**

Meanwhile, Indira Gandhi had returned to power and taken over as the Prime Minister, on the 14th of January 1980. Almost immediately after, she met the AASU leaders at New Delhi on the 2nd of February 1980. She also failed to rise over her partisan interests. In fact, she had never realized the true character of the Assam Movement, may be because of incorrect feed-back. Like her father, she also never appreciated the deep-rooted apprehensions of the Assamese race, as was borne out by historical facts of more than a century. Anyway, AASU leaders placed, *inter alia,* the following demands before her:

1. Detection and deportation of foreigners.
2. Deletion of foreign voters' names from the ERs before holding any election in Assam.
3. Constitutional safeguards to the people of Assam.
4. Issuance of identity cards to all Indian citizens in Assam.
5. Rejection of all citizenship certificates issued by West Bengal and Tripura Governments for use in Assam and transferring the power of granting citizenship from the State to the Centre and so on.

It will appear that none of these demands were unconstitutional, nor were these beyond the power of the Centre to grant. AASU had also insisted that for identifying the foreign infiltrators and voters, the National Register of Citizens (NRC), 1951 and the ERs of 1952 should be used. This was also neither irrational nor impossible to fulfill. As aleady mentioned, she never understood the rationale behind AASU's demands and even refused to use the NRC as suggested by AASU. Briefly speaking, she failed to create an atmosphere of mutual trust. She suggested 1971 as the cut-off date for detection of infiltrators. The year had no relevance in context of the provisions of the Constitution. It transpired that this suggestion had been made by her, keeping in mind the Indira-Mujib pact which had nothing to do with the country's Constitution, nor was it validated by acceptance in the Parliament. No wonder that the constitutional validity of this arrangement has since been challenged in the Supreme Court of India.

With the aid of hindsight, one may well conclude after more than three decades of her assassination, that in this respect she betrayed complete lack of statesman-like quality and foresight. A statesman thinks of the next generation and not of the next election, which is thc domain of petty politicians. By proposing 1971, as the cut-off date, she practically proposed to grant citizenship to those foreign nationals who had migrated to Assam between 1951 and 1971, without going through the constitutional procedure and Rajiv Gandhi materialized the proposal by one stroke of the pen while inking the Assam Accord, a copy of which is reproduced in Appendix 5. It is significant to note, that the same standard has not been applied to other States of India. If she had permanent welfare of the country in her heart, she should have thought in terms of promoting friendly equation between the immigrant sector of the society and the indigenous sector. Certainly, she had the potential to impart constructive leadership in this regard. Instead of solving the problem and promoting harmony, Indira Gandhi went all out to politicize the issue and evinced more interest in persuading the student leaders to lift the oil blockade. Another round of discussion was held at New Delhi on the 7th and 8th of March, 1980. This time, the AASU and AAGSP delegation had submitted a draft agreement incorporating all the salient features of their demands to the Central government. But the later rejected the draft without assigning any reason thereof. As a result, the resentment against Indira's leadership was further aggravated and the Movement was all the more intensified.

Having failed to persuade the Movement leaders to cry a halt to their agitation, this time, Mrs. Gandhi took measures for sabotaging the Movement and blackmailing the leaders. In fact, she never seemed to be a great believer in applying the instrument of negotiations. Instead, she believed more in the 'divide and rule' policy and in resorting to application of brute forces. The promotion of national integration was certainly not very high in her list of priorities. She wanted to teach a lesson to Assam by resorting to 'Tit for tat' policy and an 'Assam Blockade' programme was organized for a week, under the leadership of Subrata Mukherjee, the youth Congress leader of West Bengal with the slogan –'No oil, no food'. No food, because most of the essential food items were being imported to the entire North East from other States of India. She did not care to realize that such a step might alienate the North-East further from the rest of the country. Even Jyoti Basu, the Chief Minister of West Bengal, defended the 'Assam Blockade' programme without considering that his support might cause a rift between the Assamese and the Bengali of Assam; but the Bengalis of Assam did not fall a victim to such divisive reaction. Not remaining content with defending the 'Assam Blockade', Jyoti Basu went to the extent of ridiculing the Movement as a 'picnic'. Such ridicule might have been a reaction against the bitter confrontation between the Leftists of Assam and the Movement leadership. Even then, it certainly did not befit the image of a leader like Jyoti Basu; by such an utterance, he did not promote the cause of the Leftists in Assam. On the other hand, Indira Gandhi was ahead of Jyoti Basu by condemning the Assam Movement as communal and secessionist. Efforts were now afoot to impart an 'anti-Bengali' and 'anti-Muslim' image to the Movement, obviously at Indira Gandhi's behest, and she followed it up by promoting the AAMSU. Clearly, her intention was to drive a wedge between the Assamese and the Bengali people of the State. The Indian Bengali of the State, however, refused to respond to such a divisive policy.

There was no end to steps taken for bamboozling the Movement. On the 5th of April 1980, the entire State of Assam excepting the district of N.C. Hills (now Dima Hasao), was declared a 'Disturbed Area', thereby bringing into operation the *Assam Disturbed Area Act*, a law originally intended to control militant insurgency and combat secessionism. Along with it, *the Armed Forces Special Powers Act* was also made operative. The intention was clear - just to bulldoze the Movement! Some prominent national leaders like A.B. Vajpayee, George Fernandes, Chandrasekhar condemned this action strongly. The State government employees also strongly reacted against this declaration, by resorting to *Satyagraha,* while Indrajit Barua, once again, went to the Court by filing a writ petition in the High Court, challenging the validity of the declaration. The High Court passed a stay order on the 7th of April 1980. Thus, the civil life in Assam was dragged into a topsy-turvy situation!

Subsequently, Mrs. Gandhi must have had possibly some rethinking and during her visit to Guwahati on the 12th of April1980, she took the plea of adopting a humane approach while once again insisting on 1971 as of the cut-off date; but the Movement leaders were unyielding. She had also referred to some international obligations, obviously in terms of the Indira-Mujib pact. Here it may not be out of place to point out that Mujibor Rahman had categorically refused to take back those who had infiltrated from East Pakistan, although he was ready to take back those who had taken shelter in India during the 'Liberation War of Bangladesh'. Unfortunately for Assam, millions of those who had crossed over to Assam during the war did not go back and there being no official registration of all these refugees, it subsequently became almost impossible to pin-point them.

Anyway, the next day, a fresh and reasonable proposal was offered through Zail Singh, the Union Home Minister. According to this proposal, either the 31st of December 1966 or the 1st of January 1967 was offered as the cut-off date, for the purpose of identification of the infiltrators. This was considered reasonable by the knowledgable circle because the PIP scheme was operational in full swing till 1969, and the number of those who had escaped scanning under the PIP scheme cannot but be insignificant But the prominent student leaders once again refused to abandon 1951 as the cut-off date. Then, it was not evident that these student leaders were entertaining very high political ambition and therefore, they had a secret agenda unknown to the other members of the AAGSP. Little reflection on this secret agenda may be of interest: As the Movement gathered momentum, these student leaders gradually developed the ambition of capturing political power on their own. But they had to keep this design a well guarded secret so that the people in general and the other non-student members of the AAGSP in particular, did not withdraw their unflinching support to the Movement, supposed to be a non-political movement. Needless to mention that an agitation with ulterior political motive would not have attracted such wide-spread support from all sections of the society—all committed to the cause of preserving the distinct identity of Assam, which was presently being threatened by unabated influx of Bangladeshi nationals. But the problem arose from constitutional requirement that every candidate contesting in an election either for Lok Sabha or for Legislative Assembly Constituency must be, at least twenty-five years old; most of the prominent student leaders were yet to be of that age. The way out was to lengthen the Movement so that these student leaders became constitutionally eligible for contesting in the next elections. Nobody had seen through this strategy. To be very candid, uppermost in their mind, was their respective personal ambition to capture political power. They refused to reason out and did not relent from their demand - for accepting 1951 as the cut-off date; a proposition no government could have accepted. Such a step would have amounted to moving the clock of history in the reverse gear. As the years went by and with the unfolding of subsequent political scenario, it became evident that the then AASU leaders had a deeper design in lengthening the Assam Movement. As it transpired subsequently, they were not serious about solving the problem of infiltration from Bangladesh. They had led the entire people of Assam up the garden path and once they captured power, the issue of infiltration was dropped like a hot potato!

There were other adverse fallouts also from the rejection of 1967 as the cut-off date in 1980: Firstly, there would have been no need to hold the catastrophic election of 1983. Secondly, the possibility of passing the controversial, pro-infiltrators IMDT Act would have been very remote, if not absent. Above all, being what she was, Indira Gandhi would have honored and implemented whatever agreement would have been arrived at, in 1980, whereas the Assam Accord signed in 1985, was yet to be implemented even after the passage of more than three decades, since the signing of the Accord. Most ridiculously, another agreement was signed on the 5th of May 2005, in a tripartite conference of AASU/Central/State Governments for implementing the Accord, but even then no perceptible progress was noticed in its implementation. The same set of student leaders made a turn of 180 degrees and accepted 1971 as the cut-off date while signing the Assam Accord on the night of the 14th of August, 1985! They had by then attained the age of twenty-five; making themselves eligible candidates in any elections to be held subsequently!

What followed next, was the greatest ever betrayal perpetrated on the people of Assam. Still more mysterious and intriguing, was the fact that the non-student leaders and the executive committee of the AAGSP were not taken into confidence, while secretly preparing the draft of the Assam Accord, with the help of some officials of the MHA. Subsequently, it was learnt that Hiteswar Saikia, who had taken over as the Chief Minister on the basis of the results of the elections held in 1983, was behind the entire exercise and he had agreed to resign once the agreement was signed, so that fresh elections could be held in the State. Executive members of the AAGSP were flown to New Delhi only in the morning of the 14th of August, but the AASU leaders had gone few days earlier. The executive members of the AAGSP had played no role in drafting the Accord. Infact, some of them refused to attend the Accord-signing ceremony and the party thrown by the Prime Minister; Rajiv Gandhi in celebration of inking the Accord. Theyleft New Delhi by the next available flight. It also subsequently transpired that the student leaders in their haste to capture power, were holding secret parleys with few MHA officials and the Cabinet Secretary for quite a while, keeping the Executive members of AAGSP in the dark. Needless to mention that the student leaders were no match to the talents of these officers. In this background, it should not be difficult to understand why the talks so far held in New Delhi, particularly during Mrs. Gandhi's regime did not succeed. On the other hand, because of such selfish and obdurate stance of a handful of student leaders, the people of Assam had to undergo untold sufferings and inhuman atrocities for six long years. 855 participants of the Movement had to sacrifice their lives during this period!

The latest version of Quisling surfaced in Assam, with the consequent fallouts to be suffered by the indigenous people of Assam.

That the State Administration during the President's rule was totally divorced from ground realities, was in full evidence on the 20th of April 1980: The oil-blockade of the Narengi oil installation at Guwahati, manned by hundreds of unarmed picketeers, both men and women drawn from cross sections of the society, had already completed more than a hundred days. Early morning, 20th of April, 1980, the Army and the Police moved in and took position, in order to remove the blockade as if they were about to start an operation against some well-armed enemy outfit! Needless to mention, the curfew orders were clamped down and during the previous night, many arrests were made, including some senior citizens of the city. The news of these arrests, promulgation of curfew orders and the deployment of the Army and the Police had spread like wild fire, generating explosive reaction from the public, already surcharged with intense emotional involvement with the Movement. The multiple intelligence agencies had miserably failed to assess the depth of such public involvement, with the result that the disastrous consequences of such a move could not be anticipated. Maybe that nobody wanted to anticipate, the only concern being to please Indira Gandhi. It is significant that most of the leaders were either behind the bar or had gone underground. That is to say, there were no leaders or any organization to channelize the instantaneous public reaction against the high-handedness of the government. Whatever happened that morning, in the process of breaking the curfew order, was a spontaneous outburst of lakhs of commoners, reminding one of the storming of the ***'Bastille'*.** More than three lakh people gathered at Narengi, the site of the oil installations and made a total mockery of the curfew orders. Certainly, the District Magistrate did not want a repeatition of *Jalianwalabagh* and had no other alternative than to withdraw the curfew.

> H.C. Sarin was appointed at one stage of the Movement as the Chief Adviser to the Governor, during the President's rule. He made no secret of his strategy of defaming the Movement and bulldozing it. His ICS mindset possibly did not allow him to understand the agonies of the Assamese and he intensified the repressive measures. Thousands were arrested and sent to jail. Many arrested leaders were

> transferred to the infamous Bhagalpur jail. He even did not hesitate to spread canards against female participants of the Movement, so that the guardians of the female wards would prevent them from going out to participate in the agitation. He did not succeed. Not only Indira Gandhi, but also her advisers had failed to understand the character of the Assam Movement and the rationale behind it. Instead, they treated the matter as a 'law & order' issue! That the government employees had also responded actively to the various agitation programmes, announced from time to time by the AASU and the AAGSP, thereby paralyzing the administration, enraged Sarin, and in the process, goaded him to take more stringent measures.

The formation of the AAMSU made the foreigners' lobby more courageous to get organized and start a counter-movement inspired by Indira Gandhi herself. Even the State administration did not hesitate to extend its helping hand to them. As for instance, Barpeta was under curfew orders. The curfew orders were withdrawn so that they could hold a rally. They took out mammoth rallies in the districts Goalpara, Nagaon and the sub-division of Barpeta, thereby they themselves identifying the strong-holds of the 'Bangladeshi lobby'. In Barpeta subdivision alone, more than three lakh people of foreign origin participated in the processions, holding nine rallies on the 26th of April 1980. As already mentioned, the flag of Bangladesh was unfurled and the slogan 'Jai Bangla' was shouted along with displaying the portrait of Sk. Mujibor Rahman – all with impunity. The administration remained a silent spectator. The pro-Bangladeshi stance of Indira Gandhi was fully exposed. True, the partisan interests of Congress (I) were promoted, but a strong undercurrent of communal tensions was built up, to be released at the opportune moment. In any case, the emergence of AAMSU had crystallized in an unmistakable manner, which would create complications in coming days also. Thus, an atmosphere was being built for the final count down. The subsequent inhuman massacre of innumerable immigrant Muslims including innocent women and children was the logical retaliation by the indigenous tribal people. Without understanding the origin, it will be unwise to blame only one faction. Towards the end of the month, Assamese Hindu villages were attacked, particularly inthe Nagaon district. 300 houses were torched; 1,200 hundred Assamese people were rendered homeless and they had to be sheltered in the relief camps in their own homeland. Manywere killed and hundreds injured. Such organized violence continued almost for a week in the district. In all, thirty-nine people were killed. At many places, the Police had to resort to firing for bringing the situation under control. Thus, the chain of events was contributing to the occurrence of the inhuman massacre at Nellie. Most of the Movement leaders were in jail while none of the Congress or Leftist leaders came forward to take an active role in pacifying the situation. Thus, throughout 1980, the atmosphere continued to be explosive with the government confining its attention only to repressive measures. Non-co-operation by the government employees and police atrocities continued. The lives and properties of the people had become insecure with the student community becoming the special target of police atrocities. The academic atmosphere was put on heavy premium. Virtually, the entire Assam was converted into a battle-field, as if it had become a 'free for all' situation! Already, we have referred to the terror unleashed during the short regime of Anowara Taimur. As a last resort, press censorship was also introduced, but it also failed to defuse the explosive situation. The only success achieved during this period against the Movement, was to break the oil blockade with the help of the army. The services of military engineers were utilized to operate the oil refineries, as the regular employees of the refineries were non-cooperating because of their support to the Movement. The flow of crude oil to Barauni refinery could only be resumed in February, 1981. But the situation turned worse. Violence erupted. Series of bomb blasts took place, the main targets being the oil pipe-line and the railways. Thus, because of the severe repressive measures, the non-violent character of the Movement was gradually eroded and non-violence was yielding place to violence. Indira

Gandhi, once again, failed to understand the reasons for this transformation. She became more determined to teach Assam a lesson. Then followed the forcibly held elections of 1983, which had already been discussed elsewhere. Sinning Indira totally forgot the lessons of 1975! Her upbeat mood overjoyed the Congress (I) activists of Assam, without ever realizing that they were gradually being mortgaged to the 'Bangladeshi lobby', which would not hesitate to leave them high and dry, once it ensured a dominant role. This is what exactly Maulana Badaruddin Azmal was trying to do on the eve of the general elections of 2016, although his communal strategies seem to be miscalculated, as a sizeable percentage of the young generation does not seem to be communally motivated.

The emergence of AAMSU had already engulfed Assam in an ambience of communal divide and the forcibly held elections of 1983, accentuated this very process. The holding of 1983 elections without removing the names of alien voters from the ERs, witnessed the following developments:

1. The Movement leadership had to undertake many fresh agitational programmes for resisting the imposed election and these programmes were, by and large, successful. This time, the indigenous segment of the population of Barak valley had also responded to these programmes.
2. The Administration had to resort to unprecedented repressive measures and unconstitutional activities for frustrating the election-boycotting programmes, the only tangible object being to satisfy the whims of Indira Gandhi and promoting her partisan interests. She simply did not listen to the call of quite a number of national leaders for abandoning such an undemocratic act.
3. Indira's refusal to see the writings on the wall and her all out efforts to install a government of her own party at Dispur, had emboldened the anti-national communal forces to commit violence against the indigenous people.
4. Such high-handedness, committed by the administration, had been certainly instrumental in causing many socio-political-administrative upheavals, detrimental to the

healthy functioning of the democratic process, the very life-blood of the traditional Indian society. With the help of hindsight, one is easily convinced that the happenings of 1983, had been the major factor in helping the emergence of ULFA as a strong militant secessionist outfit and building up its anti-Delhi agenda.

The Movement leadership had exhibited tremendous innovative and organizing ability in chalking out various programmes, for resisting the holding of elections in 1983. Its innovative capacity also proved to be a great stumbling block on the way to maintaining the normalcy of the situation for holding the elections. The leadership innovated the system of ***Janata Curfew***—not imposed by the government, but by the Movement leadership. In fact, wherever Indira Gandhi was to go for her electioneering campaign, Janata Curfew was promulgated, with the result that the people would not come out to attend the electioneering meetings. As a result, she had to keep her programmes confined to only immigrant Muslim areas, trying to prove that she was their savior and unless they voted for her party, the Assamese would drive them out. Also on all the three days fixed for holding elections, Janata Curfew was promulgated. It was to the credit of the leaders that they could motivate the indigenous people for boycotting the elections. The State government employees had paralyzed the State administration for a long period of seventeen days and the authorities had to import officers and employees from outside the State for completing the show of holding the elections. All the State government employees had risen to the occasion, as one man, for boycotting the elections.

The second phase of the Movement came to an end with the assassination of Indira Gandhi. The sad and cowardly assassination of Indira Gandhi was followed by Rajiv Gandhi becoming the Prime Minister and with this, commenced the final phase of the Assam Movement.

I had the privilege of representing the prestigious **Axom Sahitya Sabha** in the AAGSP for four years and had had therefore, the opportunity of interacting with the student leaders from close quarters. Before delving deep into the matter, let it be crystal clear that during the entire Movement, the people never betrayed the cause of the Movement but the leaders did ultimately, as was hinted upon elsewhere. Most unfortunately, Late Tapan Deka who was in charge of recording the proceedings of the meetings of the AAGSP, was no more and with him, had disappeared all these proceedings which would have been otherwise a vivid picture of the contemporary situation and the inside story of the functioning of the AAGSP. It is a matter of anybody's guess if somebody had taken the custody of these proceedings. But what was most surprising, was lack of any anxiety for recovering these proceedings after Deka's expiry. Else, many of the leaders would have stood thoroughly exposed. Ever since my participation in the meetings of the AAGSP, I had noticed that the proceedings were entirely dominated by the student leaders. An allergy to any opposition to them was easily discernible. Rather, they had manipulated to expel senior leaders like Nibaran Bora, Jatin Goswami and Atul Bora from the AAGSP as they, on one or the other ground, proved to be inconvenient to the AASU's way of functioning. Besides, an undercurrent of rivalry, if not animosity, was discernible between AASU and Axom Jatiyatabadi Yuva Chhatra Parishad, another prominent member of the AAGSP as also a prominent youth organisation of the state. There was no shortage of fund; rather some of the student leaders were seen to be lavishly spending to feed fat their luxurious habits. In fact, while in Delhi for participating in the talks with the Central government, some of these student leaders were noticed to have gone on shopping spree. Nobody knew where the money came from. None of these student leaders were in a position to defray such expenses from their regular monthly budgets. Donations were collected from various sources but no receipts were issued. Likewise, no account was ever submitted in the periodic meetings of the AAGSP. That is to say, they were not the least bothered to cultivate the principle of accountability, so vital for a clean public life. Habits die hard and such irresponsible conduct was evident during both the tenures of AGP rule. Thus, some of these student leaders got addicted to easily available, unearned money, a habit quickly getting into vogue in the days to follow. In fact, this has been one of the worst banes of Assam's socio-economic life. With the ever growing unemployment problem, this social evil has assumed epidemic proportion and an upward tendency, since the days of the Assam Movement. AASU's hold over the student community in the Brahmaputra valley was all pervasive; but the top leadership did not pay any attention to creating healthy tradition and practices amongst the students. Since the academic atmosphere had deteriorated during the days of the Movement, the practice of resorting to unfair means in the examinations had surfaced in full vehemence. AASU leaders never realised the baneful consequences of such evils. Even some teachers were reported to have connived in such academically harmful ventures. Still worse, some of the top leaders got graduation and post-graduation degrees with distinction without ever attending the class room!

Anyway, the most damaging trait was their fascist tendency of not tolerating any opposition. After assumption of powers, they also went on a spree of self-aggrandizement, as if a competition had commenced for acquiring movable and immovable properties.

Also, the latent Assamese middle-class chauvinism found expression in the field of politics while forming the two AGP governments. As a result, ethnic divergence tore apart the otherwise composite character of the traditional Assamese society. These leaders had neither the foresight, nor the requisite education to realize the likelihood of adverse fallouts of such chauvinistic stance. The State Language Act, passed in 1961, had already created a suspicion, that the Assamese chauvinists were out to perpetuate their dominance over all the ethnic groups of the State and promote the cause of the Assamese language, exclusively by denying similar opportunities to the development of the languages/dialects of all other ethnic sub-nationalities. Particularly, the Bodos were evidently sore about it. (The Bodo language has since been recognized as one of the State languages.) The historic Assam Movement had released tremendous socio-political forces for organizing the civil society of Assam on a solid basis. But the process came to a halt, as a result of the myopic perspectives and absolute selfishness, on the part of the AGP leadership, which failed to reckon with the hopes and aspirations of various ethnic groups. Thus, the collective entity engendered by the Assam Movement, gradually betrayed symptoms of being extinct so much so that a strong agitation swept the valley once again for the creation of a separate Bodoland. The agitation ultimately ended in the creation of the BTAD—a state within a State, although the demand for a totally separate Bodo State was yet to die out.

Such lack of a broad-minded approach and record-breaking corruption, put the Axom Gana Parishad (AGP) on a downhill journey. They refused to introduce new blood into the party with the result that since 2001, AGP had to fight for its very survival as a leading regional party. The people had ultimately rejected them and the resultant vacuum was being gradually filled up by the BJP and few other small political parties organized on ethnic basis.

The betrayal perpetrated by these erstwhile AASU leaders, embarrassed the next generation of AASU leaders and they had to work very hard to recover their credibility. However, it must be admitted that the present leadership of the AASU has remained committed to the implementation of the Assam Accord, although nothing much has so far been achieved in respect of the problem of infiltration.

The six year long Assam Movement culminated in the signing of the Assam Accord (Copy at Appendix 5) on the night of the 14th of August1985, in presence of Rajiv Gandhi, who proudly informed the country the next day, about the signing of the Accord, while delivering his Independence Day speech. True, the country might have heaved a sigh of relief without, however, realising that the Assam Accord had promised much but delivered nothing, towards the solution of the ever expanding problem of illegal trans-border migration, even after three decades of signing the Accord. Though the government frequently points out about its success in implementing many provisions of the Accord, one cannot get away from the fact that the main objectives of the Movement were not to establish an IIT, two universities and revive a few sick industries. Taking advantage of the immaturity of the student leaders, the core issue of the Movement was obfuscated in addition to shrewdly begetting recognition to the controversial IM (DT) Act. Now the possibility of detecting and deporting the illegal migrants has been becoming more remote with the passage of each day, whereas various data and so many census reports of India and Bangladesh, as analyzed above, clearly indicate that the rate of such illegal migration has assumed serious and ever expanding proportion as were envisaged and contemplated by Sadiqeue Khan and Abdul Momin, two prominent persons of Bangladesh. As narrated above, in the process, the indigenous people of Assam irrespective of their language, caste, creed, religion are gradually becoming minority in many LA constituencies.

The turn of events had since exposed the fact that Rajiv Gandhi never intended the Assam Accord to solve the problem of illegal migration from Bangladesh, his only intention seeming to be, as it transpired subsequently, to diffuse the Assam Movement. Thus, the country was deceived by creating an illusion of a solution of the vexed problem of massive infiltration from Bangladesh. However, the Accord certainly paved the way for the contemporary AASU leadership to capture power at Dispur almost immediately after the Accord was signed. Still worse, no specific commitment was included in the Accord for updating the National Register of Citizens (NRC) which should have been the main basis for detecting illegal migrants. Thus, the Assam Accord amounted to a deed of total betrayal perpetrated by Prafulla Mahanta and his colleagues, against the people of Assam.

And now, in the absence of any definition of the Assamese people as stipulated in the Accord (which should have been indigenous people), the most important clause of the Accord pertaining to constitutional safeguards against being overwhelmed by illegal alien migrants, has still remained confined to the file, besides cultivating enough scope for politicizing the entire matter. Prafulla Mahanta formed two governments in 1985 and 1996 but did nothing worth mentioning for implementing the Assam Accord. Incidentally, BJP, despite being a participant in the Assam Movement, also let down the people of Assam when it was in power in New Delhi for six long years. Particularly, the Union Government headed by the BJP failed to take any effective preventive measures against fresh infiltration.

Briefly speaking, the Assam Accord was a still-born baby. Besides, it was a very poorly drafted document, leaving enough scope for defeating the purpose of the entire exercise. Late Kirtinath Hazarika, the then Editor of Dainik Axom, had observed in his book captioned '*Chari Dasakor Jalangaidi*' (Page number 227) that '— the drafting of the accord was so weak and the provision for detecting the foreign national so shallow that it would afford many opportunities to the Centre to retrace its step. The provisions for detecting the foreigners were so loose, cumbrous and pro-infiltrators that the steps stipulated in the Accord for detecting the foreigners, divesting some of them of voting rights for ten years and deporting some others, would become totally ineffective.' No wonder that Rajiv Gandhi had subsequently announced in a meeting held at Lataseel Field of Guwahati, that the Accord was aimed at offering protection to the minorities!

What is still more disturbing, is that most of the persons declared as foreigners by the Tribunals concerned, could not be deported physically from the State because they were missing. 42,000 persons were declared to be foreigners by the Tribunals concerned, but only 2221 of them could be deported. This state of affairs also raises the doubt about the sincerity of the government in detecting and deporting the infiltrators from the State. On the other hand, the Central government has failed to seal the border even after three decades of signing the Accord, nor has it taken any effective steps to conclude an *Extradition Treaty* with Bangladesh. Bangladesh government has not been known for accepting the findings of Assam Police or for that matter, even the verdict of any Tribunal deciding the status of a foreigner, particularly in the absence of a mutually accepted Extradition Treaty. The Home and Political Department of Assam, had pointed out on the 20th of October 2012 in a White Paper, published by this department that 'In the absence of a properly laid down procedure for deportation of illegal migrants between the Government of India and the Government of Bangladesh, it has become difficult to carry out deportations—'. This has amounted to a glaring omission on the part of the Indian authorities. As such, a 'repatriation treaty' between the two countries has become imperative. Even the reports of neutral agency like the UNO, stated in its UN Population Facts Number 2013/3 made public in 2013, that the people from Bangladesh residing in India constituted the single largest 'bilateral stock' of international migrants (3.2 million). After such revealation by UNO, there should have been no hesitation in formulating a 'repatriation treaty' between the two countries for repatriation of the illegal Bangladeshi migrants. Emphasizing the importance of a 'repatriation treaty', The Assam Tribune wrote an Editorial in its issue of March 26, 2016 and its relevant portion is reproduced below '....... Last but not the least— and unfortunately kept ignored by successive Central governments in India—is the issue of having a repatriation treaty with Bangladesh under which it should take back illegal migrants living in India, especially in Assam. The absence of a repatriation pack has hit at the very core of the process of detection and deportation of illegal Bangladeshi migrants. This is because even after the determination of their illegal citizenship status through the judicial process, sending them back to Bangladesh has remained a non-starter because of the latter's reluctance to accept them. With a friendly government in Bangladesh, the Centre should be proactive in settling this contentious issue— something having disturbing socio-political fallouts for Assam— once and for all.'

The pro-talk ULFA faction is, however expected to salvage something on the basis of their Charter of Demands. It can be ignored only at one's own peril, that besides threatening the distinct identity of the Assamese, now the unabated infiltration is posing a great threat to the security of the country also

The preparation of correct ERs divested of foreigners' names without an updated NRC, is simply inconceivable under the present situation. The NRC must be not only updated but also regularly maintained flawlessly. The editorial column of the Assam Tribune had highlighted the issue on the 9th of August 2007. The particular *editorial* is reproduced at Appendix 6. After a good deal of idling, the modalities of updating the NRC, were finalised only after the Supreme Court interfered in the matter and issued specific orders in this regard. The H'nble Court has gone to the extent of appointing an one-man commission headed by Advocate Upamunya Hazarika. The revelations made by this Commissions have since been creating fresh waves of consternation amongst the indigenous people, albeit much to the embarrassment of the state government. A correct NRC is not only a *sine qua non* for the detection of the illegal migrants, but also, after it is updated, there will be no scope left, for raising the oft-repeated hue and cry that genuine Indian nationals are harassed, in the name of detecting foreigners. Of course, the process of updating the NRC has to be a continuous process so that it cannot be distorted. Meanwhile, as reported in Dainik Axom of the 20th of February 2015, the one man Commission headed by Advocate Upamunya Hazarika has pointed out certain other anomalies which may create unforeseen difficulties in preparing a correct NRC: 25th of March, 1971, has been accepted as the cut-off date for updating the NRC, which contravenes section 3 and section 6(a) of the Citizenship Act, 1955. It has been pointed out by certain quarters that the children of infiltrators born after the 25th of March1971, will be entitled to Indian citizenship unless the Citizenship Act is amended before the final shape is given to the NRC. Advocate Hazarika has pointed out that according to the amended Citizenship Act, those born within the 1st of July 1987, will be entitled to Indian citizenship; but if one of the parents happens to be Indian, then those born between the 1st of July1987 and 2003, will also be deemed as Indian citizens. The Law also states that only those born of alien citizens, after the 3rd of December 2004, will not be entitled to Indian citizenship.

(For all practical purposes, such legal provisions have nullified the Assam Accord.) Briefly speaking, all children born of Bangladeshi infiltrators within 2004, will have to be treated as Indian citizens. As a result of such legal provisions, Advocate Hazarika observes, lakhs of persons of Bangladesh origin will acquire Indian citizenship. Now, for all practical purposes, the cut-off date for identifying Bangladeshi infiltrators will be the 3rd of December 2004. It may be pointed out that, as was the case with the since repealed IMDT Act, 1983, such provisions related to acquisition of citizenship in Assam by Bangladeshi nationals are discriminatory in nature, since the cut-off date for acquiring Indian citizenship for the rest of the country has been fixed as the 19th of July 1948. It is extremely unfair to Assam because Assam had already accepted the stream of Bangladeshi immigrants who had infiltrated up to the 25th of March 1971. Thus, the likelihood of a fresh confrontation against the Centre in the future, cannot be ruled out.

The media has been constantly pressurizing the State Government to complete the updating of the NRC. In its Editorial column dated The 8th of October 2014, The Assam Tribune had unequivocally stated, inter alia, that 'The Supreme Court recently gave a directive to the Government of Assam to complete the process of updating the National Register of Citizens (NRC) of 1951 in the first part of 2016, that is before the next State Assembly elections. — The process of updating the NRC remains slow and only after the intervention of the Supreme Court, the process may be expedited.' But the State Government has belied such pious hopes also. The full text of the Editorial is reproduced at Appendix 7. In fact, the lack of strong political will, has been so far the main obstacle to complete the updating process. Now, it has been stated that the entire process will be completed by December, 2016 and this is certainly, a welcome development. The Register General of India is reported to be monitoring the process. However, the completion of the updating process will, to a great extent, depend on how quickly the cases pending before the Foreigners Tribunals are disposed of. Needless to mention that vested interests are already creating lot of delaying tactics and also many cases of using forged, false and inadmissible documents for the inclusion of names in the NRC, have been detected and according to Press reports, quite a few criminal cases have already been registered in the context of fraudulent practices resorted to, for inclusion of names in the NRC. Lately, advocate Rafiqul Islam of Barpeta districts has been arrested on the 22nd of April 2016 for forging the name of the Electoral Officer, in order to facilitate the inclusion of the names of one of his clients in the NRC. In its editorial column of the 23rd of April 2016, The Assam Tribune observed that 'With the process of updating the National Register of Citizens (NRC) in the final stage, the onus lies squarely on the State Government, to ensure that the all-important exercise of identifying the genuine Indian citizens remains a foolproof one. Disturbingly— even though it merits little surprise—there have been reports of submission of forged documents by many people of doubtful identity in a bid to register themselves as bona fide Indian citizens. Given that the stakes are high for the large number of illegal migrants living in the State, it should not come as a shocker that such elements would be hell-bent on entering their names in the NRC by hook or crook. — It also needs to be found out if the sinister developments are part of a deep-rooted conspiracy to enlist names of foreigners in the NRC. —'. Will these cases be sent up for trial in the Court and necessary steps taken to ensure conviction? As such, it is going to be a lengthy process, although much will depend upon how the new state government will deal with the matter.

It is in this context, the national media must also be activated and ceaseless pressure maintained on the Central and the State governments.

Though the question of granting constitutional safeguards to the indigenous people of Assam, has been mentioned in the Assam Accord, nothing has materialized so far on this count also. Clause number 6 of the Assam Accord envisaged that 'Constitutional, legislative and administrative safeguards, as may be appropriate shall be provided to protect, preserve and promote the culture, social, linguistic identity and heritage of the Assamese people.'

The use of the word 'Assamese' in clause number 6, has created lot of controversies, intensifying the feelings against Assamese chauvinism and therefore, efforts for correct interpretation of this word are still continuing. At the time of preparing the draft of the Accord, the people involved failed to foresee the controversies that may arise for the use of this particular expression. There is no denial that the proposed safeguards were not meant only for the Assamese-speaking people. So, the correct expression in place of 'Assamese people' should have been the 'indigenous people'. Much time has already been lost in search of a correct interpretation of the word 'Assamese'. Even a debate took place centering around this issue in the State Assembly. Sri Pranab Gogoi, the Speaker of the Assembly, had offered a reasonable definition of the word, so that all the indigenous people could be covered by this provision of the Accord; but Tarun Gogoi, the Chief Minister had outright rejected the Speaker's suggestion, for reasons not explained in understandable terms. But in terms of what has been visualized in the Accord, there should be no ambiguities in defining 'Assamese'.

CHAPTER 9

ACROSS THE SEAS

The geo-political, socio-political and socio-economic equations in North-East India are undergoing silent yet rapid inauspicious changes. Unfortunately, the rest of the country is hardly aware of the same. But there is no reason to believe that the Central and the State Governments, with their widespread networks of Intelligence Services, are unaware of the gathering storm. Neither the government, nor the illegal migrants seem to have as yet reckoned with the recondite militant nature of the tribal people of the area, The same has already betrayed its manifestation from time to time in some of the tribal areas and the appearance of the *jihadis* in the scene, had not eased the situation either. In fact, this is one of the main reasons why quite a few of the ethnic tribal groups are agitating for separate States, so that they can deal with the situation on their own and not fall victims like the Assamese-speaking people to the insensitive and apathetic attitude of Assam Government.

Oflate, the illegal migrants are overflowing to the neighboring States of Arunachal Pradesh, Nagaland, Meghalaya, Manipur, Mizoram amidst others and creating socio-political unrest. Communal violence in erstwhile East Pakistan had displaced from the CHT, a large number of native Chakma people and about 60,000 of them migrated to Arunachal Pradesh, thereby creating a huge hullabaloo. They had entered India between 1964 and 1969. On the 9th of November1996, the Hon'ble Supreme had passed an order, directing the government of Arunachal Pradesh, not to deprive these Chakmas of their life and liberty without due process of law. On the other hand, in Nagaland, the illegal migrants have adopted an ingenious strategy by marrying local girls, with the sole purpose of ingratiating themselves with the indigenous population of the state. This is resulting in gradual emergence of a hybrid race, popularly being referred to as Nagamia. If the mother is a Sema girl and the father a Muslim, then the offspring are classified as Semia. Likewise, Aomia, Zeliangmia, Angamia amidst others are re-emerging as separate sub-races, thereby silently changing the demographic pattern. Besides, as already discussed, these illegal migrants have already usurped a major chunk of the labor and the business sectors of the State. Fortunately enough, the Bodos of Assam and the Assamese Muslims have not yet fallen victims to such unholy alliance. These immigrants, both legal and undocumented, are yet to develop any sense of belonging to the region.

Nagaland recorded the highest rate of population growth in India, from a growth rate of 56.08 per cent in 1981-1991, to a growth rate of 64.41 per cent in the period between 1991 and 2001. This growth rate is not uniform all over the State. Very high growth has been recorded only in the two districts of Wokha and Dimapur bordering Assam. It is significant to note that the district of Wokha recorded a growth of 95.01 per cent during the period between 1991 and 2001, this being the highest rate of decadal growth district-wise in the country. A section of the Naga society has been viewing this as a threat to their distinct tribal identity. It may be noted that Nagaland does not have a border with Bangladesh. The illegal migrants have been coming via Assam after managing to procure some kind of identity documents in Assam for proving their Indian Citizenship and there are reasons to believe, that many of these documents were procured by fraudulent means. As in Assam, in Nagaland also, the dislike of the native young generation for manual labor has been a major factor in causing influx of these illegal migrants. Such influx detrimental to the national interest, has been happening despite the system of Inner-line permit. As in Assam, in Nagaland also the construction sector has harbored the highest immigrant labors. Monalisa Changkija, the Editor of the Nagaland Page, had observed that 'Land is prestigious for the Nagas. However, inability of the locals to work in the field compelled us to depend on non-locals, many of them Bangladeshis to till or plough. The hospitality of the Nagas coupled with the erosion of community-based values among the contemporary Naga society patronized immigrants to work for us. We are now increasingly dependent on them. In their absence will we the Nagas fill up the vacuum created?' (Interview held on the 12th of November2005 by M. Amarjit Singh with Monalisa Changkija.)

West Bengal is another State which has been bearing a heavy load of illegal migrants; both Hindu and Muslim from Bangladesh. It may be noted that the density of population in West Bengal is one of the highest in the country. The Indo-Bangladesh border in West Bengal is 2,204 kilometers long and is divided among the nine border districts of West Bengal. The Islamic character of Bangladesh has prompted a large number of Hindus to migrate to West Bengal, who did not find any difficulty in ingratiating themselves in the Bengali society of West Bengal for obvious reasons. The nine districts of West Bengal, which have been the main bearers of this load, have, as in Assam, recorded abnormal growth of population. The decadal growth of population between 1981 and 1991 is shown in the table below:

District	Population	Decadal growth	Density Per square kilometer.
South 24 Parganas	5,708,260	30.08 per cent	573
North 24 Parganas	7,280,261	31.66 per cent	1778
Nadia	3,818,247	29.82 per cent	980
Murshidabad	4,734,278	28.04 per cent	889
Malda	2,633,942	29.63 per cent	706
West Dinajpur	3,132,374	30.25 per cent	585
Darjeeling	1,335,618	30.40 per cent	424
Jalpaiguri	2,789,827	25.96 per cent	448
Cooch Bihar	2,158,169	21.82 per cent	637

(Source: Demographic Diversity of India, 1991 Census by Ashish Bose, Page 386)

It may be noted that during this period, the population growth in West Bengal was 24.55 per cent as against the national average of 23.50 per cent. Such abnormal growth has also resulted in abnormal growth of Muslim population in these districts, mainly in the districts of Murshidabad, Malda and West Dinajpur. Sri T.V. Rajeshwar, the ex-Governor of West Bengal, like Lt. Gen S.K. Sinha, ex-Governor of Assam, had also highlighted the above quoted menace in an article published in 'The Statesman', dated the 6th and 8th of April, 1990. Relevant parts of the article are reproduced in Appendix 8. Some Muslims of Murshidabad district had even gone to the extent of shouting slogans that since they were in majority, they should secede from India and amalgamate with the Islamic Republic of Bangladesh! Given the present state of affairs, some districts of lower Assam may follow suit, in not too distant a future. In fact, in the heart of Kolkata, a mini Bangladesh has already surfaced in Metiaburuz, harbouring many fundamentalist, anti-India elements.

Shonu Nangia in his **'Demographic changes: Is Bengal sitting on a jihadi volcano?'** (www.bharatniti.in) published on the 10th of April, 2016, has given a more alarming account of what has befallen West Bengal. Apart from his own observations, he has quoted American thinker Janet Levy (www.americanthinker.com/articles/2015/02/the_muslim_takeover_of _west bengal. html#xzz40fID8Iwh) who reported in her article that 'At partitioning, the Muslim population of West Bengal stood at 12 per cent and the Hindu Population of East Bengal, at 30 per cent. Today, with massive Muslim immigration, Hindu persecution, and forced conversions, West Bengal's Muslim population has increased to 27 per cent (upto 63 per cent in some districts), as per the 2011 census and Bangladesh's Hindu population has decreased to 8 per cent. While the situation for Hindus in Bangladesh is certainly dire, life has become increasingly difficult for Hindus in West Bengal, home to a Muslim appeasing government and a breeding ground and safe haven for terrorists. For several years, West Bengal has suffered under apparent Muslim-planned riots designed to implement shariah, extract government concessions and grab more territory.' These are not the remarks of any Hindu communalist but of an American thinker and researcher. (Shonu Nangia is an Associate Professor of Foreign Languages at the Louisiana State University at Alexandra, USA) The situation in West Bengal is not different from that of Assam. What is more significant, is that Mamata Banerjee's government of Trinamul Congress, has not been averse to following the policy of her arch rival CPM. Without being under any compulsion to subscribe to his political prescription, the reader may go through Shonu Nangia's article to get a better view of the Islamist expansion under political patronage.

For the benefit of the reader, the treatise by Shonu Nangia is reproduced at Appendix 10.

The Muslim infiltrators from Bangladesh have been mainly responsible for the abnormal growth of Muslim population in Katihar and Purnea, two districts of Bihar. In Bihar, quite a few districts like Bhagalpur, Saharsa, Champaran, Dhanbad, Singhbhum amidst others, have been also subjected to very heavy infiltration by Bangladeshi Muslims. In Bihar also, helpless tribal people have been victims of infiltration from Bangladesh. Already clashes have taken place between the infiltrators and the indigenous Santhal people of Purnea district.

In backward states like Arunachal Pradesh, Nagaland, Sikkim and so on, the process of development commenced rather lately. In the wake of such developmental activities, the contractors and even the government agencies, in search of cheap labor were instrumental in engaging labors of Bangladeshi origin. The case of Nagaland has been already discussed. The following table will illustrate the abnormal growth of Muslim population due to infiltration of non-citizens.

Name of states	Decadal growth of Muslim population between 1971-1981
Sikkim	867.46 per cent
Arunachal Pradesh	502.49 per cent
Nagaland	298.04 per cent
Meghalaya	57.26 per cent

> >

> >

Name of states	Decadal growth of Muslim population between 1971-1981
Manipur	39.95 per cent
Tripura	33.76 per cent
Assam	No census was held in 1981

Lately, labors of immigrant stock have been engaged in large numbers in mining activities in Meghalaya and also in Assam. Exact figures are not yet available. Arunachal Pradesh has been lately targeted because of abundant availability of land and fairly low density of population.

After the army crackdown and eruption of communal violence in South-West Myanmar, there has been exodus of large number of Rohingiya Muslims who were never given citizenship status in Myanmar. They were treated as Bangladeshi Muslim migrants by Myanmar. In 1978-1979, the Rohingiya infiltrators were detected by the mobile team of Border Police Organization in quite a few trains. However the Rohingiyas have mostly infiltrated into Mizoram, where they are working as both, skilled and unskilled labors.

The Rohingya Muslims inhabit the Rakhine State of South-West Myanmar, bordering the Bay of Bengal. The population of this community is estimated to be about 1.2 million. They have throughout been treated as Bangladeshi Muslims and never as citizens of Myanmar. They are accused of illegally settling in Myanmar. The Myanmarese government has been discriminating against them and also they have been subjected to violence by the Arakanese Buddhists. The violence committed against them in June and October, 2012, compelled thousands of Rohingyas to flee their place of habitation. It has been estimated that 1,40,000 Rohingya Muslims have been driven out of their homes and most of them have slipped into the North-Eastern region of India with many others taking shelter in relief camps. The concept of ethnic cleansing seems to have surfaced with full vehemence, as the Rohingyas are being perceived as a threat to Myanmar's national security, given the expansionist designs of the fundamentalist forces of Pakistan via Bangladesh.

According to the World Migration Report of 2011, the trend of migration to developed countries like the USA, the UK and others had shown signs of slowing down because of global economic crisis. For instance, in the USA, the number of migrants came down to 1,042,625 in 2010 as compared to 1,130,818 in 2009. In the UK, the number came down to 4,70,000 in 2009 from 5,05,000 in 2008. Likewise, the number of migrants dropped in Spain and New Zealand also. Even then the general pattern did not betray any drastic change as the total number of international migrants was estimated to be 214 million in 2010. Briefly speaking, as of now, one out of seven people of the world population is a migrant. Some of the key trends are as follows:

The political turmoil in the Middle East and North Africa in 2011, coupled with the emergence of the ISIS phenomenon had a tremendous impact on the migration trend. However, by the middle of 2011 more than a lakh and half of these migrants were evacuated from 50 different countries. Most of these evacuees hailed from Bangladesh, Chad, Egypt, Sudan, Nigeria, Ghana and Mali. The deportation of such huge number of migrants may, however, accelerate the problem of unemployment in their respective countries which, in its turn, may have grave bearing on the economic stability of these countries. In addition to such unforeseen developments, these countries will also be deprived of the remittances these migrant labors used to send home. The issue of reintegrating these evacuees/deportees has attracted the attention of the UNO and the World Bank which has approved of a project, namely, 'Repatriation and Livelihood Restoration for Migrant Workers Project.' No data are available if India has mooted any plan for availing of this project. Bangladesh is, however, reported to have availed of the scheme. Nepal has also followed suit. The number of displaced persons also increased beyond usual calculation because of natural disasters. A relevant report of the IOM reads as follows: 'In 2010, the estimated global number of displaced persons due to sudden-onset natural disasters was over forty-two millions, which represents an increase of six and twenty-five millions, in comparison with 2008 and 2009, respectively. The large majority (thirty eight million) were displaced by climate-change related disasters (primarily flooding and storm (IDMC/NRC, 2011). The significant overall rise in 2010 was mainly due to the unusually heavy flood in mid-2010 in China (which displaced over fifteen millions) and Pakistan (which displaced at least eleven millions), as well as the earthquakes in Chile, Japan, Haiti, Bangladesh, India and the Philippines were also severely hit by natural disasters, making Asia the most affected region.....' This report is all the more relevant for India, because of the havoc likely to be caused in Bangladesh due to global warming in next few years.

The United Nations Anti-Trafficking (Palermo) Protocol was signed by eighty nations; of course, this number has since risen to 117. But the number of displaced persons being on the rise, it is doubtful how much this particular Protocol will be, in the near future, successful in controlling the international trend of migration. However, such efforts on the part of a growing number of nations signal a growing interest in the international pattern of migration, both legal and illegal. It has been generally accepted that the Intergovernmental Authority on Development Regional Consultative Process (IGAD-RCP) and other similar inter-regional platforms, can play an effective role on the migration issue for rationalizing the trend, particularly in the sector of international labor market. The International Labour Organisation (ILO) is also taking keen interest in such rationalization for synthesizing all applicable principles and guidelines so that it may also contribute to the formulation of sound migration policies.

In the above-mentioned background, Asia is the top emigration region, as also the top receivers of remittances in the world. According to the World Bank's report of 2011, Bangladesh, China, India, Pakistan and the Philippines are the top emigration countries. Singapore, Hong Kong, the Republic of Korea and Malaysia top the list in respect of emigration within the region. The same report points out that a significant number of migrant workers hail from Bangladesh, Indonesia,

Nepal, Cambodia and the Philippines, mostly their targets being Malaysia, Singapore and Thailand.

The havoc being caused by Bangladeshi migrants has already attracted international attention. Bangladesh has been all along denying the presence of her nationals in India. Also Bangladesh has so far refused to accept any Bangladeshi deportees from India. In 'The Bengal Borderland, Beyond State and Nation in South Asia' penned by Williem van Schendel published from London, Schendel said: 'The desperate tenacity with which Bangladeshi officials clung to their discourse of denial was the result of an acute sense of vulnerability vis-à-vis their huge neighbor, India. Rooted in partition, this feeling was boosted by Indian adoption of the discourse of infiltration. To the Bangladeshi state elite, acknowledging the unauthorized movement of Bangladesh citizens across the border would reveal the inability of their state to control this movement, or worse, suggest its complicity. In their anxiety to avoid owning up to the failure of their state's strategy of territoriality – and hence, its claim to full statehood – the Bangladeshi authority chose to disown their citizens in Indian Territory.'

Schendel observed that Bangladeshis in India are 'Truly transitional'. Firstly, they are not accepted as Indian citizens and the world over, they are called illegal immigrants. They do not belong to India. Secondly, at present they are not motivated by nationalist ideologies. (However, I'm convinced that presently they are under heavy influence of fundamentalist forces, the ulterior motive being to cause polarization of voters on communal line). According to him, their motive is to avoid the hard life at home and pursue the good life not available back home. Thirdly, Schendel says that 'like their counterparts all over the world, they think transitionally, when they remit money and make occasional visits back home'. Further, Schendel adds an additional subjective perspective that' it was not impossible for Bangladeshi opinion leaders to start portraying migrants to India as 'Cultural heroes'; people who against enormous odds were able to rely on their own wits to survive and create new cultural and social forms of transitional

Bangladeshi identity. Until that time, Bangladeshi discourse or migration to India is likely to be marked by denial, disdain and disinformation" which is why lurking suspicions have been agitating the minds of the indigenous people of Assam, that the dream of a 'Brihattar Islamistan', if realized, will be followed by the conceptualization of distinct cultural identity. The gradual emergence of this situation is also communalizing the issue of illegal immigration as already discussed in details, thus creating mistrust and tension between Muslims and non-Muslims. Besides, in this developing situation, external forces will not certainly fight shy of promoting anti-India feelings.

With the pace of development being accelerated in Bangladesh, a large number of Bangladeshi students are going abroad for higher studies with the UK being the most coveted destination. According to the World Migration Report, 2005, Asia accounts for about two million students. However, student migration from Bangladesh is yet to be brought under close analysis and research. It may, however, be pointed out that Japan has stood out to be a popular destination of Bangladeshi students – obviously because of Japan's technological superiority.

The services rendered by migrant workers, are being increasingly appreciated in the receiving countries. The case of Assam is entirely different for reasons already explained. Wherever the fundamentalist expansionism is not in the agenda of the migrant workers, the migrant workers are receiving sympathetic treatment. Migration protection and support services, according to World Migration Report of 2011, are being offered by the new labor migration policies undertaken by quite a few developed countries coupled with memoranda of understanding with the main destination countries. In 2010, Philippines and Pakistan either adopted new migration policies or amended the existing ones. Again, according to the same Report,' The Philippines 1995 Migrant workers and Overseas Philipinos Act was amended in 2010, to include stricter penalties related to illegal recruitment as well as the extension of services.....' In order to combat the growing menace, similar strict legal provisions have become imperative in Assam and the other adversely affected Indian states. In fact, there is provision in the Foreigners Act, 1946 for dealing with harboring illegal alien migrants. Not lagging behind, Indonesia has also signed a number of memoranda with quite a few destination countries. Sri Lanka has also undertaken certain measures to protect the interests of her migrant workers. The International Migration Annual Review of 2010/2011 reports that 'Irregular migration within and from Asia remains a primary issue. In an effort to regularize the situation of migrants in Thailand, the Thai Government introduced a registration programme that would grant a two-year work renewal permit to those who completed a nationality and biographical verification process by the end of February 2010. The process was applied to certain categories and primarily targeted the 60,000 migrant workers (mainly Burmese), whose permits were due to expire in January 2010. Meanwhile, the Korean Government granted amnesty to 1,78,200 irregular migrants, authorizing their departure (without the payment of the usual fines) between May and September 2010(UC Davis, 2010c).

At a regional level, the Bali Process on People Smuggling, Trafficking in persons and Related Transnational Crime organized different workshops throughout the year 2010—for example, on regional cooperation regarding refugees and irregular movements and on repatriation and reintegration assistance. In March 2011, it held its fourth ministerial meeting, discussing possible strategies for revitalizing cooperation on trafficking in persons (including, for the first time, a proposal for a regional cooperation framework to address the irregular movement of people and to combat people smuggling) and reaffirming the commitment of participating States to effective cooperation on border control and law enforcement initiatives to combat people smuggling.' (for more details, the reader may refer to www.baliprocess.net).

However, the manner of dealing with the issue in the developed western countries is different in many ways. Developed countries with capitalist system of economy have been, throughout the history, on constant lookout for earning more profit and being richer than others. One of the main factors in maintaining the economy at profitable level, is to ensure low cost of production as much as possible. Living standard in Asia not being as high as in the developed Western countries, the cost of labor is also not as high. Here one finds the benefits of the system of outsourcing as well as utilizing the services of low-cost labors, mostly available in the shape of migrant workers coming from Asia, either legally or illegally.

As such, the trend of migration to Europe and the manner of dealing with it, are different from migration to and within Asia. Over the years, European countries have evolved a more utilitarian approach to the issue with a bias in favour of Christian values. Even the Pope has pleaded for a humanitarian approach to the issue. Efforts have been made for rationalizing the trend in European Union countries. The trend presents a more calculable picture because of comparatively more accurate documentation. Still, the situation cannot be accepted to be stable. This is evident from the fact that after the massive exodus from the Middle East, Africa, Pakistan etc. coupled with the rise of the ISIS, some of the EU countries have perforce tightened their belts and enhanced their vigilance against illegal migrants and been deliberating upon a common security and border management system. Because of the flow of migrant workers, both legal and illegal, coupled with the aforesaid massive exodus, the security consciousness, unlike in India, has recorded a rising graph. The concept of a common security and border management is, in fact, gradually taking a concrete shape. Unfortunately, India in general and Assam in particular, lags far behind in this regard. Of course, India's Western international border is far more protected and better managed as compared to her Eastern sector of the international border, a phenomenon being taken advantage of, by the illegal migrants from across the border.

The European Union had to face the problem of large scale unemployment in the wake of the global economic and financial crisis of the first decade of the present century.

The average unemployment rate in the EU increased from 8.9 per cent in 2009 to 9.6 per cent by the end of the year 2010. As a result, the number of jobless migrant workers also recorded a sharp rise. According to World Migration Report, 2011 '....... In Spain, at the end of 2007, 12.4 per cent of immigrants were jobless, compared with 7.9 per cent native-born Spaniards. By mid-2010, those figures had gone upto 30.2 per cent and 18.1 per cent, respectively....' (Quoted from IOM, 2010a; MPI, 2010a.) According to The Economist, 2010, in Italy, joblessness created unprecedented social tensions and even anti-migrant riots. On the other hand, such problem of unemployment also gave rise to emigration from within Europe. It has been estimated that by the end of 2010, an unprecedented number of 60,000 nationals emigrated from Ireland alone in search of better working conditions. Such large-scale emigration had a negative effect on the migration of alien migrant workers into Europe and the end result was the eastward journey of the floating migrant labors.

In any case, the migration of foreign workers in large numbers, both legally and illegally, has attracted very serious attention of the EU authorities. According to World Migration Report, 2011,' The EU Global approach to migration originated from a need for a common global immigration policy, widely recognized and encouraged by the European Commission and EU Member States. Partnership with third countries, solidarity and shared responsibility are at the core of the approach, with the aim of promoting comprehensive and coherent policies that address migration-related issues, bringing together different policy areas (development, social affairs and employment, external relations and justice, and home affairs) and taking both short-term actions and a longer-term vision to address the root causes of migration and forced migration.' (More details available at www.europa--eu--un.org/articles_7589_es.htm.) In Nvember, 2010, the European Commission recommended 'Several actions targeting the most urgent security threats facing Europe....' (More details available at www.eur--lex--europa.eu/LexUriServ/LexUriServ.do/uri). Thus, the EU is gradually developing a global approach to the issue of immigration in its entireity. In the Stockholm Programme, the European Council announced in 2010 two main objectives: '.... More effective control over external borders to preserve internal freedom of movement, and cooperation with the sending countries to accept the return of their citizens and to cooperate to reduce illegal out-migration....' With such target in view, the role of the EU Border Agency Frontex has been defined and expanded with necessary budgetary support. An agreement has already been signed in this context with Pakistan in October, 2010 which states that 'The main objective of this agreement being to establish rapid and effective procedure for the identification and safe and orderly return of of Pakistanis staying illegally in the EU territories.' The alarming situation created by Bangladeshi infiltrators in Assam and its neighboring States, should have prompted India long back to sign such an agreement with Bangladesh at the time of the emergence of the latter as an independent sovereign State. But even after forty-five years of her liberation, Bangladesh is yet to be brought under any such obligation. It is significant to note that because of the fundamentalist back-up and self-destructing political machination, the common Assamese could not develop any sympathetic attitude to the Bangladeshi infiltrator whose struggle for survival was yet to be channelized in a rational manner on long term basis as if the expansion of the Bangladeshi domain was the only way out!

Alien migrants have created many legal and anti-social problems in the EU countries also and as already pointed out elsewhere, some of the EU countries have adopted stringent measures against such violation of their laws. Despite all the problems created by the alien migrants, the EU have been taking measures for facilitating the migration of alien labors in legal manner and as already shown above, such measures have been envisaged in the Stockholm Programme. In fact, in its totality, it envisages a meaningful and legal partnership with the third-world countries in respect of regulating the flow of migrant workers so that the need of cheap labor, though not formally announced, is not ignored. It even envisages a phase of integration of these alien migrants, as well as a system of intra-corporate transfers. As a strategic move, the European Blue Card system has been introduced in order to ensure a common labor migration policy for skilled migrants. Also in 2010, the European Council adopted the Europe 2020 Strategy so that 'Along-term, well-organized legal immigration policy will continue to play an important role in filling labor shortages and meeting the EU's demographic challenges.' (More details are available at www.ec.europa.eu/commission2014/malmstrom/archive/malmstrom_speech_oecd_migration_outlook_12_july_2010. pdf). However, in a capitalist economy, the main motivating force is to earn as much profit as possible and this motive is couched in some technical terms. In this vein, the World Migration Report stated that the objective of such a move was to promote Europe's sustainable economic development with the help of free international movement in response to the skill needs of the labor market. But one cannot get away from the impression that in the entire exercise, the supreme consideration continues to be the beneficial outputs to the EU countries and their corporate houses. However, the question of security has never been low in the EU's list of priorities. As such, a department has been created for the Director General of Home Affairs. The opening of this department aims at ensuring European security and consolidating the EU's migration policy. According to the same Report, 'The Stockholm Action Plan constitutes the road map for implementing these priorities.' (For details see www.ec.europa.eu/dgs/home-affairs/index_en.htm). It may be also noted that in the same context that the European Commission adopted in 2010, a strategic policy, namely, Internal Security Strategy in Action for ensuring strict action against security threats befalling Europe. Even then, some governments adopted at the national level, more stricter measures on their own, in a bid to regulate the influx of migrants. Of course, though these measures are apparently anti-migrants in nature, the real intention behind such measures was to stave off the impact of the global economic crisis on unemployment rates at domestic level so that the number of immigrant labors could be maintained at a secure level. As for instance, only 20,700 foreign skilled workers were permitted by the UK to work for the period 2011–12. Likewise, Switzerland reduced the quota of foreign workers by half—to a maximum of 2,000 only for long stays and to 3,500 for short stays. Few other EU countries had also adopted similar measures with the additional objective of reducing the flow of illegal migrants. No doubt, comparatively low density of population in some of the EU countries has enabled these countries to accommodate migrant workers Not remaining content with the adoption of so many protocols/ agreements, some of the EU countries have also resorted to physically deporting the illegal migrants.

Thus, the EU countries have been ardently trying to strike a balance between rationalizing/tightening their immigration policies and punitive measures against illegal migrants.

Emigration from Africa and GCC, is also quite pronounced. According to the World Bank's Report of 2011b/2011c, thirty million Africans, constituting 3 per cent of the population, have migrated internationally and in 2010, they remitted forty billion US dollars— 2.6 per cent of Africa's GDP. 90 per cent of African migrants hail from North Africa and eight out of ten move out to the EU countries. Because of the affluence of the ME countries and the GCC, most of the migrant workers hailed from the Eastern region of the ME or the Gulf countries. These countries are Bahrain, Qatar, Oman, Israel, Saudi Arabia, Jordan, Kuwait and the UAE. Contractual labors have been targeting the receiving countries of the EU. These alien labors also come from South America, the Far East, besides India and the Philippines. Now, the growing presence of Chinese labors has been also evidenced. The shortage of low-skilled labors in the developed countries, is filled up by these temporary workers of foreign origin. Remittances attributed to these temporary workers constitute a significant percentage of the GDP of their countries of origin. According to the World Bank Report, 2011b, remittances to Lebanon and Jordan by the temporary workers in 2009, represented 22.4 per cent and 15.6 per cent of GDP respectively.

With spread of higher education coupled with emergence of higher living standards, even the labor market of the Middle East countries are experiencing shortage of low-skilled labors. Hence the migration from outside. As for instance, 4.7 million foreign workers outnumbered 4.3 million Saudi nationals in the labor market (ILO, 2011). But the foreign migrant workers were not fortunate enough in the Middle East countries to have been protected by any legislation in their favor. Many of the foreign labors including Indians, were subjected to mal-treatment, abuses and delayed payment, of their wages and even non-payment in certain cases. However, of late, few countries like Bahrain, Kuwait, the UAE amidst others, have been gradually adopting an attitude of empathy. Lately, some legislations were introduced to give relief to the unskilled labors. In fact, human rights activists helped in improving the state of affairs in this regard, albeit to a certain degree.

Significantly, it has become almost an axiomatic truth that unlike in developing countries, such as, India, Bangladesh, Nepal, Pakistan amidst others, the more a country is developed and urbanized, the more is the shortage of low-skilled labor.

In the wake of globalization and consequent lift in economies of many countries, the pattern of migration has also undergone changes. There has been perceptible rush to countries like Australia, New Zealand amidst others viz the Oceania region. Earlier, Australia used to be the targets of migrants from the UK and Europe; but lately, there has been a spurt in the number of migrants from Asia to countries of Oceania region. In 2010, Oceania countries had to receive six million international migrants and this accounted for only 3 per cent of global migrants; but this six million migrants accounted for 16.8 per cent of entire Oceania's population with Australia and New Zealand receiving the highest number. However both these countries witnessed a preference for highly skilled migrants, although in the wake of the global economic crisis, Australia had taken steps to cut down the intakes of international migrants. New Zealand also perforce had taken similar steps, although such steps had added to the shortage of labor force.

Trans-border migration to the USA had already been hinted upon. Some significant details with bearing upon the global pattern are as follows:

Next to Bangladeshi infiltrators, Mexican migrants, both documented and irregular, have been in the headlines for quite a few decades. Mexican migration have a long history, dating back to the last quarter of the nineteenth century. Divested of land ownership during this period, a sizeable percentage of the rural population had to perforce, turn towards low wage occupations, and the population explosion between 1875 and 1910, created a considerable surplus in the labor force. Then, the political instability between 1910 and 1920, did not help matters either. Briefly, this was the background which compelled lakhs of Mexicans to look Northwards for accommodating themselves in the rapidly expanding agricultural sector of South-Western regions of the US. The graph of Mexican immigration to the US had been rising rapidly, until the Great Depression of 1929, which had certainly applied a break to the migration of Mexican labors. Wide-spread unemployment caused in the US by the Great Depression also reduced the demand for Mexican labors. But the unforeseen hands of the World War-II, were instrumental in reviving the flow of Mexican labors. USA entered the World War in 1941 and immediately after, the American economy was relieved of the pains of the Great Depression. War efforts resulted in new and large demands on the agricultural sector of the US as also in other production-oriented activities. Bilateral agreement was entered into and Mexican government agreed to export Mexican labors on short-term contract for the duration of the war. This bilateral agreement is known as the Bracero Program. Because of limitations imposed by this agreement and the need of short-term workers being very high, the number of undocumented Mexican labours recorded high rise. Once the gate was reopened, the process of migration has since continued at different pace at different periods, even necessitating the introduction of regulatory measures because of large-scale illegal migration in violation of the US border security arrangements. In 1965, USA passed the Immigration Act of 1965, in order to regulate immigration. A numerical limit was placed on the entry of immigrants. The adverse impact was felt in Mexico when steps were taken in 1968 for strictly implementing the Act. Still, USA cannot ignore its trading relations with Mexico, which certainly exercise significant impact on its policy, in respect of Mexican migrant workers crossing the border for better economic prospects. In this context, it is relevant to note that Mexico is the fourth largest exporter of oil and the US's second largest trading partner. Bilateral relations have even transcended economic relations. In 2002, it has been estimated that 277 million people entered USA by land from Mexico; most of them being Mexicans. The number of permanent Mexican residents and workers, has recently recorded an enormous rise.

The Table inserted below is illustrative of the volume of Mexican immigration into the US:

Year	Number of Mexican migrants admitted officially
1990	6,79,068
1991	9,46,167
1992	2,13,802
1993	1,26,561
1994	1,11,398
1995	89,932
1996	1,63,572
1997	1,46,865
1998	1,31,575
1999	1,47,573

Table: Number of Mexican immigrants admitted to the United States, 1900—1999 (Source: INS statistical yearbook, 1999)

It has also been estimated that the cross-border trade is today accounting for about 270 billion US dollar annually. This is what Stewart Verdery, Assistant Secretary for Border and Transportation Security Policy, testified before the US Senate Committee on foreign relations on the 23rd of March 2004. In fact, such cross-border legal crossing in Mexico-American border, is by far the largest in the world. On the other hand, the huge volume of illegal immigrants crossing the Mexican border into the US, has been also causing serious concern for both the countries. Before 1990, about two million Mexican immigrants were estimated to have been staying in the USA illegally. But this number has been estimated to have more than doubled in next ten years. According to the Immigration and Naturalization Service (INS), about 70 per cent of the illegal immigrants staying in the US, were Mexicans. The INS's latest calculation is that 4.8 million illegal Mexican immigrants are staying in the US. Circumstances betraying symptoms of gradual deterioration compelled the US authorities to be more vigilant against illegal entrants. The number of arrests made by the US Border Patrols in ten years, between 1990 and 1999, is reflected in the following table:

Years	Number of apprehended illegal migrants
1990	1,169,939
1991	1,197,875
1992	1,258,481
1993	1,327,261
1994	1,094,719
1995	1,394,554
1996	1,649,986
1997	1,536,520
1998	1,679,439
1999	1,714,035 (ibid)

It may be noted that many more must have escaped the Police patrols, because the US border, like the Indo-Bangla border continues to be porous.

Nationals of other countries also find it more convenient to enter the US via Mexico. Such illegal entries into the US have also volubly contributed to the proliferation of drugs trafficking, amidst other smuggling enterprises, thereby throwing a serious challenge to the law-enforcing agencies, as highlighted by Jon E. Dougherty in his discourse 'Illegals'. Dougherty has observed in the same book that 'An increasing number of immigrants, however, come merely to clamor for opportunities and benefits not available to them in their home countries— and not ones they necessarily earn for themselves. Worse, there is a growing faction in America assisting them, knowing all along these immigrants aren't interested in enriching American society, but rather to take what they can from it.' But Dougherty also admits that 'Today, however, the process of immigration - indeed, the requirement that our immigrants assimilate into our society—has changed dramatically.' However, both the US and Mexico became more concerned about border security—particularly after the 11/9 catastrophe sounded the alarm bell and both the countries entered into mutually agreed arrangements in 2002. The US-Mexico Border Partnership Agreement, popularly known as 'The Smart Border Plan', was signed on the 22nd of March 2002. The US authorities certainly want to ensure that no terrorist may infiltrate through the Mexico border and have, therefore, intensified its efforts for very high degree of co-ordination of security measures taken by both the countries. With this end in view, the Department of Homeland Security (DHS) was established by the US in January, 2003 so that 22 disparate departments of the US government dealing with different aspects of foreign relations, including the control of international border, its security, immigration laws and allied matters, could be brought under a unified, central command. The detailed 22-point agreement for collaboration between the two countries under The Smart Border Plan, may be reduced to three general heads:

1) Improved system of border control and its infrastructure.
2) Secure and efficient management of cross-border travels.
3) Safe trading activities by ensuring efficient and secure transportation and flow of commercial goods.

Even prior to implementing the aforementioned 'Smart Plan', both the countries were exercised over ensuring stricter border control and the process had commenced in the wake of the World War II, as already referred to. The bilateral agreement between Mexico and the US, signed in the wake of the World War II, is known as the Bracero Program which was solely intended to promote war-efforts. It was, therefore, limited in its scope of absorbing migrant workers whereas the demand for low-cost labors was much higher than what was envisaged in the Bracero Program. As a result, the flow of undocumented Mexican labors had assumed a rising trend and the number of such labors out-numbered the Bracero limits. As for instance, Mexican labors admitted in 1945 had numbered 49,454 whereas the number of arrested immigrant Mexican labors trying to illegally enter, was 63,602 and border security being rather lax and unscrupulous entrepreneurs netting for low-cost labors, many more thousands had escaped the border patrols. Besides, the implementation of the Bracero scheme also suffered because of paucity of resources, not upgraded till then.

The Bracero programme did not end with the end of the war. It was kept alive in reduced form; but the Korean War of 1951 resulted in the restoration of the Bracero Program in its original form as the US was in need of marshalling additional resources—particularly in the agricultural sector. The following table illustrates the rising trend of admitting more and more Mexican labours under the Bracero Program:

Year	Number of Braceros admitted
1950 (prior to the Korean war)	67,500
1951 (During the war)	1,92,000
1952	1,97,100
1953	2,01,380
1954	3,90,033
1955	3,98,650 and so on. (ibid)

Again, the apprehended migrants out-numbered the legally admitted ones as shown in the following table year-wise:

Year	Number of apprehensions by US Border Patrols
1951	5,00,000
1952	5,43,538
1953	8,65,318
1954	10,75,168
1955	2,42,608 (ibid)

However, with the end of the war, the number of apprehensions gradually declined. Mexico also took advantage of the increased demand, to ease its mounting unemployment. It has been observed that any decrease in the number of Braceros, had invariably led to increase in the number of undocumented immigrant Mexican labours. The Bracero Program was ended in 1965; but the undocumented migrant workers continued to take full advantage of the network, that the Bracero program had built, even after a halt was called to the Program. Previously, there was no limit imposed upon the number of immigrants admitted to USA, as per the provisions of the National Origin Act of 1924. But under changed circumstances, due to various international developments and after the winding up of the Bracero Program, The Immigration Act of 1965 was introduced and this Act imposed a numerical limit of 1,20,000 persons to be allowed annually to enter into the US from South America/Central America/Carribean/Canada/ and Mexico. Though, for the first time, a limit was imposed upon the admissible number of the Mexican immigrants, the flow of undocumented Mexican immigrants could not be slowed down. By the time (1968) the Immigration Act was fully implemented, many crisis's overtook the growth of Mexican economy. During this period, the American economy was prospering while the Mexican economy was facing crisis after crisis. The issue of continued illegal immigration from Mexico was heating up the political atmosphere. Strong public opinion compelled the Congress to pass the Immigration Reform and Control Act (IRCA) in 1986. This Act's main objectives were as follows:

- To strengthen the US Border Patrol.
- To introduce strict punitive measures against the employers of undocumented Immigrants. (It may be noted that similar provisions are there in India also, in its Foreigners Act, 1946, albeit without being purposefully implemented.)
- To ensure that those immigrants, who were staying for a long time, were granted amnesty. (It may also be noted that similar steps have been envisaged in the Assam Accord.)

- To regularize the stay of many undocumented agricultural workers.

But IRCA has not been able to stop illegal cross-border immigration, despite the strengthening of the border patrols. The infiltrators have now resorted to using more hazardous routes through the desert. But bilateral co-operation has certainly been lifted to a new height as an aftermath of 11/9 catastrophe. Particularly in the post- 11/9 period, a personal factor played a great role in shaping the bilateral relationship: The emergence of close personal relationship between President Bush and President Fox at the political scene in the wake of 11/9, with its 'ups and downs', ushered in a new era of bilateral co-operation on the security front which went a long way in rationalizing and controlling the problem of Mexican immigration to the USA. New channels of interaction were opened up and in this context, the US-Mexico Binational Council started playing a major role in identifying the areas of bilateral co-operation, which necessarily included the issue of immigration, both legal and illegal. Bush-Fox understandings have led to considerable progress in securing the shared border against terrorist activities, trafficking of drugs and people and fraudulent trading practices. Such steps have been greatly responsible for placing the issue of immigration on a rationally effective level and this has proved to be mutually beneficial. Above all, US- Mexico relationship is playing an important role as the global security agenda is evolving. The US- Mexico Binational Council has since made a number of recommendations which highlight the entire issue of immigration and steps needed to be taken as well. According to the council's report, following priorities have been fixed for the flow of people:

- 'Pre-cleared travellers.
- Advance travellers' information.
- NAFTA Travel.
- Explore methods to facilitate the movement of NAFT Travelers, including dedicated lanes at high-volume airports.
- Safe Borders and Deterrence of Alien Smuggling.

- Expand Alien Smuggling And Trafficking Task Force.
- Visa Policy Consultations.
- Joint Training.
- Compatible Databases.
- Screening of Third-country Nationals.'

The success of the aforementioned plan of action will, however, largely depend on a well-oiled border infrastructure. With this end in view, the Council has identified the following priorities:

- 'Long-Term Planning.
- Develop and implement a long-term strategic plan that ensures a coordinated physical and technological infrastructure, one that keeps pace with growing cross-border traffic.
- Relief of Bottlenecks.
- Infrastructure Protection.
- Harmonize Port-of-Entry Operations.
- Demonstration Project.
- Establish prototype smart port-of-entry operations.

However, immigration of Mexican labors, both legal and illegal, into the US, cannot be equated with Bangladeshi infiltration into India in general and Assam in particular, as there is neither any ethnic clash nor any fundamentalist design on the part of the migrants from Latin America, their prime motivating force being economic. Besides, more than 90 per cent international migrants entering India are infiltrators and a sizeable percentage of these infiltrators are being attracted to the fundamentalist network. In fact, President Obama believes that '... immigration remains good for the US economy and that there is a need to attract skilled workers.' He is firm in his conviction that '..... the large flows of immigrants into the United States, throughout history have made the country more prosperous.' *No wonder that USA is a nation of migrants.* Still public opinion in the US, is perceptibly opposed to illegal migration. That is to say, President Obama, while appreciating the role of migrants, speaks of legal migrants only. Many of the American states are, however, in favour of introducing measures against illegal migration. In fact, reflecting the local perception on illegal migration as many as twenty-four States had introduced restrictive measures against illegal migration.

To sum up, it may be stated that:

- The global economic crisis of 2008/2009 had certainly slowed down the pace of international migration.
- The said crisis had forced many countries to tighten their International migration policy.
- Though the movement of low-skilled workers was discouraged, the preference for highly skilled international migrants remained more or less static.
- Many migrant workers, mainly low-skilled workers, had to either return to their respective countries of origin or in many cases, the receiving countries had deported them.
- Ultimately the crisis in the international labor market turned out to be short-lived.
- The Global Forum for Migration and Development (GFMD) has raised hopes for more meaningful dialogue and accepting the concept of shared responsibility, collective benefits and partnership.
- The 11/9 terrorist attack made many countries, mainly the EU Countries and the Western hemisphere countries, extremely cautious about promoting their respective national security. Consequently, such steps created an impact on their policies, in respect of receiving alien migrants and guarding against undocumented migrants.
- Remittances to migrants' countries of origin also did not betray any decline of long duration.
- Environmental disasters, too, had an impact on the number of displaced persons including migrant workers, thereby contributing to the shape of migration pattern to some extent, which necessitated fresh legislation for managing population movement. Besides, environmental changes have roused active interests in the world of science for containing the impending danger, although many governments are yet to rise to the occasion. But some of the world bodies are devoting serious attention to the gathering cloud.

- Also World Migration Report, 2011, states that 'More recently, social and political upheavals (most notably in the Middle East and North Africa) have given rise to a type of population movement, rarely seen on such a scale in the past: flows of migrant workers caught up in conflict situations in their destination country and requiring assistance in returning home. Each of these situations is a reminder of the vulnerability of migrant workers who may see their jobs (and employers) disappear overnight, and then have to make the difficult choice between weathering the hostilities, at the risk of their lives, or fleeing to a neighboring country in the hope of obtaining a passage home.'

However, the situation is not as hopeless as it may appear, because the Global Forum for Migration and Development is making efforts for improved dialogue, notwithstanding complications being created by unregulated immigration while means must be devised, both at regional and international levels, for solving the problems of illegal migration, particularly by bilateral and multilateral agreements.

Meanwhile, The New Observer has reported on the 7th of May 2016 that 'Russia Offers Free Land to Foreigners'. Of course, this may be a counter measure against the hordes of Chinese migrants. According to this report 'The Russian State Parliament will pass a bill on the 12th of April 2016, which will offer free one hectare (2.5 acres) of land, in that country's Far Eastern Federal District, to both Russian and non-Russian nationals, wishing to settle the region.'— Deputy Prime Minister Yuri Trutnev is reported to have observed, that such a step would 'strengthen the tendency of people's migration to the far East.' (www.newobserveronline.com/russia-offers-free-land-foreigners/).

Anyway, whatever the political motives may be, the allergic attitude to foreign migrants is gradually undergoing a perceptible change all over the world, excepting those regions where the migrants are threatening to overwhelm and outnumber the native inhabitants. India may possibly negotiate with Russia to find out if some of the Bangladeshi migrants, who are not likely to be accepted back by Bangladesh, and are good tillers of land, may be settled in the Russian far East districts. At present, such a proposal may sound to be far-fetched, but in the fast changing international scenario, nothing seems to be impossible, although white-skinned migrants may receive priority.

CHAPTER 10

THE WAY AHEAD

The oft-repeated adage, 'Prevention is better than cure', is relevant to States like Assam, West Bengal, amidst others, while dealing with the problem of infiltration from Bangladesh. Despite all that has happened till now, it should be possible to maintain the distinct identity of Assam and its people, provided foolproof preventive measures are adopted and bilateral agreements are implemented. But, in this respect, the most essential *'sine qua non'*, is strongest possible political will, which has so far been conspicuous by its absence. A pertinent question agitating the minds of the thinking section of the people is: 'If the Indo-Pak border may be well protected and vigilantly looked after, why not the Indo-Bangla border?' It should not be an insurmountable problem to deal with the difficulties presented by the adverse topography, particularly in these days of so much technological advancement. In any case, in Assam, the situation vis-à-vis the problem of Bangladeshi infiltration, calls for a sustainable action plan. The action plan may be classified under three major heads: Cultural, political and administrative. Political and administrative measures suggested for Assam may be equally applicable to West Bengal; but on the cultural front, it may be a different story altogether. For, the situation in West Bengal is not bedeviled by ethnic divisions but by political factionalism, a factor common to both the States. Another factor common to both the States, revolves round the emergence of jihadi networks. Which is why, a unified front has become imperative in Assam to fight the jihadi menace.

As such, for Assam, the need for cultural integration can hardly be over-emphasized. It has been felt that only cultural integration may overcome the hurdles created by the ethnic divisions so that cultural exchanges may evolve a common front against the threats held out by the Bangladeshi infiltrators and jihadis. In fact, the potential of a common entity has been dormant, whereas the Assam Movement had really given birth to such a common front backed by emotional upheavals. But the chauvinism betrayed by the middle class, young Assamese leaders while forming the two Axom Gana Parishad governments in 1985 and 1996, ignored the common bond created by the Assam Movement, thereby alienating a major section of the tribal population, ever eager to maintain and promote their own ethnic interests. Late Upen Brahma, acclaimed as *Bodofa* (father of the Bodos) was totally undermined by the governments of Prafulla Mahanta and late Upen Brahma was left with no other choice than to open his own Bodo front, which ultimately resulted in tremendous degree of ethnic divisions; even the demand for an independent Bodo state had also surfaced, accompanied by armed insurrection. However, the situation was brought under control by the creation of the BTAD under the sixth schedule. But the party in power before the 2016 LAC elections, viz., the Congress (I), can hardly be accused of any anxiety for promoting ethnic integrity. On the other hand, in order to cultivate political gains, it has created so many Development Councils for so many ethnic groups, thereby, in the ultimate analysis, perpetuating ethnic divisions and greed for political powers. These bodies have been created with the sole aim of cultivating political influence and favouritism. Besides, these councils are not elected bodies. The origin of such a policy, camouflaged as developmental venture, may be traced to the British policy of 'Divide & Rule'. In the wake of such steps, one is led to question whether the 'Panchayat System' has been given a goodbye. Besides, such a step has also opened the floodgate of malpractices. Has it been considered where the necessary funds will come from, particularly in view of the fact that current financial health of the State, is not in a position to sustain so many disparate ventures? How the councils will be elected, if at all elected, in distant future and who will prepare the ERs for such elections? One must find out the answers to these questions before approving of such ventures of dubious intention. Knowledgeable quarters are entertaining grave doubts about the need of such councils and their sustainability.

Still, one cannot ignore the fact that socio-economic, socio-cultural and socio-political exchanges between the Bodos and the Assamese mainstream are in evidence. The latest round of electioneering campaign for the 2016 LAC elections, has brought the Bodos and few other tribal sub-nationalities still closer to the mainstream, a phenomenon which must be taken full advantage of, in order to evolve a common front against the common danger looming large in the horizon. In fact, such ventures should not be confined to Assam only but should encompass the entire North East. An MP from Arunachal Pradesh is presently a minister of State in the MHA. His services may be also utilized for promoting the aforesaid common front. Besides, it is certain that the North Eastern Regional Students Union (NESU), the AASU and the AJYCP will also actively lend their support to such a move.

Only for the purpose of informing the reader and placing it on record, it may be mentioned that late Bimala Prasad Chaliha, the then Chief minister of Assam (1957 – 1970), had in 1968 visualized such an cultural approach in collaboration with late Bishnu Rava and Late Dr. Bhupen Hazarika, who were then MLA, because at this time, some recalcitrant Bodo youths were smarting under a feeling of discrimination by the Assamese and demanding a separate state for the Bodos, namely, the Udayachal. But the project could not take off the ground because of the untimely death of Chaliha, closely followed by Rava's terminal ailment. However, the project may be revived now with the help of the patriotic artists of the State, belonging to different ethnic groups, which are popular with the indigenous people. It also must be mentioned that Shri Kanaksen Deka during his two tenures as the President of the Axom Sahitya Sabha, had formed a common platform for all the Sahitya Sabhas of different ethnic groups, which had taken a concrete shape in the Sipajhar (Darrang district) session of the Sabha. If sustained, this platform would have gone a long way in achieving the much needed common cultural front, which might have received better response from all sections of the people. But that was not to be. For some unknown reasons, the platform organized by Shri Deka, was allowed to become defunct.

The political front is going to prove to be the most difficult front because of the 'vote bank' legacy. While one political party craves for votes of the Muslim infiltrators, another party is working overtime for legalizing the infiltration by Hindu Bangladeshis, instead of devising an integrated approach. On top of such political schism, the supporters of the fresh infiltrators, jihadis and immigrants of Bangladesh origin had organized their own political party in 2006, named as All India United Democratic Front (AIUDF), and have been dreaming of forming the government at Dispur in alliance with the Congress (I), thus communalizing the political scenario for causing polarization of votes on communal basis. As such, vested interests devoid of patriotic farsight will prove to be the main stumbling block and this is where emerges the need for educating the general public. Anyway, a consensus at national level must be worked out while not ignoring the humane aspect of the issue and at the same time, adequately redressing the grievances of the native people. Lessons may be taken from the arrangements made by the EU countries and the countries of the Western Hemisphere which have been analyzed in details in chapter no 9.

Administrative measures calls for maximum attention. These measures may be roughly classified into the following:

- Strict preventive measures. In fact, the prevention of fresh infiltration is not as difficult as the problem of identification and deportation, provided both the Central and the State Governments come forward with strong determination to introduce stringent preventive measures and enact an independent **Central Immigration Control Authority,** instead of leaving the matter to be dealt with by some bureaucrats in the MHA and the External Affairs Ministry.

- The BSF manning the Indo-Bangla border must not be diverted for any other Police duties.
- Bilateral agreements with Bangladesh including the signing of Repatriation/Extradition Treaty.
- A firm land policy for preventing alienation of land/full control over land/resources/territories.
- A well spelled out labor policy.
- An equally strong conservation policy.
- Preparation of correct ERs divested of the names of foreign nationals on the basis of the updated NRC which must be updated every year.
- Collaboration at international level for adjusting to Global Migration Policy.
- Stop denudation of forests and degradation of water bodies.
- A bicameral legislature for ensuring the political rights of small/numerically weak ethnic groups so that they are not overwhelmed by numerically stronger immigrant Muslims of Bangladesh origin.
- Ensuring regular and efficient functioning of the Foreigners Tribunals.

These issues have been discussed in more details later on. However, recommendations made in this discourse, may not be the last words on such a vast and complex subject. Besides, future unforeseen developments may call for fresh adjustments for all the countries concerned, particularly in view of the globalization of the entire issue.

There must be sustained operation against the infiltrators as was done while implementing the 'PIP Scheme' instead of haphazard sporadic operation and dependence on chance detection and detection by the public. No doubt, the 'Infiltration Lobby' has been considerably enthused by the statement of Chief Minister Tarun Gogoi, that there is 'no foreigner in Assam', followed by his stupid statement that 'if there be any, let it be pointed out'! In other words, the Chief Minister wants the public to undertake the responsibility of detecting the infiltrators. Then what the Home Department exists for? Nothing reflects better the attitude of the ruling party than these statements of the Chief Minister himself! Then another disturbing factor has been the 'hue and cry of harassment to the minority community', resulting in apprehensions in the minds of the minorities, raised whenever and wherever any operation is undertaken for detection of infiltrators and foreign voters without, however, considering the apprehensions being caused to the majority community/indigenous people. Besides, the expression 'Minority' is in itself a misnomer with 34.2 per cent of the population of the state being Muslim. Let us consider another phenomenon: More than 90 per cent persons accused of committing heinous crimes, belong to the immigrant Muslim stock and in case of their arrests no such hue and cry is raised, the difference in respective perspectives being caused by ulterior political/fundamentalist motive. Such factors must not be allowed to intervene while chalking out preventive and detective measures.

Preventive measures must be such as to discourage fresh infiltration, even if these appear to be cruel, because an extreme situation deserves extreme measures. In respect of taking measures for preventing fresh infiltration, the Central Government must discharge its constitutional obligations so that political, economic and social interests of the Indian citizens of Assam are safeguarded. Rapid economic development of Bangladesh with equitable distribution of self-sustaining resources may also, to some extent, reduce the pace of infiltration. The grave situation created by the incessant flow of infiltrators from Bangladesh was brought to the notice of the President of India by the then Governor of Assam, Lt. General S.K. Sinha in a letter written on November 8, 1998 which is reproduced below:

'***Rajbhavan***
Guwahati
D.O. No GSAG. 3/98
November 8, 1998.

Dear Adaraniya Rashtrapatiji,

Large-scale illegal migration from East Pakistan/Bangladesh over several decades has been altering the demographic complexion of this state. It poses a grave threat both to the identity of the Assamese people and to our national security. Successive Governments at the Centre and in the State have not adequately met this challenge.

As Governor of Assam, I feel it is my bounden duty both to the Nation and the State I have sworn to serve, to place before you this report on the dangers arising from the continuing silent demographic invasion. I have also formulated my recommendations for dealing with this issue of vital importance. I earnestly hope that this matter will receive due consideration and suitable action taken to avert the grave danger that has been building up for some time.

With profound regards,
Yours sincerely,
Sd. (Lt. General (Retd.) S.K. Sinha, PVSM)

Shri K.R. Narayanan
President of India,
Rashtrapati Bhawan.
New Delhi'

(Because many of the points raised by the Governor, have already been discussed and analyzed in some of the earlier chapters, only relevant portion of the Governor's Report is reproduced as Appendix 11)

Salient features of the Governor's recommendations:

1. Awareness should be promoted about illegal migration into Assam, not only as a threat to the identity of the Assamese people, but to our national security. It may be noted that awareness has since certainly increased and the campaigns for creating such awareness.

2. Border fencing in Assam should be completed on a war-footing. Observation towers and lighting should be provided on the same scale as in Punjab.
3. BSF battalions deployed in Assam should not be given responsibility to hold unduly extended frontages. As in the case of Punjab, BSF battalions should hold a frontage of thirty kilometers. Additional BSF battalions should be provided for this purpose.
4. Diversion of BSF battalions from the border in Assam for other tasks, when the battle against infiltrators is on, must be scrupulously avoided.
5. All country boats, plying in the river near the border should be registered and their registration numbers marked on them.
6. Medium crafts for floating BOPs with adequate speed boats for the riverine sector, should be made available as early as possible
7. Multi-purpose photo identity cards should be provided to all our nationals. Districts bordering Bangladesh should be accorded higher priority.
8. Effective arrangements should be made for registration of births and deaths.
9. The National Register of Citizens should be updated and computerized. A separate register of Stateless citizens should also be maintained.
10. Vacant Chars in the river should be handed over to the Forest Department and trees planted on them.
11. As far as possible, we should assist in the process of economic development in Bangladesh. Socio-economic programmes designed to improve the lot of women should be given priority due to its multiple beneficiary spin offs—improving the family's income, women's education, curbing population growth and educated women becoming a bulwark against the spread of Islamic fundamentalism.
12. Hindu illegal migrants who have infiltrated after the 24th of March 1971, should not be given refugee status. They should be treated as illegal migrants.

13. While maximum effort must be made to stem the ingress of illegal migrants, those who have already infiltrated after the 24 of March, 1971 to date, may not be deported.

These recommendations were made by the Governor, about two decades back. However, most of his suggestions continue to remain unattended, excepting that because of the Supreme Court's intervention, the process of updating the NRC has reached the final stage despite many hurdles created by 'Bangladeshi lobby' and politically motivated vested interests. Following in the footsteps of Gen. Sinha, Ajoy Singh, another Governor of Assam had in May, 2005, prepared another report on infiltration which was ridiculed, as was evident from a press report of The Telegraph (Kolkata) dated the 20th of May 2005, by Chief Minister Tarun Gogoi as 'A worthless document based on heresay rather than facts. We would have examined the report had it contained facts.' Gogoi further told the press in Guwahati that 'I had not given any importance to the report submitted to the Centre by the previous Governor, S.K. Sinha, on the issue of infiltration and I am not according any importance to this report too.' Gogoi saw the hands of RSS and BJP in preparing such reports. Such full-throated denial by no less a person than the Chief Minister himself, simply betrays the absolutely motivated purpose of Tarun Gogoi's government. Such difference of opinion at the highest level of the State government, in respect of such a serious problem threatening the very identity of the Assamese people, is certainly not conducive to working out a permanent solution of the problem. But most unfortunate was the total inaction on the part of the NDA Government, headed by the Prime Minister, A.B. Vajpayee. Back then, L.K. Advani was the Union Home Minister. This NDA Ministry was in power for long six years, between 1998 and 2004, a period adequate enough to implement, at least some of the suggestions made by Gen. Sinha. Even the representative from Assam in the Union ministry preferred to remain silent on the matter for reasons best known to her only whereas all of them were active participants in the Assam Movement!

The Central Immigration Control Authority (CICA) should be a statutory autonomous body with legal power necessary for detecting and deporting illegal foreign migrants. A Task Force, if need be more than one, should be formed under this Authority under a senior Police officer entrusted with the responsibility of keeping all forest/government/land in the tribal blocks and belts /riverine areas free from encroachment and illegal transfer of ownership. Branches of the Task Force may also be formed in each district. And for this purpose, the required number of officers/employees should be deputed from the Revenue/Forest/and the Police departments to assist the Task Force in discharging its duties. This Task Force should not be burdened with the responsibility of detecting and deporting alien infiltrators. This responsibility should be entrusted to a separate body to operate under the CICA. The antecedents of those persons, whose names do not figure in the updated NRC, must be subjected to thorough enquiry and necessary steps taken on the basis of such enquiry. If the CICA feels it necessary, it may also be empowered to include members of the civil society in the Task Force. The CICA must also be empowered to scrutinize the proposed firm land policy. Briefly speaking, the Central Government must spell out a precise immigration policy; its implementation must not be left to some bureaucrats or the 'Bureau of Immigration', handicapped by their myopic perspective and career-promoting agenda. In fact, the Bombay High Court had, in 2013, castigated the Central Government for not spelling out any policy in respect of the illegal migrants in *Siraj Khan Vs. the State case.*

The non-formulation of a firm land policy has very much facilitated the acquisition of vast track of land by the Bangladeshi migrants. In this context, the reader may please recollect the glaring instance of Zahidulla, a promonent jihadi activist and a non-citizen having acquired landed property and married a local girl as referred to in Chapter 4 above. (Of course, he has since been absconding. Most unfortunately, no enquiry was ever instituted to ascertain how could Zahidullah get permission to acquire immovable property.)

All encroachment upon forest/government land/riverine areas/particularly lands of tribal block & belts/PGR's & VGR's must be restored to their original status. All char areas should be cadastrally surveyed and cleared of all Bangladeshi settlers. Scientific measures also should be adopted to prevent formation of 'chars' (sand bars) on the bed of the Brahmaputra, which had been so far main targets of the Bangladeshi migrants. All transactions involving sales/transfers of land to foreign nationals with special emphasis on the tribal blocks and belts constituted under chapter X of the Assam Land and Revenue Regulation, 1886, as amended in 1947, should be declared illegal with retrospective effect. The foreign nationals found to be in possession of such land must be ruthlessly evicted. Also encroachment upon lands of Satras, Mosques and Waqf properties, must be cleared. There are 909 Satras (865 registered) in Assam. It has been reported that infiltrators have encroached upon the lands of as many as twenty-six Satras. Some foreign nationals had even gone to the extent of murdering Muktinath Goswami, the head of the 'Adi Alengi' Satra with the State Administration remaining a mere spectator! Such lawless misdeeds must be put down mercilessly. The implementation of a firm land policy will necessitate the maintenance of National Register of Villages (NRV) like the NRC. The unusual increase in the number of villages as shown in another chapters, simply confirms the presence of new arrivals. All villagers of such new villages must be subjected to thorough scrutiny in order to determine their antecedents. No new village should be allowed to surface in forest land, government land, PGR/VGR/char areas and all other prohibited/reserve areas. Lately, there have been instances of new villages sprouting overnight under political patronage. The Char Areas Development Authority of Assam had carried out two socio-economic surveys in 1993-94 and in 2002-2003. Dhubri district, the main entry point of the infiltrators had 303 char villages in 1992-93 and by 2002-2003, this number had shot up to 480. In the survey conducted in 2002-2003, it transpired that during the intervening period, the char population had recorded an increase of more than eight lakhs (from 1,60,0244 in 1993-94 to 2,49,0397 in 2002-2003). In 1965, late B.N. Mullick, the then Director of Intelligence Bureau had, in a report, observed that 'The main attraction of the immigrants is land, and the land that is available in the char areas and in the Government Reserve Forest and other Government Reserve areas. Encroachment is a revenue offence and legally a trespasser can be evicted, but due to the inadequacy and corruption of subordinate revenue staff this work has practically not been done and encroachment has gone on freely and at the will of the infiltrators. We feel that the only way to find a permanent solution to infiltration is to deny the infiltrator the main attractions which draw him into Assam that is the arable land or forest.' (Quoted from Annexure 5 of the book 'Prabrajan aru Anupravesh' by H.K. Deka.). However, it must be noted that new factors resulting in incessant flow of infiltrators, have emerged after Mullick had submitted his reports, which might not have been foreseen or anticipated.

As a long-term measure, in order to undo a historic wrong being committed since August 15, 1947, a **Judicial Commission of high standing** should be appointed to determine the extent of encroachment by non-Indians, in violation of laws of the land and identify these areas so that necessary legal proceedings might be undertaken, to restore such areas to their original status and the violators were proceeded against for defying the law. It may be noted that any crime, if detected after the lapse of several decades, the offender could not be treated as innocent, only because the commission of the crime had been detected after lapse of a long period. It does not matter even if the proposed Judicial Commission has to operate for a number of years. But the formation of such a Judicial Commission is a 'must' in order to restore to the native people of Assam (those who were residing in Assam on the commencement of the Constitution), the control over their land and resources. All non-cadastral land must be surveyed and included in relevant book of records. Also the disappearance of any village due to erosion and washing away of any 'char', must be recorded with the list of persons displaced by such natural disasters.

Indo-Bangla border must be completely sealed in all the states bordering Bangladesh. The sealing of the Assam border only will not yield the desired results. The quality of the border fencing must be the same as on the Punjab border. After clearly demarcating the Indo-Bangla border, an area of about hundred meter width, must be cleared of all human habitation and vegetation all along the Indo-Bangla border. These areas also must be put under dusk to dawn curfew with flood-lighting arrangements. Besides, CCTV cameras should be installed at points considered vulnerable by expert opinions and local contacts. The BSF manning the Indo-Bangla border must not be used for law & order duty as is being done presently. Even any temporary withdrawal of BSF personnel for such duties must not be resorted to. Any vacuum created by such withdrawal, is invariably taken advantage of, by the touts. The Group of Ministers (GOM) on National Security had the following to report on 'Border Management' in 2001: 'The repeated withdrawal in large numbers of Para-military forces from border guarding duties for internal security and counter insurgency duties has led to a neglect of the borders. The present tendency on the part of each agency to guard its turf, even at the cost of compromising national interests, needs to be deprecated and put down sternly.'

Occasionally reports of corrupt practices indulged in by BSF personnel, appear in the press. Confessional statements made by some arrested infiltrators also point to such direction. Not that all BSF personnel are corrupt, but there are black sheeps. In order to rule out such possibility, BSF personnel should be put through a motivational course and serious implications of infiltration by Bangladeshi nationals, explained to them before they are deployed in the border. In-service training is also necessary for acquainting with the current situation on both sides of the border. In this connection, inhabitants of the villages of the border should also be properly motivated and encouraged to extend a helping hand to the BSF in their own interests. A plan for raising a Village Volunteer Force, for better co-ordination with the BSF and mutual assistance may also be considered as long-term policy so that the villagers of the border may also be properly motivated and the level of motivation sustained.

Most of the Muslim infiltrators, as seen from past experience, use the riverine routes of the Brahmaputra and the Barak, although some others travel by train also after crossing the borders of West Bengal, Tripura and Assam border in Karimganj district. In any case, it must be made compulsory to register all rivercrafts, mechanized or otherwise, operating in the Brahmaputra/the Kushiars/and the Barak and all their tributaries. Any boat, small or big, found without registration certificate must be consficated. The responsibility of registering these boats must be entrusted to the River Police Organisation (RPO) and certainly not the Inland Water Transport Department, so that vigilant control may be ensured. If need be, some officers and employees of this department may be deputed to the RPO. With this end in view, the RPO will have to be adequately modernized, strengthened and equipped with all modern gadgets. The RPO also must have a well equipped, trained and motivated RPO battalion of full strength, so that all operations by the RPO get the benefits of armed coverage. It may not be out of context to mention here that such a scheme for modernizing the RPO was envisaged by CM Golap Barbara in 1979 and its implementation was to be carried out in two stages, obviously for financial compulsions. But the successive AGP and Congress governments did not bother to pursue Barbara's plan. The files concerned must be collecting dust in the Home Department and the Border Police Organisation. The scheme may be revived and updated. There should be dusk to dawn curfew in all the rivers/tributaries. Also, curfew should be in force all along the Indo-Bangla border during the same period. There must be floating Police stations to be manned by the RPO in the Brahmaputra between Majuli and Mahamayarchar. Also such floating Police station must be opened in the Barak as well. The number of such Police station may be determined on the basis of strategic requirements after proper survey by experts. All such floating Police stations must be given few bulletproof speed boats, particularly in the Dhubri/Mahamayarchar sectors. In the dry season, the Brahmaputra multifurcates into number of channels downstream of Dhubri, presenting a width of 9/10 kilometers, if not more, thereby creating opportunities for the infiltrators to sneak in unnoticed. Hence, the need for speed-boats, which may be utilized for the purpose of chasing as well.

Also all water bodies, about 4,000 in number, dotting the plains of Assam, must be surveyed and mapped and then cleared of all encroachment and habitation/cultivation within the aforesaid mapped areas. Also, persons of doubtful origin and even people of non-indigenous stock should not be allowed to form forest villages and even if found to have formed such villages, must be evicted.

The Citizenship Act must be suitably amended to ensure that the children of Bangladeshi infiltrators do not get Indian citizenship only because they were born in India/Assam/other North-Eastern States, particularly if the fathers of such children are Bangladeshi nationals. Only on following grounds, anybody born in Assam should be treated as Indian national:

- If the persons concerned satisfies the requirements as stipulated in Article 5 and 6 of the Constitution.
- If the person's or his forefather's name is in the NRC of 1951.
- If his or his forefather's name is available in the ER of 1952 or 1971.
- If his or his forefather's mother tongue is either Assamese or any other language/dialect, spoken by the people of native origin in Assam.

(The fore-father mentioned above should be of the paternal side and not of the maternal side.)

The Registration of Birth and Deaths Act was passed in 1969 but the implementation of the Act has been tardy, and the scope of mandatory provisions very limited. The registration of births and deaths must be made compulsory. Some responsible persons must be put in charge at the level of each village panchayat and each municipal ward, for maintaining correct account of births and deaths. Names of dead persons must be removed from the ERs. It may be noted that in the past, instances of using dead persons' names for casting votes, had come to notice. Of course, with the issuance of photo identity cards, the number of such instances will be reduced to great extent, but such possibility cannot be ruled out. The Act should be amended, to make it mandatory to produce birth certificates at the time of applying for ration card, driving license, opening of bank account, passport, enumeration as voter, admission into primary school, job card under the MGNREGA and the like. All the data in respect of birth and death should be computerized and stored in a data-bank.

The employment of foreign labors not in possession of valid travel documents, by the government, semi government agencies, private contractors and individuals must be specifically banned and official announcement made for the knowledge of all concerned. Anybody found to have done so, should be prosecuted Under Section 14 of The Foreigners Act, 1946. Also, the earnest and security money of the defaulting contractors should be confiscated, followed by their blacklisting for life. Such steps will also create avenues for employment of local unemployed youths. In order to attract the local youths for filling up the resultant vacuum, the rate of wages also must be made more attractive. If the unskilled labors of Bangladesh origin are deprived of easy availability of employment, the pace of infiltration to Assam will certainly slow down.

As have been found out, presently licenses for operating cycle-rickshaws, push-carts and even motor transports, are being issued without verifying the citizenship of the applicants. Some drivers of motor transports are also reported to be using forged licenses. In Guwahati alone, it has been reported; more than 20,000 cycle-rickshaws are plying without valid license. Not only it must be made obligatory to verify the citizenship of all applicants, but also, the police must be empowered to seize all such vehicles, as found to be operated without valid licenses. Such steps do not require any empowerment by the Central Government. The State Government and the Municipal authorities have the powers to take such steps on their own, the only stumbling block being the lack of political will coupled with the urge for enriching the respective vote-banks.

The increase in the number of private unregistered Madrassas, coming to the notice for imparting lessons of fundamentalism and selling the dream of a Brihat Islamic Bangladesh, must be brought under strict surveillance and if considered necessary, banned. The sources of fund received by such Madrassas must also be thoroughly enquired and steps taken against illegal receipt of money from abroad.

Serious concern has been voiced by very responsible quarters including High Court Judges about the irregular, if not perfunctory, functioning of the Foreigners Tribunals. The number of such Tribunals has since been raised to hundred; but for want of infrastructural facilities and logistics, these Tribunals have not been able to function at the desired level and adequate pace. The Tribunals have to depend upon the mercy of the District Magistrates for necessary funds. Obviously, the State Government is solely responsible for forcing these Tribunals to helpless situation. Presently, as per a press report (Amar Axom of the 25th of April 2016), as many as 4,32,149 cases including those referred by the screening committee formed under the repealed IMDT Act, are pending for disposal. This number is increasing every month. On the other hand, there is no provision for arresting the persons accused of being foreign nationals and sent up for adjudication in the Foreigners Tribunals. As such, most of the persons declared to be foreigners by the Tribunals, abscond and evade deportation. According to a source of the Home Department, of 51,766 persons declared as foreigners by the Tribunals, 51,749 of them have absconded. No better instance is required to illustrate the callous manner in which the entire issue has been dealt with. As such, it is emphasized that (1) the efficient and uninterrupted functioning of the Foreigners Tribunals must be ensured; and (2) provisions should be made for the arrest of the accused persons or in the alternative, they should be interned in detention camps until the Tribunals dispose of their cases and the offence should be made non-bailable. However, a fresh ray of hopes has surfaced with the assumption of office by the newly elected State government under the leadership of Mr. Sarbananda Sonowal, who since his student days and as the President of AASU for two consecutive terms, has been committed to solve the problem of Bangladeshi infiltration. A report of Assam Tribune of June 6, 2016, states that ' No other State in the country is facing a grave situation because of infiltration of foreigners like Assam, observed Chief Minister Sarbananda Sonowal.

Addressing a meeting of the members of the Freigners Tribunals here today, Sonowal said that the entire country is keeping a close watch on the functioning of the Foreigners Tribunals and the process of updating the National Register of Citizens and these works would become role models for all the States.

Sonowal said that the Tribunal members have got a golden opportunity to work for a national cause and they should not let goof up such an opportunity. He said that the government would provide all necessary facilities to the Tribunals, so that the process of detection of foreigners can be expedited. He said that along with the government, the people should also cooperate with the Tribunals, to ensure their smooth functioning. If anyone tries to pose hurdles in the functioning of the Tribunals, strong action would be taken, warned the Chief Minister —'. It is significant that for the first time ever, a Chief Minister has taken so much keen interest in respect of detecting the foreigners. It is, therefore, expected that equally strong follow-up action will also be taken. In the same issue of the Assam Tribune, it was observed in the Editorial column that 'Chief Minister, Sarbananda Sonowal, deserves credit for exhibiting some much-needed alacrity in resolving the vexed issue of cross-border infiltration and fencing the porous Indo-Bangla border. This is an issue that had a big role in propelling the BJP into power in the state in a manner that surprised even the party itself. More than that, illegal migration from Bangladesh is having disturbing the socio-economic and political implications, that are not in the best interests of the State's indigenous people.

This has to be acknowledged even while maintaining that not all immigrant Muslims are Bangladeshis as many of the saffron brigade would have us believe. A sizeable segment of the immigrant population who migrated before the cut-off date of March 25, 1971 has assimilated with and became a part of the composite Assamese identity. A witch-hunting campaign in the name of detecting and deporting Bangladeshis is totally unacceptable and will end up doing more harm than good. At the same time, the legal mechanism to identify illegal migrants must be strengthened—.' Thus, Sonowal's observations have already cultivated rich dividends.

People belonging to diverse ethnic, racial, linguistic, religious, cultural groups have been coming to and settling down in Assam from pre-historical times. Comparatively advanced ethnic groups have been enjoying the benefits ushered in by Independence to the exclusion of the backward, numerically weak marginalized groups, all the more aggravated by discriminatory policies. As a result, many of the ethnic tribal groups have become restive and been agitating for due place under the sun, thus giving rise to fissiparous and separatist tendencies, a phenomenon fully taken advantage of, by forces not known for their friendly attitude to India. According the Report of the Anthropological Survey of India (2003), Assam is the habitat of 114 ethnic groups and these diverse groups speak forty-five different languages and they do boast of distinct cultural heritage. Also they belong to different religions, including tribal religions, for the apprehensions of losing their distinct identity and existence; many of the ethnic groups have been agitating for autonomous status. Peaceful co-existence of so many tribes and races, had been, in the past, the key to Assam being a self-sufficient, conflict-free land. But the advent of the British with sheer colonial purposes changed the scenario. Their colonial exploitation created a class of deprived people. For example, the cases of the Moran and Motok tribes may be cited. They were driven out of their age-old settlements without any compensation for the sole purpose of making suitable plots of land available to British tea planters. This is how many big tea gardens owned by British companies had surfaced in today's Tinsukia district. Nor were they provided with the benefits of modern education. As such, the educative sensitivity necessary for voicing their demands was conspicuous by its absence which deprived them of the opportunities for facing so many British Commissions appointed for liberalization of the Administration. Nobody from amongst them was competent enough to represent their cases before these Commissions. Unfortunately, no other leaders also took up their cases in 1909, 1919, 1929 and 1935. This is how their cases remained unrepresented by default. No wonder that the Moran community proved to be a very fertile ground for recruiting cadres of the ULFA. The Assamese middle class has been accused of ignoring the demands of these backward communities, whereas the latter had invariably veered round the larger interests of the Assamese society, whenever any crisis befell the larger Assamese society. The so-called Hindu class stratum of the Assamese society has, therefore, been frequently accused, rightly too, of failing to rise above their caste consideration. As quoted by Indibar Deuri in *'Axom Andolan: Pratisruti aru Falasruti', (Page 288),* Late Bhimbar Deuri in no uncertain terms had, while speaking in the Assam Assembly, emphasized upon 'The right of every community to have a share in administration, a right of every community to serve the province, or to serve the people at large —.' Unfortunately, quite a few communities still remain unrepresented in the political bodies because of the lack of their numerical strength. Socio-political and socio-economic safeguards for all the communities are not of uniform pattern. Meanwhile, six ethnic communities, namely, Ahoms, Koch-Rajbangshis, Chutias, Mataks, Morans and the Tea Tribes/ Adibashis have been agitating for many years for getting the status of scheduled tribes. They feel marginalized not only in economic spheres, but also in respect of representation in the administration and in the legislature in proportion to their numerical strength. The grant of scheduled tribe status to these communities is sure, if nothing else, to safeguard the LA constituencies reserved for them against being captured by hordes of illegal foreign migrants. No doubt, the issue of self-determination is at the root of all these demands accentuated by a long history of deprivations and undermining their right to survive as distinct identity. It is once again emphasized that the numerical strength of some of the ethnic tribes of Assam is so low, that they can never expect to have any say in the legislative activities of the State nor do they have any chance of their voices being heard in any other platform. In order to allay their apprehensions of losing their distinct identity, there should be a legislative council for ensuring their representation in legislative activities. This should be the Upper House of the Assam Legislative Assembly. It has, therefore, become absolutely necessary to amend Article 171 of the Constitution to constitute an Upper House, viz., 'Legislative Council of Indigenous Tribes/Communities' in accordance with Article 167 of the Constitution. Its composition, functions and powers may be worked out in due course, by experts in consultation with the representatives of each ethnic group.

All these discussions and recommendations emanating there from, will be an exercise in futility unless their implementations are in the hands of those people whose interests are intended to be safeguarded. In the explosive situation which has surfaced in Assam, constitutional safeguards to the Indian citizens of Assam have become imperative. In the list of priorities of such safeguards, the top-most is the political right for electing the state Assembly. Only the Indian citizens should have the right to occupy the seats in the Assembly so that representatives of infiltrators and the immigrant Muslims, passing themselves as Indians, may not overwhelm the representatives of the native people and snatch away political power for ever. In this context, it has to be ascertained which of the native communities have been reduced to insignificant presence by illegal migration from East Pakistan and subsequently from Bangladesh. In the first General Elections held in 1952, Assam had 108 LA constituencies. Now, it has to be ascertained which communities were prominent, (not necessarily majority community but prominent) in these 108 LA constituencies and since reduced to numerically insignificant position by hordes of infiltrators from across the border. The cases of these communities must be given priority while taking measures for reservation of seats in the Assembly. Realizing that number plays the most decisive role in an elective democracy, fundamentalist Islamic forces have not only been instrumental in distorting the ERs in their favour, but lately they are trying to distort the compilation of the NRC also as already highlighted. Therefore, the prime objective must be to neutralize the impact of such motivated designs. The number of LA constituencies has since been raised to 126, during the last phase delimitation of constituencies. Presently, there are only twenty-four reserved LA constituencies – sixteen for scheduled tribes and eight for scheduled cast – which do not suffice for ensuring the political survival of the categories of people determined to be Indian as per norms stated above. Already in as many as fifty LA constituencies, the immigrant Muslims have become decisive factor in determining the results of elections and in as many as twenty-six constituencies, no candidate of indigenous stock may ever expect to win in any election. In such a situation, the only way to ensuring political survival of Assam and her people, is to have 90 per cent reservation of LA seats for the Indian citizens of Assam, as also for Central Legislature. The same norm should also be applied to all other elected bodies pertaining to governance and administration in Assam. This norm of reservation must also be extended to all other sectors of economic activities, so that the benefits of development are available only to Indian citizens.

Assam has already agreed to take the load of pre-1971 stream of immigrants from Bangladesh. AAsu has reiterated its stand that illegal migrants, both Hindu and Muslim, who came from Bangladesh after 1971, will not be accepted by Assam. (As reported in Assam Tribune of the 6th of June2016.) Quite likely, that the presence of a huge number of illegal immigrants from Bangladesh will emerge after the compilation of the NRC is completed. Their continued presence in Assam will be constant source of irritation, if not communal clashes. Assam will not be in a position to host such huge additional load of illegal immigrants. Nor Bangladesh is likely, under the present circumstance, to accept them in the absence of any bilateral agreement. In fact, Bangladesh has been throughout denying the presence of any Bangladeshi citizens in India. Seven Sisters Post, an English daily (since defunct) had reported on the 17th of August 2012 as follows: '— Deputy High Commissioner of Bangladesh, Mahbub Hassan Saleh, said that the illegal entry of citizens from his country into Assam has never been raised by the Indian government.' 'I have been in New Delhi since the Awami League coalition-led coalition government assumed power in Dhaka and the issue of illegal migration has never been taken up by the Indian government', Saleh told reporters on the sidelines of an international conference. 'This clearly shows that illegal migration from Bangladesh is not an issue at all between the two neighbours', He added—.' So according to the present state of affairs, Bangladesh is not at all likely to accept back millions of Bangladeshi infiltrators. As such, they may be dispersed all over the country and issued work permits for earning their bread. But what will happen if other States refuse to accept them? In such eventuality, all the identified Bangladeshi illegal migrants should be organised into a labor force which may also include unemployed youths of native stock. With the growing number of middle-class families and expansion of the industrial base, the demand for low-skilled labors, domestic aides and the likes, is also recording rapidly rising trend. In other words, labor market is also growing at rapid pace. The surplus number of the proposed labor force may be exported to other states in need of such labors and, for that matter, even to other countries in such need. A well spelled out labor policy may envisage such arrangements. Thus, Assam may earn the distinction of a labor exporting State and convert a liability into a revenue earning source. According to a report published in Amar Axom (Local Assamese Daily) dated the 20th of October 2016, remittances made by Bangladeshi labors constitute a major source of revenue for Bangladesh. According to their government report of 1980, Bangladeshi labors sent home 349 million dollars and this remittance jumped to 14.9 billion dollars in 2014. Such remittances contribute 9 per cent of the country's GDP. As reported in Amar Axom, in 2014 the number of Bangladeshi labors in the following countries was as shown below:

Name of the country	No. of Bangladeshi labors engaged therein till December 2014
India	32,30,025
Saudi Arab	13,09,004
UAE	10,89,917
Malaysia	3,52,005
Kuwait	2,79,167
Great Britain	2,39,610
Pakistan	1,86,114
Oman	1,48,314
Singapore	54,750
Other countries	10,68,756

Source: Amar Axom, as noted

It is significant that no country is under any obligations to honour the judicial verdicts of another country, in the absence of any bilateral agreement. Hence, the need for a bilateral agreement with Bangladesh, which must ensure a stringent policy in respect to issuance of visa and proper vigilance over the incoming traffic. Already more than 80,000 Bangladeshi nationals entering India with proper passports and visas are reported to be missing, like lakhs of Mexicans who also entered the US legally but overstayed in violation of conditions stipulated in their visas.

The problem of illegal migration from Bangladesh is not going to be solved only with the adoption of the measures highlighted above. The phenomenon of global warming has already been causing overflow of Bangladeshi nationals, with India being the most accessible target. This will assume a permanent nature with the shrinkage of living space in Bangladesh. As such, the problem must be raised at the proper international forum while also opening bilateral dialogue with Bangladesh. Consequences of such climatic changes must be anticipated and the administration geared up to deal with the crisis. But it must be realized that the internationalization of the issue may entail fresh obligations, which may not be conducive to solve the problem bilaterally. As such, above all, a bilateral understanding in respect of controlling illegal migration must top the list of priorities.

The Central Government had entrusted in 2001, a Group of Ministers (GOM) with recommending measures for stopping illegal immigration as well as for developing border areas. The GOM's recommendations have covered most of the issues discussed above with special emphasis on border management. They had also recommended the establishment of a Border Management Department under the MHA. In addition, they had also recommended the issue of multi-purpose national identity cards so that the detection of illegal immigrants could become easier. The same purpose is likely to be served with the updating of the NRC. They further recommended better co-ordination among all the central and State agencies concerned with border management and border guarding. This GOM in its report on national security had passed a severe indictment on the vote-bank politics in the following words: 'Such large-scale migration has obvious social, economic, political and security implications. There is an all-round failure in India to grip with the problem of illegal immigration. Unfortunately, action on this subject invariably assumes communal over-tones with political parties taking positions to suit the interest of their vote banks.'

Meanwhile, we had gone through the MHA's Annual Report for the year 2014-2015, which seemed to conceal more than reveal. It, however, reported that the Department of Border Management was created in the MHA in January, 2004 which was entrusted with the task of border policing, border fencing, construction of Border roads, flood-lighting and implementation of the Border Area Development Programme. But even after eleven years of its formation, the department is yet to complete the job it was entrusted with. However, in the month of June, 2016, the Union Home Minister has announced that the border fencing will be completed within next one year; that modern electronic gadgets will be also put into use for uplifting the border vigilance. This annual report has failed to give a full insight into the current state of affairs in respect of unabated infiltration from Bangladesh. The Report says that between 1946 and 1971, 52.31 lakhs of displaced people migrated to India and of these, 31.32 lakhs were settled in West Bengal and the rest in other States. But which are the other States and why these could not be mentioned? According to the Report, India has signed bilateral agreements on combating drugs and related matters with a number of countries including Bangladesh. But the Report is silent on results achieved so far on this count whereas smuggling activities through Indo-Bangla border of the Assam sector have been rampant, as is evident from reports emanating from so many sources, including the print media. Besides many observers of the North-Eastern affairs are of the opinion that Assam is being used as the corridor for cross-border transportation of narcotics, mainly from the infamous golden triangle. Also instances of smuggling of cattle-heads and human trafficking across the same border are being frequently reported and the performance of the security forces in this regard has left much to be desired. The report is silent on such matters of vital public interest. The report is also significantly silent about the number of illegal migrants and forged Indian currency notes detected so far and if detected at all, what has been done with these illegal migrants and what action has been taken to prevent the circulation of forged currency notes. Likewise, nothing has been indicated about the functioning of the Foreigners' Tribunal. In respect of North East, emphasis has been given mainly to highlight the steps taken to contain insurgency and related militancy. But even after the Supreme Court's instructions in respect of the Bangladeshi infiltration, this report seems to have paid only lip service in this regard. An Extradition Treaty is reported to have been signed with Bangladesh in 2013, but nothing has been indicated to highlight the consequences of signing the

Treaty. One is inclined to believe that the report has carefully abstained from furnishing some vital data. As for instance, according to the report, 5,24,923 documented Bangladeshi's visited India in 2013, but the report is silent about the number of the Bangladeshi's who did not go back to their home country on expiry of the validity of their visas. Apparently, the problem of illegal migration from Bangladesh has not been discussed at bilateral conferences, held at different levels. Then does such apathetic attitude mean that India also agrees with Bangladesh, that there are no illegal migrants staying in India? How many Bangladeshi illegal migrants were apprehended by the BSF while trying to cross over into India? Since there is an Internal Security Division, one would have expected that more light was thrown on the jihadi activities, particularly after the Burdhaman exposure, coupled with the sensational detection in Assam At least, all the private Madrasas (Quami) should have been brought under strict vigilance, particularly after a Maulana of a privately run Madrasa was arrested for having been involved in jihadi activities. Further, due investigations should be done about the various sources of money received by these Madrasas. Also while reporting on militancy, no mention has been made about the activities of MULFA/MULTA/and other fundamentalist Muslim Organizations. Is there any need for maintaining secrecy in this regard? Also one gains the impression that more attention has been devoted to the international border in the Western sector, while the Eastern sector does not seem to receive the same degree of attention, although India extends much beyond Siliguri.

Satras are the focal points of Assam's rural life which, by and large, revolves round the Satras. In para 2.7.9 of the MHA's Report, it has been stated that 'The security of religious shrines/places in the country is primary the responsibility of the concerned State Governments—. However, the Ministry of Home Affairs issues necessary advisories for strengthening the security of such religious shrines/places— when any specific threat inputs are received in respect of them.' Didn't MHA receive any inputs from its Intelligence Agencies about the encroachment into the land of quite a few Satras by persons of Bangladesh origin? Thus, if analyzed word by word, there may not be an end to the seemingly casual manner in which the affairs of the North East has been dealt with. A serious scrutiny of the report creates that impression on one who should have nothing otherwise against the MHA.

In any case, the degree of awareness in the MHA about the cancer of unabated Bangladeshi infiltration and the serious consequences thereof, certainly deserves to be upgraded. One can only ignore at one's own peril, that the geographically inevitable neighborhood of Bangladesh will continue to create problems ceaselessly for the Eastern and the North-Eastern parts of India for how long nobody can foresee at present.

It may not be out of context to note that the Indira-Mujib Pact was signed on the 19th of March1972 for a period of twenty-five years; but the Treaty was not renewed after it expired in 1997. Presently, the constitutional validity of many of the provisions of this Pact and the latest amendment of the Citizenship Act, have been challenged in the Supreme Court of India and the matter has since been referred to the constitution bench of the Court. As such, any bilateral agreement with Bangladesh on the issue of illegal immigration may have to wait until the verdict of the Hon'ble Supreme Court is available. In any case, a bilateral agreement in this respect will be very much imperative in due course. The Indira-Mujib Treaty had created unnecessary and unforeseen complications in respect of cut-off date for detection of illegal migrants and Justice M.C. Chagla had seen no logic in setting up such cut-off date and questioned '— What does it matter when a person comes to Assam if he is not a national but a foreigner? The year of entry does not change his legal status. 'Such a situation could emerge again because of the lack of knowledge and far sight on the part of the signatories of the Assam Accord.

In fact, the UN Convention also envisages bilateral understanding for action against trafficking of persons and India and Bangladesh being a members of the UNO, both the countries should have worked to implement such provisions of the UNO's convention – particularly in view of the fact that criminals of both the countries are reported to have taken shelter in the neighboring country. In Article 9 of the Preamble of the Convention, it has been stipulated that 'State Parties shall establish comprehensive policies, programmes and other measures (a) To prevent and combat trafficking in persons; and (b) To protect victims of trafficking in persons, especially women and children, from re-victimization.' Similar measures have been envisaged in Article 11 also in respect of Border Management; but perceptible and effective steps are yet to be in evidence. If proofs given by India, along with judicial verdicts are not accepted by Bangladesh, there is also scope for any particular dispute being taken to the International Courts of Justice. These are certain matters which may certainly be sorted at the bilateral level.

Some international observers have even indicted Bangladesh as a failed State. Certainly that is too harsh a statement made without considering that Bangladesh is in a transitory stage. Internal dissensions coupled with unceasing fundamentalist efforts for converting it into a main base for extending the jihadi network, have not allowed her to stabilize the situation in the home front. The span of forty-five years (2016) of independence is too short a period in the life of a nation, to formulate certain policies having international implications. Consequently, it has failed to evolve a well defined policy on international migration, although it is now more than three decades that the Emigration Ordinance was framed in 1982 and on the other hand, it has not been averse to immigration of its nationals, legally or illegally, to foreign countries with two main objectives being the motivating force: (1) To reduce the pressure of unemployment at home. (2) To welcome remittances from abroad. In the process, Bangladesh has been well ahead in respect of capturing the market for unskilled and menial labors, the world over. One may safely assume that the present government of Bangladesh, headed by Sk. Hasina has no intention of abetting the spread of the fundamentalist network through the medium of immigration of Bangladeshi nationals, although the above quoted two factors may weigh in favor of such immigration. On the other hand, the civil society of Assam has totally failed to come to grips with such, almost aggressive, conduct of the Bangladeshi immigrant labors. Sadiq Khan's advocacy for 'lebensraum' and a free world trade for labors, is making rapid progress.

Main constraints in respect of taking effective, result-oriented preventive measures may be summed up as follows:

- Inadequate Policing of the border and absence of a second line of defence at strategic areas. The Watch Posts set up under the PIP scheme, were supposed to operate as second line of defence but these posts were allowed to become defunct.
- Adverse topography.
- Tardy progress in land acquisition for constructing border roads.
- Close ethnic affinities in both sides of the border.
- Lack of strong political will as well as national consensus cutting across all partisan motives.
- Communalization of the issue.
- Indifferent and non-cooperative attitude of Bangladesh. As for instance, in January, 1999, Sk. Hasina Wajed had announced that 'There are no Bangladeshi infiltrators in India.—'
- Non-availability of a correct NRC till now as also a correct ER.
- Corrupt practices of government officers and employees.

Of course, there are many other allied factors which have been already highlighted. This scribe has been dealing with and studying the issue of illegal immigration both as a Police officer and also as a public activist. During all these days, it has transpired that the lack of political will to solve the problem has been mainly instrumental in perpetuating it while, at the same time, the rest of the country was kept in the dark about the serious and dangerous nature of the problem. It has been only after few other states have come face to face with the problem, some awareness is gradually taking shape. At the end of the day, after having gone through reports of Pamela Geller and Shonu Nangia, one is constrained to wonder whether the national press of India has considered it necessary to delve deeper into the seriousness of unabated infiltration and proliferating jihadi activities, with the sole exception of The Indian Express. Sekhar Gupta was in Guwahati for a long time and also was an eye witness to the historic Assam Movement. He was subsequently the Chief Editor of The Indian Express for quite a few years; besides, Samudragupta Kashyap was the local correspondent of this English daily. One is convinced that because of these two senior journalists, Indian Express paid attention to the issue it deserved. Else, whether in the North or in the South, the national press had hardly bothered to inform the rest of the country about the dangerous development of anti-national elements in West Bengal and the North East. It is noteworthy, that was despite the fact that the entire country's attention was attracted by the Assam Movement. In fact, I was surprised to find that the university students in Kerala and Karnataka were hardly aware of such catastrophic developments in the East and the North East! Instead, in a seminar held at Bangalore, a Muslim student of engineering discipline accused me openly of being anti-Muslim and left the meeting without waiting to listen to my deliberations and illustrations of the growing menace.

Unprecedented, mind-boggling changes on many fronts, are sweeping the entire globe with the dynamics of the entire range of human relations also undergoing concomitant changes, resulting in the emergence of new equations, previously unknown, all over the world as has been stated by Jaswant Singh in his book 'A Call Of Honour'. The rapidly growing urban centres are also exercising growing impact on the socio-political and socio-economic sectors of the world. True, there will be reaction and stiff resistance against such changes and presently, such resistance is mainly manifesting in the shape of religious fundamentalism and its aggressive posture as is being betrayed by the ISIS.

In fact, the distinctive feature of illegal Bangladeshi infiltration into India, unlike in the EU and the USA, has been the hidden agenda of full scale Islamisation, taking advantage of India's liberal heritage and total failure of the governments. Fundamentalists are yet to realize that since the dawn of the emergence of religion, religions irrespective of their hues, have failed to be self-sustaining as political force. The stability of the nationhoods of countries like the UK, USA, France and even for India, are not based on religion. Religion has, in fact, failed to keep the Arab world together. Near home, religion could not keep Pakistan in tact. Even in Bangladesh, despite all-out efforts by Gen. Zia and Gen. Ershad, religion could not be sustained as a political force. Rather opposition to religious fundamentalism has emerged as a political force.

In the present situation, the deportation of millions of infiltrators, is an impossibility; but their identification is not. Such persons identified as infiltrators must be treated as stateless individuals and dispersed all over the country after issuing work permits to them. How this strategy may be implemented, has already been explained above. Assam has an advantage over West Bengal, as Marxist indoctrination could not do the damage it had done in West Bengal. Its present problem is to arrest the growth of Islamic fundamentalism amongst the illiterate immigrant Muslims who may not otherwise subscribe to the policy of 'live and let live' as well as to ensure that fresh infiltration is prevented.

In the case of Assam, the society has remained content with only blaming the politicians while ignoring the subservient role played by the bureaucrats empowered to deal with the ever expanding menace of infiltration. In the past two or three decades, quite a few Chief Secretaries (CS) and DGP's of native stock were in power, to deal with the problem but preferred to remain silent. I, having been a Police officer of high rank, had come across only three or four bureaucrats like Late B.N. Mullick (the then DIB), R.S. Paramasivam (CS), Late B.K. Barua (IGP) and Late Ghanakanta Medhi (DIGP), who had on their own taken active interest in confronting this 'life & death' problem of Assam. Ultimately, it was at the behest of the Supreme Court only, that the process of updating the NRC could take a final shape, despite all the hurdles created by the State government of Tarun Gogoi. The SP of a district has the power to initiate action under The Foreigners Act on his own, against any foreign infiltrators, but he would not do so, for fear of incurring political displeasure, thereby fecundating the vote bank politics! There is a full-fledged Border Police Organization under an officer of DGP's rank. If the performance of this branch of the State Police department would have been enterprising, there is no doubt that the problem could have been contained to a considerable extent. The Border Police Organisation has miserably failed to persuade the powers that be, to augment the strength of the ROP and fully modernize it, as per the demands of the situation. How can one ignore the fact that a fearless, patriotic bureaucracy has always been in a position to influence the functioning of the political executives?

EPILOGUE

The problem of Bangladeshi infiltration has kept the ambience of Assam agitational for decades, with no acceptable solution emerging as yet. In this context, there have been accusations and counter accusations galore. At times, variance of opinions has clouded the main issue. It has so far been impossible to determine the correct number of illegal migrants staying in Assam. Deductions have so far been made by analysing the various census reports and the abnormal growth in the number of electorates. Opinions vary in all respect. Some quarters try to justify the abnormal growth of population and the number of electorates on seemingly legitimate grounds, while others outright reject their pleas. Some are even thinking in terms of ethnic cleansing. AASU has been consistently demanding fhe detection and deportation of the infiltrators, in terms of the Assam Accord which stipulates that the 25th of March, 1971 be held as the cut-off date for detection and deportation, while some other quarters do not agree with AASU, and have demanded to determine the cut-off year to be 1951. The matter is now in the Supreme Court, where the issue is subjudice. Meanwhile, the trend of human migration, both legal and illegal, has assumed global proportion, resulting in unforeseen developments and new equations. In any case, in the context of what has been analysed in this discourse, any easy and immediate solution of the problem of illegal migration from Bangladesh does not seem to be on the card in the immediate future, although the arrest of the ever rising trend of such migration may be possible on the basis of what has been suggested by various quarters. In the context of this complex problem, some prominent personalities of Assam were interviewed and their statements recorded. Excerpts from these interviews are reproduced below.

Interview with Senior Advocate Abdul Hafiz Rashid Choudhury:

Mr. Choudhury is a senior advocate, presently practising in the Guwahati High Court. He has been a teacher of Law in Sokoto University, Nigeria, Africa and in the Gauhati University Law College. He is also the former Principal of A.K. Chanda Law College, Silchar, Assam. He is also the Chairman, Executive Committee, Bar Council North Eastern States. Having belonged to a Freedom Fighters' family, he has been active in politics also and was the founding President of the United Democratic Front[UDF], since renamed as All India United Democratic Front. But he resigned in 2011 from the AIUDF on grounds of ideological differences with Badaruddin Azmal, who had succeded him as the President of the party. Presently, he has been the President of the Assam unit of the Samajvadi Party since 2012. He is one of the prominent personalities of Assam and known for championing the cause of the minorities. Basically he is an anti-Congress and anti-BJP politician. He was responsible for naming the aforementioned party as United Democratic Front in place of United Minority Front, so that the party did not assume a communal colour and instead, could embrace in its fold members of all the communities, the whole intention being to build up a viable opposition to the Congress and the BJP.

Excerpts of our interview with him are reproduced below in questions & answers form:

Q: Mr. Choudhury, do you subscribe to the 'two nation' theory?

A: Certainly not. I was never a Muslim League activist. In fact, I belong to a Freedom Fighter's family.

Q: Between 'Religion and Nation', which one receives priority over the other in your scheme of things?

A: Well Mr. Bhattacharyya, Islam is my faith which is entirely a personal and hereditary matter and it must not be mixed with politics, a matter with public involvement and public causes. There should be no doubt whatsoever that in case of need, the nation and public interests must get priority and my religion also preaches the same tenet.

Q: Why did you leave AIDUF?

A: For more than one reason. Azmal Sahab's inclination to woo the Congress, proved to be a constant irritant. Then his close proximity to religious organisation and betrayal of communal bias, proved to be the main stumbling block in maintaining AIUDF's secular image. Also Azmal Sahab's dictatorial way of functioning coupled with his naked nepotism, made it impossible for me to continue my political association with him. Briefly speaking, I could not compromise with the process of his derailing the AIUDF.

Q: Now let us deliberate upon the more contentious issues. Do you agree that there has been infiltration from Bangladesh on massive scale and now the situation has taken a worse turn with the arrival of the jihadis in the scenario? What is the role played by the Madrasas in this context?

A: There is no denial that there has been infiltration from Bangladesh. Without being in possession of reliable information, I am not in a position to comment on the jihadi issue. If such anti-national underground activities come to notice, all Muslims of Assam should oppose such conspiracies. There are two types of Madrasas, namely, Madrasa registered with the government and privately-run Madrasas known as Quami Madrasa. The registered Madrasas cannot afford to induldge in anti-national activities. In the Quami Madrasas, only religious teachings are imparted. Lately, there have been some instances of such Madrasas coming under suspicion of induldging in anti-national activities. Thorough Police investigation should unearth the real position. In any case, such anti-national activities must not be allowed to continue. At the same time, it must be admitted that some such Madrasas are being used by vested interests for political purposes and in the process it is not unlikely to promote communal divide.

Q: If there are infiltrators, then why a hue and cry about harassment to minorities is raised whenever any operation against alien infiltrators is undertaken?

A: Because in many cases, innocent persons are subjected to uncalled for harassment and demands made for payment of money in exchange for letting them free. In fact, in 1965, I was myself a victim of such harassment at Lumding while travelling by train. At this time my father was serving as a teacher in the Silchar Government High School. So you can well imagine the predicament likely to be faced by an illiterate innocent villager. Secondly, many innocent villagers, after having become suspects, are deprived of the benefits available to a citizen in due course. I should have no objection to impartial investigation made in this context. Further, I would suggest that there should be committees at Panchayat levels, comprising impartial and prominent persons of all communities as also government representatives to regularly scrutinise minutely and impartially every case of suspects instead of allowing the Police to take arbitrary action. Such steps will not only greatly reduce the incidence of harassment but will also relieve the Police of the allegation of malpractices.

Q: Do you think that religion may be a political force and may sustain a political system?

A: It cannot be a ever sustainable political force but it can certainly become a factor whenever a polarization of voters on communal basis takes place. This is how the United Minority Front and the AIUDF tried to use religion as a political factor by calling upon the Muslim voters to vote for them but they failed to monopolise the Muslim votes. Thus it cannot be sustained as a permanent political force. Still some leaders, both Hindu and Muslim, never tire of trying to divide Hindu and Muslim voters on communal basis. Unfortunately, this is the curse of electoral politics.

Q: Don't you agree that the emergence of AAMSU has been a heavy constraint on communal harmony? In presence of

AASU which represented students of all communities, what was the need to create AAMSU?

A: Those who promoted AAMSU, wanted to create a counterforce against AASU. Another target was to create division between, on the one hand, Hindus and Muslims of indigenoue stock and Bengali-speaking Hindus and Muslims, on the other. The entire exercise was motivated by vested political interest by whom you know already. The response from Bengali Hindus not reaching the expected level, AAMSU gradually for all practical purposes, became the champion of the causes of immigrant Muslims. Certainly its activities have not been conducive to building up communal harmony.

Q: My last question: How do you envisage prevention of fresh infiltration?

A: First prerequisite is a strong and uncompromising political will. Secondly, the Indo-Bangla border must be fully sealed in its entire length. And thirdly, the strength and intensity of patrolling and vigilance by BSF must be enhanced in proportion to the existing ground realities.

The Author: Thank you so much, Mr. Choudhury. It will be great pleasure to place your views before the readers.

Interview with Dr. Samujjal Kumar Bhattacharyya, Chief Adviser of AASU and Adviser of North Eastern Students Union:

Dr. Bhattacharyya has been a public activist since his student days. An M.A. in Political Science, his thesis for his Ph. D degree was on 'The role of ST members in Assam Assembly since 1971.' He has been making tremendous impact on moulding the public opinion of Assam and guiding the course of AASU's role in the post-Assam Accord period. Prior to this, he was the General Secretary of AASU for three consecutive terms between 1989-91, 1991-94 and 1994-99. Most significantly, Mr. Bhattacharyya along with AASU, has been unrelenting in maintaining that the Assam Accord must be fully implemented and the problem of Bangladeshi infiltration must be solved in terms of the Assam Accord.

Our interview with him is reproduced below:

Q: Dr. Bhattacharyya, How do you envisage the solution of the problem of unabated infiltration from Bangladesh?

A: There is no ambiguity whatsoever in our stand. We have been insisting with all the vehemence at our command that the problem must be addressed in terms of the Assam Accord only. Any favourable improvement will certainly be welcomed.

Q: Will you please specify the steps you consider to be imperative in this context in terms of the Accord?

A: Following are the steps which must immediately be taken:

1] Complete sealing of the Indo-Bangla border in all the sectors withou further delay.

2] Completion of updating the NRC within next 100 days.

3] Our formula of 'Three D's' must be fully implemented. In other words, all illegal Bangladeshi migrants from Bangladesh irrespective of their religions must be detected, deported and their names deleted from the ERs. We have already taken the load of pre-1971 stream of infiltrators and now we refuse to take any more load of migrants.

4] In order to preserve the distinct identity of the native people of Assam, there must be specific constitutional safeguards like 100 per cent reservation of seats for the native people of Assam in all elective bodies ranging from Panchayats to the Parliament as also in case of all other government benefits available under reservation scheme; we also fully support the proposal for granting Schedule Tribe status to the six ethnic communities which is being processed; but after holding threadbare discussion with twenty-six ethnic groups, we have formed the firm opinion that while granting such benefits, care must be taken to ensure that benefits already available to the presently recognized sixteen Schedule Tribes are neither interfered with nor subjected to any sharing; an Upper House of Legislature for the numerically weaker sections of the Assamese society; By the word 'Assamese', we mean all the indigenous people of Assam who were living in Assam in 1951—let there be no controversy created by professional politicians in this regard; under the present circumstance, Assam must be granted a special constitutional status so that our rights over land and natural resources, may be ensured; introduction of Inner Line Permit; full protection to the lands of *Satras*/ Tribal Belt & Blocks.

5] The reservation policy must be based on well specified grounds.

6] As per admission of the Central Government itself, there are at least fifty lakh infiltrators. There must not be any hesitation in excluding their names from the NRC and deporting them outright.

The Author: Thank you so much, Dr. Bhattacharyya, for having spared your valuable time.

Interview with Assam Chief Minister Sarbananda Sonowal

Sonowal is a highly educated and vastly experienced person. Since his school days, he has exhibited his unending quality of leadership. He was a student of English literature but could not complete his post-graduation in the subject for reasons beyond his control. Then he got his degree in Communication and Journalism from the Guwahati University. He has also got a degree in Law. A public activist since his student days, he has been, to a great extent, responsible for organizing the AASU network on wide scale in Upper Assam. Twice the President of AASU in two consecutive terms, he has also got the distinction of being an MLA and an MP. He has been acclaimed as the 'national hero' of Assam because it was in response to his writ petition that the Supreme Court invalidated in 2005 the IMDT Act by declaring the Act ultra vires of the Constitution. He joined the BJP in 2011 and on being returned to the Lok Sabha as a BJP nominee in 2014, he was inducted into Modi's Council of Ministers. He was the guiding force behind successful holding of the SAARC Games at Guwahati and Shillong in 2015. He was sworn in as the Chief Minister of Assam on the 24th of May 2016. Our interview for more than hour with him is reproduced below:

Q: What preventive measures do you propose to take against illegal migration from Bangladesh?

A: We propose to proceed step by step. To start with, we want the updating of the NRC to be completed within next hundred days. The NRC itself will be a great preventive measure. There are hundred Foreigners Tribunals, but necessary infrastructural facilities are not yet available to them with the result that the Tribunals are facing many difficulties in performing their duties. As such, all the Tribunals must be made fully functional at optimum level so that all the pending cases may be disposed of, within a reasonable period. Additional preventive measures will be determined after analyzing the current situation and consultation with experts.

Q: How do you propose to deport the infiltrators after their judicial identification or deal with them otherwise?

A: It has to be planned very carefully to develop proper constitutional mechanism.

Q: Priority wise, what will be the first steps?

A: I have already indicated that the first priority will be to identify the infiltrators without causing any harassment to genuine Indian citizens and also any apprehensions in their minds.

The Author: Thank you very much, Mr. Sonowal for having spared so much time despite your busy schedule.

We discussed a few other topics related to Assam's socio-cultural life and conservation of environment etc which may not be relevant for the purpose of this discourse.

Interview with D.R. Nabla alias Ranjan Daimary, President of NDFB, presently engaged in Peace-talk with the government.

Born in 1960, Ranjan Daimary graduated from the St. Anthony College, Shillong with honours in Political Science and took his MA degree from the NEHU, Shillong in 1985. Suave and soft-speaking, he speaks fluent English unlike many other leading insurgent leaders of the North-East. Of medium height, he possesses a pleasant personality, although he seems to be very firm in some of his convictions. He hails from the Odalgoory district of Assam, now a part of the BTAD. Immediately on coming back from Shillong after doing his MA, he founded the Bodo Security Force on October 3, 1986. Since he turned a rebel immediately after coming back from Shillong, it is obvious that the plan for forming the insurgent unit was formulated during his long stay at Shillong. Subsequently, the name of the Bodo Security Force was changed into NDFB in 1994. The objective of the NDFB was to create an independent sovereign socialist republic of Bodoland. He has widely travelled in Bangladesh, Myanmar, Thailand, Singapore, Malaysia etc, during the course of his campaign for marshalling resources necessary for NDFB's fight for an independent Bodoland. He had also stayed in ULFA's camp in Myanmar for quite sometime and then in 1987, held long discussion with Isak Chishi Swu, the President of NSCN. In pursuance of the decisions arrived at during the above quoted meeting, Swu deputed three instructors to train up the cadres of the NDFB in handling of various arms and explosives. Needless to mention that before coming forward for holding the Peace-talk with the GOI, NDFB was responsible for committing number of subversive acts and violence of different magnitude. The story of Ranjan's turn around for peace-talk may not be relevant for this discourse. But he was certainly very much concerned, if not bitter, with the unabated flow of infiltrants from Bangladesh. As such, our questions to him were mainly focussed on infiltration from Bangladesh as narrated below:

Q: From our discussion it transpires that you are very much worried about the menace of illegal migration from Bangladesh. How do you visualize to deal with the problem? What specific measures you would suggest to prevent fresh infiltration?

A: The first prerequisite is strongest possible political will to combat this silent invasion. Only border fencing is not sufficient to stop infiltration. The government must free itself from the influence of the pro-Bangladeshi lobby and enact tough anti-infiltration law and amend the Citizenship Act so that the children of Bangladeshi infiltrators may not be entitled to Indian citizenship. Quite likely that lakhs of such infiltrators will be detected after the updating of the NRC is completed. After the process of identification is completed, national identity cards must be issued to all Indian citizens. Those who are not in possession of the said identity cards, must be deprived of all government facilities/benefits available to an Indian citizen. Licences/ permits for operating cycle rikswas, push-cart, small trading activities, educational facilities, must not be made available to non-holders of this identity cards. Native people found to have engaged non-holders of identity cards, must be severely penalized under the relevant laws. Documented migrants from Bangladesh may be issued temporary work permits for limited period entirely on economic grounds so that cheap Bangladeshi labors could be made available in those economic sectors where there are seasonal needs for such labors. But steps must be taken to send them back on expiry of the time limit so that they cannot disappear in the midst of their co-religionists. Besides, in order to ensure full control of indigenous people over land and resources, alienation of land must be prevented. Sale of lands and other immovable assets to foreigners both in tribal and non-tribal areas must be totally banned.

Q: As visualized by you also, it is very much on the card that lakhs of undocumented Bangladeshis will be identified after the updating of the NRC is completed. Now, how would you deal with these illegal alien migrants, particularly in view of the fact that neither it might be possible to deport them physically to Bangladesh nor will Bangladesh, as on today, accept them back?

A: Irrespective of the stand taken by Bangladesh, our government must keep on pressurizing the Bangladesh government for taking back these immigrants. Meanwhile, after identification, they must not be allowed to mingle and interact freely with the immigrant component of our population. Instead, they should be isolated and confined to either detention camps or earmarked areas. Also, they may be engaged under strict supervision in productive activities so that they may earn their own bread. They also must be ruthlessly evicted from any land they might have encroached upon or acquired by other means. Also the possibility of dispersing them all over the country must be fully explored. In any case, Assam must not be compelled to take the entire burden, particularly after Assam had agreed to accommodate the pre-1971 stream of immigrants in terms of the Assam Accord.

Q: What happens if other States donot agree to accommodate them? Or even after some of them are accepted but still a huge number of these illegal immigrants is left to be sent away from Assam, then what do you propose to do with them?

A: In such an eventuality, there would be no way out other than what you have already suggested. They should be organised into a labor force and then undertake marketing of labor at various levels. Of course, very strict labour laws must be enacted.

Q: In the wake of so many violent disturbances, the concept of etnic cleansing was doing the rounds. That the concept had gained some acceptability, is apparent from the pattern of ethnic clashes. Do you think that the concept of ethnic cleansing is still gathering momentum? If so, how do you propose to eradicate such inhuman approach to solving the ethnic problems and clashes?

A: Now that we are engaged in peace-talk, the question of resorting to violence simply does not arise. But more militant elements might not have altogether banished the concept and this was where the government might fully assert itself and eradicate the sources of friction with long term planning and preventing further encroachment into the region of tribal existence instead of waiting for violence to erupt once again. I have already stated about measures to be taken in this regard.

Author: Thank you so much, Mr. Daimary for having spared so much time and favouring me with the opportunity for recording your views.

Author's note: As our meeting was drawing nigh to the end of the interview, Daimary referred to a very significant development which had so far escaped our attention. This is about the inter-state migration which we had no reason so far to object to. But Daimary had a different story to tell. He observed that as Lower Assam is about to be overwhelmed by illegal immigrant Muslims from Bangladesh, so also Upper Assam and the inter-state borders of Nagaland and Arunachal are being inundated by unabated flow of Adivashis from states like Jharkhand, Satisgarh,

Madhya Pradesh and so on. The violent clashes on these interstate borders are entirely due to the aggressive postures of the Adivashis. Still more dangerous, he further stated, is that some of these Adivashi's are being used as a medium for silent spread of **Maoism.** As such, he demands that there must be a system for controlling interstate migration as well. He further stated that the possibility of future violence against the aggressive Adivashis in the BTAD areas cannot be ruled out. Very significantly he pointed out that the Adivashis have already organised so many fronts including some underground armed outfits. In fact, he stated, most of the Adivashi villages are sheltering many cadres of the underground militant outfits and Adivashi population is proliferating in an unimaginable rate.

What Ranjan Daimary has stated before us, sounds like a wake-up call for all concerned.

APPENDICES

Appendix—1

Names of CEC's who held office since 1950		
1.	Sukumar Sen	1950 to 1958
2.	Kalyan Sundaram	1958 to 1967
3.	Gagan Jinwala	1967 to 1972
4.	Nagendra Singh	1972 to 1973
5.	T. Swaminathan	1973 to 1977
6.	S.L. Sakhder	1977 to 1982
7.	R.K. Trivedi	1982 to 1985
8.	R.V.S. Pery Shastri	1986 to1990
9.	V.S. Rama Devi	She held the office for a short period, between 26/11/1990 and 12/12/1990.
10.	T.N. Seshan	1990 to 1996
11.	M.S. Gill	1996 to 2001
12.	J.M. Lyngdoh	2001 to 2004
13.	T.S. Krishnamurthy	2004 to 2005
14.	B.B. Tandon	2005 to 2006
15.	N. Gopalaswami	2006 to 2009
16.	Nabin Chawla	2009 to 2010
17.	S.Y. Qurashi	2010 to 2012
18.	V.S. Sampat	2012 to 2015
19.	H.S. Brahma	He was the CEC between 16/01/2015 and 18/04/2015; when he retired
20.	Nasim Zaidi	from 19/04/2015 till date

(We had occasions to interact personally with Mr. Sakher and Mr. Seshan.)

Appendix—2

To

The Chief Election Commissioner of India, New Delhi

&

The Chief Electoral Officer, Assam, Guahati 27/10/1992

Dear Sirs

Namaskar!

We are constrained to draw your pointed attention to the following and demand that you clarify your position vis-à-vis the points raised below.

Lately, lots of controversies have been raised and apprehensions voiced in respect of cleansing the electoral rolls of Assam of foreign voters. It has been alleged that the Election Department of our state has succumbed to the influence exercised by the State Government with the result that the guidelines issued by the Election Commission for deleting the names of foreign nationals from the ER's have been totally ignored. On the other hand, the Chief Minister has totally denied any such interference. We, the Indian citizens of Assam have a right to know, whether the Election Department of the state is discharging its duties in faithful obedience to the aforesaid guidelines.

In the All Parties Conference held on September 22, assurances were given that these guidelines would be strictly implemented; but it seems the CEO had found it more convenient to forget these assurances. Else, why would he remain silent about the allegation that the guidelines issued by the Commission had not been circulated among the Deputy Commissioners and the Electoral Registration Officers? If the allegation is correct, then this amounts to a total betrayal of the people of Assam, if not a heinous crime committed on them. The Chief Election Commissioner and the CEO owe it to the people of Assam to clarify their position on the following counts also:

What prevents the CEC from identifying the infiltration-prone constituencies on his own, instead of passing on the bulk to the state government? With little application and objective analysis, it should be possible for the CEC to determine these constituencies from his own office records. We are ready to furnish the names of these constituencies, but will accept them?

The Commission has betrayed the people of Assam time and again. In the past, it has gone back on many of its own assurances and this time seems to be no exception. For, the Commission seems to be intent upon converting a simple operation into an unnecessary complex problem for reasons which cannot be considered constitutional and to be in conformity with their constitutional duties. Both the CEC and the CEO must be aware of the provisions of the *Assam Accord*, which stipulates that all the post-1971 foreign infiltrators should be deported. That they have not been deported is another matter; but what prevents the Commission from accepting the 1971 (1972?) ERs as the basis for using of the names of lakhs of foreign nationals from the voters' list, is not explicable. If the Commission is true to its salt, then they would even now refrain from accepting the 1990 rolls as the basis for preparing the 1992-draft rolls. Even after doing so, it can certainly atone for its sin by comparing the draft rolls with the 1971 rolls and delete the names of those from the draft rolls whose names do not figure in the 1971 rolls. This, however, willnot apply to the children of the Indian voters enumerated in the 1971 rolls as they have by now attined the age of 18 and over as well as those genuine Indian nationals who have since taken up residence in Assam. It will be also pertinent to point out that there is absolutely nothing sacrosanct about the 1990 rolls. Despite all these, if the Commission yields to political design of the party in power by treating the 1990 rolls as the basis for correcting the current draft rolls, then this will be nothing short of total abdication by the

Commission, besides being another sin committed on Assam and her people. The Commission also possibly cannot ignore the threat held out by the fundamentalists promoting the cause of the Bangladeshi infiltrators, that if need be, they can throw out the Saikia government within 'five minutes'.

Do the CEC and the CEO also, like a particular lobby, consider the foreign nationals illegally registering themselves as Indian voters and Indian voters belonging to the religious minority community, are identical? If not, then they better say so instead of remaining silent on such claims being constantly put forward by the fundamentalists with transborder inspiration.

Between 1958 and 1969, about 3,10,000 foreign infiltrators were deported from Assam under different laws of the land. This figure also includes about 2,50,000 infiltrators deported under the *PIP Scheme.* Besides, between 1978 and 1980, another number of about 10000 foreign infiltrators was deported from Assam. Both the CEC and the CEO will certainly agree with us that these deportees cannot be voters here by any stretch of imagination. Names of these deportees were not deleted from the ERs even during AGP rules also. Will the Commission now make it bold to assure the people of Assam that all the names of these deportees will be deleted from the from the 1992 rolls? This is the minimum the Commission can do without raising any fresh controversy. The Commission may also do well to note that taking advantage of the existence of these names in the ERs, many fresh infiltrators are reported to have assumed many of these names and been exercising voting rights. All the names of these lakhs of deportees are available either with the DIGP (Border) or with the respective Police Chiefs of all the districts of Assam unless these have been destroyed at the instance of ever manipulating fundamentalist politicians who had in the past captured power in the state.

Successive Chief Election Commissioners have been categorically admitting for years on end that the ERs of Assam contain names of foreign nationals; but surprisingly, the Commission has never considered the question of initiating necessary action on its own for deleting the names of foreign nationals from the ERs, although the Commission has the power to do so under the relevant law without taking any dictation from the state government. That being so, how does the Election Commission expect the people to believe that its independent constitutional status has not been sacrificed under political pressure? On this count also, the Commission owes an explanation to the country in general and to Assam in particular. If this time also, the Commission sabotages the process of preparing a correct voters' list excluding the names of foreign nationals, then this will be an act of treason in the face of the silent invasion of Assam by millions of Bangladeshi nationals with active support from their government and politicians of this side of the border, All said and done, the Commission cannot afford to be a party to the diabolic action of suppressing the Commission's own instructions and this is where the Chief Electoral Officer of the state has to assert his independent status.

While anxiously waiting for a reply to clarifications on the points raised above, we conclude by quoting from a statement made by the then External Affairs Minister Mr. Atal Behari Vajpayee on the floor of the parliament on November 2, 1978:

'It has come to the notice of the Election Commission from time to time that large-scale inclusion of foreign nationals in the electoral rolls, especially in the north-eastern region, has been taking place.

In August, 1975, the Ministry of Home affairs instructed all the state governments that the state criminal department may be instructed to take immediate steps to check the electoral rolls, and if they discover the names of foreigners in the rolls, the fact may be brought to the notice of the concerned Electoral Registration Officers for getting such names deleted from the electoral rolls.

The Election Commission has also has issued instructions to the electoral officers of the states and Union Territories concerned that if it is found that a large number of foreigners have managed to get their names registered in the electoral rolls, recourse should be had to provisions of section 22 of the Representation of People Act of 1950 for getting the names of such persons deleted from the electoral rolls on the ground that they are not Indian citizens.'

What prevents now both the CEC and the CEO from taking recourse to this provision of the law and thereby end all controversies once and for all?

Thanking you.
Yours faithfully
Hiranya Kumar Bhattacharyya
Beltola, Guwahati.'

Appendix—3

Govt. ensures neat burial of CEC guidelines. Enumerators get vague orders on making draft rolls

By a Staff Reporter

Guwahati, Oct 23: The State Election Department has taken up the preparation of draft electoral rolls without having undertaken the enumeration work as laid down by the Chief Election Commissioner in respect of identifying the foreigner infested constituencies first. On the other hand, none of the over a dozen guidelines issued by the State Chief Electoral Officer to the Deputy Commissioners and Electoral Registration Officer etc. has a word on foreign nationals and vaguely asked the enumerators to 'include names of eligible citizens who are members of the household or are ordinarily residents in that house' etc. Meanwhile, the other state governments' constituencies as have already identified foreigner-infested constituencies as asked by the CEC.

The State government and the Chief Electoral Officer have not circulated the guidelines of the Chief Election Commissioner among the Deputy Commissioners and the Electoral Registration Officers. The CEC guidelines (details of which were published in The Sentinel on Oct 18 at page 3) have been kept by the government and the Chief Electoral Officer though the State government is required not to interfere in the works of the Election Department. Meanwhile the works on the preparation of the draft rolls are going on in full swing.

The first instruction of the CEC guidelines has specially asked the state government to fully implement the instruction in respect of first identifying the constituencies with substantial population of foreign nationals. But now that the enumeration works have been stated to be over to take up the preparation of draft electoral rolls, the CE guidelines seem to have been given a neat burial by the Chief Electoral Officer and the State Government.

The CEC guidelines, it may be noted, after it was widely published that illegal infiltrators from Bangladesh had swamped vast areas in neighboring States and the Government of India decided to convene a conference of Chief Ministers to discuss the problem. The guidelines were issued to the governments of the North-eastern states, West Bengal and Bihar.

They laid down that after having identified the foreigner dominated constituencies, such areas covered by each polling booth in such constituencies had to be identified. It was only after such identification that the enumeration was to be taken up. The CEC also fixed August 31 as the date for completion of the identification process.

When asked if the state government would start the identification of the foreigner-infested constituencies a senior official told The Sentinel that the state government had no data or records to show which constituency was foreigners-infested. However, if the Chief Election Commissioner furnished such data, the state government would immediately start the work to identify such constituencies, he said. It was only after the draft rolls were published that the exact position could be ascertained; he said and suggested that before the position was ascertained, it would not be proper to act on the CEC guidelines.

On the other side of the scenario, the state Election department is still waiting for a positive decision from the state government on the CEC guidelines. 'We are still waiting for the government to first identify the constituencies with large foreigner population', Election Department Official told The Sentinel. He agreed that much time had already been wasted by now.

The state government has not informed the CEC that it had not implemented its guidelines. It may be recalled here that a meeting of all political parties convened by the state government on September 22, had lent its full support to the CEC guidelines and asked the state government to implement them fully.

What, however, has baffled the concerned citizens is government's explanation that it had no data or records to identify the constituencies with substantial foreigner population. The CEC guidelines were the only rational and correct ones under the circumstances, but with the non-implementation of the very first instruction contained therein by the State government, the whole exercise has been a non-starter.

The Election Department is, meanwhile, working within its limitations to publish a revised voters' list. It has already appointed sixofficials.

It may also be noted here that the CEC has not asked for any information from the state governments whether its guidelines had been implemented or not till today.'

(Source: The Sentinel, 24 October 1992)

N. B: Other press reports are also available, but the above quoted one is illustrative enough – Author.

Appendix—4

SHRI AFZALUR RAHMAN
MINISTER, PANCHAYAT &
RURAL DEVELOPMENT, ASSAM
DISPUR, GUWAHATI – 781006

Ashoka Logo

Name: Atawar Rahman.
Father's/Husband's name: Mega Moulavi
Village: Boro-Udmari, PS: Lakhipur, District: Goalpara (Assam).

Certified that the above mentioned person is known to me. He/She is known to me. He/She is a permanent resident of the said village and is an INDIAN (*emphasis mine*).

To my best knowledge he/she bears good moral character. I wish him success in life.

Also another press report mentioned in the main text as published in The Assam Tribune of October 18, 1992 in the same context reads as follows:

'From our Correspondent

Dibrugarh, Oct 2017 – Detection of a Permanent Resident Certificate here apparently issued under the seal and signature of a Cabinet Minister of Assam has caused many an eyebrow to raise. The certificate in a printed format in the letter-pad of Sri Afzalur Rahman, Minister for Panchayat & Rural Development, was reportedly detected here from the possession of one Sri Atawar Rahman, said to be a permanent resident of Boro Udmari village under Lakhipur PS in Goalpara district. He is at present a licensed richshaw-puller here, residing at Naliapool area of the town.

Sri Bhudeb Phukan, President of the Dibrugarh district unit of the Bharatiya Janata Party, in a memorandum addressed to the Governor of Assam and submitted to the Deputy Commissioner here for onward transmission, sought to draw the attention of the Governor to the matter. The memorandum referred to the printed format of the certificate issued under the seal and signature of the minister, and expressed apprehension that the minister must have issued such certificates in large numbers. The memorandum demands a CBI inquiry into the matter and dismissal of Mr. Rahman from the Cabinet.'

Appendix—5

ASSAM ACCORD
(MEMORANDUM OF SETTLEMENT)

Government have all along been most anxious to find a satisfactory solution to the problem of foreigners in Assam. The All Assam Students' Union (AASU) and the All Assam Gana Sangram Parishad (AAGSP) have also expressed their keenness to find such a solution.

The AASU, through their memorandum dated the 2nd of February 1980, presented to the Late Prime Minister Smt. Indira Gandhi, conveyed their profound sense of apprehension regarding the continuing influx of foreign nationals into Assam and the fear about adverse affects upon the political, social, culture and economic life of the State.

Being fully alive to the genuine apprehensions of the people of Assam, the then Prime Minister initiated the dialogue with the AASU/AAGSP. Subsequently, talks were held at the Prime Minister's and the Home Minister's level during the period 1980-83. Several rounds of informal talks were held in 1984. Formal discussions were resumed in March 1985.

Keeping all aspects of the problem including constitutional and legal provisions, international agreements, national commitments and humanitarian considerations, it has been decided to proceed as follows:

Foreigners Issue

5.1 For purpose of detection and deletion of foreigners, 01.01.1966 shall be the best data and year.

5.2 All persons who came to Assam prior to 01.01.1966, including those amongst them whose names appear on the electoral rolls used in 1967 elections shall be regularized.

5.3 Foreigners who came to Assam after 01.1.1966 (inclusive) and up to 24th March, 1971 shall be detected in accordance with the provisions of the Foreigners Act, 1946 and the Foreigners (Tribunals) order 1964.

5.4 Names of foreigners so detected will be deleted from the electoral rolls in force. Such person will be required to register themselves before the Registration Officers of the respective districts in accordance with the provisions of the Registration of Foreigners Act, 1939 and the Registration of Foreigners Rule 1939.

5.5 For this purpose, Government of India will undertake suitable strengthening of the government machinery.

5.6 On the expiry of a period of 10 years following the date of detection, the names of all such persons, which have been deleted from the electoral rolls, shall be restored.

5.7 All persons who were expelled earlier, but have since re-entered illegally into Assam shall be expelled.

5.8 Foreigners who came to Assam on or after March 25, 1971 shall continue to be detected, deleted and practical steps shall be taken to expel such foreigners.

5.9 The Government will give due consideration to certain difficulties expressed by the AASU/AAGSP regarding the Implementation of the Illegal Migrants (Determination by Tribunals) Act, 1983.

Safeguards and Economic Development

Constitutional, legislative and administrative safeguards, as may be appropriate shall be provided to protect, preserve and promote the culture, social, linguistic identity and heritage of the Assamese people.

The government take this opportunity to renew their commitment for the speedy all-round economic development of Assam, so as to improve the standard of living of the people. Special emphasis will be placed on education and science and technology through establishment of national institutions.

Other issues

8.1 The government will arrange for the issue of citizenship certificate in future only by the authorities of the central government.

8.2 Specific complaints that may be made by the AASU/AAGSP about irregular issuance of Indian Citizenship Certificates (ICC) will be looked into.

The international border shall be made secure against future infiltration by erection of physical barriers like walls, barbed wire fencing and other obstacles at appropriate places. Patrolling by security forces on land and riverine routes all along the international border shall be adequately intensified. In order to further strengthen the security arrangements, to prevent affectively future infiltration, an adequate number of check posts shall be set up.

9.2 Besides the arrangements mentioned above and keeping in view security considerations, a road all along the international border shall be constructed as to facilitate patrolling by security forces. Land between border and the road would be kept free of human habitation, wherever possible. Riverine patrolling along the international border would be intensified. All effective measures would be adopted to prevent infiltrators crossing or attempting to cross the international border.

It will be ensured that the relevant law restricting acquisition of immovable property by foreigners in Assam is strictly enforced. It will be ensured that Birth and Death Registers are duly maintained.

Restoration of Normalcy

The All Assam Students' Union (AASU) and the All Assam Gana Sangram Parishad (AAGSP) call off the agitation, assure full cooperation and dedicate themselves towards the development of the country.

The central and state governments have agreed to:

Review with sympathy and withdraw cases of disciplinary action taken against employees in the context of the agitation and to ensure that there is no victimization.

Frame a scheme for ex-gratia payment to the next of kin of those who were killed in the course of the agitation.

Give sympathetic consideration to proposal for relaxation of upper age limit for employment in public services in Assam, having regard to exceptional situation that prevailed in holding of academic and competitive examination etc in the context of agitation in Assam.

Undertake review of detention cases, if any, as well as cases against persons charged with criminal offences in connection with the agitation, except those charged with commission of heinous offences.

Consider withdrawal of prohibitory orders/notification in force, if any.

The Ministry of Home Affairs will be the nodal ministry for the implementation of the above.

Signed/-
(P.K. Mahanta)
President
All Assam Students' Union

Signed/-
(R.D. Pradhan)
Home Secretary
Govt. of India

Signed/-
(B.K. Phukan)
General Secreatary
All Assam Students' Union

Signed/-
(Smt. P.P. Trivedi)
Chief Secretary
Govt. of Assam

Signed/-
(Biraj Sharma)
Convenor
All Assam Gana Sangram Parishad
In the presence of

Signed/-
(Rajiv Gandhi)
Prime Minister of India
Date: 15 August 1985
Place: New Delhi

Election Commission will be requested to ensure preparation of fair electoral rolls.

Time for submission of claims and objections will be extended by 30 days, subject to this being consistent with the Electoral Rules.

The Election Commission will be requested to send Central Observers.

Signed/-
Home Secretary

Oil refinery will be established in Assam.

Central Government will render full assistance to the state government in their efforts to re-open:

Ashok Paper Mill/Jute Mills

IIT will be set up in Assam.

Appendix—6

UPDATING NRC (1)

'Updating the National Register for Citizens (NRC) of 1951 is vital for the detection of foreigners living in Assam, but the process of updating the vital document is very slow and at present the state government is not even in a position to declare as to when the process will be completed. The decision to update the NRC was taken at a tripartite meeting to review the progress of implementation of Assam Accord on May 5, 2005 and though the state and central governments promised in the meeting, chaired by the Prime Minister, to complete the process in 2 years, the promise has remained on paper only. Of course immediately after the meeting, the state government created a separate directorate to carry out the job and the data entry process started soon thereafter, but the government has not yet been able to finalize the modalities for updating the NRC till date. Now the government has decided to form a Cabinet Sub-committee to hold talks with all concerned, including the All Assam Students' Union (AASU) to finalize the modalities. However, one fails to understand what took so long to start the process. If the government is serious in updating the NRC on time, it should have started the process of finalizing the modalities immediately after the decision to update the vital document was taken and there was no reason to wait for two years to form the Cabinet Sub-committee. Moreover, the central government is yet to amend the Citizenship Act to give the required authority to the State government to carry out the job of updating the NRC and the Chief Minister recently admitted that the Act would be amended only after the modalities for updating the NRC are finalized. The NRC is not only vital for detection of foreigners, but after it is updated, the harassment of genuine Indian citizens during the process of detection will also be stopped. If the government is really serious in solving the problem of infiltration of foreigners, the process of updating the NRC should be expedited and all political parties and students' bodies should also mount pressure on the government to complete the process in a stipulated time frame. It is also a fact that the process of detection of foreigners living in Assam is very slow as only 42,000 foreigners were detected since signing of the Assam Accord and only 2,221 of them could be deported. The government should initiate probe to ascertain the reasons for the failure to deport all the persons detected as foreigners, or else there is no point in carrying out the process of detection of foreigners.'

Appendix—7

UPDATING NRC (2)

'The Supreme Court recently gave a directive to the government of Assam to complete the process of updating the National Register of Citizens (NRC) of 1951 in the first part of 2016, that is before the next State Assembly Elections. Now it remains to be seen whether the government can complete the job within the stipulated time frame. The process of updating the NRC remains very slow and only after the intervention of the Supreme Court, the process may be expedited. The decision to update the NRC within a couple of years and to give photo-identity cards to the Indian citizens on the basis of the same was taken way back in May, 2005 in a tripartite meeting involving the state and central governments and the All Assam Students' Union (AASU) to review the progress of implementation of the Assam Accord. The meeting was chaired by the then prime Minister Dr. Manmohan Singh himself. But unfortunately, the Assam government took a long time to formulate the modalities of updating the NRC. Though the pilot project of updating the Citizenship Document was launched in 2 revenue circles of the state in 2010, the government suspended the process after violent protest by one organisation in Barpeta and the modalities were re-formulated, which resulted in loss of time. Unfortunately, though a judicial probe was ordered into the violent protest in Barpeta, no action was taken against anyone on the basis of the report of the probe, which raised doubts on the sincerity of the government in dealing strongly with those opposing the process of updating the NRC.

The state government, under pressure from the Supreme Court, has appointed a senior Indian Administrative Service (IAS) Officer as the Nodal Officer for updating the NRC. But appointment of only one officer will not be enough and a full-fledged team of senior officers should be constituted for the job. The government should also appoint district and sub-divisional nodal officers for the job and the officers engaged in the process should not be engaged in any other job. If the government is really serious on the job, the police force should be directed to take strong action against anyone making any attempt to destabilize the process. Moreover, the political parties and organizations should not make it a political issue and extend cooperation to the administration for completing the job within the stipulated time frame. The parties and organizations should also play the role of watchdogs to ensure that no foreigner can register his/her name in the NRC with false documents. The NRC is vital for a state like Assam facing serious problem of infiltration of foreign nationals and all indigenous persons of the state should come forward to extend a helping hand to the project to ensure its early completion.'

Appendix—8

(STATESMAN, APRIL 6 & 8, 1990)
'SERIOUS INFLUX FROM BANGLADESH'

'The basket case of Asia, as Henry Kissinger described Bangladesh, pours out in thousands each teeming millions all over the sub-continent, not to speak of West Asia and elsewhere abroad. They have sneaked into the remotest parts of Arunachal Pradesh, the Inner Line Permit system notwithstanding. The Inner Line Permit is a must even for Indian nationals entering Arunachal Pradesh. But the Bangladeshis have managed to seep through to offer their services for cultivating forest lands cleared by the local tribals......'

'The Bangladeshis have been spread out all over India. In Punjab and Haryana they are indispensable as farm labors during the harvest season. They are used as expandable couriers both by the Punjab terrorists and Pakistan Rangers. There is a Bangladeshi in trans-Jamuna area in Delhi......'

'However it is in the neighbouring states of Assam, Tripura, West Bengal and Bihar that the impact of Bangladeshi immigration is overwhelming. In Tripura, the demographic picture has undergone a total change after partition with a predominantly tribal territory being overwhelmed by the influx of plainsmen...... In Bihar some of the north-eastern tracts adjoining West Bengal, particularly the Purnea district has a sizeable Bangladeshi presence.....'

'The narrow neck of Indian territory in the Kishenganj sector is favourite infiltration route for Bangladeshis via West Dinajpur especially for the non-Bengali infiltrants.....'

'It would not be an exaggeration to say that the problem of Bangladeshi influx in West Bengal is indeed very serious.......

As per the 1981 census, while the Muslim population in West Bengal constituted 21.51 percent, it accounted for a percentage ranging from 31 in Birbhum district to 58.66 in Murshidabad district. The district of West Dinajpur, Malda and North and South 24 Parganas, accounted for figures ranging between these two percentage. What the current figures are cannot be said with any accuracy but it can be safely assumed that a serious demographic change has taken place in these districts due to continuous influx of Bangladeshi migrants........'

'...............According to the state government about 28 lakh Bangladeshi nationals entered West Bengal between 1972 and 1988, of whom over five lakhs stayed back. The pre-1971 influx is apparently covered by the Mujibur Rahman-Indira Gandhi pact. The figures for 1988 and 1989 are not known.'

'However, according to BSF authorities the Bangladeshi infiltrants apprehended, both by the BSF and the state police, constituted only about 20 per cent of the actual number who managed to infiltrate into West Bengal.'

Appendix—9

Greater Islamic Bangladesh is a serious threat to Indian Integrity, Sovereignty and Hindu Majority By Pamela Geller

Of the following article, Dr. Richard L. Benkin, author of A Quiet Case of Ethnic Cleansing: the Murder of Bangladeshi Hindus, writes, 'I can confirm this. I have spoken with Bangladeshi schoolchildren and older students who are being taught that there is 'no reason for Dhaka [capital city of Bangladesh] and Kolkata [Calcutta] to be separate' and that they should both be part of Bangladesh. When I ask them why they both should not be part of India if they should be one (and given the fact that Bangladesh is a failed state), they are left without a response. But this is how they are being prepared. When we see how ruling WB [West Bengal] parties are willing to lay down for this in order to hang on to vote banks, we see the importance of elections.'

'Greater Islamic Bangladesh is a serious threat to Indian Integrity, Sovereignty, and Hindu Majority,' Hindu Existence Upananda Brahmachari, |HENB|New-Delhi & Kolkata|29 Oct 2014: The NIA (National Investigation Agency) has smelled a deeper conspiracy of the establishment of a Greater Islamic Bangladesh hatched by the ISI (Inter service Intelligence) of Pakistan and DGFI (Director General of Foreign Intelligence) of Bangladesh with other terror modules engaged in Burdwan Blast. As per revealation through recovered documents by the NIA suggest that a bigger conspiracy was being materialized in different parts of Burdwan, Murshidabad, Birbhum, Nadia, Jalpaiguri and different Madrasas stretched out in the border areas of West Bengal. The documents reflect that the terror modules working on brain-wash of the Bengali Jihadis to establish a 'Greater Islamic Bangladesh' considering the territory of the last nawab of Bangladesh Siraj ud-daulah (1733-1757), as on 1750 AD. who was infamous for his anti-Hindu cruelty and debauchery. The proposed Greater Islamic Bangladesh includes whole of present Bangladesh, West Bengal, Assam, Tripura, Meghalaya and parts of Bihar, Jharkhand and Orissa.

But an exposed leaflet distributed by the Islamists active in West Bengal and Bangladesh goes further. 'If we manage to establish a Syria-like (ISIS) reign here (in Bangladesh) then Muslims from Assam, Arakan (former name of Burma's Rakhine State) and West Bengal too would be able to come here for hijrat (migration with religious agenda). Simultaneously, anti-India revolts would intensify in seven eastern Indian states,' says the pamphlet. 'This would be a huge blow for India, one of the key non-Muslim states in the changed situation of the world.'

The discovery of the jihadi literature comes after al Qaeda announced its plans in September to open a branch in the Indian subcontinent. Through a pamphlet generated by Al Qaeda and ISIS modules, urging people to restore the Isalamic rule of pre-colonial India, is oviously arising a serious security threats amid growing communal polarization in West Bengal, analysts opine.

The officers of Indian Intelligence say that the ISI and DGFI were taking the help of Jamat-ul-Mujahideen (JuM) of Bangladesh, Harkat-ul-Jihadi-Islam (HUJI), Arakan Rohingiya Islamic Front of Myanmar and Pan South Asian Militant Organisation of foreign roots. Simultaneously, Muslim United Liberation Tigers of Assam (MULTA), Muslim United Liberation Front of Assam (MULFA), Muslim United Volunteers Force (MUVF) are also engaged in this anti-national subversive and Anti Hindu conspiracy. These Islamic force are also active in various social media and internet by instigating Muslim youths to join in the module of ISIS (Islamic State of Iraq and Syria, now renamed as IS (Islamic State). They are depicting India as a 'Fascist Force') and 'Slumdog' and trying hard to raise social unrest and communal hatred. The unsanctioned Islamic seminaries (Khariji Madrasas) are working as the hatchery for supporting Jihadis, and bomb making factories to challenge the Hindu majority in West Bengal, as well as pseudo-secular goverment. in Bangladesh.

The Islamists engaged in this conspiracy by calculating a demographic change of West Bengal through massive infiltration of illegal Muslims through West Bengal, Assam, Meghalaya and Tripura. The investigations suggest that a huge influx through Karimganj, Dhubri, Kacchar, Barpeta, Hylakandi of Assam, North and Western districts of Tripura; Western Jayantia Hills, Western Garo Hills and South-East Khasi Hills of Meghalaya and the districts of Coochbehar, Dinajpur, Nadia, Murshidabad, Malda, Nadia and North 24 Parganas of West Bengal is perpetuating the demographic change of West Bengal to the goal of Greater Islamic Bangladesh.

As per Central Home Ministry statistics, some 577 infiltrators were arrested by the Police and BSF in 2011, while rise of 2851 of infiltrators were seen in 2013, as a bigger threat to demography in West Bengal. But the actual figure of Muslim infiltrators in Bengal as well as India is higher as unimaginable five crores in numbers. Dr. Mohit Roy, an expert on demographic changes and Indi-Bangladesh relation suggests the number of Muslim infiltrators from Bangladesh into India has a size of 4 per cent of total population in India as broad day light.

In course of 'Khagragar (Burdwan) Bomb Blast' and 'Shimulia Madrasa Bomb Making Factory investigations NIA recovered documents containing the Bengali versions of the speech of Ayman AI Zawahiri and Mufti Fazlul Haq of Taliban School. The infamous Mufti Fazlul Haq of Bangladesh propagates the unification of Dhaka and Kolkata in a Greater Islamic Bangladesh.

It is now obvious that various terror modules along with some state authorities in Pakistan, Bangladesh and Saudi Arabia are also engaged in the dangerous conspiracy of establishment of Greater Islamic Bangladesh. Sources said that huge funding was entered in the Bengal Terror Modules through Rabat-al-Islami and Islamic Bank of Bangladesh. Central IB (Intelligence Bureau) sources revealed that a huge amount of 3.5 crores of US dollar was arranged and donated by ISI through Islamic Development Bank of Islamabad to make a success of 'Operation Pin Code', the secret code for Greater Islamic Bangladesh through fanatic Islamic terrorism.

On the other hand, a Kuwait based Islamic NGO named RIHS (Revival of Islamic Heritage Society) is helping a huge jihadi fund In India in their recepients' end in Dhaka, Kolkata and Guwahati and for fanning jihadi fume spread over Burdawan Blast and Shimulia rackets through Jamat-ul-Mujahideen-Bangladesh.

The Terror module of Burdawan Blast and Shimulia Madrasa Jihadi Rackets have earned and are procuring funds for the Talibanisation of Bengal as well as India through Saradha Money laundering to JuM, Fake Currency networks, Cross border Cattle Smuggling, Bank robbery and from other sources hitherto unknown.

The Quaeda's brain-storming in both West Bengal and Bangladesh is taking a shape of whirlpool. In its recently launched English mouthpiece Resurgence, Islamic terrorist outfit al Qaeda has called upon Indian Muslims to regain their lost glory by visiting 'Free Afghanistan' and then return to India to engineer jihad. 'The time has come for the Muslims of India to play a proactive role in the jihad in Afghanistan and benefit from the experience of forty years of jihad so that they may build a better future for coming generations,' the outfit claimed in an article titled 'The Future of Muslims' in India.

The article is written by Maulana AAsim Umar who is the ameer jama'ah quaeda al-jihad means the head of operations in Indian subcontinent. Umar has urged Muslims of Indian subcontinent, specially the Muslims of India and Bangladesh to regain the lost glory of Islam in the region.

As per Mr. D C Nath, an ex-Deputy Chief of Central IB, the ruling state government, headed by Smt. Mamata Banerjee of AITC (All India Trinamool Congress) has an utter indulgence for making West Bengal—a terrorist state, for the purpose of vote bank politics and culpable Muslim appeasement in Bengal.

NIA has cautioned the State and Central authorities that there are fifty-eight existing terror modules in West Bengal, that are working for waging the jihad against India. National

Security Advisor; Mr. Ajit Doval handed over a list to the CM West Bengal comprising 180 Islamic Terrorists hiding in West Bengal for showing their jihadi power in awaiting.

But, in an urgent report Mr. Ajit Doval mentioned the proactive twenty-five to thirty terror modules of the Bengal are catering all these activities of subversiveness, treason and terrorism in entire Eastern and North Eastern region connected with Burdawan blast and Shimulia Mafrasa networking. The report was also submitted to the Central Home Minister Mr. Rajnath Singh. Most of these Jihadis are working in a camouflage of working as 'Attar' (essence), Burqa selleror otherwise engaged in 'Jari' embroidery work.

Now, it is a high point of perception that Jihadi modules of West Bengal and adjacent region that the Jihadi's of Bengal are Kolkata as their safe and central place of of entire operation. The alleged MP of AIUDF, Mr. Badaruddin Ajmal connected with terror link and his lieutenants, Mr. Sidiqullah Chowdhuriy and others, have penetrated in the politics of Kolkata and they are using politics as the front office and fuelling the jihdi activism from the respective back office, as suspected.

Kolkata and its suburbs are being used as the sleeper cell of JuM to assassin Bangladesh Prime Minister, Sheikh Hasina in Dhaka. Is Talibanisation of West Bengal eventually posed as a major threat to the majority people in Bengal while such planning of 'Bengal Caliphate' and 'Greater Islamic Bengal'are spreading its wings in a clear sky of Jihad?

However, experts say that Greater Islamic Bangladesh may be a part of another dangerous part of 'Mughlstan' and obviously a threat for majority of peace loving and law abiding citizens of India. NIA thinks the 'Greater Islamic Bangladesh' is a threat to Indian Integrity and Sovereignty.

Retrieved from:

(www.pamelageller.com/2014/11/greater-islamic-bangladesh-is-a-serious-threat-to-indian-integrity-sovereignty-and-hindu-majority.htm/)

Appendix—10

Demographic Changes: Is Bengal sitting on a jihadi volcano?

By Shonu Nangia

Demographic changes in West Bengal and Assam have been going on for years. There is nothing new in it. Mass infiltration and settlement of Bangladeshi Muslims coming in search of *lebensraum* into these regions has been taking place for decades. India has always known this but always been complacent. After independence, Muslim migrants into India had, in fact, been encouraged due to vote bank politics and the hunger of the Congress party and CPI-M for Muslim Votes.

Designs for a 'Greater Bangla Islamic Calipha

According to Dr. Mohit Roy, an expert on Indo-Bangladesh relations and demographic changes, Muslim Bangladeshi infiltrators now make up 4 per cent of India's population (www.pamelageller.com/2014/11/greater-islamic-bangladesh-is-a-serious-threat-to-indian-integrity-sovereignty-and-hindu-majority-.html), but in vast areas of Bengal and Assam, the situation has reached a tipping point.

American Thinker Janet Levy in her article reports: 'At partitioning, the Muslim population of West Bengal stood at 12 per cent and the Hindu population of East Bengal 30 per cent. Today, with massive Muslim immigration, Hindu persecution and forced conversions, West Bengal's Muslim population has increased to 27 per cent (upto 63 per cent in some districts), as per the 2011 Census and Bangladesh's Hindu population has decreased to 8 per cent. While the situation for Hindus in Bangladesh is certainly dire, life has become increasingly difficult for Hindus in West Bengal, home to a Muslim-appeasing government and a breeding ground and safe haven for terrorists. For several years, West Bengal has suffered underapparent Muslim-planned riots designed to implement shariah, extract government concessions and grab more territory.'

The demographic changes in West Bengal have reached a point where the consequence has been a wave of aggressive Islamisation, a jihadi consolidation, and a suicidal politics that harks back to the genocide era of 1946-1947. The congruence of all of these resulting in a fresh Hindu Bengali exodus from what have traditionally been Hindu lands.

Remote, and thus vulnerable and mostly poor villages are being targeted under a greater project to merge West Bengal and Assam with Bangladesh by driving out non-Muslims. According to a report titled 'Greater Islamic Bangladesh'-A Serious Threat to Indian integrity, Sovereignty and Hindu Majority published on the Pamela Geller website (http://pamelageller.com/about/) which monitors global jihad, 'The NIA (National Investigation Agency) has smelled a deeper conspiracy of the establishment of a Greater Islamic Bangladesh hatched by the ISI (Inter Service Intelligence) of Pakistan and DGFI (Director General of Foreign Intelligence) of Bangladesh with other terror modules engaged in Burdawan blast. The revealation through recovered documents by the NIA suggest that a bigger conspiracy was being materialized in different parts of Burdawan, Murshidabad, Birbhum, Nadia, Jalpaiguri and in different madrassas stretchet out in the border areas of West Bengal.

'The documents reflect that the terror modules are working on brain-wash of the Bengal jihadis to establish a 'Greater Islami Bangladesh' considering the territory of the last Nawab of Bengal Siraj ud-daulah (1733=1757) as on 1750, who was infamous for his anti-Hindu cruelty and debauchery. The proposed Greater Islamic Bangladesh includes whole of present Bangladesh, West Bengal, Assam, Tripura, Meghalaya and parts of Bihar, Jharkhand and Orissa.

Bangladesh authorities also acknowledge jihadist plan for an eastern Islamic Reporting on the killing of a Hindu priest of the Deviganj temple who was beheaded on February 21, 2016 near Panchagar about 500 kms north of Dhaka, by militants suspected to belong Jamatul Mujahedeen Bangladesh (JMB). Pakistani newspaper ***Dawn*** (http://www.dawn.com/news/1240961/Bangladesh-hindu-priest-killed-by-suspected-islamist-militants-plice) quotes deputy director general of police, Humayun Kabir, as saying that 'The motive for the killing was probably to create an unstable situation in the country and ultimately establish a caliphate'.

This side of the border, in West Bengal, the vote bank politics of the Communist CPI-M government earlier and the pro-Islamist stance of the TMC government subsequently have facilitated the Mughalistan project by emboldening the jihadi forces in the state. State patronage under TMC rule has rendered Islamists untouchable even by the Central Government security forces.

Mamata Banerji's policies have resulted in a rapid Islamisation of West Bengal (www.indiafacts.org/west-bengal-jihadi-playground/) and the concomitant creation of a sociopolitical climate in which Hindus are attacked, killed and prevented from practicing their religion, Hindu homesteads and properties are looted and destroyed (www.indiafacts.org/falta-extensive-violence-against-hindus/), and young Hindu girls are kidnapped, raped, and forcibly converted to Islam and then often sold into prostitution or killed.

In areas where there is a substantial Muslim presence, entire villages are being targeted where the Hindus are terrorized, demoralized and displaced. The Hindu population is losing land and livelihood and is migrating to safer places.

Since 2011, in this silent war on Bengali Hindus, 380 Hindu temples have beeb reportedly destroyed or vandalized, 2134 confirmed rapes by Bangladeshis have taken place, state money to the tune of Rs 2,000 crores has been disbursed to mosques, and seventy Hindu leaders have been murdered in West Bengal. In addition, it is believed twelve lakh Bangladeshi's have illegally crossed into India through Bengal in the same period.

Marxist Islamist Nexus in the Garb of Secularism

Human rights abuses against the Hindus of West and East Bengal have been going on for years, yet the elite, Leftist, intellectual class and the 'secular' media and journalists in Calcutta and Delhi chose to be blind to it. None of the secular Bengali writers, journalists and intellectuals who try to dominate public discourse in India and constantly attack the Hindu civilization foundations of India have questioned Mamata on Muslim appeasement like Taslima Nasrin did recently.

While Islamist forces prepare the ground for the inclusion of West Bengal in an Islamic Caliphate, mainstream media in West Bengal and rest of India seems to be completely disinterested and disconnected, and does not cover any of this stuff. Calcutta's two leading English dailies, *The Statesman and The Telegraph* (www.epaper.telegraphindia.com/paper/1-0-22@2016-1001.html), mouthpieces of Bengal's entrenched communist ideology, for example, routinely black out such news. With reference to The Telegraph, this is what Shefali Vaidya (www.facebook.com/shefv) writes in the context of *l'affaire JNU* 'This is the front page of an Indian newspaper. The biggest and most prominent headline that covers 75 per cent of the space is dedicated to a thirty-year-freeloader who shouted anti-India slogans and organised a march to protest against the hanging of a terrorist after a full trial. This is the same man who hid like a sewer rat for one week only to resurface now to play the 'minority' card. A twenty-two-year –old man made the supreme sacrifice to defend that very freedom that Umar Khalid abused with such impunity, and the Telegraph dedicates the bottom corner of the front page to him.

On social media, one encounters throngs of Leftist Bengali 'intellectuals' who have now fanned out all over India. Many of them are themselves from refugee families who fled East Bengal (former Bangladesh) during one of the cynical periods of Hindu mass killings there, and who were completely unable to resist Islamic fundamentalism there in any meaningful way. They all seem to be cut from the same cloth—that of Marxist ideology—who now bemoan the new awakening of Indian Hindu political and social consciousness as evil or communal, and are unable or unwilling to see reality of jihad in their own backyard. It is also a fact that politically correct Western media does not tell the story of Muslim persecution of Hindus in India. Neither does mainstream media in India report violence against Hindus, especially when it is committed by Muslims.

The sorry condition of Hindu Bengal

One thus feels compelled to signal Tapan Ghosh (www.facebook.com/Tapan Ghosh.official/), founder of Hindu Samhati (http://hindusamhati.blogspot.com/), who has been documenting and raising awareness about the atrocities on the simple and helpless Hindu victims of Islamic jihad, who up until the very recent Malda riots that began on the 4th of January 2016, tended to be mostly poor, rural agrarians, with low educational attainment levels.

His organisation, Hindu Samhati, curageusly investigates, documents and reports on the Islamic persecution of Hindus in West Bengal, often times at great risk to the lives of the investigators. According to Ghosh, there are abut 32,000 villages in West Bengal that are sites of active ethnic cleansing. There are multiple acts of violence against Hindus in many places daily and only some get noticed. In many villages and towns, the Hindu population has dropped below 50 per cent due to an earlier exodus of middle-class Hindus, and now only the poor Hindu segment is left to bear the brunt of ethnic cleansing. Thousands of Hindu girls disappear in the state every year.

If this entire situation does not change, the story of East Bengal will soon be repeated in West Bengal. Hindus, just a few decades ago, were 40 per cent of the population of East Bengal. Today they make up just 8 per cent of the populatin there.

While the disenfranchised rural Hindu segment has been enduring soft jihad for years now and their victim, isation was never reported in mainstream media, the recent Malda attacks show how the organizers of micro level jihad in Bengal have upped the the ante by expanding the magnitude and the focus of their operations. A mob of 2,50,000 Muslims wreaked havoc in Malda district, West Bengal, ostensibly over a blasphemous remark. After Malda the violence also spread to Birbhum and to Purnea in Bihar state. The events in Malda, which secularists have tried to pass off as a simple law and order related disturbance, are a warning signal that West Bengal may be heading towards a Kosovo-like situation with the rise of Islamism, which poses a great danger to India's security and territorial integrity by creating a civil-warlike situation. Sheikh Hasina has done more to combat Islamic fundamentalism in her country than Mamata Banerjee, who has actually encouraged it in her State.

It must be remembered that 'West Bengal was created by negotiating about 35 per cent area from erstwhile Bengal as a safe sanctuary for the Hindus'. Given the demographic changes that have already taken place and the damage that has already been done, feasible options to correct the situation seem very few.

How do you integrate a large powerful, and aggressive minority that has an exponential growth rate, looks upon the Mughal Empire and past Caliphate as Utopia, considers national borders as irrelevant, demonstrates a strong will to not assimilate, overwhelms a meek majority, and bides its time as it waits for the day it can fully impose its sharia on the rest of the population?

Noting that 'The land was partitioned on the basis of religious demography alone but unfortunately unlike Punjab (both, East-Indian and West-Pakistani) population exchange was not done,' and that 'crores of illegal Bangladeshi Muslims invaders have captured major parts of the state with the help of local Muslims, who were not sent to Bangladesh as Punjabi Muslims from Indian Punjab to Pakistan.'

While this may be a new dream of many a Hindu Bengali, who now clearly sees the writing on the wall, and while this may not be very different from Malaysia's Bhumiputra (sons of the soil) policies designed to ensure the domination of Malay Muslims, it might already be too late for such measures in Bengal. Time has come to oust Mamata Banerjee from power so that further ethnic cleansing of Hindus can at least be stopped.

Why is the 2016 election critical for an Indian future?

In 2014, a serious allegation 'leveled against Mamata Banerjee and her closer aides for helping Jamaat-e-Islami in Bangladesh to promote a political jihad in West Bengal with Saradha cheat fund money' was not persued to its logical conclusion by her political opponents. The Central investigative agencies also dropped the ball in this regard. Nevertheless, public discontent against Mamata is at an all-time high, State Assembly elections will take place in April-May this year. And Mamata will be more than ever dependent on the Muslim vote to stay in power.

As Bengal goes to election in April-May 2016, a shocking front page news item published in The Telegraph on the 17th of February, 2016, indicates how Mamata Banerjee plans to increase the number of Muslim votes to augment her share of votes. The Telegraph reported that Mamata Banerjee has declared that 'the Bengal government will urge the Centre to give citizenship to all Bangladeshis living in the State for five years or more, a move that will impact Assembly poll results as ten districts share border with the neighboring country.'

According to the news report, state officials themselves admit that there are 'huge' numbers of undocumented Bangladeshis in ten districts bordering Bangladesh. The piece also quotes an unnamed TMC minister as saying, 'People who have identity documents but want citizenship certificates can decide the electoral outcome in at least fifty Assembly seats in the ten districts. They are mainly from the minority community. We want to get their votes.'

The brazen anti-people and anti-national strategy that TMC is plotting to add more Bangladeshi Muslims to the electoral rolls should be of grave concern to all right minded people, and especially to all Bengalis.

Nationalist forces in the state should not hesitate to vocalize and propagate the truth to raise the political consciousness of the majority Hindu population. This will be a difficult process given the previous long term communist indoctrination of Bengal's masses, the anti-Hindu bias of the state's administrative apparatus, and the stoic silence of the state's Marxist controlled media outlets who have a long tradition of censoring all information relating to anti-Hindu violence and jihad. With Modi at the Centre, a BJP government at the state level might just be the only way to keep Bengal from slipping away from its Hindu identity and from India.

Given TMC's nefarious plan to court the Islamist lobby further, perhaps the biggest challenge and ultimate obstacle for the BJP this time will not be how to awaken or win the confidence of the Hindu voters, but rather the usual rigging of elections and booth capturing by the TMC goons who will be inside and outside the polling stations when elections take place this summer.

Shonu Nangia
Author is Associate Professor of Foreign Languages
At the Louisiana State University at Alexandra, USA.

Retrieved from: www.bharatniti.in/story/demographic- changes–is-bengal-sitting-on a-jihadi–volcano/138.

Appendix—11

(Personal DO letter written to the President of India is available at Chapter 10)

Relevant Excerpts From The Report Submitted
To The President Of India by Gen. (Retd)
S.K. Sinha as Governor of Assam in 1998
Introduction

1. The unabated influx of illegal migrants from Bangladesh into Assam and the consequent perceptible change in the demographic pattern of the minority in the State, has been a matter of grave concern. It threatens to reduce the Assamese people to a minority in their own State, as happened in Tripura and Sikkim.
2. Illegal migration into Assam was the core issue behind the Assam student movement. It was also the prime contributory factor behind the outbreak of insurgency in the state. Yet we have not made much tangible progress in dealing with this all important issue.
3. There is a tendency to view illegal migration into Assam as a regional matter, affecting only the people of Assam. Its more dangerous dimension of greatly undermining our national security is ignored. The long cherished design of Greater East Pakistan/Bangladesh, making inroads into the strategic land link of Assam with the rest of the country, can lead to severing the entire land mas of the North East, with all its rich resources, from the rest of the country. This will have disastrous strategic and economic consequences.
4. I have held prolonged discussions about illegal migration with a large number of people in Assam of different background and with different shades of opinion. This has included politicians, leaders of the minority community, journalists, lawyers, Government officials, both serving and retired, social workers and so on. I have also discussed this issue at length with the Indian High Commissionm at Dhaka. Besides,

I have extensively toured the border areas of Assam with Bangladesh, visiting a number of land and riverine BOPs of the Border Security Force. Further I have studied the relevant literature and statistics on the subject. On this basis, I have formulated my views and recommendations contained in this report. Different aspects connected with illegal migration have been examined. Recommendations have been made for more effectively arresting the ongoing influx of illegal migrants and taking practical steps to soften the adverse fall outs from the large scale infiltration that has already taken place.

(Then Gen. Sinha has traced the entire background of the problem of migration and illegal migration which have been highlighted by us already.)

Consequences

22. The dangerous consequences of large scale illegal migration from Bangladesh, both for the people of Assam and more for the Nation as a whole, need to be emphatically stressed. No misconceived and mistaken notion of secularism should be allowed to come in the way of doing so.
23. As a result of population movement from Bangladesh, the spectre looms large of the indigenous people of Assam being reduced to a minority in their home State. Their cultural survival will be in jeopardy, their political control will be weakened and their employment opportunities will be undermined.

This silent and invidious demographic invasion of Assam may result in the loss of geostrategically vital districts of Lower Assam. The influx of these illegal migrants is turning these districts into a Muslim majority region. It will then only be a matter of time when a demand for their merger with Bangladesh may be made. (Emphasis mine. Already demand for separate autonomous Council has been made as narrated elsewhere). The rapid growth of international Islamic fundamentalism may provide the driving force for this demand. In this context, it is pertinent that Bangladesh has long discarded secularism and has chosen to become an Islamic State. Loss of Lower Assam will severe the entire land mass of the North East, from the rest of India and the rich natural resources of that region will be lost to the Nation.

Chapter lll
PREVENTING INFILTRATION

1. ----------
2. ---------------------------The large scale movement of Bengali population, both Hindus and Muslims into Assam, caused considerable resentment among the Assamese people and there were instances of anti-Bengali riots.
3. -------------------
4. -------------------
5. --------------------
6. --------------------

Border Fencing

7. A border fencing may not be a fool proof method of preventing infiltration but there is no better way of doing so. To be effective, border fencing has to be supplemented by vigorous patrolling and other measures. The motivating factors behind infiltration must be addressed. If this can be done successfully, then a permanent solution of the problem can be found.
8. Border policing in both Punjab and Assam should prevent trans-border movement of smugglers, militants and infiltrators. In the case of Assam, infiltration has a much bigger and more dangerous dimension. Despite this, the measures to counter trans-border movement in Assam appear to have been given a lower priority than in Punjab. This is evident from the following facts:--
   (a) The decision to fence the border was taken in 1985 and reflected in Assam Accord but the work on fencing started seven years later in 1992. 13 years have elapsed since this Accord and fencing has not yet been completed. Whereas in the Dhubri sector of Assam it is nearly complete, in the Cachar sector, only a little over half has been completed. As against this, fencing in Punjab started in 1988 and was completed in three years by 1991.

(b) The quality of fencing in Punjab is superior. It is two feet taller. Observation towers and lighting of the fence have been provided in Punjab, all along the border. In Assam, the observation towers have been constructed in the Dhubri sector only and there are none in Cachar sector. There is no lighting of the fence anywhere in Assam.

(c) The density of troops guarding the fence is higher in Punjab. A BSF battalion in Punjab holds a frontage of approximately thirty kilometres. In Assam, BSF Battalions in Dhubri sector are deployed over frontage of seventy kilometres and in Cachar sector over a frontage of forty kilometres.

9. ------------------------ there must be lighting arrangements for the fence. Observation towers must be provided in Cachar sector.

10. Additional BSF battalions should be provided in the East with each battalion having a frontage of thirty kilometres. -------------------------------- diversion of forces from border policing to other duties, when the battle against illegal migrants is on, cannot but have adverse effect. The shortage of BSF units must be made up on priority through new raising.

11. The present arrangement of guarding the riverine border with some speed boats and out-board fitted country boats, is not adequate. There is a need to have floating BOP's on medium watercraft with four to five speed boats attached to them. A proposal for nine medium crafts has been put up by DG BSF. This should be sanctioned soon.

12. All country boats plying on the river near the border must be registered with their registration number marked on them and the registration papers available with the crew for verification, when required. (Our recommendations in this regard, cover the entire State and not only the rivers near the border).

Other measures

13. Certain other measures are also required to be taken to deal with illegal migration. These are as follows -

(a) Our nationals in the border districts and for that matter in the whole State, should be provided multipurpose photo identity card. This task should be completely on high priority.

(b) Effective arrangements must be made for registration of births and deaths in the State.

(c) The 1950 National Register of Citizens should be updated. Computerisation will facilitate this process. A separate register for illegal migrants (stateless citizens) should also be maintained.

14. The Brahmaputra is normally five to seven kilometers wide and during floods has only one water channel. However, in the lean season, there are two, three or even more water channels throwing up chars (river islands). Due to changing river configurations, it is difficult to survey the chars. The Bangladeshi Muslims settle on these chars. They are hardy and prepared to face difficult living conditions, particularly when the chars get submerged for a few days during floods, which come three to four times in a season. Chickens are put on roofs, cattle herded on platforms above the water level and in emergent situations men and cattle live in boats. This hardy community has been living on chars in the Brahmaputra from Dhubri (near the international border) to Lakhimpur. There are still several chars which are uninhabited. These should be handed over to the Forest Department and notified as forest land. Trees which can withstand one to three feet of water during the flood season should be planted on them. (I, personally, do not agree with this suggestion. Instead of forestation, measures should be taken with the help of modern technology, to ensure that such chars may be washed away).

15. The measures recommended to arrest the influx of illegal migrants may not completely stop their ingress but will go a long way in reducing it to a small trickle. A more lasting and effective solution can come about through economic development in Bangladesh. This will remove the motivation behind trans-border migration. ---------------------------------------.

Chapter IV
DETECTION AND DEPORTATION

1. ------
2. -------
3. International law does not provide for unilateral deportation in defiance of the views of the country to which the deportation is to take place. With the stand now taken by Bangladesh, it will not be possible for India to deport millions of illegal migrants to Bangladesh. ---. Moreover, the bursting population of Bangladesh creates a Malthusian nightmare and is not conducive to that country accepting them. Further our capability to identify and deport over ten million such people is questionable. In these circumstances, deportation of these illegal migrants is not now a practical proposition.
4. The survey should be completed in a fixed time frame4. The repeal of IMDT Act and its replacement by another Act, must take into account the legitimate fears of the minorities. They should be assured that the new Act will be fair, just and transparent, leading to expeditious disposal of cases. --.
5. Although illegal migrants, who came in after the 24th of March, 1971 will not be deported, they must be identified and after identification denied voting rights and certain other facilities like acquisition of immovable property. Suitable process of doing so which may have acceptability and command credibility should be evolved. This exercise should be completed expeditiously. The process for doing so should be on the following lines:
   (a) Ground survey teams each under a Magistrate assisted by the Border Organisation, should extensively tour the areas allotted to them, to identify illegal migrants. To ensure maximum objectivity and freedom from local pressure, political or otherwise, Magistrates from outside Assam be deputed for this task. The survey should be completed in a fixed time frame of a few months. Inducting Magistrates

from outside will be on the lines of what happened in 1983 elections, when officers were brought into Assam from different States on temporary deputation.

(b) Individuals identified as illegal migrants should be allowed the right of appeal before Foreigners Tribunals set up under the Foreigners Act. This will provide necessary judicial sanctity to this exercise.

(c) Foreigners identified as illegal migrants should be denied voting rights and their children born in India should not automatically become eligible for Indian citizenship. (This is where the amendment of the Citizenship Act becomes imperative.: This author's own recommendation.) Disenfrancisement may be a big issue for political parties who so assiduously try to build vote banks But is no hardship to the immigrants. The denial of voting rights to these migrants can by no stretch be deemed to be unjust. Over one lakh Hindu and Sikh refugees from West Pakistan, who settled in Jammu region in 1947, have to this day, after a lapse of over fifty years, not been given voting rights. However, refugees from West Pakistan who settled in other States were given full citizenship rights and many amongst them became Union Cabinet Ministers and one became Prime Minister.

6. The proposed arrangement should adequately assuage the legitimate fears of the minority community and will also be a humane measure for illegal migrants. Pre-1971 illegal migrants stand already legitimized and the post-1971 illegal migrants, now not to be deported, will be partially legitimized.

7. The minority community in Assam now comprises nearly 30 per cent of the population and with their tendency to vote as a block, they can hardly be considered a minority, in real terms. (According to 2011 census, they have gone up to 34.2 per cent. – author). They have come to acquire a decisive role in Assam's democratic polity, which the majority community with its split votes, cannot match.

So far as the majority community is concerned, they may resent the decision not to deport the illegal migrants but in the present circumstances, there is no other alternative. They should get reconciled to it. Illegal migrants upto the 24th of March 1971 have been made Indian citizens, and this has been accepted by them. Illegal migrants of post the 24th of March 1971 vintage will not be deported but will be made Stateless citizens... This will also reduce political patronage for illegal migration and will be yet another disincentive to prospective illegal migrants.

Abbreviations

AASU	All Assam Students Union
AAGSP	All Assam Gana Sangram Parishad
AJYCP	Assam Jatiyatabadi Yuba Chhatra Parishad
ABSU	All Bodo Students Union
AAMSU	All Assam Minority Students Union
ABMSU	All Bodoland Minority Students Union
AIUDF	All India United Democratic Front
BTAD	Bodoland Territorial Autonomous Distr
BSF	Border Security Force
CHT	Chitagong Hill Tracts
CEC	Chief Election Commissioner
CEO	Chief Electoral Officer
CRPF	Central Reserve Police Force
CICA	Central Immigration Control Authority
DGFI	Director General of Foreign Intelligence
DHS	Department of Homeland Security
EC	Election Commission
ER	Electoral Roll
EU	European Union
GDP	Gross Domestic Product
GOM	Group of Ministers
GCC	Gulf Coast Countries
ISI	Inter Service Intelligence
IED	Improvised Explosive Device
IGAD—RCP	Inter Governmental Authority on Development—Regional Consultative Process
ISIS	Islamic State of Iraq and Syria
INS	Immigration and Naturalisation Service
IRCA	Immigration Reform and Control Act
JMB	Jamatul Mujahidin Bangladesh
IMDT Act	Illegal Migrants Determination Act
MHA	Ministry of Home Affairs
MULTA	Muslim United Liberation Tigers of Assam
ME	Middle East
NGO	Non Government Organisation

NRC	National Register of Citizens
NRV	National Register of Villages
NDFB	National Democratic Front of Bodoland
NSCN	National Socialist Council of Nagaland
NEFA	North East Frontier Agency
NESU	North Eastern Students Union
PGR	Professional Grazing Reserve
VGR	Village Grazing Reserve
PIP Scheme	Pak Infiltration Prevention Scheme
ROP	River Police Organisation
ROP Act	Representation of People Act
SAARC	South Asian Association of Regional Cooperation
UNO	United Nation Organisation
ULFA	United Liberation Front of Assam
UAE	Unite Arab Emirate
UNDP	United Nation Development Programme
WMR	World Migration Report